A LONG WAY BACK

A LONG WAY BACK

1997

Dear Heydays fans
    Hope you enjoy
    this + pass it on.
        Love,
        Liz W.

Liz Wainwright

Book Three of the Lynda Collins Trilogy

Elizabeth Wainwright asserts the moral right to be identified as the author of this work.

This novel is entirely a work of fiction. The names, incidents and characters portrayed in it are entirely the work of the author's imagination. Any resemblance to actual persons living or dead, events or localities is entirely coincidental.

Printed and distributed by Createspace Ltd

Loveday Manor Publishing

ISBN-13: 978-0957227934

ISBN-10: 0957227930

www.lizscript.co.uk

For Glyn
and
our wonderful family.

CHAPTER ONE

'Oh, dear God,' Lynda whispered to herself. 'Who'd have thought that it would be like this?'

She'd never imagined that she'd be walking up to her own front door with her key in her hand, and have to stop and wonder if she'd a right to walk in.

The thought made her clench hold of the key even more tightly as she approached the front door of 24 Beechwood Avenue, a 1930s semi-detached with a bay window and a neat garden. This was the home she'd walked out of in March 1985, not long after her fortieth birthday. Over ten years ago.

Lynda brushed back a strand of hair which had strayed from the immaculate styling she'd checked before she got off the train. Her golden hair had sometimes caused envy as well as admiration, but had always made her feel good.

Before she'd reached her fortieth birthday, it had startled her by beginning to turn grey. Lynda had immediately bought some cheap hair colouring which had, indiscreetly, covered up the evidence that she was no longer as young as she wanted to be. Her daughter, Carolyn, had, of course, disapproved.

Lynda paused to look towards the end of the avenue and the view of the town in the distance. She'd always loved the way the rough edges of the moors pushed their way in among the rows and rows of weather worn sandstone terraced houses.

These 'two up and two down' houses had once been the soot-blackened homes of a resourceful, determined army of workers who, early in the morning, had put on their black leather clogs and marched their way to the Lancashire cotton mills. Among them had been Lynda's grandmother, Madge Collins, from whom she had inherited not only her strength and resilience but, unfortunately, also more troublesome characteristics.

'You do what you want, Lynda, love,' Madge had told her granddaughter when she was a teenager. 'There's always folks that think they know better than you. Take no notice, or tell them to go to hell. You've had it tough all your little life, just like your poor Mother did, God rest her. You hang on to your dreams, my girl, be happy. You deserve it.'

There had been a shower of rain, and it had polished the slate roofs so that they'd shone silver and black as the taxi-driver had driven her from the station, through some of the old streets where Lynda had played, worked and flirted as a girl.

It wasn't raining, thank goodness, when the taxi drew up outside her home. The last thing Lynda wanted was to arrive wet and bedraggled, she needed to look good, to give her the courage to face them after all these years.

It wasn't like her to be scared but, as the train had been about to set off from Guildford station, Lynda had panicked, getting up from her seat for a moment, ready to get off, to run for home. And she would have done, if she'd been sure where 'home' was.

Tom Meredith's jealous ex-wife, Suzanne, had made it clear that, in her opinion, Lynda Collins didn't belong at Loveday Manor.

'We don't want you here!' she'd screamed hysterically when Lynda had tried to talk to her. 'You might have fooled my husband, but you've never fooled me. You're a common little tart who's done too well for herself down here. But it's over now.

So get out. Go back to where you came from!'

The woman who had sat opposite Lynda on the train had made the journey even worse. She was in her sixties, and wore a hideous green and purple lumpy tweed suit. She'd squeezed herself in at the other side of the table and had informed Lynda, in a voice shrill with self-importance, that she was going to visit her son and daughter-in-law.

'I'll have to give the place a good spring clean as soon as I get there, of course. They both work, so they'll be glad of the help.'

She had organised this pilgrimage dedicated to inflicting order and censure, on a self-catering basis, and soon unwrapped a grease-proof package, thrusting it towards Lynda.

'I always bring my own, you know what you're getting then. Do you want a tuna sandwich?'

Lynda recoiled from the combined smell of tuna and the hard-boiled egg the woman had cracked open. 'No, thank you.'

Wishing she'd booked a seat in first-class, Lynda had tried to retreat into the glossy shallows of the magazine she'd bought. It had served as a limited barrier to conversation but then, foolishly, Lynda had been unable to resist taking the small album from her handbag, and looking at the slightly faded, treasured photos.

She'd wanted to seek some reassurance from the smiling faces from the past, especially the photo of little Michael Sheldon at three months old, his tiny hands clutching at a teddy bear bigger than he was. But almost immediately the nosey, beady-eyed woman had leaned across to peer, uninvited, at the photos.

'Is that your grandchild?'

'Yes.'

3

'A boy or a girl?'

'A boy,'

Lynda had moved the album closer to her, and focused solely on its contents, but the woman wasn't the sort to take a hint.

'What's his name?'

'Michael.'

'Has he any little brothers and sisters?'

'I don't know.'

The woman had had her mouth open like a bulging-eyed carp, and was wrapping her lips round the hard-boiled egg, but she almost spat it out in her haste to pursue this intriguing line of inquiry.

'You don't know?'

'No. I've been away.'

'Oh.'

The woman had leaned forward eagerly, almost lying across the table to see the next picture in the album, a tall, good-looking man with a blonde on his arm.

'Is that you and your husband?'

'Yes,' Lynda said curtly, snapping the album shut and staring pointedly out of the window.

The front door of 24 Beechwood Avenue had a delicate Art Deco style flower etched in the glass panel in the centre. Lynda stared at the pale reflection shimmering back at her, not a young face, but strong and beautiful. The notoriously blonde hair, now more subtly coloured, was today drawn up behind her head in the kind of elegant, classy style she remembered Carolyn had once admired in one of her Nana's 'Vogue' magazines.

As a teenager Carolyn had attached herself to a group of friends who came from families who had money. Her friends' fathers were local business men, and their mothers didn't go out to work but stayed at home; they were smart and sophisticated, and wore stylish, expensive clothes. Carolyn had been ashamed of Lynda, the brassy blonde working Mum who served pies in a café, and talked and laughed too loudly. And she'd let her know it.

Lynda had never forgotten one particular confrontation.

'It's a parents' evening. I'm your Mother, why can't I come?'

'I promised Nana that she could come with me and Dad. You can't both come.'

'Why not?'

'You're only allowed two people.'

'Then your bloody Nana can stop at home.'

'No. I promised. And I want her to come.'

'But you don't want me, your Mother, there.'

Carolyn had lost patience then. 'No. If you must know, I don't.'

'Well, hard luck. I'm going!'

'No, you're not! I don't want you to! You'll embarrass me.'

'I won't.'

'Yes, you will. Look at you! Cheap flashy clothes, and all that mascara and bright red lipstick.'

'Anything else?' Lynda had demanded angrily.

'Yes! You talk too loud.'

Lynda hadn't talked much after that, not to her daughter anyway. She'd also found it got harder to talk to John, her husband, who always took Carolyn's side. And then there was his Mother. Too often John Stanworth had been forced to choose between her and his wife, and too often he had not chosen Lynda.

Sheila Stanworth had been an ever present cloud over their marriage, clinging to her son, and taking over her granddaughter. She had, in her quest for supremacy, quietly convinced Carolyn that it was she, not Lynda, who was the one who cared the most, and who knew what was best for her.

Sheila had insidiously worked at convincing Carolyn that Lynda didn't want to be at home looking after her. As a child she hadn't understood why her Mummy wasn't there. She hadn't really been aware that Lynda had had to work, that there was no choice, financially, if Carolyn was to have all the clothes and opportunities that her Mother had never had.

So they'd stopped talking, Lynda and her daughter, because their conversations always turned into arguments which neither of them had been willing to lose. And in the end they had lost each other.

Today Lynda was returning to Milfield to try to put everything right, but now, as she stood looking at her reflection in that door, she noticed the fear in her eyes. It had come back, even after all this time, that old fear of not being good enough, of being rejected.

Even now, at fifty-two, she could still be frightened like a child in the schoolyard, and still react by lashing out instinctively to defend herself. That old fear always brought out the worst in her, it could still make her forget all that she'd learned in the last ten years, all that Tom Meredith and his love had taught her.

Straightening her shoulders, Lynda drew up the deep, soft collar of her black cashmere coat so that it framed her face, gently comforting her. Then a dark cloud of memories suddenly blurred the image in the glass, and made her turn and walk hurriedly back down the path.

She knew she was running away from that house, just as she had in 1985, which seemed a lifetime ago now. She knew she would probably never have come back to Milfield if Tom Meredith hadn't needed her to promise to find the courage.

Lying there against the cluster of soft pillows on their bed, with Lynda sitting beside him, he'd tried to make a joke of it, like he did with everything that really mattered to him.

'You don't want me to have to hang around as a restless spirit, to make sure you're all right.'

He'd stopped there, because he'd seen her tears. He'd held her hand even more tightly, and made her look into his eyes.

'It's worth a try, love, everything's worth a try,' he'd said in that gentle voice which, for the last ten years, had been the only voice she had needed to hear.

Tom had looked up at her with those blue eyes which almost matched her own, those loving eyes which, so often, had sparked in her the strongest passion she had ever known. Those eyes which had had to close to end the pain.

'They might not want me,' she'd whispered.

'They're your family. And that's what you'll need now.'

He was right of course, as always. Tom would know her thoughts before she'd found the words, or the courage, to deal with them. How could she live without him? She'd never ever felt as safe as she had with Tom Meredith, or as happy.

She paused and looked back at the bay window of the house and, although she knew he'd still be at work, she pictured John Stanworth sitting in the living room, watching television, cosy in his armchair by the fire. It used to drive her crazy, the way he'd sit there all the time, mesmerised by whatever was on the magic box. She hesitated again, but then walked along

Beechwood Avenue and up to the main road. Of course it would have to start raining again.

She hurried along to the bus shelter, and shivered as she stood there alone, looking around at the past. The shops across the road and next to the bus stop didn't look to have changed much while she'd been away, except that the corner shop now sold take-away pizzas and baked potatoes instead of wool and embroidery silks. She remembered buying balls of green wool there and knitting John a disaster of a sweater, trying, and failing once again, to impress his Mother.

Sheila Stanworth had been appalled at the idea of her son marrying Lynda Collins, whom she considered to be 'a common, flighty piece'. But John had stubbornly refused to listen, and in the end Sheila had realised that if she tried to stop him, she would lose him.

Her opposition had upset Lynda, but after the first year of their marriage she'd given up trying to get along with her mother-in-law, and had settled for tongue-biting animosity instead.

A cold, damp, chilling wind, having whipped its way across the rough grasses of the Lancashire hills which cradled the town in a begrudged embrace, thrust Lynda against the glass of the shelter, and made her shiver even more.

A short distance away, a little, sharp eyed woman in her late sixties was battling to stop the wind snatching hold of her red umbrella and empty grey shopping bag. Alice Smith was a bright little finch of a woman, always alert for the crumbs of life she needed from other people's tables. She compensated her self-esteem by observing, and sometimes playing with, the weaknesses of her patrons.

As she regained control of her umbrella, Lynda's luxurious coat and small expensive suitcase caught her eye. Alice stopped and gazed up at her.

'Is it Lynda?'

Trapped in her wide-eyed stare, Lynda tried to smile.

'Yes. Hello, Alice.'

'You're back then. How long has it been?'

'Over ten years.'

'Yes, it must be. You've come home at last, eh?'

'Yeah. Sort of.'

Relieved to see the bus approaching, Lynda managed a tense smile and said, 'Nice to see you again.'

The woman's small dark eyes glittered with the excitement of speculation, as she anticipated the effect of Lynda's return on certain inhabitants of Milfield.

'Yes. I'll say the same,' Alice responded. 'Though there's those that wouldn't.'

Lynda quickly got on the bus, and Alice smiled and waved, thinking that, although there would, indeed, be people who would not welcome this woman back to Milfield, she was glad Lynda was back.

Alice, an incurable gossip who couldn't always resist doing mischief, had never had many friends. When her widowed father, her sole companion, had died, people had offered polite sympathy, and then swiftly move on.

Apart from Dan Heywood, the owner of the bakery where Alice worked, Lynda had been the only person who had called, not once, but several times during those desperately lonely months, to sit and talk, and comfort her. Alice had never forgotten that.

It was a long time since Lynda had been on a bus.

Tom had taught her to drive and, as well as the Mercedes, he'd even allowed her to sit behind the wheel of the classic red MG that had been his pride and joy. He'd wanted to leave it to Lynda, in memory of the happy times they'd had driving around in it together, but Suzanne had insisted that he gave it to their son, Mark. Lynda loved Mark almost as much as Tom had, so she'd been able to accept his having the car. But she'd hated Suzanne for arguing with a dying man.

The bus was comfortingly warm, with red and grey plush seats, it was a different creature from the draughty old brown and yellow double-decker buses that used to rattle into town, but the scenery it toured hadn't changed much.

A few of the tall chimneys which had stood guard beside the old cotton mills were still there, black against the sky, standing now in stubborn defiance against the modern age. They towered above the sexy images on the billboards placed in front of the crumbling buildings of the now derelict local brewery. Grass was growing from the gutters and windows, but the walls still bore the faded name of what had been a favourite local beer.

It reminded Lynda now of her teenage years when she'd served drinks behind the bar in The Black Bull, working as cheap labour for the landlord, her unappreciative father. But she didn't want to revive those bad memories, she'd enough to think about, starting with John, and Carolyn.

In Milfield town centre traffic had been moved aside to make more room for shoppers. The bus route now went along the back of the main road, Broad Street, which Lynda and her teenage friends had nicknamed 'Broadway' in the days when it had been lit up with theatres, cinemas and a dance hall.

'Broadway' was the street she had giddied along arm in arm with girlfriends, laughing at the lads who had huddled in groups to smoke, and to shout comments aimed at provoking a response from the girls and, if they were lucky, a bit of encouragement.

Now the bus squeezed its way past the offices of estate agents and solicitors as well as local council organisations. Lynda looked out of the windows eagerly, just in case she might by chance catch a glimpse of her daughter, her only child. Would she recognise Carolyn, though? She'd be thirty now, and would probably have a different hairstyle.

Lynda hunched her shoulders in embarrassment at the thought that she might not recognise her own daughter. Then she sat up straight and told herself not to be stupid, of course she'd know her, nobody changes that much. And yet she was hoping that Carolyn would have changed.

CHAPTER TWO

Lynda's son-in-law, Steve Sheldon thought that Carolyn had changed, a lot, in the last few years. Sometimes he hardly recognised the girl he had married, it was as if she wasn't 'his Carolyn' any more. His Carolyn was the one who laughed at his jokes, who nestled in his arms, grateful for the warmth and reassurance he offered when she was hiding from demons of self-doubt.

His Carolyn was the Mum who would go without to give their children the things they needed, who was proud of even their smallest achievements, and who would hold them in her arms every chance they gave her to show how much she loved them.

But this new Carolyn, this ambitious business woman who, these days, appeared even more proud of wearing smart suits, and working longer hours seemed, especially over the last few months, to be constantly moving further away from him. And he felt powerless to stop her.

Steve Sheldon was good looking, with steady brown eyes, shoulders you could lean on, and a smile many girls had remembered in their dreams. As a teenager he'd kept up with his mates as far as having girlfriends was concerned, but he'd never even looked at another woman once he'd kissed Carolyn Stanworth.

There never seemed to be time for hugs and kisses now, and Steve was worried about the rows they'd been having lately, like the one that had flared up this morning in their bedroom.

Everything had seemed fairly normal. He'd been putting on his faded shirt and battered jeans, getting ready to go to work and take the kids to school on the way, and Carolyn had been carefully applying her make-up. She was wearing her dressing gown over her underwear, waiting to slip her still slender body into the new, designer-label suit which was hanging on the front of the wardrobe.

Steve had built that wardrobe a few years ago, and he was still proud of its quality and design. Carolyn had loved it, too, and had been even more proud of it than he was. He had impressed her in those days, but not now.

He sighed as he looked at her slim figure, and the pale golden hair which was smoother and shorter than he liked it to be; he saw that, in her head, his wife was already half way into the career woman persona which carried her away from him. Sitting on the end of the bed, lacing up his work boots, Steve had tried to ignore the items which signalled that today was not routine: Carolyn's smart new suit, dark blue with velvet lapels, the small suitcase she had almost finished packing, her new black leather briefcase lying beside it on the bed. It was as if these objects were forming a barrier between them.

Carolyn was leaving for another two day conference and her boss, Paul Ferris, would be coming at 9.30 to pick her up and drive her to the hotel in his silver BMW.

The kids were arguing downstairs as they packed their school bags, but Carolyn had ignored it. She'd wanted to think only of the pleasures ahead, the freedom from domestic responsibilities, but guilt elbowed its way in and crowded her mind with small anxieties.

Watching herself in the mirror, she'd suddenly

pictured her Dad alone in his flat, the tired, haunted look which was too often in his eyes. She loved her father very much, wanted him to be happy, but she also felt guilty that she couldn't devote more of her life to him.

'You won't leave them too long with Dad, will you?' she said.

She knew the hint of exasperation in Steve's voice was justified; he cared about John Stanworth as much as she did, perhaps more in some ways.

'Of course, I won't. I'll pick them up as soon as I finish work.'

Then Carolyn had heard herself adopting the assertive tone she used in the office.

'Don't say anything about the re-organisation, he'll only start worrying.'

Steve had turned to face her reflection in the mirror. His stubborn, determined expression had made it clear to Carolyn that she'd made no progress with her arguments during these last few weeks. When would he see that they had to leave Milfield?

'Your Dad would be right to worry - if we were moving. Good thing we're not, eh?'

'We could be, if I get that job at head office.'

'I don't know why you applied,' Steve had muttered.

Carolyn's mouth had tightened. 'Because it's a good job, and a promotion I deserve. And Leeds isn't that far away. I wish you'd at least think about the possibility of moving.'

'I've thought about it, we've talked about it.' He'd moved to stand behind her. 'Now give us a kiss and forget about it,' he'd said.

He'd tried to embrace her but, not wanting her make-up ruined, Carolyn had turned away.

'Steve. I'm serious. You're not happy at

14

Randerson's. And there are no prospects for you there, or anywhere in Milfield as far as I can see.'

Steve had stood up, solid and resolute. He was calm, in control, knowing he had made his decision. She'd seen that gleaming certainty which always shone in his eyes once he'd made up his mind about something.

That look of his used to excite her. It had been there when Steve had made up his mind, all those years ago, that she was going to be his, and it had made her lose all reason. And look where that had got her, she'd often thought, still living in the same old semi-detached house in Milfield.

Steve's words had come steadily.

'I don't want to move, it's a simple as that.'

'Is it? What about what I want?'

'Nobody knows what that is, least of all you!'

She'd turned to face him.

'I do know. I want to get away from Milfield. If I get that job, I'm going to take it, Steve.'

'Even though it'd mean all our lives being turned upside down? And for what? Just so that you can earn some more money.'

'There'd be nothing wrong with that.'

He'd looked at her, and she'd seen that that old feeling of guilt was fuelling a resentment he was ashamed of.

'What are you saying, Carolyn? That I'm sabotaging your plans for the future, again?'

He'd picked up his jacket, once quite smart but now shabby even for work. He'd looked at it, and then met Carolyn's eyes. She'd stared at the jacket, and he'd seen that it hurt her to have him wearing a coat like that. She wanted him to have the best, always and in every way - he knew that. Like he knew that she loved him, even when she was fighting as she

15

was now, against him and all the kinds of things he based his life on.

She'd tried again. 'It'd be a different life'.

'What's wrong with the one we've got here?'

'It's not the life I want.'

He'd shaken his head and, putting on his jacket, was already moving towards the door. In a few minutes he'd be gone. They'd go their separate ways, and today, Carolyn knew, the way she was going might take her too far, far enough to be lost.

She'd sprung to her feet, angry but also desperate at the possibility of losing everything she wanted to hold on to.

'Steve!' she'd shouted, 'Why can't you listen? Why can't you damned well hear what I'm saying for once?'

He'd stopped and stared at her, then shaken his head slowly in that patronising way she hated, so she'd ended up yelling at him.

'What the hell do I have to do to make you hear me?'

He'd had enough now. His tone was sardonic and incisive.

'Shout a bit louder - we don't want the kids to miss it, do we!'

A few minutes later it was all over, but not forgotten. Carolyn had kissed Michael and Gemma goodbye. She'd hugged and kissed her daughter, but Michael had moved his head away, so that only a fleeting whisper of his Mother's lips touched his forehead, and Carolyn had tried not to mind.

Steve had minded that Carolyn had only given him a cool, light kiss on the cheek before stepping back before he could put his arms round her. It was this physical withdrawal which upset him more than

16

anything. It made him very unsure every time she held herself away from him like that, giving out the message that she didn't want him to touch her.

He didn't know that his wife had not meant to let him walk out of the door with his head bowed like that, but her anger hadn't died away in time for her to call him back. In fact the anger had stayed with her so strongly that Carolyn had been overwhelmed with the need for some kind of petty revenge against Steve.

Later, when she was dressed, she'd looked again at her reflection in the mirror, and seen not only the designer suit and smooth blonde hair, but also the cold eyes, and she hadn't liked the image which confronted her. The collar of her silk shirt lay cool and pristine white against the midnight blue of her jacket. Too clinical, too masculine. She didn't want the career image to take away her womanhood.

She'd heard Paul's car draw up outside, and slowly she'd undone another button of her shirt and pulled the collar aside to reveal more of the smooth white softness of her skin.

Moving across to the window, she'd watched Paul getting out of the sleek, powerful car. Tall and lean, he looked like a fashion model in his perfectly tailored grey suit, and carefully chosen, expensive silk tie. His dazzlingly white shirt showed off his smoothly tanned skin as a light breeze had lifted his dark blonde hair away from his handsome face. Sensing he was being observed, he'd looked up and, with a smile, walked round the car and given a gallant salute as he'd positioned himself to wait to open the passenger door for her.

As she'd leaned towards the window Carolyn had glanced down and seen that her breasts had now eased forward to form a provocative cleavage within the white fold of the collar. She'd looked down at

Paul again and, before picking up her case, had carefully re-fastened the button.

CHAPTER THREE

The bus eventually reached the other side of the town, and Lynda got off at the end of Bridge Street. The small suitcase was beginning to feel heavy, and again she wished she'd left it with its larger companions in the locker at the train station. She was ashamed that she'd chickened out of walking into her own home. And she knew she'd look a fool turning up on Jean's doorstep with a suitcase when Beechwood Avenue was only a couple of miles away.

She could afford to stay in a top class hotel, no problem, but it would make her think too much of Loveday Manor, and anyway it seemed wrong somehow to stay in a hotel in your own home town. After all, that was the reason she'd come back to Milfield, she wanted to come home, to belong. But it wasn't going to be easy, any of it. Even knocking on her best friend's door meant a deep breath and a flutter of fear inside her.

Jean Haworth had tagged along with Lynda since that first day at primary school when Lynda Collins, as she was then, had placed herself between Jean, cowering in a shabby brown raincoat that was miles too long for her, and the bullies who had gathered to mock.

The Collins family had also been having a hard time in those days, but at least Lynda's Dad had worked for a living. He wasn't like Stan Clayton, Jean's big fisted, uncaring father, who'd only take a job if it offered quick and easy cash in the hand, with no questions asked. Lynda had been Jean's best friend since those early schooldays, and the friendship had even survived Lynda having married John Stanworth, the boy Jean Clayton had set her heart on.

Lynda had thought that Jean would always be her friend, until that final phone call in 1985, several weeks after Lynda had walked out on her husband, her daughter and baby grandson.

'I'm sick of this, Lynda,' Jean had shouted at her down the phone. 'I'm not playing go-between any more. If you want to know how they are, you can damned well phone them, or come back and see them!'

'No, I can't. It's taken all my strength to do this, and if I come back now, nothing will be different, except that they'll want me even less.'

'What else can you expect, after what you've put them through? You don't deserve a good husband like John. The poor man doesn't know what to say to people when they ask where you are.'

'He knows where I am. I left a letter for him to find, and sent him a birthday card with my address on it, but he hasn't written to me.'

'Oh? Well, he hasn't said anything about it. All I know is that he used to tell people you'd gone for a few days holiday. But he can't keep saying that when you've been away for months! It makes him look a fool, not knowing where his wife is.'

Lynda had felt tears on her cheeks as she'd pictured the tall strong man she had married reduced to looking foolish in front of his mates. Then the memories of the battles she had lost had made her stiffen, as if someone had wrapped a cold, heavy mantle around her body. Her next question had gone to the heart of the matter.

'Has Carolyn asked you about me?'

That had silenced Jean for a moment, then she'd had to give Lynda an answer she knew would hurt.

'No.'

'Then I'm doing right to keep away, aren't I?'

'No. You can't do this. You've got a baby grandson here, little Michael, who won't remember what his Grandma looks like. You've got to come home, back where you belong.'

'But that's the point, Jean, I don't belong.'

Jean had never been able to cope with complex relationships, and her inadequacy made her angry.

'Oh, you're just being stupid, Lynda, and stubborn, and selfish. And I've just about had enough of it all. Don't phone me again, phone your family!'

Jean had slammed down the receiver, and Lynda had never phoned again. She hadn't written to her family either, not after the Christmas present she'd sent for Michael had been returned unopened.

Lynda noticed that the front door of Jean's small terraced house needed a lick of paint, and wondered how Jean was doing, moneywise, and whether she'd married again.

Jean's sensible and adoring husband, Gordon Haworth, had bought this cosy little house, and Jean had tried, unsuccessfully, not to show her disappointment that they'd had to move out of his much grander family home when his mother had died.

Even though she'd been only twenty-two, Jean Clayton had felt in danger of being left on the shelf. Lynda and almost every other school friend had married, and many of them already had children. So, when gentle, hard working Gordon Haworth, encouraged by his enthusiastic Mother, had carried out the most romantic of courtships, Jean had eventually agreed to become his wife.

She'd tried not to notice that he was ten years older than her, and that he wasn't tall and handsome, with thick dark hair and big brown eyes like John Stanworth.

Gordon had been the assistant manager in the furniture department at the Co-op, and Jean had been thrilled to be able to live in his Mother's large and relatively grand semi-detached house, but only Lynda knew the truth.

It had been a love match for Gordon Haworth, but one girls' night out, when she'd had a few drinks, Jean had confessed to Lynda that she wasn't sure whether she should have married him.

Lynda sighed as she remembered Gordon. He was a good man and a devoted husband, and he hadn't deserved the heart attack which had killed him when only in his forties. After he died Jean had tried to convince herself that she'd made him happy, and that he had never guessed that she hadn't loved him. Lynda had had to spend a lot of time comforting Jean, and helping her cope with her feeling of guilt.

Standing at this neglected front door, and thinking about the death of Jean's husband, made Lynda think of Tom Meredith, whom she had married barely two months ago, on Valentine's Day, just four weeks before he died.

Lynda fought back the tears, pushed those thoughts away, and pinned a smile on her face as she heard a scrabbling at the lock, followed by the rattle of a security chain. The door opened a few inches, and then was pulled back to reveal a slightly shapeless figure in a brown A-line skirt and a washed-out blue cardigan. Jean Haworth's face was pale beneath her short, dull brown hair, and her eyes were tired; but then it was if a light had been switched on.

'Oh! It isn't, is it? Lynda?'

Lynda shook her head in mock reproach.

'Oh, you do know how to make a girl feel good, you! I know it's been over ten years, but I haven't aged that much, have I?'

'No. No, of course not.'

Then, for a moment, the delight faded and anxiety took its usual place among Jean's thoughts.

'No. It's such a shock, that's all. Do you want to come in?'

Lynda laughed, picked up her case and drove Jean back into the house towards the strains of Elvis Presley rumbling out 'Good Luck Charm' from the radio-cassette recorder on the sideboard in the living room. Lynda had for years teased Jean about her Elvis obsession.

'Of course I want to come in! Get the kettle on, for god's sake! And turn him off!'

Lynda had to blink back tears as she stood looking round Jean's living room, full of mementoes of the past they had shared. She gazed fondly at the souvenirs from Blackpool, Jean and Gordon's silver framed wedding photograph, and the daft looking china dogs Jean had inherited from her aunty Daisy.

Lynda used to feel at ease in this room, and in the old days she would have just plonked herself down on the settee and made herself at home. Now she stood there awkwardly.

Jean was aware of the tension, too, and felt a ridiculous combination of shyness and defiance. They heard Elvis again, now pleading to be their Teddy Bear and suddenly their eyes met, and they laughed.

'I can't believe you're still mad about Elvis!'

'I always was, and I always will be, but seeing as it's you.'

Jean switched off the tape, and when she turned back to Lynda she found her friend was holding her arms open wide and had tears in her eyes. Jean hesitated for a second, and then let herself be enveloped in the old warmth and feeling of safety Lynda had always offered her.

'I wondered if you'd let me in,' Lynda said, her voice hoarse with emotion.

Jean looked at her, and shook her head gently.

'We both said things we shouldn't have.'

'That telephone line must have nearly blown a fuse!'

Jean laughed a little nervously as she watched Lynda take off her coat.

Gently and lovingly, Lynda asked, 'How are you, love?'

'I'm all right.' Jean said, and was dismayed at how unconvinced she sounded. She looked at Lynda and, with her heart suddenly full of memories of their friendship, she sighed, 'Oh, it is nice to see you.'

'I'm glad to see you as well.'

'Have you been to Beechwood Avenue?'

'Yeah, but I hadn't told them I was coming, so they weren't in.'

'No, they'd be at work.'

Jean took hold of Lynda's elegant black coat and smoothed its collar, appreciating the quality. She looked at Lynda, and had so many questions in her head, if they'd been a pile of books they'd have toppled over. But she just said, 'Well?'

Lynda gave one of those enigmatic little smiles that had always signalled she wasn't telling, but Jean knew she would, when she was ready. Jean went back into the hallway to arrange the coat carefully on a hanger.

Lynda still didn't sit down, but felt more confident now.

'I'm gasping for a cuppa.'

Jean slipped back years into the old habit of playful rebuke.

'You always did time it right, you. I'd just boiled the kettle'. Then concern altered her tone, and she looked anxiously at her friend. 'How are you doing, Lynda?'

Lynda grinned, flung out her arms and did an extravagant twirl, letting her image speak for itself. Jean smiled, and nodded approvingly, but then turned quickly away as she couldn't stop the old envious resentment shadowing her eyes.

She headed for the kitchen but then, again assessing Lynda's professionally styled hair, and expensive clothes, she went instead to the display cabinet which had belonged to her mother-in-law, and took out rose-sprinkled china cups and saucers. Lynda put down the photo she was smiling at.

'Your best cups and saucers?' she exclaimed. 'Good heavens, what have I done to deserve this?'

To her surprise, Jean blushed and looked guilty as she replied, 'Nothing.' She forced a laugh, 'You don't deserve it!'

Lynda winced. 'That's true.'

Jean scuttled into the kitchen, and then darted back to the cabinet for the matching milk jug and sugar bowl, taking them to be dusted and filled. With a sigh, which held more relief than she expected, Lynda snuggled herself into the cushions in the corner of the settee, and tried to look relaxed.

Jean returned with the jug of milk and teaspoons.

'Do you still take sugar?'

'Yes. Haven't managed to lose all my bad habits.' Lynda paused for a moment, and then stated firmly,

'I have changed, though.'

Jean's lips tightened a little.

'I should hope so. You've been away long enough.'

Lynda took a deep breath, trying to keep her voice steady, as she asked, 'How are they all?'

Jean stopped setting out the cups and saucers, and started to give a brief account which, even as she very carefully uttered the words, seemed to her stupidly banal in the context of Lynda's sudden re-entry into their lives.

'They're fine. Carolyn's got a good job, she works at Addison Financial Services now, and it sounds like she's going to be a manager one day. She's earning more than Steve already, I think. He's still in the same job. And Michael and Gemma are both doing well at school.'

'Gemma?'

The old disapproval was back in Jean's eyes now. 'Yes. You've got a granddaughter. She's ten.'

Lynda was too delighted to take any notice of Jean's expression.

'Oh! Lovely! I wondered if they'd have another.'

Jean wasn't impressed with the enthusiasm. 'Did you?'

The guilt which had haunted Lynda for the last twelve years, made her shift her eyes away from Jean's, like a cat needing to slink away. She had to swallow hard before asking the next question. Oh, there were so many questions she wanted to ask, and some she didn't, but would have to.

'And John?'

'He had a heart attack last year.'

Jean heard Lynda catch her breath, but waited a little before giving reassurance. Jean had always fought hard to push away her malevolent little demon of resentment and envy, nurtured within her by her miserable childhood, but it wouldn't leave her. Now it was there again, inducing her to inflict a small moment of suffering.

Lynda's eyes were wide with fear, and Jean felt ashamed at having made her wait.

'He's O K. but it was very frightening. I'd have phoned you if I'd had a number.'

CHAPTER FOUR

In the stone-flagged yard of what once had been the Victoria cotton mill, Steve Sheldon was dying for a cup of tea. The employees at 'Randerson's Bedroom and Kitchen Design Ltd.' had managed to hang on to the tradition of tea-breaks by ignoring the owner when he glowered, grunted and looked at the clock. Tony Randerson had eventually learned to avoid coming into the workshop at tea-break time, and that was why he had called Steve out into the yard.

He wanted to get this matter sorted quickly because he'd planned, as usual, to take the Friday afternoon off to play golf with business associates. Many of these suspected that golf wasn't the only game Randerson played on Fridays. Tony Randerson's wife, Angela, worked hard to support children's charities, and was the daughter of the late owner of the company, Ralph Bentham. According to local gossip, her husband had always been more attracted by Angela's wealth than by her womanhood.

Randerson always left Steve in charge when he took time off. He depended a lot on him as his production manager, and main design talent, but he'd never admit it. He would have been furious if he'd known that Steve was planning to leave.

Steve Sheldon was determined that he would, one day, be a designer of all kinds of furniture, that his designs would be bought all over the world, and would make everyday living a sensuous pleasure. And he wasn't just a dreamer who sketched ideas on paper and put them away in a drawer. Steve could make these works of art, like the one he was going to deliver to Bob Horton's Victorian mansion that evening.

Steve hated working for a bullying chancer like Randerson. He was desperate to be his own boss, and his dream was to own his own company. Fortunately for Randerson, that dream, at the moment, didn't stand much chance of coming true.

And what Steve had to deal with now was the reality of the pieces of paper Randerson had handed to him. Steve, after the upset of the row with Carolyn earlier this morning, had hoped to avoid Randerson today.

Steve couldn't stand this arrogant, middle-aged man who was standing in front of him, smoothing back his carefully tinted dark hair which curled on to the collar of his Armani suit.

'It's the Sheffield order. They want it delivered by Thursday.'

'That's a week earlier than we agreed,' Steve protested.

'They can do it.'

Steve thought of the men he supervised and the grim faces whenever mortgages and M.O.Ts for their ageing cars were talked about. He decided to go for it.

'On overtime,' he said firmly.

'No chance,' snarled Randerson and walked back across the yard and into the office. Steve watched him resentfully, and sighed as he walked into the workshop.

As part of a former cotton mill the workshop, with its bare stone walls and draughty metal-framed windows, offered all the features of an age when the comfort of the workers was a rare consideration. Randerson had seen no reason not to adopt the same approach, he was a man who simply shrugged his shoulders at any complaint about inadequate heating or out-dated machinery.

The labour force at Randerson's consisted of Steve, his mate, Gary Pearson, a couple of men who worked part-time, and the big, fresh-faced eighteen year old apprentice, Matthew Crowther.

Also, up in the office, there was Josie Williams, a bright twenty-one year old from a straight-talking, mixed race family. Josie played the role of PA in a way designed to massage Randerson's ego, but she understood much better than he did the spreadsheets she produced on her computer. She also liked talking to people on the telephone.

The April weather wasn't warm enough to counteract the cold in the workshop. All the men wore old, baggy woollen sweaters to ward off the chill of the damp air, which seemed to creep off the walls and attach itself to their skin as they bent their backs to make the units which sold cheaply, and hid no quality beneath their veneer.

Gary Pearson, a wiry, healthy cynic in his thirties, was cursing as he screwed a kitchen cabinet together. He looked up as Steve entered.

'Bloody hell! What am I supposed to do with wood like this? It's like bloody egg-carton!'

Steve knew he was right to complain, and hesitated before sharing the bad news with Gary. Steve always went to him first, even though he worried about some of the things Gary did, and his nonchalance about bending any rules.

Gary had been a mate of Steve's ever since they'd played together as scrawny kids, who'd preferred to be on the street rather than in their cramped, cheerless, terraced homes where there was always a war on.

'Randerson wants the Sheffield order ready to be delivered by Thursday.'

Gary's answer was automatic. 'Can't be done.'

'That's what I said.'

Matthew heard this and, always wanting to be helpful, made a suggestion. 'We might be able to do it if we work this weekend.'

Gary turned slowly to face him.

'I worry about you, Matthew, a young man of your age.'

Matthew was wary of Gary. His Mother had warned him about the Pearson family, but there was something about Gary's street-wise manner that was compelling, so he had to ask. 'Why?'

Gary sighed heavily.

'Because, young Matthew, you need to get yourself a woman. You should be devoting the weekends to your primal instincts, looking for a mate, not offering to spend them making a profit for Tony Randerson.'

Matthew tried to reassert himself as a man of the world.

'He'd pay us double time, wouldn't he?'

Gary straightened up to his full five-foot five and smiled wryly as he shook his head. He reached up and patted Matthew on both cheeks, like a little old lady congratulating a talented child.

'Aaah. You keep on believing, don't you?'

'What?'

Gary's smile disappeared. 'That Randerson can't really be the bastard we all know him to be.'

The Cedars Hotel and Conference Centre was so beautiful that, as soon as you saw it you knew you

31

wouldn't want to leave. The distinguished golden sandstone Edwardian mansion had, a few years ago, been acquired by an entrepreneur with sound ideas as well as money to invest. He had appreciated the house in every way, and when tastefully converting and extending it he had taken care to maintain its aura of calm.

Along the front of the house was a wide stone terrace, leading down to a long lawn and fragrant and colourful flower beds. There was a rose garden with a fountain, and, a little further away, the shade of horse-chestnut trees, willows and, of course, magnificent cedars.

As soon as Carolyn saw the house the desire to belong in such surroundings made her breathe out a sigh, like she used to as a child gazing longingly at the windows of expensive toy shops.

Paul Ferris, easing the BMW along the driveway, heard this small sound and saw the look on Carolyn's face. In that moment he discovered the source of the weakness he had perceived beneath the surface of the diffident, business-like manner she presented at the office. Carolyn Sheldon coveted the precious delights of a life far beyond the little world she inhabited.

'Lovely, isn't it?' he said.

'Oh, yes. It's perfect'.

'A pity we're here to work. It will seem a shame to waste these surroundings on seminars and workshops. Especially in such attractive company.'

Carolyn knew that, if she looked at him, the smiling eyes would offer an invitation as well as the compliment. She turned away to gaze out of the car window and concentrate on the pretty flower beds with their daffodils and pink and gold tulips.

Paul had been making his admiration obvious for months now. She was sure the other women at work were beginning to notice the attention he paid her, and the way he stood very close to her at every opportunity. His closeness made her feel the warmth of sexual longing within her, but experience had taught her, more than once, that it was a mistake to let yourself get carried away by such an impetuous physical response.

When she was seventeen Carolyn's passion and need for Steve Sheldon had overpowered her. It had destroyed all the dreams she had focused on at school, where she had far less money than all her friends but more brain-power than any of them.

With her Nana, Sheila Stanworth, and Sheila's wealthy friend, Ellen Heywood, as her champions she'd been about to break free, and escape to a different world, to go to university and a future away from Milfield. Then she had shocked and disappointed them both by getting pregnant.

Carolyn didn't regret having Michael, she loved him with a fierce protectiveness which sometimes made him resent her supervision of his life and his behaviour. She was not happy that, at twelve years old, he was already starting the phase of shrugging away from her as he focused on his determination to belong in the world of men.

What Carolyn did regret was that her life, and that of her husband and children, had not moved on. It drove her mad that they were still living in a semi-detached house in Milfield, when she had dreamed of spending her life in a house more like this one.

As if he'd read her thoughts, Paul Ferris smiled at her again.

'You'd make a wonderful mistress for a house like this.'

She noted the slight emphasis on the word 'mistress', and tried to ignore the flutter of excitement it caused her. She'd also pretended to ignore it when, during their journey to the hotel, Paul had brushed his hand along her thigh in a casual way which could have been excused as 'accidental', but which both of them knew had been absolutely intended.

Paul Ferris frightened her. Carolyn couldn't tell Steve that one of the reasons she wanted to apply for promotion to head office, was to get away from the temptation of this man to whom she was so unwillingly attracted.

He was well thought of in the office, he used his charm to make his junior colleagues forgive the pressure he put them under. His experience had been, without exception, that all the women who had ever worked for him would do almost anything for him, even those who studiously disregarded the power of his very handsome and very masculine presence.

Carolyn had been one of those who had resisted acknowledging his attraction, but Paul had seen that she was having to work hard at defending herself from enticement. He knew she was vulnerable to his wanting her.

Paul Ferris had taken care in the office to be discreet with his gradual seduction, but knew he was achieving some success when he'd felt Carolyn tremble a little if he brushed against her. When he took hold of her hand for a brief moment, he'd smiled at the way she hesitated before withdrawing from his touch. It had become a game of sex for him , and one which he intended to win.

CHAPTER FIVE

The afternoon sun which shone on the lawns at The Cedars Hotel struggled to gain access to John Stanworth's flat through the lace curtains which shrouded its windows. The light from the television set was brighter, and John was gazing at it in the hope of a few minutes of distraction from the silence which otherwise would fill every corner of the tiny living room. He sat in his armchair and zapped at the channels of day-time television, until the babble of female trivia exasperated him and he turned it off.

He was a tall, lean man with thick, wavy hair which he used secretly to brush with colour, but which he was now allowing to fade into greyness. As a good-looking teenager he had sauntered through town, enjoying admiring glances from girls, and in his twenties he'd been a man other men used to look for when they walked into the pub seeking good company.

And now here he was in a poky flat crammed with furniture which, like him, was too big for it. He stood up and moved around restlessly in his restrictive surroundings. As he paused to look in the mirror over the fireplace, he wondered where the real John Stanworth had gone, because that pale defeated face couldn't really be him, could it?

Walking past large school photos of his grandchildren, Gemma and Michael, their parents' wedding photo, and a studio portrait of Carolyn as a teenager, he selected an Elvis Presley LP from the collection in the cabinet next to his stereo. He placed it carefully on the turntable of his stereo system and released its wave of nostalgia into the room.

In a reflex reaction he flashed his arms out wide in an Elvis pose, and flicked his hips as the notes of the bass guitar pounded energy back into his limbs. He began to dance, but then caught his reflection ridiculing him and stopped.

John looked at the clock on the mantelpiece below the mirror, and at the two tablets next to the clock, and remembered he hadn't yet taken his midday medication. He stuffed the tablet into in his mouth and wandered across to the window, lifted the net curtain and peered outside. With a sigh he turned away from the light and, looking round the room, he sought the company of the faces in the photos on the sideboard.

He focused on the one of Carolyn. Ever since she was born, he'd loved to look at her and hear the compliments. And people were right, she was a lovely looking girl, and her hair was pure gold, like her Mother's. His body tensed at that thought, getting ready for the pain as he opened a drawer in the sideboard and slowly took out another photograph, one of a young woman who had the same golden hair, but very different in style.

Lynda's hair had always been allowed to curl and cascade over her shoulders. The vitality of the photograph always surprised him, it was as if the big smile on her face was flashing around to try to light up the room. Lynda. His lips parted to speak her name but then he felt his heart contract a little. He quickly put Lynda's photograph away, so that again it was hidden, almost like a guilty secret, in the back of the drawer.

The doorbell rang and John answered it cautiously, he wasn't expecting anyone. On the doorstep, hands in his pockets as usual, stood Alan Whittaker, a sixty-five year old as indefatigable as a Jack Russell terrier.

Alan, who seemed to spend most of his retirement constantly trying to outmanoeuvre his wife, Beryl, lived in one of the bungalows opposite. These and the block of two storey flats formed the senior citizens reservation allocated by the local council and optimistically christened 'Sunnybank'. Milfield councillors were renowned for their selective use of statistics and in this case had completely disregarded those relating to the weather in the area.

'Hey up, John! She's sending me to Asda, thank god! Are you coming with me?'

'No, thanks.'

'Come on, keep me company.'

John felt the fresh wind on his face and smelled the stale air of the flat behind him. A trip round the supermarket - hardly a lads day out, was it? But he swallowed his masculine pride and told himself to be thankful for small mercies.

'OK. Hang on a minute.'

He stepped back inside to get his jacket, and locked the door behind him. Alan's battered blue Metro was parked outside the bungalow.

'Is there anything you want?' Alan asked, trying to instil some sense of purpose into the outing for John.

'I don't think so.'

Alan tilted his head towards the window where his wife Beryl was peering out. She was just checking he really was going at long last, and that she could have a quiet hour with her Catherine Cookson.

'There's a lot I want,' Alan said with a wink and a lecherous smile, 'but I won't get it, not while I'm married to Beryl!'

John laughed and got into the car. Alan, starting the engine, glanced across at him.

'It's a hard life when you can't have what you want, isn't it?'

'Yeah.'

'Women,' Alan snorted as he eased the car into second gear, 'pleasure and pain, eh?'

John remembered his feelings as he'd looked at the forbidden fruit of Lynda's photograph. It was ridiculous that he felt he had to keep it shut away in the drawer, but he knew Carolyn couldn't bear to be reminded of her Mother.

Alan held strong views about the women in John's life, and liked to pour out a dram of the spirit of rebellion whenever he could.

'You and me ought to make a break for it.'

John, finding some of the humour he'd salvaged from his youth, responded with a sly, mocking smile.

'What? You and me? Run away together?'

Alan gave him a shove. 'You know what I mean! Get away from these bloody women, my Mrs and your Carolyn, and maybe the nursemaid you've been courting as well.'

'I think it might be a bit too late.'

Alan couldn't stand the resignation in his friend's voice.

'For me, perhaps, but not for you, John, surely?'

John shrugged, but rubbed his fingers thoughtfully across the stubble on his chin as he stared out of the car window.

In the little terraced house in Bridge Street Jean, still playing hostess, had managed to find a packet of biscuits.

'They're only cheap, not the sort of thing you're used to now, by the look of you.'

Lynda reached out and took one, 'Custard creams, my favourite.'

38

Jean, sitting opposite her, leaned forward, wanting to find out everything. She already knew the answer to her next question, but asked it anyway.

'So where was it you waltzed off to?'

'Cornwall.'

'Oh, yes, to see your friend.'

'Yeah. To see Rose.'

'Wasn't she the woman John's father ran off with?'

'Yes, you remember. Ted went to live with her in Blackpool. When he died she moved to Cornwall, a place called St Benedict, she had friends there.'

Jean pursed her lips, but her eyes betrayed her excitement at the scandal. 'I remember seeing her at Ted's funeral, and John's Mother chasing her away. You had to feel sorry for Sheila, having her husband leave her for another woman, and at his age.'

'It was Ted I felt sorry for. Sheila had been making his life a misery for years, he deserved a bit of happiness.'

Jean was familiar enough with John's family to know that there was more than a little truth in that.

'So you went to stay with her. How long for?'

'I didn't stay with Rose, I stayed at a hotel, The Springfield, owned by Robbie Skelton, a friend of hers. And he offered me a job there.'

'And you decided to take it, and not to come home to your family.'

'Yeah, Carolyn had made it very clear they didn't want me back.'

'Carolyn? Did she?'

'Yes. I didn't tell you, but I phoned her the first week I was away, and we had a helluva row, and she told me not to bother ever coming back.'

'Oh. I didn't know that.'

'No, I remember, you thought I was just being

selfish, and having a lovely long holiday.'

'Well, that's what it looked like. And why did you have to go so far away? Cornwall!'

'I couldn't think of anywhere else to run to. And I had to go, Jean, I really did. My life here wasn't worth living.'

'Don't talk rubbish!'

'I'm not! I was close to a nervous breakdown, but I didn't realise it till I got away.'

Jean shook her head.

'Lynda, it's no good making excuses. What you did was wrong! Like I said, I don't understand how you could do it. Walking out on them like that!'

Lynda looked at her friend beseechingly.

'Jean, you know I tried to make it work, but Sheila Stanworth didn't give me a chance, did she?'

Jean suspected that was true, and listened carefully now.

'She never forgave me for marrying her son,' Lynda continued. 'And she turned Carolyn, my own daughter, against me. I was nobody in my own home, Jean!'

'You left your family, and your first grandchild. Did you never wonder how little Michael was, what he was like?'

'Of course I did. That's why I tried to keep in touch through you, till you didn't want to bother any more.'

Jean folded her arms again. 'Don't you start blaming me!'

'I'm not. I know who was to blame, Sheila Stanworth, and our Carolyn. And me.'

Lynda brushed away a tear, her hand shaking a little. Jean noticed the diamond and sapphire ring she was now wearing next to her wedding ring. She wondered about it, but Lynda had always liked rings,

40

and had worn them on any finger, according to her whim rather than convention.

Jean sat back and watched her friend in silence for a while.

Lynda, trying to remain calm, said, 'So John's had a heart attack, but he's all right now?'

Jean unfolded her arms and placed her hands in her lap, unaware that she was twisting Gordon's wedding ring round her finger.

'Yes. He has to take it easy, though.'

'Do you see much of him and the family?'

Jean got up and went to stand by the table, picking up the teapot.

'Do you want another cup?' she asked, without looking at Lynda.

'Please.'

Lynda tried to relax as she drank her tea. Jean still sat upright in the armchair, worrying about what she knew she would have to tell her friend. She looked at the clock.

'What time are you going back to Beechwood Avenue?'

'I don't know.'

Lynda stood up and walked over to the side-board, pretending to look again at the photographs arranged there.

'Like I said, I went there, but I didn't go in. I had my key but I didn't feel I could just let myself in.'

'Oh. Well, perhaps it's as well you didn't.'

Lynda could see that Jean had some news she was dreading having to deliver.

'What is it? Is there something you're not telling me, Jean?'

'Lynda, that's not your house any more. John's got a flat now. He sold, well, more or less gave the house to Carolyn and Steve.'

'He's sold our house? What the hell for?'

'It was after Gemma was born. They needed more room for their family, and Steve wasn't earning enough to cope with a bigger mortgage.'

'Oh. I see. Bloody hell! That's my home we're talking about.'

'I know. I thought it was wrong at the time. But apparently John didn't need your permission.'

'No, because it belonged to him, not both of us. His Mother made sure of that when she lent us the money for the deposit. It was on condition the house was in John's name only.'

'Oh.'

'She never thought the marriage would last, you know. She hoped it wouldn't.'

Jean was still thinking about John's house. 'Like I said, I didn't think it was right. You can give your children too much, and be left with too little of your own.'

She stopped herself there. Jean didn't like to criticise Carolyn, she had always loved being the adopted aunty of the pretty child with golden curls.

'I'm sorry, Lynda.'

'So am I! I've no home to go to!'

Lynda suddenly felt close to tears. Again and again on the train journey, she'd imagined walking straight into the house and being in her own familiar rooms. She'd treasured the image of the furniture and the bits and pieces of memories like Jean had here in her living room.

'Where's John living?'

Jean leaned forward eagerly again, remembering the drama.

'That was another thing. Sheila had borrowed money against her house, so when she died there wasn't the money John and his sister had hoped to inherit. Not that Sylvia needed money! But it meant that John couldn't buy a house, and he really wanted a garden like his Dad. Anyway, in the end, he found a nice little flat at Sunnybank.'

'Sunnybank? Isn't that those flats and bungalows the Council built for pensioners?'

'Yes, originally. It was the only place available that John could afford at the time. It was only meant to be temporary.'

Lynda's mind was struggling to find a way through the maze of defeated expectations.

'What the hell is a man like John doing living in a poky little flat surrounded by old people? He is all right, you said, after his heart attack?'

'Yes,' Jean said cautiously. 'But he has to take it easy.' Then she thought for a moment and, with a meaningful look, added, 'And a shock wouldn't be good for him.'

Lynda was quick to realise what she was hinting at.

'Like me turning up on his doorstep, you mean?'

'Yes.'

Jean took both their cups and poured more tea. Trying not to let her anxiety show in her voice, she asked, 'Why have you come back, Lynda?'

A good question, and Lynda stared out of the window, avoiding Jean's eyes, and wishing she could think of a true answer which didn't sound totally self-centred.

'To see everybody I suppose. And to make things right, if I can. To be honest, I suddenly felt I wanted to come home.'

In an attempt to cover the emotion that caught hold of her breath, Lynda tried to put a joking tone over the next question, but failed.

'Do you think they'll have me?'

'I don't know. You'll have to ask them that.'

Lynda steeled herself to ask the next question. There was a lot riding on the answer.

'Has John divorced me? Nothing to stop him after so many years, so I assumed he had.'

For some reason it was now Jean's turn to look away.

'No. No, he hasn't divorced you. Not yet.'

Lynda felt a blurring of sensation in her head and thought she was going to faint.

They had convinced each other, she and Tom, that she was Lynda Collins again, that John would have got a divorce. And anyway, they'd had no choice, no time for doubt in the end. They had wanted to be married, even if it would only be for a few weeks. Marriage would be, for them, the eternal blessing on their love, the declaration that they would always belong to each other.

Tom Meredith had had another reason, too. He had wanted to make sure there would be no challenge to the will he had already made. As his wife, Lynda would definitely legally inherit her share of Loveday Manor.

But now, in law, she wasn't Lynda Meredith, she still belonged to John Stanworth. Lynda glanced down at the wedding ring next to the heart shaped sapphire and diamond engagement ring which her beloved Tom had given to her that wonderful morning in Paris.

The wedding ring she wore now was the one which Tom Meredith, held upright by pillows and cushions on their gold velvet sofa, had placed on her finger and sealed there with a kiss.

CHAPTER SIX

At The Cedars Hotel the prey was still being pursued. The sound of the cool water trickling from the outstretched hands of the cherubs on the fountain at the centre of the lawn, was very soothing. To Carolyn it was a welcome relief from the clatter of coffee cups and the barbed chatter of competitive colleagues.

Paul Ferris walked out on to the ornate stone terrace. He sipped his cup of coffee and stood watching Carolyn, with confidence and intent. She had left her jacket on a chair, and the sunshine made her white shirt gleam as it stretched its silkiness over her as she'd walked down to stand by the fountain. She was tilting her face towards the sun, and letting the tension slip away from her body.

She looked at her watch and reluctantly turned to look back towards the hotel. She saw Paul looking down on her from the terrace. He smiled and lifted his hand. Carolyn was embarrassed to realise that he'd been watching her.

Paul handed his cup to a waiter and stepped down on to the garden, away from the observant colleagues standing by the windows. He walked across the lawn, and then stood in the shade of a large rhododendron and waited for her, like a lord of the manor watching an obedient spaniel walking shyly towards him.

'You're wearing the wrong outfit, Carolyn.'

Carolyn suddenly felt anxious, vulnerable to his criticism. Paul smiled reassuringly.

'A romantic evening dress would go much better with the surroundings.'

She laughed with relief, and then was annoyed with herself for having cared what he thought of her, for having wanted him to be watching her with only male admiration in his eyes.

He looked towards the house. 'I suppose we do have to go back in.'

'Yes,' she sighed, but looked longingly at the garden.

Paul had thought out his strategy. 'Beautiful place, isn't it? It's a shame there isn't the opportunity to enjoy its pleasures.'

'Yes.'

'Perhaps I can arrange some more time here,' he paused just long enough to add meaning, 'for the two of us.'

He watched carefully for her reaction, and was satisfied to see she didn't immediately reject the idea. They turned to walk back towards the house. Paul placed his hand gently on her back and allowed it to slide slowly down to her waist. Then he stopped and turned her to face him, standing so close that the heat from their bodies formed a connection between them.

He smiled, and his eyes glittered as he presented the opportunity he had planned. His voice was low and enticing.

'I need you, Carolyn,' he held his face close to hers so that his words sighed on to her lips, 'to stay until tomorrow.'

Carolyn felt the breath in her body being held still for a moment, and then heard herself ask, 'Oh. Why?'

Immediately she was aware of how stupid she sounded, how pathetic to make a last pretence of being just a work colleague. The question had come out with a breathlessness which betrayed the warmth of the sexual response within her body.

His eyes flickered over her face and breasts with a look that could not be misunderstood.

'Oh, I think I could find a reason. If you want me to?'

Carolyn looked up at him, her eyes opened wide with both excitement and fear. He was waiting, and she knew the time had come. Paul laughed softly as he watched her glance at the observant women standing on the hotel terrace and, relishing the danger, he drew her on to his body for a brief moment. and felt the shudder of her pleasure.

'Do you?'

'Yes.' One word, only a breath above a whisper, but it was enough to change her future.

Carolyn's husband was lined up in Randerson's yard with his mates, all of them weary from their morning's work, and the burden of knowing they could have no pride in what they'd produced.

In the office which looked down on the yard, Josie checked the time, still only two o'clock. She stretched her shapely legs in front of her, signalling to her body that she was ready to escape from her desk. She yawned as she leaned back in her chair and then, lifting her bushy hair up off her neck, she clasped her hands behind her head as she looked out of the office window to observe the scene in the yard. She thought it looked as if Randerson was enjoying himself.

She was right. Her employer felt a malicious satisfaction in knowing he was being unreasonable, but that they'd have to do what he wanted. Steve recognised the look in his eyes - he'd seen that look on his Dad's face often enough as a kid. George Sheldon's eyes had flickered like that as he'd stroked his right hand, easing it slowly into the fist which would exact obedience.

47

Steve had only stood up to his father once and had been knocked from one side of the room to the other before his mother's screams had finally penetrated her husband's fury. Not long after that, Steve had seen it as a kind of victory when his father had left them.

Steve felt that same urge to hit Randerson now, but jobs were scarce and he needed the money to appear in his bank account at the end of the month.

Gary needed the money even more than Steve did, but was angry enough to forget that, and inform Randerson, 'We work for you Monday to Friday, anything else is up to us.'

'Is it?' Randerson retorted in mock surprise.

Steve's voice was steady and calm.

'Carolyn's away, I need to be at home with the kids.'

'You'll find somebody to look after them.'

'No.'

Randerson didn't blink.

'I need this work done by Monday. And you need a job.'

'Is that a threat?'

Randerson turned on Gary pityingly.

'No, it's a fact.'

'You can't force us.'

'No, you can't,' Matt echoed Gary's bravado, before stepping back with uncertainty as Randerson's eyes flickered in his direction.

'Can't I?'

Steve saw that Gary's fists were clenched, and touched his arm gently as he stepped forward to challenge his employer.

'No, Mr Randerson. We have a right to please ourselves about working at the weekends.'

'You'll work if I say so, or you're out of here.'

Gary wasn't taking any more of this.

48

'Don't come it, Randerson. We'll have you if you threaten us with that.'

'Oh, yes? What are you going to do? Take it to a tribunal?' He was sneering at them now.

Steve stood his ground. 'If we have to.'

Randerson laughed, and started to walk towards his car. 'Go ahead, lads, you do that. It won't bother me. Because, do you know something? I haven't lost one yet.'

He turned his back, got into his Jaguar and drove at full revs out of the yard, leaving Steve, Gary and Matthew standing there looking at each other. Matthew felt like he used to when the headmaster had ordered him and his mates to go on litter duty.

'We'll have to do it, won't we?'

Steve nodded. 'Yes.'

Gary clenched his fists and looked hard at Steve.

'We'll have him one day.'

Steve met the challenge in Gary's eyes. 'Yeah, we will.'

Later that afternoon Steve and Carolyn's children were happily sitting watching television in their Grandad's flat, enjoying the crisps and Coca Cola that he'd brought back from the supermarket. John was always glad when their parents had to arrange for them to come to his house after school, they filled his flat with noise and life.

Gemma had entered in high spirits and had flung her arms round him, but Michael had followed her wearily. School was tough for a boy approaching his teens. He could compete in the playground, but struggled sometimes in the stuffy environment of the classroom, which he often found boring and too restrictive.

Gemma was fed up with Michael zapping from

one television channel to the next, and decided to practise her adult conversation on her Grandad.

'I'm glad Mummy's coming home tomorrow, Dad can't cook properly.'

Michael turned away from the television to glare at his sister.

'He can. You're just too fussy.'

'I'm not! Anyway, I wasn't talking to you!'

In tones of deep satisfaction she continued her tête à tête with John. 'Mummy's going to be a manager at work, isn't she?'

John felt a little uncomfortable at the sound of the same tones of ambition he used to hear from Carolyn when she was a child, but was as indulgent with his granddaughter as he had been with his daughter. He smiled and raised his eyebrows in speculation,

'She might be one day.'

Gemma was eager to underline her point, 'Dad says we'll have to call her 'sir' then.'

Michael was now the young male defending territory and status.

'Don't be daft!' he snarled.

Gemma pulled a face at him.

John laughed, but it made him wonder how Steve was coping with Carolyn's progress at work. He knew his son-in-law was an easy-going and generous man, willing to give credit and enjoy his wife's achievements, but he also knew that Carolyn sometimes didn't realise that enough should be enough.

Gemma, bored now, wandered round the room and imitated her Mother. 'Have you taken all your tablets, Grandad?'

'No, not yet.'

'You should have. You must take them on time each day.'

Michael, like his Dad, didn't approve of his Grandad being treated like an invalid.

'Leave him alone, Gemma!'

'Well, he's got to look after himself.'

'He has to live as well, Dad said! Are you coming to the match with us tomorrow, Grandad?'

'No, but thanks for asking.'

Gemma shook her head at her brother. 'Mum says he shouldn't. They had a row about it, remember?'

John was beginning to be worried about the frequency of disagreement between his daughter and her husband. He knew Steve was right about him not going out enough, and he knew he should have accepted Michael's invitation to go to the football match with him and Steve tomorrow, but he couldn't face the fuss Carolyn would make about it. And to tell the truth he was still too scared, still anxiously listening all the time for any extra beat, any small contraction of the heart which had threatened to deprive him of life.

Michael heard the car pull up and went to look out of the window. 'Dad's here'.

He picked up his coat and threw Gemma's at her. As she put it on she asked, 'Is Aunty Jean coming to see you tomorrow night, Grandad?'

John paused as he collected up empty crisp packets and Coke cans, 'Yes, I think so.'

Gemma, who needed the points on the pink and yellow chart she and her friends had devised, was keen to become a bridesmaid soon.

'Grandad, are you going to marry her?' she asked.

This was one question which John definitely didn't want to answer. He was relieved when Michael, who perceived John's discomfort, told his sister to shut up. Gemma had had enough of being silenced by her brother and began to punch him. The brawl was at full onslaught when Steve walked in. John, feeling embarrassed at this breakdown of control, looked at him apologetically, but Steve just laughed.

'Hiya, John. Can I get a bucket of water to chuck over these two?'

'Help yourself,' John grinned.

Gemma fled behind the settee, shouting, 'I'll tell Mum!'

Steve grabbed hold of her and tickled her into submission. A few minutes later the children said goodbye to their Grandad and then ran out to fight over who would sit in the front seat in the car.

Steve didn't like asking, but he had no choice.

'John, can I ask a big favour?'

'Of course you can.'

'I've got to work overtime tomorrow morning. Would you come and sit with the kids for me? They'll behave themselves, I'll bribe them, and they usually watch television on Saturday morning. You could come to the match with us afterwards.'

'No problem with tomorrow morning I'll enjoy it. But I won't come to the match, if you don't mind.'

'Oh. O.K. Shall I come and pick you up before I go to work.'

'No need. I can easily catch the bus. I'll get to your place about half-seven, shall I?'

'That would be great, thanks.'

John handed Steve the bag which Gemma had forgotten, and looked at him carefully, as he commented, 'You'll be glad to see Carolyn back tomorrow.'

'Yeah,' Steve replied, without the eagerness John would have expected. John wanted to know what made Steve look so anxious these days whenever he spoke of his wife. He and Steve were good mates, close even, but they respected the bounds of loyalty when talking about Carolyn. He hesitated, wondering how to lead to the subject of his concern.

'She seemed to think this course, or whatever it is, would help her on her way.'

There was a moment of reflection before Steve looked at John, who saw the resignation and uncertainty in his eyes.

'Yes,' Steve agreed, 'but on her way to what?'

John was worried at the resentment in Steve's voice, and tried to laugh away the tension, 'The good life! Whatever that is.'

Looking at his son-in-law, he felt a sense of guilt which made him want to ask Steve's forgiveness for making his daughter a wife who wasn't always easy to love.

'Lynda always used to say Carolyn was never satisfied, and that I gave in to her too much.' He tried to laugh, 'So it's my fault if she's spoilt, you know.'

There was no way Steve was going to let John suffer any bad feelings. From the early days of his marriage to Carolyn, he had learned to love her parents, perhaps more than she did sometimes. Steve now placed this good man, who no longer stood as tall as he used to, where he belonged, right at the centre of his family's life. And John loved him.

It was not likely that they would ever put into words this bond of mutual esteem which held them so close. These two were Northern men whose inhibitions made them dependent on offhand gestures of affection; no American style hugs or arms across the shoulders for them, just small signals of acceptance and regard.

'Thanks for baby-sitting tomorrow. And you'll be coming round for your dinner on Sunday, like we'd said, won't you?'

John's face brightened 'Yes, if that's all right.'

'Of course it is.'

He gave John one of those small signals, a quick grasp of his arm as, in a conspiratorial undertone, he suggested, 'You never know, we might get to go for a pint beforehand, as well.'

The old John Stanworth responded without hesitation.

'If you go, I'll follow.'

Steve grinned and nodded as he went out, 'Right. See you.'

John closed the door behind him and felt the room regaining its silence. He went into the kitchen to heat up the steak and kidney pie he'd bought at the supermarket.

CHAPTER SEVEN

Jean was having to think fast.

'Like you said, Lynda, it would be too much of a shock for John if you just turned up unannounced at his place. Somebody needs to tell him first, and it's not the sort of thing you want to say on the phone.'

'No, I suppose not.'

Jean had made her decision.

'If you really don't feel you can go to Carolyn's yet, you can stop here, if you like.'

Lynda beamed at her, 'Can I? Oh, that would be lovely. I didn't want to go to a hotel.'

'Well, there's only Ashton House now, really. And it's very expensive.'

Lynda smiled to herself, Jean wasn't to know that money was not one of her problems but, at the moment, staying in a hotel was. And Jean had told her there was only one bedroom in John's flat. There was no way she could share a bed with another man now, not even the man she had been married to, and who was still her husband.

'Thanks, Jean.'

'I'll go and tidy up the spare room, it's a bit of a mess.'

'Don't worry, love. I'm just really glad you'll have me to stay.'

Jean was suddenly embarrassed.

'I don't know what we'll have for tea.'

'Is there still that fish and chip shop round the corner?'

'Yes.'

'Marvellous! I haven't had really good fish and chips for years. They don't know how to do them properly down in Surrey.' She answered Jean's questioning look. 'I've been living near Guildford for the past few years. I moved on after Rose died.'

'Oh. I wouldn't have thought you'd fit in down south, not with your accent.'

'No.'

Lynda had noticed that her Lancashire accent had come back quickly since she'd sat down and talked to Jean. She was pleased at that, it gave her a strong feeling of being at home, just hearing those familiar sounds and turns of phrase.

She felt so relieved. She'd be all right here, in familiar, homely surroundings. She needed to be with Jean, someone she could talk to, rely on. And Jean had been glad to see her back, hadn't she?

Lynda found herself wondering about this. She'd noticed a reserve in Jean's behaviour towards her, a holding back of confidences. 'Bloody hell,' she thought to herself, 'was nothing going to be straightforward?'

Once they were sitting at the table eating their fish and chips, accompanied by yet another pot of tea, it all felt different.

'Do you remember Duckworth's fish and chip shop?' Lynda asked.

'Of course I do. And I remember you taking me there as a special treat after we'd finished our exams. And to the Odeon to see 'South Pacific' as well.'

'Oh, yes,' Lynda exclaimed, and began to sing. 'A hundred and one pounds of fun, that's my little honey bun. Get a load of honey bun, to- nigh-ite!'

'You were so busy singing that, you nearly knocked Dan Heywood over. Do you remember?'

Lynda remembered, very clearly.

'How is Dan?' she asked, her voice soft and warm now.

'Still living with his Mother.'

'Oh, he's not! Did he never get married again?'

'No. He's had girlfriends, but nothing serious. And his Mother wouldn't let him marry any of them anyway, would she?'

'No.'

'He's still got the bakery, but spends most of his time running the café now.'

'My café, The Copper Kettle?'

'Yes. He loves it. You'll have to go and see him while you're here.'

'I certainly will. But you're talking as if you think I'm only back in Milfield for a short visit. I'm not. I might want to stay for quite a while.'

At the hotel the seminar was over and the conference delegates were drifting in groups towards the foyer and the hotel bar. A few had gathered round the desk at the front of the room, having a discussion with the consultant who had been presenting the kind of management ideas that Tony Randerson would have thought were from another planet.

Paul had given the vote of thanks and during the applause had gone to stand between Carolyn and the door. As she stood up, and hesitated about where to go he moved towards her. Casually, but with a clear signal to anyone who wished to take note, Paul placed his arm round Carolyn's shoulder, and kept it there as he introduced her into the discussion with the consultant.

Carolyn, again feeling acutely aware of Paul's closeness, tried to concentrate on what was being said, but the thoughts in her head were of managing a situation not covered in the text books being referred to here.

She became aware of being observed with a degree of speculation by two women who, in the past, had tried and failed to gain Paul's attention. She saw the look which passed between them, and decided it was time to make an excuse to move away.

Paul allowed Carolyn to slip from his grasp, but only slowly, with his hand sliding in a caress across her shoulders and down towards her waist as she moved away. His eyes lingered on the movement of her hips as she walked out into the hotel foyer.

Paul Ferris had learned, from his far from limited experience, that the waiting, too, could be pleasurable. He would enjoy playing her along until all her small gestures of resistance were exhausted. He would also give himself the pleasure of teasing the other female delegates, giving them his flirtatious attention to confuse their speculations. It was a fascinating game and one which, tomorrow, he would win.

Luckily Gemma had been invited round to a friend's home that Friday evening, so Steve only had to take Michael with him to deliver the cabinet. It had been commissioned by Robert Horton, a builder who'd come to Milfield in the 1970s and set up a very successful business.

It was raining, so before they'd loaded the cabinet into Steve's old Ford estate, they'd had to cover it with a couple of old shower curtains Steve kept in the garage as dust sheets.

The car's windscreen wipers struggled to cope with the onslaught of the rain lashing down. As they approached the driveway of the ornate Victorian mansion which loomed out of the rain-darkened sky, Michael looked anxiously at his Dad.

'Is this it?'

Steve switched on full beam and read the name, Conway House carved into the stone gateway.

'Yeah.'

They drove up to the house and Steve parked in front of the main entrance. Michael huddled down into his seat and stared up at the imposing building.

'I'll stop in the car.'

'You won't. You're my business partner.'

'Dad!' Michael groaned, with pretended exasperation.

Steve gave him a poke in the ribs.

'And, besides, I can't lift it on my own.'

He switched off the engine.

'Come on.'

'Can't you ask Mr Horton to help you?'

'Oh, no. Not professional that. He's the client.'

Michael, thinking his Dad was being pretentious now, corrected him. 'Customer.'

Steve got out of the car.

'Client.'

Bob Horton, once a bricklayer and then a builder but now, his wife insisted, a property developer, was a big, tough but kindly man who had made money but was never ruled by it. He was delighted with the cabinet, and enthusiastically supervised Michael and Steve as they positioned it in a corner of the large, slightly ostentatious lounge.

'A bit more this way, Steve. Marvellous. Goes well with the other stuff, doesn't it?'

'Yes.'

Steve allowed himself to be very proud when he saw how well his elegant walnut cabinet matched the grace of the antiques Horton's wife invested in.

Frances Horton was very particular about her home, where everything was arranged in a manner

59

which would guarantee to garner little gasps of admiration from those she judged wealthy and worthy enough to be invited to visit. She'd be pleased with the way the cabinet would conceal the television she looked upon with disdain.

Bob Horton often hid a wry smile when his wife, who professed to the 'high society' of Milfield that she never watched any of the soaps on television, could, if the need arose, voice detailed opinions about the on-going storylines.

'Your Dad knows a bit about furniture, Michael,' Horton told the boy. 'And football. Do you want a drink?' he asked, opening a well-stocked drinks cabinet. 'Coca Cola all right for you, Michael?'

'Yes, please,' Michael said, staring wide-eyed at the range of bottles in the cabinet.

'And for me, please,' Steve requested, 'I'm driving.'

They sat down with their drinks and Horton again looked admiringly at the television cabinet.

'I reckon even my lady wife won't be able to find fault with that.' He looked over his glass of whisky and winked at Michael. 'Take my advice, lad, don't get married.'

'I'm not going to.'

Steve and Horton both laughed at his vehemence, then Horton leaned forward and gazed intently at Steve.

'It's quality work this. You could set up your own business, Steve, with your talent.'

Steve smiled ruefully.

'I'd love to. And I will, one day.'

Horton shook his head. 'No, lad. 'One day' never comes. You have to take the risk. I did, and this is what you get.'

Horton, not wanting to show off, but simply to make the point, indicated the signs of wealth which surrounded them.

'I know, and I really want to, but . . .'

Horton saw Steve glance momentarily at his young son, and knew that, as always for people like Steve, it was a question of money. It was Horton's nature to be tough, but his advice was given out of kindness.

'Like I said, 'one day' never comes. Do it now.'

'Yeah.' Steve's longing was beginning to hurt again, and he didn't want Horton to see it, so he changed the subject.

'Have you got somebody to wire this up for you?'

Bob Horton, being the man he was, had already seen the opportunity to help somebody.

'I thought I might ask your father-in-law.'

Steve's eyes lit up.

'John? That'd be good. I'll give you his number, shall I?'

'Thanks.'

Steve wrote down the number and gave it to him. 'Thank you, Mr Horton.'

They shook hands, and as they said goodnight, Steve found himself wishing that his father had been a man like Bob Horton.

CHAPTER EIGHT

At eleven o'clock on Saturday morning, little Alice Smith trotted up to the very grand front door of Kirkwood House, the majestic home of Ellen Heywood.

She carried her shopping bag only as an excuse, she'd no shopping to do, she'd finished it yesterday, after she'd seen Lynda Stanworth waiting at the bus stop. Alice squeezed her shoulders together with glee, anticipating the expression on Ellen's face when she told her Lynda was back in town. Being the one to break that news to the woman whose patronage she both sought and resented, was to be the highlight of Alice Smith's day.

Many years ago, in 1961, according to Alice's excellent memory, she had watched the drama of true love being denied. Ellen Heywood had forced her eldest son, Daniel, to abandon his romance with beautiful, sixteen year-old Lynda Collins. She had thus, inadvertently, enabled John Stanworth to get the girl he desired.

Alice had been a witness to the start of that romance, too. She'd been in her mid-thirties then and, still shying away from the prospect of eternal spinsterhood, she'd been disguising her wall-flowering by serving drinks at the Saturday night dance at the Carlton Ballroom.

She had watched John Stanworth have his first dance with Lynda, who'd been wearing a tight red dress. Alice guessed she had adjusted its neckline downwards as soon as she'd managed to get away from her Dad and her duties behind the bar at The Black Bull, a run-down pub in one of the poorest areas of Milfield.

Later that night Alice had watched Jean Clayton, her young cousin, being very disappointed and upset. And one Sunday, after church, she'd observed the horrified look on Sheila Stanworth's face, as she'd seen that her only son had fallen in love with Lynda Collins.

Watching people was Alice's passion. This was understandable, as other passions had been denied her since that terrible day when, wearing white lace, she'd walked into that cold, very quiet church. She had stood there, tiny and pathetic, and had had to endure the silence and then the pity of the shocked congregation, who had realised before she did, that the bridegroom no longer intended to arrive.

Alice had to reach up on tiptoe to lift the heavy iron knocker on the door of Kirkwood House. Ellen's home was still the imposing Victorian detached residence which her wealthy parents had purchased when her father had moved his family down from Scotland in the 1940s.

Richard Alexander Buchanan had come to Milfield to take up the post of manager at the town's largest building society, and had quickly established himself as one of the leaders of the small élite of self-righteous, self-appointed aristocracy in the thriving cotton town. His daughter had carried on the family tradition of superiority.

After a little while Alice heard Ellen's footsteps on the once luxurious, but now a little faded and worn, claret coloured carpet in the long hallway. Then the door was slowly opened to reveal the tall, elegant seventy-five year old lady of the house.

'Good morning, Ellen.'

Alice, all consideration and smiles, stepped forward as she spoke, but Ellen did not move aside to allow her to enter.

'I'm going into town, and just wondered if you wanted anything?'

'No, thank you.'

'Oh? Are you sure?'

There was a moment's silence. Ellen Heywood's shrewd eyes had quickly perceived, from the expression on Alice's face, that there was much more to this visit than a desire to be helpful.

Ellen had made an accurate, and not very favourable, assessment of Alice Smith's character many years ago, when Alice, as a schoolgirl, had first become one of her tolerated, less fortunate followers, but Alice's company had always offered Ellen the entertainment of outwitting her. And Ellen had little enough to entertain her during the long lonely days of her old age.

Oh, so casually, Alice dropped what she hoped was her bombshell.

'You never know who you'll meet when you're out shopping, do you? I saw a mutual acquaintance yesterday.' Hoping to tantalise Ellen into a response, she paused, but was disappointed and had to continue. 'Lynda Stanworth.'

Ellen saw Alice was watching her carefully, and smiled to herself as she denied her the treat of a dramatic reaction. Self-control had been inculcated into Ellen Heywood's soul ever since, as a small child, she had been relentlessly disciplined, held in the corridor of stillness between her Father's rasping, demanding tones and her Mother's anxious eyes.

'Oh, yes?' said Ellen, easily feigning indifference.

Alice, although disappointed, persevered.

'I wonder why she's come home after all this time?'

She had her reward. The instinctive animosity Ellen Heywood had felt ever since that first encounter, when teenage Lynda Collins had dared to defy her, surfaced in habitual scorn.

'A woman like Lynda Stanworth has nowhere else to go in the end, unfortunately for her family. I'm not at all surprised she has come back.'

Alice had long ago mastered the art of oblique comment.

'It might be a welcome surprise for some people, though.'

They both knew she meant Daniel, but Ellen had no intention of discussing her son in the context of Lynda's return. She replied in a dismissive manner.

'Possibly. But let us hope it's a short visit, shall we? Goodbye, Alice.'

She swiftly closed the door to end her caller's occupancy of her doorstep, and Alice, disappointed that she'd not managed to be invited in for a cup of tea, slowly made her way home.

Ellen went back to sit in the now slightly faded glory of what she had always insisted should be referred to as the drawing room. Like her bedroom, this was adorned with silver framed photographs of her dead son, Richard, and still furnished with many of the antiques inherited from her parents. She sat by the fire in the chair which had been her Father's, and her mouth involuntarily shaped itself into a tight little smile.

She almost welcomed the news of the return of Lynda Collins, it provided something to think about at least. She would have been horrified, however, had she known that, very soon, her other son, Daniel, would be in that woman's arms.

65

Lynda was having to kill time in Milfield's shopping centre. She'd been to hire a car, and had chosen a red Vauxhall Cavalier, which she parked outside the library. Now all she had to do was take a walk round Milfield, and wait for the end of the football match and her opportunity to see Steve and her grandson.

She'd thought she would enjoy looking round the town and the shops, but she saw no-one she recognised. It was depressing to feel like a stranger in the place that had once been her home, and Milfield town centre had changed a lot.

What had once been a confident, friendly, bustling main street had been turned into a half empty pedestrian precinct with quiet looking shops. She felt like crying when she thought of how it had been in the days of her childhood, before some of the sandstone buildings had been demolished and replaced by the 'modern' concrete and glass, and blank blue panels of the sixties.

They'd built a bandstand in the centre of the pedestrian precinct to try to hold on to some of the sense of community from the past, but there was no band playing. Lynda could have done with some music to cheer her up.

She looked round the precinct and wished she was back at the Loveday Manor Hotel, which she and Tom had developed into a four-star wedding venue. She pictured the large country house where ancient stones sat comfortably side by side with Georgian elegance and Victorian eccentricity, and imagined herself walking hand in hand with Tom again along the river which meandered through its beautiful garden.

She felt tears begin to make their way on to her cheeks, and quickly brushed them away with a tissue.

She sat down on a bench by the bandstand and took out her mobile phone. She wasn't too keen on this new technology which sometimes seemed to be taking over people's lives, and often she left it at home, but she needed the comfort of its company today. She needed to talk to Mark, the closest she could get to her beloved Tom.

'Oh, I'm so glad you've phoned,' he said, his voice full of emotion.

'Is something wrong?'

'No, I was just missing you, that's all.'

She smiled to herself, there was a time when this young man would never have talked about how he felt.

'I wanted to phone for a chat,' he explained, 'but I thought you'd be busy catching up with your family. I bet your grandson is thrilled to bits to have his Grandma turn up and cuddle him.'

'Yes.'

'And what about your daughter, is it all sorted out between you now? All forgive and forget?'

'Yes, yes of course. How are things at Loveday?'

'Fine. Busy as usual. We've that wedding you booked next week.' He paused. 'It'll be really strange, not having you and Dad here making it all happen.'

She couldn't speak, the memories swept over her, warmth and colour, and love.

'Are you all right, Lynda?'

'Yeah,' she whispered. 'I'm missing him so much, Mark.'

'So am I.' There was a silence, as he tried to steady himself. 'Come back as soon as you can, won't you? Oh, sorry, I know I'm being selfish. Your family need you to be with them, and you've a lot to catch up on, but come back when you can.'

'I will. And don't worry about the wedding, you

and Amy will make it a big success.'

'I hope so. I'm sure we will, as long as my Mother stops trying to interfere.'

'Oh. Well, like I said, tell her we have our way of doing things and it's been very successful, so that's the way it has to continue.'

'Yeah. She'll be O.K. eventually. Once she stops being angry, and feeling guilty about the way she treated Dad.'

'She should be better now I'm out of the way.'

'Yes. But come back soon, won't you? If only for a visit.'

'Yeah, yes, I will.' She took another deep, shuddering breath, and knew that in a moment she wouldn't be able to stop the tears. 'Goodbye, love. Take care. Give my love to everybody.'

'Lynda?'

She switched off her phone and found that her hand was shaking as she thrust it into her bag. She hated herself for lying to Mark, but she knew that he'd have insisted on coming and taking her back to Loveday if she had told him the truth.

Mark Meredith, standing behind the reception desk in the elegant foyer of Loveday Manor, frowned as he put his phone back in his pocket; he'd not realised how much he was going to miss Lynda. He looked up to see his Mother walking towards the table at the side of the foyer, her arms full of silver and green foliage and white lilies.

'What are you doing, Mother?'

Suzanne gave her son the well-practised, condescending smile she usually directed at people she considered less intelligent than herself.

'Arranging the flowers?'

'But those are lilies.'

'Yes. Aren't they beautiful? They've always looked so good in here.'

'I told you, Mother, we don't have lilies in the hotel now. Dad didn't like them, and neither do I.'

'Your Father never objected to them, I always had this kind of tasteful arrangement in the foyer when we were running the hotel together. It was that woman who changed the flowers, just as she ruined so many other things here. Including my marriage!'

Suzanne took a handkerchief out of her pocket and dabbed away the tears which threatened her mascara.

Mark was well aware that there was little truth in those assertions. He'd been upset when his Mother had insisted that there would be lilies in the church for Tom Meredith's funeral, but had felt he had to allow her choice of her last tribute to her dead husband. He and Lynda had chosen red roses for the other displays in the church, and for their wreaths.

'Please, Mother.' He walked towards her, wanting to remove the flowers, but she stepped protectively in front of them.

'Mark, I thought we had agreed that we would run this hotel together.'

'We agreed that you would help out until Lynda comes back.'

'You think she's coming back, do you? I don't.'

'She's just gone to see her family, like Dad wanted her to.'

'He knew where she really belonged.'

'She belonged, belongs, here. Loveday became hers as much as Dad's.'

'How dare you say that! You forget it was my parents who bought this place for me and my husband. How could it ever be hers?'

Exasperation made him resort to what she would

69

understand, money. 'It's hers because Lynda owns forty-per cent of it. You know that Dad left her thirty per cent to add to the shares she already owned.'

'And you own fifty per cent.'

'Now, yes, and Nathan Tyler the remaining ten per cent. By the way,' he added, hoping to distract her away from this subject, 'he and his wife are coming over for a visit soon.'

'I know. Nathan told me.'

'Oh?' Mark was surprised. He remembered that although Helen Tyler had made polite conversation with his Mother, her husband, Nathan, had always avoided speaking to Suzanne.

There was unmistakable triumph in her smile.

'Nathan and I have had conversations about business. He no longer owns a share in this hotel, he sold his ten per cent to me a while ago. He'll be bringing the paperwork with him on this visit. We didn't want to trust postal delivery.'

Mark shook his head in disbelief. 'I can't believe Nathan sold you his shares.'

'Well, he did. And you do realise what this means, don't you, Mark? We can outvote Lynda Collins any time we like.'

Mark didn't like the expression on his Mother's face, nor the venomous tone of her voice.

'I'd never want to outvote Lynda. She loves this place, and she played a big part in making it the success it's become. And she's not Lynda Collins now, remember, she married my Dad. She's Lynda Meredith.'

'No!' Suzanne placed her hands on the shoulders of the son who resembled his handsome father so much. 'Mark, mon cheri, how can you say these things, which you know cause me such pain?'

Mark shook himself free and moved away from

70

her, but she took hold of his arm and made him turn towards her.

'Tom Meredith was my husband. He loved me. And it was because of me, and my family that he had his life here, the life he loved. We are the family who are important, la famille Marcellin! Only you and I belong at Loveday Manor. You must see that!'

Mark moved away from her again, and stared at the flowers spread out on the table as if on an altar.

'All I can see is those damned lilies. For God's sake take them away! They remind me of his funeral. And I can't stand it. I don't want reminding. I don't want him to be dead!'

Suzanne's voice became softer.

'Neither do I, but he is. So now I am all alone in the world, except for you, Mark. You are all I have, and all I need, you know that, don't you?'

CHAPTER NINE

Lynda, still in tears after her phone call to Mark, escaped from the precinct and fled down a side street until she found a boarded-up shop with a doorway where she could hide for a few minutes until she'd stopped crying.

Then she walked on and into the market, and was comforted to see that this still looked familiar. There were fewer stalls in the open market, but in the Market Hall the flower stall which had made her wedding bouquet was still there, next to Baxter's hardware store, and Hardacre's still sold black puddings and their own pork pies. And when she came out of the Market Hall, there it was, The Copper Kettle, which she'd always thought of as 'her' café.

She'd started working there while still a teenager, and Freda Wilson, who had owned it then, had given her training so that she could eventually take over from her. And that had been her job until she'd left Milfield, and was a job she'd loved. She walked towards it, and was happy to see that it had hardly changed at all.

And there he was, Dan Heywood. Not a particularly tall man, but sturdy as a rugby player, and with a wide grin and the kindest eyes in the world. His soft, wavy hair was a little thinner and a paler gold than she remembered, because of the grey hairs threaded through it. An apron tied round his waist showed a waistline enlarged a little by middle age, and a fondness for cakes, but Dan always had been a bit cuddly, like a Teddy Bear.

As Lynda approached, he was chatting to a young couple with a baby in a battered pushchair. He was leaning over to play with the child but then looked up and saw her. She blessed him with all her heart for the beaming smile of astonished welcome which lit up his eyes, and the whole of his still handsome, boyish face.

'Lynda!' he yelled.

'Hello, Danny boy!'

'Hello, gorgeous!'

He clasped her in his arms and found he didn't want to let her go. It was Lynda who pulled away from him, she wasn't ready to be held like that, by anyone, not now.

'How are you, Dan?'

'I'm fine.'

'Still keeping the family business going, I see.'

'Sort of. I've gone into partnership with another bakery firm, they do all the bread and savoury stuff now. Takes a bit of pressure off me. I'm still involved, but I concentrate mainly on the cakes. With Alice 'helping' of course.'

'I saw her yesterday. She's not still doing the cake decorating?'

'Occasionally. Her hands aren't so steady these days, but she likes to think she can still do it. She enjoys it, like I enjoy this.'

He turned and waved his hand to proudly indicate the café. 'May I serve you something, Madame?' he asked, effortlessly slipping into the old familiar way they had of teasing each other, and holding out a chair for her.

Lynda sat down with a flourish. 'Tea, if you please!'

'Right. Tea for two. And some of your favourite Eccles cakes?'

73

'Oh, yes, please!'

He hurried off to get the tea and cakes, but before entering the café he glanced back to make sure his dream really had come true, Lynda was there, she had come back.

As she poured the tea, feeling much more at home now, Lynda looked at him and said, 'Jean tells me you own this place now.'

He laughed. 'I always have done, or rather my Dad owned it and I inherited it.'

'Your Dad?'

'Yes. Apparently he bought it off Freda when she wanted to retire and Duncan wasn't interested in it. They agreed to keep it a secret.'

'Well, I never knew. So it was your Dad I was working for, not Freda's son?'

'That's right. Do you know, I reckon that my Dad bought it for you, so you'd always have a job. He thought the world of you, you know, and always regretted that he'd let my Mother split us up.'

'And you really think he bought the café because of me?'

'Yeah.'

Lynda blinked back a tear at the thought of such kindness from that dear man. 'Bless him, I'd always wondered why Duncan never got involved, he always let me do just what I wanted with the café.'

'And you made a big success of it. But what about you, what have you been up to all these years?'

'Let me have a drink of this tea, first.' She sipped it and sighed, 'You can't get a decent cup of tea down South.'

'Oh, yes, John told me you were in Cornwall.'

'I was but I moved on. I've been in Surrey for the last ten years, near Guildford. John doesn't know about that.'

'Oh. Have you been to see him?'

'No, not yet. I'm staying at Jean's at the moment.'

'At Jean's?' Dan was very surprised, for more than one reason.

'Yeah.'

Lynda was looking round, enjoying happy memories of running the café and of the celebrations held there.

'Do you still do parties here?'

'Oh, yes. Especially children's parties, They were a great idea of yours. I've even got a clown outfit I wear for them now, and I do a bit of juggling.'

Lynda burst out laughing. 'Oh, I bet your Mother loves that! Her son a clown and a juggler.'

Dan gave a sheepish grin.

'I don't think she knows. I haven't told her, and I doubt whether any of her friends would dare.'

'How is the old bag, and how old is she now?'

'Hey, that's my Mother you're talking about,' he said, feigning disapproval. 'And she'll be seventy-six in June. Just after Alex's eighteenth.'

'Oh, my goodness, is Alex eighteen?'

'Yes. And a gorgeous girl.'

'And how's Jenny? And little Katie?'

Dan smiled and pointed at the young girl serving another customer. 'Not so little.' He waved to her. 'Katie, come and meet your Aunty Lynda.'

Katie Heywood had a heart-shaped face and gentle brown eyes like her mother's, and also the same straight brown hair which, being practical, she'd managed to gather up on top of her head, partly to keep it out of the way, and partly to make her look taller. She looked admiringly at the way Lynda's hair was similarly styled, but much more elegantly.

'I won't shake hands,' she said apologetically,

'mine are a bit sticky. I didn't know I had an Aunty Lynda.'

'I'm a friend of your Mother's. You used to call me Aunty Lynda when you were little.'

'Oh. Are you the one who was a friend of my Granny Kelly? I think I've seen photos of you with her at parties.'

'Yes, that's right, fantastic parties at your grandparents' house. Kath Kelly was a dear friend of mine. And Bernie, your Grandad.'

'I don't remember them, but Alex does, a bit.'

'How is your big sister?'

'Oh, still beautiful, slender and intelligent, isn't she, Uncle Dan?'

'Yes. And so are you.'

Lynda didn't miss the under-current in that comment, or that Katie didn't believe Dan's assertion.

'So you're helping your Uncle Dan run the café?'

'Only when I'm not at school unfortunately. I'd like to do it full-time, but Mum will only let me work Saturdays and in the holidays.'

'Oh. I worked here full time after I left school, and it was good training in the catering business. I ended up managing a hotel.'

Dan was astounded. 'Did you?'

'Yeah. Not on my own.'

Although Katie had no memory of this blonde, fashionably smart woman with a mischievous smile, she instinctively liked her, and was as intrigued as Dan was by what she'd just said.

'That's what I want to do. Leave school and train in hotel management, but Mum's insisting I stay on and take A-levels.'

'She's probably right. You need qualifications for everything these days,' Lynda said.

'Mothers can't always be right,' Katie protested.

Dan and Lynda exchanged a rueful smile.

'No,' Lynda agreed, and then winked at Dan. 'But some of them think they are.'

Katie laughed. 'You must know my Grandmother.'

'Oh, yes. I know her.'

Katie was intrigued, but glancing over her shoulder she saw two customers entering the café.

'Sorry. Got to go. See you again sometime, Lynda.'

'I hope so.'

'She's a good kid,' Dan said fondly as they watched her greet the customers and make them welcome.

'I'm glad I've seen her.'

Lynda quietly poured herself some more tea, giving herself time to cope with the memory of Katie as a small child, with her plump little arms wrapped round her Mummy's neck. She'd been crying because Jenny was crying, but had not understood then that the polished wooden box being lowered into the ground signified that this was her last moment with her Daddy.

Dan, as always, could read Lynda's thoughts.

'Happier circumstances now.'

'Yeah. How is Jenny?'

'Fine. She's working at Lawson and Broadbent, with Philip Lawson.'

'Philip? Oh, I remember him as a teenager. He had a crush on our Carolyn for a while.'

'He's married now, and he's a good solicitor, from what I hear.'

'That'll have surprised his father.'

'Yes.'

'Has Jenny got married again?'

'No.'

'And what about you?' she asked, not wanting to let him know she and Jean had been gossiping about him.

'No.'

Lynda had to turn away from the look in Dan's eyes, which told her why he hadn't married again. She stood up, ready to leave.

'I'd better be going. I'm hoping to see Steve and Michael. Jean says Steve usually treats him to a burger on their way home from the match.'

'Do they know you're back?'

'No. I thought I'd surprise them.'

'Oh.'

'Don't look so worried, Dan. I know what I'm doing,' she said, wishing she sounded more confident. 'It's best if I see them one at a time, I think. And Steve is my best bet for a friendly face, apart from you, of course.'

He hesitated, but then thought of how long he had waited, and asked the question.

'Shall we meet up tonight, Lynda, if you're not doing anything? We've a lot to catch up on.'

She hesitated. 'I don't know.'

'It'd be good to have a chat.'

He paused and looked anxious. He'd realised that she might need not just a friend to talk to, but also a shoulder to cry on. He couldn't, of course, tell her that.

Lynda saw that he was afraid for her, but wasn't going to let him know that she, too, was frightened. Fixing a cheeky smile on her face, she said, 'Daniel Heywood, are you asking me for a date?'

'Of course, I am,' he replied, matching her jaunty tone. 'Eight o'clock in The Red Lion?'

'The Red Lion, eh? I saw it was still open.'

'We'll meet there, for old times' sake, and I'll take you for a meal afterwards.'

'O.K.' she said, and then mischievously added,

'Will you be telling your Mother who you're going out with?'

'What do you think?'

She laughed. Then, more seriously, she said, 'I'll have to give you a ring and cancel if I get invited round to Steve and Carolyn's this evening.'

'Of course,' Dan agreed, although he didn't think there was much chance of that.

CHAPTER TEN

Steve was feeling much happier by Saturday afternoon. He was at the football match, with his arm round his son's shoulders, and they were both cheering Andy Layton towards a goal. It was a good match, but Milfield didn't win and Michael found it hard to cope with that. He was at the age when winning is everything and resentment comes too easily. Steve gave in, as he usually did, and took him to the shopping precinct for a consoling cheese-burger.

He and Michael were standing at the counter, having ordered a burger and two portions of chips, and Michael was asking for a large Coke, when Steve heard a disturbingly familiar voice behind him.

'Hello, Steve. Mind if I join you?'

He turned and there she was. For a moment it was like seeing a ghost, but ghosts don't wear smart clothes and make-up. The girl behind the counter was impatiently asking for the order for Coca-Cola to be confirmed, but in Steve's head her words seemed to be coming from far away.

Lynda took charge. 'Yes, a large Coke, thank you. Do you and Michael want to find a table, Steve? I'll take care of this.'

Steve couldn't feel his legs beneath him as he followed Michael to a corner table. He sat down quickly.

'Oh, hell,' he whispered. 'Oh, hell.'

'Who's that, Dad?' asked Michael, wondering what was going on.

'Your Grandma.'

'I haven't got a Grandma.'

Steve looked at his son, and then leaned on the table with his head in his hands.

'Bloody hell,' he said, and Michael started to get worried.

'Dad?'

'She is your Grandma. Your Mum's mother. She went away when you were a baby.'

Michael was still trying to take this in when Lynda joined them, and just said 'Hello, Michael' to him but sounded as if she was going to cry.

'This is your Grandma,' Steve confirmed.

'Mum said you were dead.'

Lynda white-faced, looked at Steve. 'Did she?'

Steve's eyes were already begging forgiveness. 'He assumed you were, so we let him think that. It was complicated.'

She tried to ignore the pain, and said brightly, 'Well, as you can see, I'm very much alive, Michael. I've been away, but I've come back now. And I'm hoping we'll get to know each other, and have a lot of fun together.'

'Oh. Right.'

Michael smiled at her. He liked this woman with blonde hair, a lovely smile, and sparkly blue eyes which gazed at him in a very special way. He was glad she wasn't dead, and was pleased about having a Grandma as well as a Grandad now. He'd felt a bit short on grandparents, especially as quite a few boys he knew had several, as a result of their parents getting divorced.

He could see his Dad still wasn't coping very well. He was finding it hard to talk to this woman, but Michael couldn't help grinning at this newly arrived Grandma who winked at him as she leaned over and cheekily pinched his Dad's chips. There was something about the way she looked at him when she spoke, it was as if she was signalling that she would be on his side if he needed her.

'I hear you've got a sister now, Michael. That's nice for you.'

'No, it isn't. Our Gemma's a pain in the bum,' was his immediate response.

'Michael!'

His Dad spoke sharply, and frowned, but his Grandma just laughed. He noticed though, that she didn't laugh much when they started talking about his Mother. Also neither of the adults seemed able to explain to him properly why his Grandma had gone away, or why he'd been told she was dead.

Lynda took every opportunity to laugh, it made her look a lot more confident than she felt. She was finding it hard to get through the barrier of the tension in Steve's eyes. And there were things she didn't understand, like the look on his face when she told him she was staying at Jean's. There was more than surprise in his reaction, and she noticed the warning look which stopped Michael from pursuing the subject of 'Aunty' Jean. She dismissed it as unimportant, it was Carolyn she wanted to talk about.

'I hear our Carolyn's got a very good job, at some finance company.'

Michael decided it was time to join in the conversation again. 'Yeah, she's at a conference this weekend. She'll come back talking posh.'

Lynda and Steve laughed.

'She's working at AFS, Addison Financial Services,' Steve told her. 'She's a financial adviser now.'

'Oh, that should suit her. She always was good at spending money.'

Lynda had tried to make it sound like a joke, but it wasn't a good one. Steve didn't say anything, but she saw his eyes darken. Money was, as Jean had hinted, obviously an issue between Steve and Carolyn.

Lynda saw anxiety building up inside Steve, and reassured him.

'Sorry. I haven't come back to cause trouble.'

She glanced at Michael. She needed to talk about things which her grandson shouldn't have to hear. She handed him a twenty pound note.

'Michael, would you get me and your Dad a pot of tea, and whatever you want for yourself?'

'Anything?'

'Yes, go mad!'

She watched him go off happily to stand at the back of the queue at the counter.

'You're spoiling him.'

'Of course, I am, I'm his Grandma. That's partly what I've come back for, to spoil my grandchildren.' She reached out and placed her hand on his. 'I want to try to make up for the past, Steve. I just need a chance to do that.'

'Lynda, I don't know what to say.'

'How about, 'welcome back'? You are pleased to see me, aren't you?'

'Of course I am.'

The hurt she was trying to push aside, wouldn't leave, and was making her angry.

'In spite of me being dead? You'd no right to tell my grandson I was dead! Whose idea was that? Carolyn's?'

He sighed as he tried to defend his wife.

'She thought it was the simplest way to deal with it when the kids started asking questions. She didn't want us having to keep making things up, telling them lies.'

'And John went along with it, did he, me being dead?'

Steve remembered the arguments, the persistent persuasion Carolyn had inflicted on him and on John. He felt terrible that, because he understood the pain which drove her, he had let his wife bury the truth.

'No. Not really.'

'And he's sold my house as well, I hear.'

Steve couldn't look at her. 'Yeah. I'm sorry, Lynda. But we needed the room, and I wasn't earning enough.'

Lynda saw how ashamed he was, this son-in-law who had always been her friend and ally.

'It's all right, Steve. Just a bit of a shock, that's all, having no home to go to.'

'And you're staying at Jean Haworth's,' he confirmed, with a wariness in his eyes.

Puzzled, she sat back and looked at him. 'Yes. Why are you looking like that? That's how Dan reacted as well. Why is everybody so surprised I'm with my best friend?'

Steve was glad that Michael came back with the tea and a milk shake, and apple pie and ice-cream for himself. But the respite from awkward questions was short, although this time it was Lynda who didn't want to answer them.

'Are you going to live with my Grandad then?' Michael asked as he dug his spoon into the apple pie. 'There's not a lot of room in that flat of his.'

'So I've heard.'

Steve was embarrassed again. 'It's lucky it's a ground floor flat. After his heart attack, he found stairs a bit of a problem at first.'

'Mum thought he might have to live with us,' Michael chipped in, 'but there's no way I'm sharing a bedroom with our Gemma.'

Steve wished his son didn't have to take part in this conversation. 'Michael, just be quiet and get on with your meal.'

'I gather John's O.K. now,' Lynda said, 'but that I'd better let you or Carolyn tell him I'm back before I go round to see him.'

'Yes. It would be too much of a shock.'

'It sounds like I'll need permission to see my own husband!'

'It's not like that.'

'I should hope not. And he hasn't got a job either. That's no good for a man like John, sitting at home all day.'

'No. But I saw Bob Horton last night, and he's got something for him. Not much, but it's a start.'

'Bob Horton? I thought you were still working for Randerson.'

'I am, but I do my own work in my own time, kitchens and some furniture. I delivered a cabinet to Horton last night. He was really pleased with it. He thinks I should definitely set up my own business.'

'You've been talking about that for years.'

'I know. But I will do it, one day,' he said, remembering what Bob Horton had said about that.

'When you win the Lottery?'

'Yeah.' He glanced at Michael. 'Anyway we'd better be going.'

'Sorry, Grandma. We've got to pick Gemma up from her friend's. Grandma?' he repeated, enjoying being able to use that name now. 'Are you coming round to our house?'

Lynda looked hopefully at Steve, but saw him hesitate.

Disappointed, she asked, 'When does Carolyn get back from this conference?'

Michael answered before his father could stop

him. 'Not till tomorrow now. She phoned up to say her boss is making her stay another night.'

Lynda's jokey response was automatic, 'Oh, yes?' she queried with a suggestive raising of her eyebrows.

'Don't be daft, Lynda!'

Steve spoke sharply because he suddenly found himself wondering, just for a split second. Immediately ashamed, he told himself that having that disturbing thought even occur to him, showed how much of a turmoil was going on in his head. He decided then that he couldn't cope with inviting Lynda to go home with them, even though Carolyn wouldn't be there.

'Can Grandma come home with us now?' Michael persisted.

'We'll wait till your Mum's home.'

'Monday then?' Lynda suggested.

Again her son-in-law seemed reluctant.

'What's the matter, Steve?'

'It's been a long time, Lynda. I'm not sure Carolyn will . . .'

'What?'

'Want to see you,' he said quietly.

'I'm her Mother.'

Steve looked at Lynda and couldn't bear the anguish in her eyes.

'I've got to see them, Steve,' she sobbed, almost pleading now. 'Her and John. It's what I've come back for.'

'I know. Look, just give me time to talk to her.'

'This is ridiculous. All I want is to see my own daughter!'

Steve saw her need, and wished he could comfort her.

It took a lot of courage for Lynda to ask, 'Does Carolyn ever talk about me?'

Steve again was unable to look at her, and just whispered, 'No.'

He couldn't think what else he could truthfully say, what he could add to that blunt negative so as to prevent it from hurting her; and he'd never ever want to hurt Lynda.

She caught her breath.

'Such a tiny word 'No', she said to herself, 'surprising how a word as small as that can give you so much pain.'

As she drove slowly back to Jean's house, Lynda tried to focus on the two fragments of hope she had salvaged from the meeting with Steve. The first was that she had met her grandson, and he seemed to have taken to her. The second was that she'd seen that there might be a way of helping Steve and Carolyn, and of thus becoming part of their lives again.

Steve had confessed that he wanted to get out of Randerson's and set up his own business, but it was impossible because he'd no money for such a venture.

Lynda hadn't said anything when Steve had talked about that, but she'd hugged to herself the knowledge that she hadn't come back home to Milfield empty-handed. She might be short of reasons to be forgiven, but thanks to her own hard work and Tom Meredith's love and generosity, one thing she did have plenty of, was money.

CHAPTER ELEVEN

Paul Ferris, his arms stretched out along the edge of the azure tiled hotel swimming pool, leaned his head back and gazed up at the mellowing sky beyond the atrium roof. He had needed to rid himself of the de-energising stuffiness of the conference closing rituals, and he felt good now after swimming a few leisurely lengths.

He liked to look after his body, it was like a trophy he could display whenever demons of doubt threatened to take away his confidence. He'd had to work hard to reconstruct his ego after Lisa Maitland had dumped him in favour of a better prospect.

It had taken him almost five years, and a lot of conquests, to put himself back together, and soon he'd be heading for his thirtieth birthday. He felt it had to be now, the career move, leading to all the status and achievements he'd always promised himself and, though he liked to pretend this was irrelevant, his parents.

He looked round at the palms and exotic ferns which enhanced the warm, humid atmosphere of the poolside area. This hotel was very pleasant, he had enjoyed the conference and the opportunity it had given him to raise his profile in the financial world. Carolyn had done well, too, asking several thought-provoking and obviously well thought-out questions.

He'd seen quite a few of the delegates giving her an appraising stare, and the men had been assessing more than her intellect, and fancying what they saw.

When Simon Slater, an amorous opportunist he knew, had given him a knowing look, tipping his head discreetly in Carolyn's direction, Paul had smiled, and said nothing. But he had been gratified by Simon's envy and admiration.

Paul knew that he must be gaining a reputation as a womaniser, but he wouldn't have described himself in those terms. It implied one would be ruthless in the quest for sexual adventure, and that wasn't the case with him. His ego set standards; he pursued his chosen women strongly, but they had to be willing. Paul knew he would only be satisfied if his conquest adored him, and wanted desperately to be a woman who could not only attract him, but also make him happy.

Slowly he slid himself up on to the side of the pool, and wrapped himself in one of the hotel's thick white towelling bathrobes. He was relaxed now, and ready for the evening with Carolyn. He went up to his room to dress with care for the evening meal, he wanted to be at his most seductive.

There was a different, calmer atmosphere in the hotel later that evening, now that the delegates had left. Paul put his arm lightly round Carolyn's shoulders as he escorted her towards the dining-room. He was pleased to feel her trembling a little, he liked to feel protective towards the women he favoured.

'Are we too early?' she asked as she saw the dining room was still almost empty.

'Not at all.' He paused, and looked at her intently, with wicked humour in his eyes. 'I'm hungry. Aren't you?'

Carolyn blushed and looked around to see if anyone was watching them. Paul took hold of her hand, pulling her close as she walked beside him.

'Relax, there's no-one here who knows us now.'

She looked up at him, and her words came out in a flutter of panic. 'I never thought, when we came for this weekend, that we'd be here like this.'

Paul didn't want her to start having doubts. Placing his hand firmly round her waist now, he pulled her against him. 'I know,' he murmured in his sexiest voice, 'but we couldn't go on just looking at each other for ever, could we?'

A waiter arrived and, making an experienced assessment of the situation, showed them to a secluded table for two. He flashed two menus into their hands, and moved discreetly out of sight.

Carolyn could hardly concentrate on reading the list of English and French cuisine. Paul studied her until she looked up at him, then his excited pale blue eyes refused to release her from their gaze, as he said, 'I know what I want. Do you?'

She ignored the suggestive tone, and made her selection from the menu. After the waiter had taken their order and poured the wine, she continued to glance round to see if the other guests were observing them.

'Relax,' Paul said, a little irritated.

She knew very well that it was only part of the reason for her discomfort, but used it as her excuse. 'Sorry, but I got some really horrible looks from some of the other women as they were leaving.'

He shrugged. 'They were just jealous that you spoke so well at the conference. You made quite an impression.'

She smiled at last. 'Did I?'

'You certainly did. I don't think you realise, Carolyn, what a fantastic person you are. You're clever, as well as beautiful, and the most desirable woman I've ever met.'

'Oh.' Her lips parted as she gazed at him.

He kissed her hand, and smiled to himself.

In the doorway of Daniel's room Ellen Heywood silently watched him as he stood in front of the mirror, wearing one of his best jackets and a shirt she had condemned as too bright to wear in respectable company.

Her son's face had the spotless glow of a young choirboy. However, the look in his eyes, together with the way he had splashed Armani eau de toilette over his ultra smooth cheeks, indicated that choirboy activities were not the ones on his mind.

Intent on carefully combing his hair over a thin patch, Dan didn't see her standing there. He picked up a tie but then cast it aside, unfastened the top two buttons of his shirt and arranged the collar on top of his jacket lapels in an attempt to create a 1940s debonair image. Dan was passionate about the 1930s and 40s, and loved the romance of the music and films from those periods. Ellen had decided to tolerate as harmless the fact that the walls of his bedroom were adorned with posters of Frank Sinatra, Fred Astaire and Ginger Rogers, and other more voluptuous, Hollywood legends.

'Going somewhere special tonight?' Ellen asked in the dry sardonic manner she had cultivated to perfection.

Dan jumped guiltily, just as he had as a child caught prising forbidden cubes of jelly from their cellophane.

'No. No, not really.'

In the silence which followed, their eyes met briefly and Ellen's humourless smile told him she knew he was lying.

'Alice Smith told me Lynda Stanworth has returned.'

'Has she?'

'Daniel. Please don't insult me with that look of pretended innocence. It is obvious from the way you are behaving that you are going to meet with her this evening.'

Dan was staggered that his Mother could have guessed he'd arranged to go out with Lynda.

'You are fifty-three years old, Daniel, but still foolish enough to be enticed by that woman.'

'We're going out for a drink, that's all.'

'You know my opinion of her hasn't changed.'

'Yes, Mother. But Lynda has changed.'

'Not possible. People like her can never really overcome their background, and their nature. My advice is to make sure that you do not get involved with her again.'

'She's married to John.'

'Exactly.'

She saw that the happiness had left his eyes and, satisfied she still had the power to make her son obey, she turned to leave. As she closed the door her attention was caught by the poster of Mae West, leaning provocatively against another doorway, and undermining Ellen's confidence with a mocking smile.

Lynda had bought some cream cakes, and an extravagant bouquet for Jean, who almost burst into tears. It made Lynda wonder how long it had been since anyone had bought her friend a bunch of flowers. She showed Jean the Vauxhall Cavalier she'd hired and promised they'd have a ride out in it tomorrow.

When they went back into the house Lynda opened the bottle of sparkling wine she'd also brought back.

'Oh, lovely,' Jean said, impressed. 'Celebrating are we? So you had a nice time with Steve and Michael?'

'Yes. I got on really well with Michael. He's a smashing little lad.'

'Yes, he is. What did Steve say? He'd be shocked to see you.'

'Yes, he was, but we had a lovely chat. We've always been good mates, me and Steve.'

'And when are you going to see Carolyn?'

'She's away at a conference this weekend.'

'You'll see her when she gets back then.'

'Yes. Oh, I don't know, Jean.'

Lynda couldn't keep up the pretence any longer. She took a deep breath, and for a second or two couldn't remember how to breathe out. Then it came in a rush, with the words which carried intense heartache. 'They'd told him I was dead.'

For a moment Jean thought Lynda was going to faint, and guided her to sit down on the settee. Lynda looked up at her, her eyes full of misery, and the laugh she gave was closer to a cry of pain.

'Christ! Wasn't it enough that they drove me away? They didn't have to kill me off as well!'

Lynda sat very still, clutching at Jean's hand, and then the tears came, and her body shook with the sobbing which wouldn't stop.

At first Jean was frightened, she'd never seen Lynda cry, except when her Mother had died. She put her arm round her friend and held her tightly.

'Don't Lynda. I've never seen you like this. It'll be all right. People change, they get to understand things.'

Lynda pushed away from her a little, and shook her head.

'It's not looking like my daughter ever will. From what Steve said, I'll always be the same in her opinion, selfish.'

Jean flinched and confessed, 'We all are, in one way or another.'

She got up, needing an escape from her own guilt and mixed-up emotions. Jean had been out, too, that afternoon, and didn't want to tell Lynda where she'd been.

'Let's have something to eat, we'll feel better when we've had a cream cake!'

As they ate Lynda grew calmer, and even managed to joke about having a date with Dan. Jean decided not to tell Lynda that she, too, was going out, she thought Lynda had had enough bad news for one day.

She hadn't told John that Lynda was back, even though she'd been to see him that afternoon, to check that he hadn't heard about his wife's return. Jean was too scared of what his reaction might be. For the last year she and John had spent almost every Saturday evening together, and before too long they'd be married – she hoped.

It had all seemed right, at last she was going to be happy, with the man she'd always loved. She loved Lynda too, always would, but she wished she hadn't come back. Jean was wondering what would happen now, when Lynda's words broke through her anxious thoughts.

'You can come out with me and Dan tonight, if you like.' She forced herself to make a joke. 'Or I could get Dan to fix you up with a friend, make up a foursome, like we used to. Do you remember?'

Before Jean could stop them, the bad memories pushed out the angry response.

94

'Oh, yes,' Jean said resentfully. 'I remember how they were all disappointed they were going out with me, and not you. They were the most miserable nights out I ever had.'

'I'm sorry, love, I didn't realise,' Lynda said with genuine contrition. 'I've got a lot of things wrong, haven't I, in the past?' She tried to lighten the tension again, 'All right, I won't try to find you a fella, you can share mine!'

As soon as she'd said it she realised it was another bad joke.

Jean was silent, overwhelmed by the irony of that suggestion, and the knowledge that she now had no choice. She summoned all her courage and stared Lynda straight in the eye.

'I suppose it's the wrong time to tell you, but it's only fair. I've already got a date tonight.'

Lynda beamed with delight, and mischief, 'Ooh, yes? Who with?'

'John.'

Lynda stopped smiling for a moment. 'John? My John?'

'Yes.'

Lynda's eyes were dancing as they always did when she was teasing. 'Oh, I say,' she declared in a tone of mock horror, 'my best friend's trying to steal my husband!'

Then she saw the look on Jean's face. 'You are, aren't you?'

Jean nodded, and bit her lip as she always did when she was in trouble. There was a stillness between her and Lynda now, but Jean stood there, focused on her one hope of a happy future, the hope of marrying John Stanworth.

Lynda thought back to those phone calls she'd made from Cornwall, in those lonely, agonising days, and how she'd been relying on Jean to help her. There was no humour in her voice now, only a sense of hurt and betrayal.

'So that was why you refused to keep in touch,' she said accusingly, 'you thought with me gone, you could get John for yourself at long last. No wonder you didn't want me to come back!'

Jean stammered her denial. 'It wasn't like that. Of course I wanted you to come back. You're my best friend, always have been, and I've missed you, Lynda.'

'I don't believe you.'

'It's true. I didn't set out to take John from you, but it's been over ten years, Lynda! John needed me, and since he had his heart attack he's needed me even more.'

She felt numb and confused now as she faced the anger of this woman who had always been her friend, and often protector.

Lynda knew she was being unreasonable, and that it didn't make sense for her to feel jealous when she'd left her husband, and consequently found a man who was the true love of her life. But there'd been a kind of madness in her since she'd lost Tom Meredith, and in this moment the old hot-tempered Lynda took over again.

'Well, I never thought I'd see the day when Miss Jean Prissy-Knickers would have an affair – and with my flaming husband!'

Jean felt shame, but stronger than that came defiant pride, and her love of John Stanworth.

'It's not an affair! We're getting married.'

It took Lynda a minute or two to get over that one, and Jean recoiled at the cold, measured tone of her friend's response.

'Oh, are you? Haven't you forgotten something? John's already got a wife. He's still married – to me!'

CHAPTER TWELVE

Carolyn could hardly breathe, she was so on edge. She stood at the bedroom window and then turned to look at the phone by the bed. She had felt so ashamed when she'd picked up the phone that morning and had lied to her family.

Steve had been annoyed at her boss again claiming more of her free time, but had said he hoped she was enjoying being pampered at the hotel. He'd accepted her story about having to stay on to meet a client, because he had no reason to doubt her. His trust had added to her shame, and she didn't want to think about him and the children now, but it was all she could think about.

It was half past eight, and she was waiting for Paul, but she couldn't stop herself picturing her family. They'd be watching television together, Steve sprawled along the sofa with his arm round Gemma, sharing a packet of sweets, Michael slumped in an armchair wishing he was out with the friends his Mother didn't approve of.

Carolyn suddenly needed to talk to Steve, to have him pull her back from this reckless obsession she'd allowed herself to be drawn into. She began to dial her home number, but paused as she looked across the room. In the mirror she saw what seemed to her the depraved image of a woman she hardly recognised, a woman wearing a tight red dress with a low neckline. There was a tap at the door and Paul swiftly entered the room. She put down the receiver.

He'd brought another bottle of champagne and

two glasses, but when he saw her standing there by the bed, he put them down quickly on a table. He couldn't wait any longer.

He took Carolyn in his arms and pulled her hard against him. There was no tenderness, only desire, and she felt she would break as his arms crushed her and his open mouth moved rapidly over her face and then down towards her breasts. With practised skill he deftly unzipped her dress, dragged it down over her arms and body until its soft folds fell to the floor. His hands rubbed and clutched at her body and Carolyn panicked at the force of his rough haste.

She instinctively tried to push him away, but he wasn't going to stop his onslaught of male passion. With the image of her husband and children still vivid in her head, she pushed him harder, and found she was almost screaming as she staggered away from him.

'No, Paul! No! Leave me alone. I don't want to do this!'

He stood very still. Then he took a step towards her, and she was sure he was going to hit her. She stared at him in horror but couldn't move. He stood there for a moment, taking a few angry breaths, then he was in control again. He stared at her coldly, and with an expression of disgust.

'Well, well, aren't you the little tease after all? An expensive one, though, I'll give you that; à la carte and champagne, luxury hotel suite, and all the time leading me on - to this! What a greedy, tantalising little bitch you are!'

Carolyn was shaking her head, and her eyes were beseeching him to understand, but the rage of rejection drove him on. 'What else am I supposed to think, Carolyn? That you're just a stupid cow who can't make her mind up?'

He walked towards the door, but stopped as he caught sight of himself in the mirror. His wounded pride made him stand tall to display his taut body and handsome face to her once more, and his expression now was one of mockery and disdain.

'No class, that's your problem, Carolyn,' he sneered. 'You're just a silly, small town girl who wants all those things she's dreamed of, and who thought she was smart, and sexy and sophisticated. But you're not any of those things, are you?'

He paused then, because he saw from the look on her face that he was really hurting her now, and he wanted to enjoy the satisfaction of that. With real perception, and a twisted smile, he delivered a final truth.

'And the tragedy is, that you know you will never have what you've always craved, not any of it.'

He laughed with quiet confidence, as he slowly closed the door behind him.

John Stanworth paused as he set the table with the white tablecloth and napkins, and the silver candelabra Carolyn had bought for him to use when Jean came round for supper. He'd put on an Elvis LP, so that it would be playing when Jean arrived, and had forgotten that 'Always on my Mind' was one of the tracks.

And now he found himself listening as if it was the first time he'd ever heard the lyrics. He had to sit down and work hard at not allowing himself to cry. It was him and Lynda, that song. He hadn't listened to her, or given her the love she needed, and he knew she might never come back, but he couldn't stop hoping.

The song ended, but he set it to play again, and it

was still playing when Jean, using her key, walked in and found him sitting there. She sensed immediately that he was in one of his 'remembering' moods.

'Hello, love.'

He stood up, looking a little guilty, and she kissed him on the mouth, not just on his cheek as she usually did.

'The table looks nice. I see you've opened that wine I brought.'

'Yes. I was going to get some.'

'I was passing anyway, it was no trouble to call in with it.'

'I'm sorry if I was a bit irritable.'

'My fault for coming when the football was on the tele.'

'I should have gone to the Milfield match like Michael said.'

'No, wait till next season now. You still need to be careful.'

'I suppose so, but it gets me down a bit.'

'Well, a glass of wine and a nice steak will cheer you up. Do you want me to cook?'

'No, I'm doing it. Everything's ready. I'll finish cooking it while you have your glass of sherry.'

'No rush, unless you're hungry.'

'I am.'

He served the sherry and then swiftly disappeared into the kitchen, leaving her to sit and look round the room, and notice that Lynda's photo was back on the sideboard.

John was even more quiet than usual as they ate their evening meal, and Jean had to work hard to fill the silence with details of her humdrum week, and bits of gossip she'd heard.

It had become almost a ritual, 'their Saturday

100

night'. It was part of the new régime Jean and Carolyn seemed to have established for him since his heart attack. When they'd finished the meal they did the washing up together.

'Sorry,' John apologised as he bumped into her when going to get the dirty pans off the cooker.

'It's so small, this kitchen. We'll make sure we get a bigger one when we move. There's a nice bungalow gone up for sale on Westfield Avenue. Did you see it in the paper?'

'No, I haven't looked.'

'Oh.' She didn't hide her disappointment.

He scrubbed harder at the pan in the sink.

'We're not in any hurry, are we?'

She sighed as she stood and watched him.

'It doesn't look like it. Do you realise that in May it will be ten years since you and I, got together?'

'I suppose it is. Lynda's been gone twelve years now,' he said sombrely.

'Don't say it like that, it sounds as if she's died.'

'She might have for all I know!'

Jean knew she shouldn't be deceiving him like this, but she didn't want to be the one to tell him his wife was not only very much alive, but only a couple of miles away.

'No, we've told you before, John, the police would have informed you if anything had happened to her. Shall we go and sit down now?'

She walked into the living room and sat on the settee, waiting for him to join her. She saw him staring at Lynda's photograph.

'I've been thinking about her a lot lately.'

'Yes, I saw you'd put her photo back on the sideboard.'

'I just found it in the drawer and got it out.'

Jean felt a panic inside her, and it drove her to make the point again.

'Like Carolyn said, she left you over ten years ago, so you'd have no problem getting a divorce. And we can't get married until you do.'

It was as if he hadn't heard her.

'She was right to leave, you know, Jean. It was right what she said, about being nobody in her own home. What with my Mother, and Carolyn criticising her. And me, well, it was just like it says in that song.'

He sat down heavily on the settee and Jean quickly put her arms round him and started to kiss him.

'John, it wasn't your fault.'

'It was. I keep hoping she'll walk through that door, and let me tell her I'm sorry.'

Jean moved away a little and looked at him.

'And would you tell her about us, if she came back?'

He didn't reply, but just stared at her, wondering what to say. She jumped up angrily.

'No, of course you wouldn't, because there's nothing to tell, is there? Except,' she continued sarcastically, 'that we've been sleeping together for years, that we've been talking about getting married, and that you're getting a divorce. But you're not, are you?'

There was a stubborn expression on his face now.

'I'm not ready.'

'No and you never will be, will you? It's still Lynda, isn't it?'

She didn't wait for him to confirm that, but picked up her handbag. 'I'm going home.'

'Are you not staying the night?'

'Am I hell. No!'

Ellen Heywood would perhaps have been relieved if she had known that it wasn't her son who was occupying Lynda's thoughts, even though he was clinging to her as if he'd never let her go again. As far as Dan was concerned, Lynda's body was the best support in the world to lean on. And as a result of the steady stream of alcohol which had flowed so sweetly down his throat in the last few hours, he was much in need of support.

Lynda was the wrong side of sobriety too, and very confused, but not just because of the wide range and quantity of cocktails she had persuaded the bemused bar-tenders of Milfield to concoct for her.

She moved away from him, and started to walk unsteadily across the precinct. 'I'm cold, Dan.'

He caught up with her. 'Cuddle up to me, I'll keep you warm.'

He started to dance, his cheek pressed against hers, and sang a jumbled lyric.

'The snow is snowing. What do I care how much it may storm? I've got my love to keep me warm.'

Lynda, surprised at how slurred her words sounded, declared, 'Jean Haworth's got my husband to keep her warm. That's where she is now, you know, my so-called best friend. In bed with my bloody husband!'

Dan wagged a finger at her. 'Who you left, a long, long time ago.'

'Yeah. But it's still not right.'

'You're not jealous, are you?'

'No!'

Lynda knew that what was going on in her head, and in her heart, was more complex than that, and far more painful.

'What am I doing here?' she tearfully demanded to know as she gently pushed Dan away from her.

103

'You've come home,' he said.

Lynda looked round the lifeless centre of the town which had seemed to her today like a lost soul, in need of comfort and care. Like her, she reflected bitterly, perhaps she did belong here after all.

Bowing her head, she slowly knelt down. She wanted to curl up on the cold, damp paving stones and cry, but not because of John, or Jean, or anyone else. What was breaking her heart once more was the thought of Tom Meredith, the man whose arms would never hold her again. She knelt there, defenceless in her grieving. Then she heard Dan singing.

She looked up and there he was, dancing around in the mock Victorian bandstand. Ignoring his body weight, Dan was up on his toes, doing his Fred Astaire impersonation, singing 'Isn't this a lovely day to be caught in the rain?'

She smiled. Bless him, Dan could always make her laugh, and she loved him for that. She would sing away her sorrows too, but not with that song. She staggered up into the bandstand.

'Our song now,' she told Dan, pushing him away.

'We haven't got a song,' he protested, leaning against the rail of the bandstand for support.

Looking up to the stars, her arms outstretched, she began to sing Dusty Springfield's 'I Only Want to Be With You.' She and Tom had first sung this at the Springfield Hotel in Cornwall, and had adopted it as their own.

They'd sung it together so many times, at parties or riding through the countryside in his red sports car, and finally during the last few days of his life. But now she was singing it alone, and tears soon came to drown away the words.

CHAPTER THIRTEEN

It was almost ten o' clock when Carolyn entered the dining room that beautiful Sunday morning. At the windows the well-established morning sun was making the gold velvet of the elegantly draped curtains glow like melting butter.

It should have been a morning to enjoy at leisure, with succulent fresh fruit, warm croissants and the rich aroma of the finest coffee, but instead it was to be an ordeal, and one which Carolyn had delayed as long as possible. Apart from anything else, she felt so embarrassed that she had let Paul Ferris pay for her to stay an extra night in these luxurious surroundings.

As she hesitated in the doorway, Carolyn saw Paul barely acknowledge the presence of the waiter who was refilling his coffee cup. The young man looked at her, and when she nodded he filled a cup for her, too. He moved away as Carolyn sat down slowly on the chair opposite Paul. He looked at her stonily and then went back to wrestling ill-temperedly with 'The Sunday Telegraph', making it clear that Carolyn would have to be the first to speak.

'You've had your breakfast?'

'Yes.' His tone was curt and his body tense with his anger and resentment towards her.

She tried to speak calmly, 'What time do you want to leave?'

'Soon.'

Quietly she said, 'Paul, I'm so sorry.'

He laughed at her, but there was no humour in the sound, only contempt.

They hardly spoke again until the BMW was speeding along the country lanes which took them away from the hotel. Paul had planned so carefully that 'The Cedars' would be the romantic setting for the beginning of their affair. He had been so sure that Carolyn would give way to the sexual fever he'd been assiduously nurturing between them.

Now he felt he wanted to hit this woman who had rejected him, or to dump her by the roadside. But as she quietly tried to give him the explanation she knew he deserved, he found himself listening.

'It was the dress, I think,' she began. 'I looked in the mirror and saw my Mother. It was the kind of red dress she used to wear, I hadn't realised when I bought it. I felt I looked cheap, like she used to.'

'Did you not like your Mother?'

'No. We argued all the time. It was my Nana who brought me up. My Mother was happier working than staying at home looking after me. In fact by the time I was a teenager she never seemed to be at home at all, she went out every night.'

Carolyn paused, realising that what she was telling Paul wasn't exactly true, but she wanted to make her case.

'She had affairs,' she continued. 'When I was fourteen she and my Dad nearly split up over some guy she'd been seeing. They thought I didn't know, but I heard them rowing. Nan told me we had to keep it secret, so nobody ever talked about it.'

Feeling she was talking too much, she stopped, but Paul nodded, encouraging her to go on. He was enjoying her plea for understanding, and her story was making her a more interesting conquest than he had anticipated.

'I've always vowed I would never be like my Mother. So you see why I can't have an affair?'

'Yes, I understand, Carolyn,' he reassured her.

But, he decided, he didn't see why he shouldn't have this woman, and he did still desire her. He realised, though, that he must change his tactics with Carolyn Sheldon.

He stopped the car and gently took hold of her hand.

'But you obviously haven't understood me, Carolyn. This is not an affair, my darling.' He kissed her hand and looked at her, saying softly, 'It could be very, very good, you and me – you know that.'

Carolyn looked at his elegant, sensitive hands and then at his lean, handsome face, and knew for certain that she still wanted him very much.

Her relief that he wasn't now rejecting her, proved to her how much she wanted to give in to the temptations he was offering again. Paul Ferris made her feel so beautiful, so wonderful. And she needed that, because Steve seemed to have lost interest in her and what she wanted, and the way he looked at her didn't excite her like the way Paul was gazing at her now.

When Jean came downstairs on Sunday morning, heavy with the lack of restful sleep, she could have wept when she saw Lynda coming out of the kitchen. Her hair and make-up were perfect, and beneath one of Jean's faded aprons she was wearing an immaculate coffee and cream coloured outfit of matching top and well-cut trousers. 'How could she compete with this woman?' Jean thought to herself.

'I've been to the corner shop. I thought we could do with a full English breakfast before we set off for our day out.'

'Day out?'

'Yeah. I told you we'd have a run out in the car. I thought we'd go for a drive round Milfield, visiting old familiar places, recapture my youth.' She laughed then, 'God, I never thought I'd be old enough to say that!'

Jean looked down at her skirt and shapeless cardigan. 'I've not dressed for going out anywhere.'

'You'll be fine, I was thinking we could perhaps go to The Grey Horse for a pub lunch afterwards, save us cooking. Is that all right with you?'

'Yes, lovely, but I'll get changed after breakfast.'

Jean stood in the kitchen doorway, watching her friend cook eggs and bacon. Both of them knew there was a conversation which they had to have, and Jean decided to get it over with.

'Lynda, I haven't told John you're back.'

'Oh. Well somebody will have to, because I want to see him, and soon. How do you like your bacon, crispy?'

'Lynda.'

She heard the pleading in Jean's voice and saw her anguish, and realised she didn't want this. John Stanworth had always come between her and this forlorn looking woman who, she remembered, had once been the nearest thing she had to a sister.

Jean's voice was quiet and tremulous. 'What are we going to do, about you and me, and John?'

Lynda knew the answer was simple really, but something made her hesitate to give Jean the right to take her husband. She decided to postpone dealing with their dilemma.

'See how it goes, eh?'

Jean nodded.

Lynda smiled. 'And I forgot to ask, how much rent do you want? And don't say you won't let me pay. I'm not short of money, Jean.' Then her anxiety made its way into her voice as she asked, 'I can stay, can't I?'

Jean pictured the shabby curtains and the thin, cheap bed-linen in the spare room where Lynda was sleeping.

'Wouldn't you prefer a hotel? I mean, that bedroom isn't the sort of thing you're used to now, is it?'

Lynda thought of Loveday Manor, and wished she hadn't needed to leave. She touched Jean's cheek, and made her friend look at her. Jean glimpsed for an instant, all the loneliness and uncertainty Lynda had been hiding.

'I really don't want to stay in a hotel. If you don't mind, I'd rather be here, with you.'

When she saw the look on Jean's face as they drove along Raleigh Street, Lynda wished she hadn't brought her there. But it was part of their childhood, The Clough, the tightly packed rows of small terraced houses which had once been regarded as an area to be avoided by respectable people.

'I thought they'd have pulled this down by now.'

'No such luck,' Jean said grimly.

'He must have had a funny sense of humour, the fella who named these streets after explorers. He must have known that the people who had to live here would be desperate to escape to a new world.'

'I was, and I'll always be grateful to Gordon for getting me out of here. Can we go, Lynda? The last time I saw this house there was a hearse parked outside.'

'Sorry, love. I should have thought.'

'It's all right. Shall we go to The Grey Horse now? It's eleven o'clock, and I expect you'll want to go to the graveyard first.'

'If you don't mind.'

'Of course I don't. I realised why you chose The Grey Horse.'

Lynda smiled at her. 'You know me too well, Jean.'

'I ought to, we've been friends long enough.'

CHAPTER FOURTEEN

Jenny Heywood was having a hard time listening to her daughters complaining. They always objected to this ritual of Sunday lunch and having these precious hours of their weekend commandeered by their Grandmother.

They couldn't understand why their Mother refused to rebel, why she continued to be subservient to Ellen Heywood's continual demands and 'standards' just for the sake of an uneasy peace. Jenny, too, often wished she had the courage, and the hardness of heart, to break this tradition imposed by Ellen.

In the end, however, it always seemed simpler to accept this attempt to maintain the illusion of a strongly united family. Katie and Alex joked about it being the Sunday 'séance', and had to suppress giggles if they omitted to close their eyes as Ellen said grace, for then the atmosphere round the table confirmed the aptness of the comparison.

Ellen would have been appalled at such flippancy. To her, this gathering round the table together was a symbol of continuity, and it was a way of staying attached both to her parents and to her younger son, Richard, who had been so tragically taken from her. She had vowed that nothing would ever halt this family ritual.

This morning, however, there had been a serious disruption to the schedule of the event.

Dan had a hangover so huge that even his Mother's wrath had not succeeded in getting him out of his bed before midday.

Alex, hastily dusting the furniture, answered the phone.

'One o'clock? That's fine, Grandmother, no problem. I'm sure Mum can slow the cooking down. See you soon.'

'Thank goodness for that, they're going to be late,' she announced to her Mother and sister who'd come in from the kitchen. 'I've got time to phone Jamil.'

'If his Mother will let him take the call,' said Katie scornfully. 'I wouldn't bother, I'd assume she'll have thought up some more 'Indian family traditions' to keep him away from you this weekend.'

'He has some duty visits to make, but they're not setting off till half twelve. I'll phone him now.'

'Have you finished dusting?' Jenny asked.

'Yes. Well all the bits she might notice.'

'Ellen notices everything,' her Mum reminded her. 'And she won't appreciate your Dad's photo being covered with a layer of dust.'

'And you've forgotten the napkins,' Katie said, checking the table setting.

'Oh, for heaven's sake!' Alex moaned.

'I'll have to check the roast,' Jenny said. 'Ellen is never late, I wonder what's happened.'

Alex grinned. 'Uncle Dan's in big trouble. Apparently he went out last night and, reading between the lines, he has a hangover. Will you do the napkins for me, Katie?'

Not giving her sister chance to refuse, she dashed off upstairs. Katie groaned, but got the napkins out of the drawer and placed them next to the silver cutlery gleaming against the white damask tablecloth which covered the battered old mahogany table.

This solid Victorian relic, found in a junk shop, had been one of the first pieces of furniture Jenny had bought for the house she'd insisted on moving to after her husband had died. Ellen had been appalled that her daughter-in-law, so recently widowed, had sold the impressively large, modern detached house which she had helped her son to buy for himself and his family.

Jenny had told Ellen that the move to the village of Hadden Lea was made for practical, economic reasons, but the truth was she had been desperate to leave the house Richard had chosen. She'd always considered it too ostentatious but, more than that, it had held so many bad memories.

This large old stone terraced house perched on a hillside overlooking the moors had been her choice. And she'd sold much of the ultra-modern, expensive furniture Richard had bought, replacing it with more homely items which not only suited this house better, but also reminded Jenny of her parents' home.

This dining table was like the one they'd had and, like theirs, it had survived crayons, paint pots, papier-mâché, and riotous children's parties. It was now where Alex and Katie wrote essays which required the spread of reference books, and where Jenny pretended to balance her household accounts.

It stood by the window so that whoever sat there could easily allow themselves to be distracted from their task by the view, which had been one of the main reasons Jenny had bought the house. There were fields cut into irregular rectangles by the long black lines of dry stone walls, and beyond them the moors; Jenny loved to look at this landscape as it changed day by day, season by season, it provided her with much needed interludes of calm.

She wasn't at all calm now as she awaited Ellen's arrival. Her face was reddened with the heat from the oven as she hurried into the living room with the

113

horse-radish sauce she'd forgotten, and which Ellen insisted was an essential accompaniment to roast beef.

Katie, keeping watch, saw Dan's Volvo Estate draw up in front of the house.

'Grandmama has arrived,' she announced.

'Tell Alex, will you, she's still upstairs.'

Jenny looked out of the window and watched Dan, still struggling to overcome the legacy of his night out with Lynda, heave himself slowly out of the driver's seat, and take care to close the door quietly. He then stood for a moment to try to gain some relief from his hangover by breathing in some fresh air and gazing out over the moors.

Ellen tapped impatiently on the windscreen and gave him a steely look as he opened the passenger door. She dug her fingers harder than usual into his arm as he escorted her up the steps.

Once initial greetings were accomplished, the hush of enforced politeness descended over the Heywood household as they took their seats at the table. Jenny entered with a tureen of soup, but then had to dart back into the kitchen when she realised she was still wearing her grubby apron. Ellen, seated as usual at the head of the table, picked up her napkin and with her opening remark set the tone for the unsociable gathering.

'Where are my napkin rings? You haven't pawned them, have you?'

Katie, with some effort managed keep irritation out of her voice.

'No, Gran, they're in the drawer.'

Ellen, seeking a target for her ill-humour, turned to Jenny with a mixture of patronage and accusation.

'I did not give you my silver napkin rings for them to languish disregarded in a drawer.'

Katie, fuming, sprang to her feet. 'I'll get them.'

114

Ellen's hand commanded her to remain seated, 'Too late now.'

The roast beef and carefully prepared fresh vegetables, and then the fruit gâteau, provided by Dan, were duly presented and consumed in a travesty of familial harmony, until an item of local news arrived with the cheese and biscuits.

The family had for years given in to Ellen Heywood's demands, and stifled any replies to her criticisms and gibes, but today was to be the beginning of their rebellion against Ellen's rule. Lynda would have laughed out loud if she'd known that the catalyst for the insurrection was the mention of her return to Milfield.

The bearer of the glad tidings was Katie. She had meant to tell her mother earlier about her meeting with Lynda, but it had slipped into the pending file of her memory. Now, with the aim of ending yet another deathly silence, Katie asked cheerily, 'Uncle Dan, have you told Mum about that friend you saw at the café yesterday?'

Dan winced. 'No, not yet.'

His Mother, quick to note his discomfort, asked, 'What friend?'

'Lynda.'

Jenny beamed. 'Lynda Stanworth?'

'Yes,' he said, feigning neutrality, but his eyes signalled his pleasure to Jenny. 'She arrived on Friday apparently. She's come back.'

'Oh, fantastic!'

'Who is she?' asked Alex, curious at seeing her Mother so delighted.

'A very good friend of mine, and of Uncle Dan.'

'You're blushing, Uncle Dan,' Katie teased. 'I thought you fancied her. She's really good-looking,' she explained to Alex, 'and incredibly smart. Who is

115

she, an old flame of yours?'

'No. Well, yes, a long time ago,' he confessed, glancing sheepishly at his Mother.

'She is the wife of John Stanworth, who is a friend of your uncle's, but no-one you will know,' Ellen informed her granddaughters, with a finality in her tone which indicated that this should be the end of this particular topic of conversation.

Katie took delight in ignoring her Grandmother's obvious disapproval of this woman. 'I've never seen her in Milfield before. Has she been away a long time?'

'Not long enough,' Ellen hissed under her breath.

Jenny made a decision to ignore her.

'Lynda is a great friend,' she told her daughters, 'she was a big help to me after your Father died, and she was one of your Granny Kelly's best friends. I can't wait to see her again,' Jenny declared, smiling at Dan's astonishment at her boldness.

Ellen, too, was astounded and extremely annoyed at Jenny's reaction. 'I strongly advise you, Jennifer, not to associate with that woman. Richard, I remember, did not approve of her.'

'No, he didn't,' Jenny agreed, and her daughters notice the unusually hard tone of her voice.

Ellen Heywood's eyes glinted as she spoke. 'Lynda Stanworth has always caused trouble. She deeply offended, on many occasions, her mother-in-law, Sheila Stanworth, who was a close friend of mine. To be blunt, Sheila was, till the day she died, eternally ashamed and embarrassed that her son had married Lynda Collins.

She was relieved, and not at all surprised when she ran off, and deserted not only John, but their daughter, who had just had a baby.'

Jenny, tight-lipped, listened to Ellen's tirade, and

116

was remembering Richard's antagonism towards her friend, and the wariness in his eyes whenever he met Lynda.

He'd realised that she knew about him, and about his cruelty, and that, unlike his wife, Lynda wasn't afraid of him. She'd been willing to threaten to report him to the police if he harmed Jenny again, but Jenny had been too frightened to risk accepting that offer of help.

Ellen, like her son, wasn't going to be reasonable. Assuming that her ruling would be accepted, she dismissed the idea of Jenny even going to see Lynda.

'For the sake of your daughters' moral welfare, and your husband's memory, I must insist that you do not resume your friendship with Lynda Stanworth.'

Then, confident that she had thus put an end to any prospect of Lynda becoming involved with her family any further, she announced that it was now time for the coffee to be served. However, Ellen would discover in the next few weeks that her edict concerning Lynda Stanworth would not be obeyed.

Dan joined Jenny in the relative privacy of the kitchen. As he did some washing up while she made the coffee, they talked about Lynda, and supported each other in their resolution to disregard Ellen's wishes. They had both decided, for different reasons, that Lynda was once more to play an important part in their lives.

When Ellen and Dan had left Alex flung herself down on the sofa, and Katie released her frustration with a few heavy handed discords on the battered upright piano.

'Katie!' Jenny protested.

'God, I thought she'd never go,' moaned Alex. 'She gets worse every week!'

117

Katie adopted a pained expression as she mimicked her Grandmother.

'Katie, could you not find something smarter than that to wear?'

Alex joined in the mimicry. 'I am sure your Father would have insisted on your applying for Cambridge, Alexandra, so I feel it is my duty to insist on his behalf.'

'She's for ever giving us orders! Who does she think she is?' Katie grumbled.

Jenny understood their irritation but said firmly, 'She's your Father's Mother and my mother-in-law.'

'Mum, Dad's been dead twelve years, she shouldn't have any say in your life now,' Alex reasoned.

Her sister agreed. 'Yeah, why do you keep doing what she tells you?'

'I don't,' Jenny argued.

'You do!' Alex contradicted her mother. 'You give in to her nearly all the time.'

'Yes,' added Katie. 'You'll never get married again while she's still running your life.'

Jenny was taken aback. 'Who says I want to get married again?'

Alex sat up. 'Mum, we think it would be good if you could find a man to look after you.'

Jenny smiled derisively, and cupped her hand to her ear. 'What's that sound? Oh, dear, Emily Pankhurst's turning in her grave again.'

'You can have a career as well,' Alex conceded.

'Thanks a lot. But at the moment I'll settle for some help with the washing-up.'

Alex headed towards the door. 'I can't, I'm meeting Jamil, and I've got an essay to finish.'

'I thought you and Uncle Dan had done the washing-up,' Katie said.

'Not all of it.'

'You were in the kitchen a long time.'

'We were talking.'

'Oh,' Katie laughed. 'I saw you looking at each other. Plotting rebellion, were you?'

'Something like that. Now will one of you come and help me?'

Alex gave her sister a cheesy smile, and waved her fingers as if practising a scale on the piano, as she made her exit. Katie followed Jenny into the kitchen, with little reluctance; she liked the chance to spend time alone with her, and always hoped that, this time, she'd find the right tone and be able to talk to her, woman to woman, as Alex seemed to.

CHAPTER FIFTEEN

As Carolyn wouldn't be home until the afternoon Steve had decided on a pub lunch. He took John and the kids to The Fox and Hounds for a roast dinner or, in Gemma's case, scampi and chips. John insisted on paying, and Steve realised he'd have to let him.

'I had a phone call from Bob Horton,' John announced as they stood in the park later that afternoon, watching Michael play football and Gemma chatting in the playground with a group of friends.

'Oh, yeah?'

'He wants me to go round and sort out some electrics for him, a new hi-fi system and video stuff to go in that cabinet you made for him. You didn't ask him to give me the job, did you?'

'No, it was his idea. He knows how good you are.'

'He knows how good you are, too. He told me he'd give you work if you ever took the chance and set up on your own. I wish I had the money to help you there.'

'You've helped us enough, John.'

'I can see you're not happy where you are. You seem worried, Steve.'

'No, just tired that's all.'

Steve had been trying to appear relaxed with John, but seeing Lynda again had stirred up all kinds of thoughts about the past and the future.

He was also worried that he or Michael might accidentally reveal to John that his wife had returned to Milfield. He didn't want that to happen until he'd had chance to tell Carolyn.

When Michael came back to join them at the end of his five-a-side match, the conversation turned to the Milfield match again.

'Did you see anybody you knew?' John asked innocently.

Michael opened his mouth and then swallowed hard. He looked at his Dad as they both thought immediately about whom they had met.

'Only Gary.' Steve answered untruthfully. 'He was supposed to be taking Jackie shopping, but he'd sneaked off to the match.'

'Oh, he'll be in trouble, then,' John laughed.

Gemma, who'd also joined them, saw an opportunity to dive into the conversation and cause a splash.

'So will Dad,' she commented pertly, 'if he doesn't tidy up before Mum gets home.'

Steve pulled a face at her, 'I thought you were doing it,' he retorted.

Gemma tossed her head. 'No.' she stated firmly and began to walk away.

'Where are you going now?' John teased, 'off to meet your boyfriend?'

This was greeted with another forceful 'No!' but Gemma's quickly suppressed smile showed she liked the idea.

'We'll be leaving in about ten minutes,' Steve called after her.

'Can I go home with you for a bit, Grandad?' Michael asked.

'Of course you can,' John said, delighted to have company instead of watching television on his own. 'If that's all right with you, Steve?'

'Yes. But you're a lucky lad, Michael, getting out of the cleaning up.'

121

Gemma's remark had reminded Steve that he did need to have the house presentable for Carolyn's return; she was going to be upset enough, without having the annoyance of an untidy house as well.

His head was pounding with the tension of wondering how he was going to tell his wife that Lynda had come back. He was glad Michael wouldn't be there to witness it, and was hoping one of Gemma's friends might ask her back to their house.

He needed to break the news to Carolyn as soon as possible, but he knew it might completely destabilise the delicately balanced relationship that their marriage had recently become.

From the small cemetery on the hillside you could ignore the town of Milfield and fix your gaze instead on the meadows, hills and moorland which beckoned you to fresh air and freedom. That was why Doreen Collins, being insistent for once in her life, had chosen it as her last resting place.

Lynda was relieved to find that her Mother's grave was not overgrown with weeds, and Jean told her that it was Steve who quietly made sure it was not neglected. Lynda had brought some pink spray carnations and, after she'd arranged them in the little stone vase, she and Jean, blinking back tears, stood for a moment in silent gratitude.

'She was always kind to me, your Mum.'

'Yeah. She didn't have much, but what she had she gave away.' Lynda gave a sigh, 'She worked so hard, but she never saw any benefit from it. I vowed when she died that I'd have a better life than she did.'

'And have you, do you think?'

'Yes. Eventually.'

'Not here, though?'

'No, not here.'

Lynda turned her back on the view and looked steadily at Jean, with a little smile.

'Do you remember those dreams we used to have, Jean, of being like Audrey Hepburn and Cary Grant, driving through France and Italy in a sports car, and living in swanky hotels?'

Jean laughed. 'Yeah. And I remember dreaming about marrying a millionaire. None of my dreams came true, unfortunately.'

'Mine did,' Lynda said softly.

She looked away from Jean now, and there were tears streaming down her cheeks as she stared at the landscape.

She took a deep breath. 'Let's go,' she said, and turned to walk so quickly away from the graveside that Jean had almost to run to catch up with her.

'What's wrong, Lynda?'

'Too many graves lately,' she replied.

She didn't give Jean the chance to ask any more questions, but hurried across the road and into The Grey Horse.

The inn had once been known as 'None-go-Bye' Hall, for it had been the home of a local highwayman, but this century it had become more famous for its cuisine, both traditional and adventurous.

The restaurant, with its ancient oak beams and simple, dark stained furniture, was quiet now as most of the customers had left, to set off for a walk along the nearby country lanes, or to return home to doze in front of the television.

They chose a table in a corner by one of the deeply recessed small windows. Jean smiled to herself as she saw how, when the handsome young waiter approached, Lynda turned her head away from the

123

shaft of sunshine which was trying hard to unkindly highlight the signs that she was no longer a young woman.

Lynda urged Jean to order whatever she fancied from the excellent menu, and watched her taking so much pleasure from doing that. She was happy to be once more providing Jean with treats, just as she had all through their friendship. The difference was that, this time, she had plenty of money to pay for them.

They chatted and laughed as they enjoyed their meal, and the memories and intimacy of their shared past began to strengthen their friendship again. By the time Jean was spooning her way through the large dish of ice cream topped with nuts, chocolate and whipped cream, she felt she could ask the question she'd been holding back.

'Lynda, in the cemetery, what did you mean about too many graves lately? Was it a particular grave you were thinking about?'

It was a few minutes before Lynda could give her an answer, and even then she found it hard to keep her voice steady.

'His name was Tom Meredith. He was a very special man.' She paused, still unwilling to use the harsh vocabulary of death. 'He, I lost him a few weeks ago.'

'Oh, I thought you must have met somebody, to make you stay away so long,' Jean remarked, unable to keep that disapproving tone from her voice. She immediately felt ashamed as she saw the pitiful look in Lynda's eyes, and she asked, more gently, 'What was he like?'

Lynda found she was relieved to have the opportunity to talk about her man.

'Oh, blue eyes, curly hair, and full of energy. He made me feel I was the most wonderful woman in the world, and that I could do anything. He taught me so much, and he was so kind, so gentle.' She faltered as the memory of how it had felt to be in Tom Meredith's arms overwhelmed her.

She had to stop then, and tears ran down her cheeks as she looked across at her friend and whispered, 'Oh, hell, Jean!'

Jean was amazed at the depth of love and sorrow in Lynda's eyes.

'And you really loved him, didn't you?'

'Yeah.'

'No wonder you had to stay with him.'

Lynda scrubbed away the tears with her crumpled handkerchief, and forced herself back in control.

'Yes. But I'm glad to be back home now.'

Jean wiped her mouth slowly on the white linen napkin she had admired, and then clutched it tightly in front of her.

She had been appreciating how wonderful it felt now that she and Lynda could confide in each other again. That feeling of security she had missed so much while Lynda had been away had begun to come back. So it was like watching something delicate and beautiful fall to the ground when she heard herself destroying that closeness.

The question had been the unrelenting obsession in her head ever since Lynda had walked back into her life, and she couldn't stop herself blurting it out now.

'Yes,' she said, 'but do you want to be 'back home' with John?'

Lynda's expression hardened, she felt Jean had no right to ask that question, not now, at this particular moment.

She couldn't bear even to think about John as her husband, not when the pain of losing Tom was still making her heart feel that it wanted to stop beating.

Jean was twisting the napkin in her hand. Perceiving the strength of her need, Lynda felt sorry for this woman who had had so little joy in her life. But she, too, had questions that needed to be answered.

'I haven't even seen John yet.'

'No.'

Lynda sat back in her chair, and asked coolly, 'Shall we have coffee?'

Jean ignored this attempt to distract her, she had to know.

'Lynda, are you going to give John a divorce?'

Her bluntness threw Lynda off balance for a second, and her reply came unconsidered.

'If he wants one.'

In the apartment on the top floor of Loveday Manor, you could nestle among the cushions on the cosy little sofa which faced the window, and spend hours looking out at the garden. The lawns, herbaceous borders, and the trees and shrubs, formed a landscape of foliage and changing colours. You could even see the gently flowing river.

Suzanne Heston, as she remained in spirit, even though she had insisted on keeping her husband's name after the divorce, didn't even glance at the view. She was concentrating on selecting particular items and placing them in special white boxes, and packing into ordinary cardboard boxes every photograph, and every item which she thought would have been chosen by Lynda Collins.

She hadn't quite finished by the time she heard the sound of the MG's engine, and looked out to see her son arriving back from visiting suppliers in Guildford.

She picked up one of the white boxes and, locking the door behind her, she hurried out of the apartment and down the stairs which led into a corridor to one side of the foyer.

Patrick Nelson, standing behind the reception desk taking a booking, saw her and wondered what she'd been doing in that particular part of the hotel. He had been Tom Meredith's right-hand man and loyal friend for many years, and had learned not to trust Suzanne Heston. He smiled as Mark came into the foyer carrying a box of DVDs.

'Charlie Foster sent these for the kids.'

'Oh.'

'Don't look so disapproving, Patrick! I'd already given him the order before he gave them to me. And anyway, he said they were just a free sample.'

'Remember that saying of your Grandad Heston's that Tom used to quote to us. 'Only Death is for free.'

Mark laughed as he completed the sentence. 'And you pay for that with your life.'

'That's right. You shouldn't accept any gifts. You have to be careful in business, Mark.'

'I know, but there's no harm in a little present like this, and it's for the kids.'

Patrick sighed, he didn't want to get into an argument with Mark. He took the DVDs and put them behind the desk. 'I'll have to check with the boss-lady to see if they're allowed.'

Mark laughed again. 'You're a good advert for the bachelor life, Patrick Nelson, since you got married to Amy.'

Patrick winked at him. 'I play the game, Mark, and I know how and when to win. And don't forget, I did all the playing the field I wanted to as far as the ladies were concerned.'

'Till Amy got you tied down.'

'I got her, you mean.'

'In spite of your sister giving you such a hard time.'

Patrick gave one of his slow grins.

'The fact that Amy has not a drop of Jamaican blood in her, did make for some small problems, but Lucille got over it. Now, do you want to take over till Sally gets here? I need to get back to the kitchen.'

'Sure.'

Mark swiftly moved round to stand behind the desk, and automatically looked at the bookings register.

'Have you been busy this morning?'

'Yes, but not as busy as your Mother, I don't think.'

'What do you mean?'

He indicated the corridor, 'I saw her coming from that lift carrying a fairly large box. Now, she has no reason to go to that part of the hotel, unless she wanted to visit a certain apartment. Is that right?'

'Yes,' Mark replied with a frown. 'I'll go up there and check as soon as Sally comes in and takes over.'

The Gatehouse was a small, elegantly modernised, eighteenth century detached house, which stood at the entrance to what once had been the large estate of Loveday Manor. At the insistence of her Mother, Nicki Heston, it had become Suzanne's property as part of the settlement of the divorce between her and Tom Meredith.

Suzanne was in the lounge, taking a bronze statuette of a horse, and a large china jug out of the box, and was startled when Mark walked in.

'What on earth are you doing, Mother?' Mark demanded. 'Those are my Dad's things.'

128

'This horse was given to him by my Father.'

'I know. As a memento of the good times they spent together at the races. Why have you taken it from the apartment? And why have you been there and packed all those things in boxes?'

'Some of them belong to me, like this jug, it came from our château. And I thought it was time that apartment was cleared out.'

'No, it stays as it is! For heaven's sake, my Dad's been gone only a few weeks, and in any case it's still Lynda's home.'

'No, it is not.'

'It is. Dad stated that in his will.'

'His will! She made him sign that when he was too ill to know what he was doing, just as she made him go through that mockery of a marriage.'

'That's not true, any of it. Dad knew exactly what he was doing. It was he who insisted that everything should be clear, and Dad wanted to get married even more than Lynda did.'

'Then why was it done so quickly and in so much secrecy?'

Mark heard his voice growing louder. 'Partly because Dad knew that you would make trouble, and he was right.'

'Mark, my darling, don't shout at me like that. I just want you to have what should belong to you. The hotel and all the money came from my family, your family. It should all belong to you. That woman has no right to any of it. And I am going to make sure she does not keep it.'

'How?'

'By contesting the will.'

'No. You can't do that.'

'I can, and I shall.'

CHAPTER SIXTEEN

Carolyn was furious that Steve had not made sure the house was clean and tidy for her return, but she was glad of the anger. Anything was better than the feeling of guilt which had made her hand shake so much that she'd dropped her key on the front step. Paul hadn't stayed to see that happen, he'd driven away before she'd reached the door.

She used the anger to stop her thinking; she banged around in the kitchen clearing the dirty dishes, she picked up clothes dumped on chairs, shoes shoved along the edge of the sofa, and then pushed the Hoover forcefully over the carpet to pick up the crisps and crumbs. She was still cleaning and tidying the living room when Steve and Gemma arrived home.

Steve stood in the doorway, embarrassed at the mess his wife had come home to. Gemma confidently disregarded the fact that her Mother's eyes were blazing with fury, and ran to fling her arms round her neck.

'Hiya, Mum. Have you had a good time?'

Carolyn, hurting at the thought of how she had spent the extra day away from her child, held her in a fierce embrace. She smoothed Gemma's tangled curls as she looked, as if for the first time, at her daughter's smiling face.

'Have you brought me anything?'

'Yes, some sweets, and a little bar of soap and a bubble bath from the hotel for your dolls. They're on my dressing table.'

'Thanks, Mum!' Gemma was delighted, as Carolyn had known she would be. It had seemed disgustingly incongruous that she had stood in her bathroom at the hotel, collecting these foolish treasures for her daughter and then, in that same room, she had bathed and perfumed her body in preparation for her evening with Paul Ferris.

Gemma immediately scampered upstairs to give her dolls a bath, leaving her parents to stare at each other with mutual guilt. Carolyn was the first to look away.

She walked past Steve, put the Hoover back in the cupboard under the stairs, and wondered what she could say to the husband she had betrayed. She felt it had been a betrayal, even though she had held back from the submission Paul had demanded.

Steve looked at her apologetically.

'I wasn't expecting you back till later.'

'The meeting didn't take as long as we expected,' Carolyn said, aware that she was lying to him again.

'Bit of a cheek, Ferris asking you to stay on to see that client.'

She couldn't bear to listen to Steve making innocent comments about Paul Ferris. She was afraid she'd blush with shame, and so resorted to covering her guilt with vexation.

'I could have done without this mess to come home to!'

She hated and despised herself even more as he accepted her rebuke and, taking her in his arms, apologised. 'I'm sorry. I'll make up for it, I promise.'

He kissed her on her forehead and she looked up into his eyes and remembered how much she loved this gentle, good-natured, loyal man. They kissed, and held each other close, and Steve wished they were alone. He wanted to take his wife to bed and welcome her home with all the love he had to give.

Instead they sat and had a cup of coffee, and were simply glad to be together again, sitting on the sofa with their arms round each other. Steve wished that he didn't have to spoil this quiet moment, but he knew that it had to be now, before Gemma came back downstairs, and before Michael came home from his Grandad's.

'Carolyn, something's happened while you've been away.'

Immediately fearful at his tone of voice, she sat up and stared at him.

'What? Has something happened to Dad?'

'No, it's not John. It's your Mother.'

Carolyn couldn't believe that her first reaction was to be afraid, terrified that her Mother might be dead. She steadied herself as Steve, not surprised by her instinctive reaction, reassured her.

'It's all right, nothing's happened to her. She's come back, that's all.'

Carolyn felt as if she'd been turned to stone. She couldn't move, and she could scarcely breathe, until that coldness she had nurtured in her heart took over.

'What for?'

'She wants to see you, and the kids, and John, of course. She's been missing us all, a lot.'

Carolyn's sarcasm was heavy with bitterness, 'For twelve years?'

She wasn't coping, she had to have a distraction from all this emotional turmoil. She moved out of Steve's protecting arms and went to pick up one of Gemma's Barbie dolls which had fallen out of a plastic car parked near the hearth. She concentrated on the doll, so that she wouldn't have to look at Steve and let him see the pain she was suffering.

He stumbled over his words, blundering on,

132

knowing that from the start he'd had no idea how to handle this situation.

'You'll have to see her.'

'No.' Carolyn's refusal was quick, unhesitating, and sharp.

'She's your Mother.'

Steve was pleading, but Carolyn seemed to take no heed of his words. She put the doll back in its silly pink car and turned back to face him. She tried to sound calm and rational as she sentenced her Mother out of her life.

'Not any more she isn't. Twelve years, Steve, and not a word. We didn't even know if she was alive or dead.'

She was losing her usual self-control now, childlike emotions were taking over. Steve stood up and took her in his arms again, and she held on to him tightly, trying to stop the tears.

'She didn't care, Steve. She didn't care about me, or my Dad, or even little Michael. Some flaming grandmother she was!'

He felt her shudder, and kissed her gently.

'I think she wants to try to make up for all that.'

Carolyn pulled away from him, harsh and scornful now.

'Well, she can't! She can just clear off back to where she came from. I don't want anything to do with her, and my Dad won't either.'

Steve held her close again, not contradicting her even though he knew she was wrong about that. John would never dare mention Lynda in front of Carolyn, but he had talked about her to Steve.

Carolyn always maintained that John would have divorced Lynda by now if he'd known how to contact her, but Steve didn't think so. He'd seen the sorrow and the longing in John's eyes whenever he spoke of the woman who was still his wife.

Carolyn wasn't going to listen to any of that at the moment, though, so Steve just tried to negotiate for some time. Carolyn would need that to overcome some of the pain and anger which he knew had been too intense for her to fully express, even to him. So he just said quietly, 'Think about it, love.'

Angrily she pulled away from him, and stood with her arms folded across her body, clutching at what felt like physical pain.

'I have thought about it, for years! What I'd say to her when she came back, with her arms open wide, begging forgiveness. The selfish, uncaring bitch!'

Steve shook his head. 'Don't, love. You don't mean that. I know you're hurt, and that it'll take time. Lynda knows that, too. She said she'd wait.'

Carolyn stared at him, and then cried out as she struggled to put into words a lifetime of resentment. All that came was a petty, vengeful, childish response which did not satisfy her need for retaliation, but she was glad that at least it rang out, clear, and without a tremor of doubt.

'And she'll wait a bloody long time – like I've had to!'

Michael would have been shocked to hear his Mother swear, but he wasn't thinking about her that afternoon. It was his Grandmother he was interested in, and that was why he'd asked to go to his Grandad's. After they'd played a game of chess, which John managed discreetly to let his grandson win, Michael refused a second game.

'You'd only lose again, Grandad. Shall we have a choc-ice instead?'

John laughed and went into the kitchen to get the treat.

134

When he came back he found that Michael was looking through the photograph album which John had left on a chair. He had it open at a page with photos which showed both his grandparents together in the years of their courtship and early married life. With a discretion beyond his years, Michael began to find out more about Lynda.

'That's my Grandma, isn't it?'

'Yeah.'

'She was really pretty, wasn't she?'

John sat down next to him and smiled. 'The best looking girl in town.' He opened up the folded newspaper article among the pages. 'This photo was taken when she won a beauty contest in Blackpool.'

'I bet you were proud.'

John winced as he remembered his reaction. 'I should have been.'

Michael continued with his questions, and noticed there was not just a gentleness in his Grandad's voice as he answered, but also a disturbing despondency. He paused as the turn of a page revealed a sun-squinting image of Lynda and John on a motorbike.

'That's my Grandma on the bike with you, isn't it?'

John nodded, and Michael again saw his eyes crinkle to push back the tears. 'I bet she liked to go fast.'

'Oh, yes. Nothing but top speed suited Lynda.'

He smiled as he remembered the exhilaration of a hundred miles an hour over the moors with Lynda's arms clasped tight and trusting round his body. He sighed as he thought once more that he'd give anything to have those arms holding him like that again. Michael saw the smile and the longing, and decided to take the risk to find out what he wanted to know.

'Do you still miss her?' he asked.

'Yeah.'

John felt himself losing the struggle with his emotions, and gently but firmly closed the album. He took it back to its cupboard, and Michael, wary of causing upset, changed the subject.

'What happened to the motorbike?'

'I sold it, to my friend Dan Heywood.' Then, glad to let his sense of humour help him away from his thoughts, he added, 'But don't tell anyone because Dan's not supposed to have a motorbike.'

'Why not?' Michael queried.

'Because his Mother wouldn't let him.'

Michael let out a groan against the arm-folding of mothers who insisted on limiting the adventurous risks in their sons' lives.

As if on cue the doorbell gave a single chime and Carolyn walked in. John would never tell her, but it irritated him the way his daughter, and now Jean Haworth, too, didn't wait for him to answer the door, but assumed the right to invade his living space.

He was also irritated that he felt guilty because he and Michael had been daring to look at photos of Lynda, but he could tell by the traces of anger which still flickered in Carolyn's eyes that it was as well he had put the album away.

He didn't know, and Carolyn had no intention of telling him, that the hostile feelings he sensed had been engendered by the news of his wife's return.

Carolyn had been glad of the excuse to break away from arguing with Steve about her Mother, and drive round to the flat to collect her son.

'Hiya, Mum. Did you enjoy yourself at the conference?'

'I was working, Michael. How are you, Dad?'

'I'm all right, having a good time with my grandson.'

136

'Can we have a chat?'

'Of course. Is something wrong?'

'No. Michael, here are the car keys, I'll see you in a minute. You can put Radio One on if you like.'

Used to this routine of being excluded from 'grown-ups' conversation, Michael grudgingly agreed and said Goodbye to his Grandad.

Carolyn's mind was still fevered with the thought of her Mother being back in Milfield. She had decided she must act quickly to prevent Lynda destroying her Father's future. It was time to insist on her Dad taking the step she'd been telling him should be a priority.

'Do you remember I told you about the solicitor, Philip Lawson, being a school-friend of Steve's? Well, I've got his phone number for you.'

She thrust a piece of paper at John, who was immediately wary.

'What do I need this for?'

'Like we've said before, if you want to marry again, you need to get divorced. You can't keep Jean waiting for ever.'

Thinking of the photographs he'd just been looking at, and the feelings he longed to experience again, John didn't hesitate to respond. 'We're all right as we are.'

'Jean doesn't think so. It's not fair on her, Dad, and you need to be settled. Together you and Jean could have a nice bungalow with a garden. You must stop dithering about. Get a divorce, and then you can marry Jean.'

Michael, who'd forgotten to take with him the chocolate bars which John had bought for him and Gemma, entered in time to hear his Mother's instruction.

'What about my Grandma?' he demanded.

137

Carolyn turned to him in surprise. 'Your Grandma?'

'Yeah, the one you told me was dead,' Michael said accusingly. 'She's not dead, me and Dad saw her yesterday in the burger bar.'

John stared at him. 'Your Grandma? Lynda, do you mean? Are you sure, Michael?'

'Of course I'm sure, she bought me a burger and chips, and apple pie, and had a long chat with Dad. She came back on Friday. She's really nice.'

John sank down on to the settee, and stared up at his daughter.

'Why didn't you tell me she was back?'

'I was going to,' Carolyn lied. 'I've only just found out myself. Steve told me when I got home.'

'And you came round to push me into getting a divorce? When you knew my wife's come back.'

'She's come back to Milfield, we don't know what for.'

Michael stepped in again.

'To see everybody, and to make everything all right again, that's what she said.'

'Michael, shut up!' Carolyn commanded, white-faced.

'How is she? How does she look?' John asked his grandson.

'Just like in the photos.'

Michael smiled as he saw the glow of joy which had transformed his Grandad's face. Carolyn noticed it too.

The news made John feel as if a sudden infusion of life was rippling through his body. 'Lynda,' he said, needing the miracle confirmed.

'Yes.' Carolyn's tone was matter of fact, but she wanted to scream at him not to look like that, not to smile with love like that.

138

But he was excited now, impatient.

'Where is she? Why hasn't she come to see me?'

'You don't want to see her, do you?'

Carolyn's question was loaded with indignation, but John didn't care about his daughter's indignation, anger or anything else, he just cared about Lynda.

'It sounds like she hasn't changed much.' he said, aware of how much his appearance had deteriorated.

Carolyn was staring at him. She couldn't believe the way he was reacting. Surely he had cancelled her Mother out of his life just as she had. She had to stop this.

'Michael, go back to the car, please.'

'Do I have to?'

'Please!'

She watched him through the window, and when she'd seen him safely in the passenger seat, she turned back to John.

'You can't want to see her.'

'Of course I do!'

'She walked out on you, Dad,' she reminded him. 'She left us, as if we meant nothing to her. I can never forgive her for that. And I'm sure you can't.'

Her eyes defied him to contradict her, and he'd got in the habit of backing down when she looked at him like that. But not this time. He spoke quietly, but with all the certainty in his heart.

'I already have.'

'No.'

John, his hands clasped tightly in front of him, said 'I want to talk to her. Like I didn't do before. She came back on Friday, you say?'

'Yes.'

'So where is she?' he asked again.

Carolyn gave a grim little smile.

'She's staying at Jean's,' she informed him, and saw

139

the shocked expression on his face, as he quickly realised what Lynda must know by now.

Carolyn was glad she'd made him stop and think, but she was not prepared to let her Dad suffer any feelings of guilt over his relationship with Jean.

'What are you looking like that for, Dad? You don't think she's not had other men all these years, do you?'

John had his head in his hands now.

'What a mess. What a bloody mess.'

He looked up at his daughter and, afraid of the answer, almost whispered the question. 'Does she want to see me?'

'Yes.' Carolyn knew it was no use lying about that, but she was determined to have some control over the situation. 'I'll arrange for her to come and meet you at our house.'

'Yes, it's right that we meet at home.' He paused, aware that a lot had happened since Lynda had left. 'Of course, it's not her house now. Mind you, it never was, thanks to my Mother.'

'I wouldn't worry about that, she's done very well for herself by the look of it, according to Steve.'

'Oh. What has she been doing?'

'God knows! Anyway you can ask all these questions when you see her. I'll arrange a meeting.'

'Soon.'

'I suppose so. I've got to go now, Dad.'

He stood up and she kissed him on the cheek.

'Bye Dad. Take it easy, you've had a shock.'

After she'd gone, John looked at his image in the mirror, and didn't like what he saw.

CHAPTER SEVENTEEN

On Monday morning the centre of Milfield was doing a fair imitation of a busy town, with people hurrying into shops to replenish their stock of food after the weekend, or meeting friends in cafés. Lynda was there among all these busy people, and feeling pretty lonely.

She'd come to town to see Dan, who was going to help her look for a second-hand car, and she'd also promised to call at Frances Horton's dress shop, Francesca's, to take Jean a prawn sandwich for her lunch. She'd allowed herself time to wander round the town centre again, still hoping to come across people she knew, but there was no-one.

She was beginning to find it very depressing, when she spotted Katie sitting in the burger bar. She had a friend with her but the friend was leaving, while Katie had obviously decided to stay a bit longer. Lynda waved and when Katie smiled she went in.

'Do you mind if I join you? Or are you leaving?'

'No, I'm not going back yet. It's only P.E.'

'I used to avoid that when I was at school, back in the Dark Ages! Can I get you another coffee?'

'Thanks.'

Katie smiled when Lynda came back with a couple of cream doughnuts as well.

'Thanks. I know I shouldn't but school dinners are so lousy.'

'They were in my day as well. Oh, I sound like an old lady.'

'You're not old, though.'

'Oh, you're my friend for life!'

'I like your outfit.'

'Thanks. Clothes are a bit of a weakness of mine. I could only afford cheap stuff when I lived in Milfield. Oh, I love doughnuts,' she said as she bit into hers. 'They always remind me of America.'

'Have you been there?'

'Yes, quite a few times. We, I've some good friends in Virginia.'

'I'd love to go to America. Have to wait a while for that, though,' she added dolefully.

'School and exams to get through first. Not easy, is it?'

'No, especially when your sister's done it all before you, and you know you can never do as well as she did. Oh, I'm sorry, I'm in a moaning mood this morning.'

'I understand what it's like being the second child. I had an older brother.'

'Oh? Where does he live?'

'Australia. I never hear from him. Alex will be eighteen soon, won't she?'

'Yes. My Mum's been saving up to give her a good night out with her friends to celebrate. Unfortunately it's also our grandmother's birthday the week after, and she's already been talking about having a 'joint party' at her house, featuring Alex playing some classical piece on her grand piano!'

Lynda laughed scornfully. 'I bet Alex loves that idea!'

'She couldn't believe she'd suggested it. And she's furious that Mum thinks she might have to go along with it. She always ends up doing what 'Grandmama' says.'

'That's Ellen Heywood for you! She likes to be in control. That's one reason she's never liked me, she knew I didn't see why she had to be obeyed.'

'Oh, yeah. I gather you and she don't get on. She wasn't at all happy about you being back in town. But my Mum was.'

'Oh, good. I can't wait to see her. Ask her to give me a ring, or to come round to Jean Haworth's tonight, if she can.' She scribbled on a piece of paper, 'Here's Jean's address and phone number.'

Katie put the paper carefully in her bag. 'My Mum will be really happy to do that. She said it will be great to find out what you've been up to, and to be able to reminisce about her Mum and Dad.'

'Yes, they were lovely people your grandparents. They'd no money but were the most generous people I've ever known. And, as you've heard, they gave great parties at Bennett Street, with your Grandad playing the piano and your Grandma looking after everybody.'

Lynda blinked back a tear as she remembered the couple who had rejoiced in being easy-going to the point of recklessness.

'You knew my Dad as well,' Katie prompted, hoping to find out more about a subject which she sensed was only given limited coverage by her uncle and her mother.

'Yes. Can I be nosy and ask why your Mother hasn't married again?'

'She's not allowed!' Katie declared angrily. 'Grandmother has threatened to disinherit us all if she does. Alex and I are very keen for Mum to find somebody. We don't want her to be on her own when we go off to college or university.'

'Has she been out with anyone?'

'Once or twice, but it never lasted long. She said they'd make life too complicated. We never even met them.'

Lynda nodded thoughtfully. She knew Jenny

Heywood well enough to realise that she wouldn't bring a man home to meet her daughters unless she was going to marry him.

'Perhaps I can help her find somebody.'

'Oh, that would be good.'

Lynda would have withdrawn that charitable intent sharply, had she known that Jenny Heywood had already fallen in love with someone.

He didn't know, no-one knew, but Jenny had loved him for a long time. In her secret dreams, he was the one she would marry, though her conscience told her that even to think of having him was sinful. The man she loved, unwillingly and guiltily but with a passion so strong it threatened to corrupt her, was Steve Sheldon.

After Katie had left, feeling glad that she'd found someone she could talk to, Lynda drank a second cup of coffee, and thought about Jenny Heywood. She felt sorry for her friend who had obviously not been having an easy time. It was hard enough being a single Mum, without also having to cope with a demanding and domineering mother-in-law like Ellen Heywood.

Then, foolishly, Lynda allowed her thoughts to edge their way back, via Jenny and her teenage daughters, to some of the terrible confrontations between her and her daughter. By the time she headed back out into the precinct, Lynda was feeling depressed, and lonely again.

Jean Haworth was, as usual, having a dreary day behind the counter at 'Francesca's'. Only one customer had walked through the door that morning, and she hadn't bought anything.

Jean was glad, at first, to have Lynda enter the shop and shatter the silent inactivity of the pink and cream parlour, created by its owner as a 'Continental'

144

oasis of fashion for ladies with impeccable taste. She was less pleased when Lynda, playfully taking dresses from the rails, starting making fun of them.

'Plenty of choice for old ladies here, isn't there?'

'They're not all old lady dresses. I've had quite a few nice ones in the sales,' Jean retorted defensively.

'Sorry, I was only joking. I've brought lunch. Any chance of a cup of tea to go with it?'

Jean noticed that Lynda was unusually quiet as they sat in the little room at the back of the shop, sharing Marks and Spencer's prawn sandwiches and slices of gâteau.

'Have you had a nice walk round town?'

'No, not really. I saw Katie Heywood and had a coffee with her, but apart from that it's been horrible. Has everybody I know died or left town?'

'Twelve years is a long time.'

'I suppose so. It's just, I was hoping I'd feel at home here, or that something magical would happen. You know, like seeing John walking down the street, and him starting to run towards me with his arms open wide like they do in the films.'

'You always did have too much imagination,' Jean said, her mouth turned down in a tight-lipped refusal to contemplate what was, to her, a very unwelcome fantasy.

The conversation over lunch was very limited after that, but a little while later, standing in the shop doorway and watching Lynda once again walking alone across the precinct, Jean forgot her irritation and jealousy. She felt nothing but pity as she screwed up her eyes against a scene she didn't want to witness.

Carolyn had had an exciting but also disquieting morning in the office. Paul had hung around her like a dog pursuing a bitch on heat, and her two female colleagues, Julia and Michelle, had left her in no doubt that they had noticed, and had drawn conclusions about the weekend.

Carolyn had felt foolishly gratified that she'd at last overcome their prejudices, she knew that they had regarded her as someone too strait-laced ever to be accepted as 'one of the girls'. At the same time, however, she felt shame and embarrassment.

At lunchtime she'd been glad to escape from the speculative atmosphere in the office and take a walk across town. She'd decided to see if she could find out more about her Mother from Jean.

Her mind was focused on the questions she wanted to ask, and it wasn't until she was walking towards the dress shop that she noticed the sharp-edged sound of a pair of high-heeled shoes crossing the echoing wasteland of the now almost deserted precinct.

Carolyn looked up and saw a woman coming towards her, hips swinging as her high-heels struck the ground. Carolyn recognised that confident, strutting walk, and blonde hair.

Lynda's eyes opened wide as she saw her daughter, and for a moment she looked scared, but then, in tears and with her arms outstretched, she ran towards her child.

'Carolyn!'

The air seemed to freeze into a stillness around Carolyn as she stood there, not able to believe that at last her Mother was coming towards her, just as she had dreamed so many times. Then it was as if a shutter crashed down, and Carolyn turned and began to walk away.

For a moment Lynda was shocked to a halt, her arms fell to her side and suddenly all the strength drained from her body. Then anger took over, and in a rage she ran after her daughter and grabbed her by the arm, roughly turning her to face her.

'Hey! Don't you turn your back on me!'

Carolyn looked at her coldly. 'Why not?'

'Because I'm your Mother, that's why not.'

Carolyn's shrug and look of contempt challenged Lynda's claim to maternal status, and for a few silent seconds the two women stared hard into each other's eyes. Then Carolyn, determined to remain calm, asked a question designed to offend.

'Why have you come back?'

For a moment Lynda was thrown off balance, did Carolyn really not know why? Lynda heard herself stumbling over the words which sounded pitiful, stupid even.

'To see you. And John.'

Carolyn didn't care how much she hurt this woman. She spoke slowly, proud of the control of her measured, condescending tone.

'But I don't want to see you. And neither does my Dad.'

The finality of that statement, and the tone in which it was spoken, should have been enough; but a brief shadow slipped across Carolyn's face as she spoke, and Lynda remembered it from her daughter's childhood, it had always been a sign that what Carolyn was saying was not the whole truth.

'Have you told him I'm back?'

Carolyn saw that her Mother would not be deceived.

'Yes, I've told him. But I don't want you to see him, I want you to go back where you came from, and leave us alone.'

They began to argue, stepping without effort into the old pattern of cold words and closed hearts. Jean, standing helplessly in the shop doorway with her hand to her mouth, watched mother and daughter face each other in anger as if time had never moved on. In the end, it was Lynda who won.

'I'm going to see your Dad, whether you like it or not.'

'I don't like it. But, all right, you can see him,' Carolyn condescended. 'Tomorrow night at our house.'

That was it, there was no more to be said, was there? Carolyn again deliberately turned her back, and walked away. Aware that she was standing there alone and vulnerable for all the world to see, Lynda couldn't resist a final thrust, and shouted after her.

'Don't you mean, my house, my home?'

Carolyn paused, but didn't turn round. She straightened her shoulders and walked steadily away from her Mother, blinking back tears which, she told herself firmly, were caused by nothing but anger.

Lynda watched her for a moment, and then discovered that she was shaking. She didn't see Jean withdrawing sorrowfully into the gloom of the shop, as she watched Lynda set off, almost running, towards the market square, to seek refuge in Dan's comforting and loving arms.

At the other end of town Gary Pearson was in the office at Randerson's, negotiating for a handful of teabags, and the packet of shortbreads he knew Josie kept in a drawer in case a client called in. Matthew had forgotten it was his turn to buy the tea and biscuits, but Gary knew that Josie had a soft spot for Matthew and would protect him from suffering for such forgetfulness.

Gary and Josie communicated well, they were both adept at the games of politics and intrigue. It made life more interesting for them both, so it was only natural that Gary should stay for a chat.

Josie was a good PA, and Randerson felt he could trust her, because he knew that Josie wanted to keep her job. Racial prejudice was deeply embedded in the psyche of quite a few employers in Milfield. They knew the rules, but they were practised at finding reasons why someone with a non-white complexion 'wasn't quite right' for the jobs they advertised.

So Randerson, who liked having a skilled, good-looking girl like her working for him, felt he could rely on Josie to be a 'confidential' secretary. He was right, up to point, but Josie also knew that Tony Randerson didn't deserve any loyalty, and she, too, had learned how to manoeuvre within the rules.

And Gary knew what questions to ask, and how to interpret her looks and silences.

'Randerson was in a good mood this morning, must have had a good weekend,' Gary commented with a wink.

'Yeah. That's one of the reasons I suppose.'

Gary was quick to pick up the lead. 'And what's the other?'

'He thinks he's heading for the big time. He's been oiling his way round a wealthy guy called Nigel Kavanagh, who's into homes and lifestyle complexes, for those with money, of course.'

'Oh, yeah? And Randerson wants in on that, does he?'

'It looks that way, if he can raise the sort of money Kavanagh requires his partners to have.'

'There's only one way Randerson can get his hands on big money,' Gary judged, 'and that's by selling this place.'

'Yeah, that's what I reckon.'

'And where will that leave us lot?'

Josie was under no illusions.

'Who knows?'

Gary gathered his workmates round him and, as they drank their mugs of tea, told them what he'd heard from Josie.

'I knew he was up to something. And he can't borrow any more from the bank, so there's only one way he can raise the capital.'

'By selling this place,' Steve stated grimly.

'Exactly.'

'But that means we'll be out of a job,' wailed Matthew.

'Got it in one, my son,' Gary said wryly.

'Why does he want to sell?' stammered Matthew. 'It's a good business this, he's making money.'

Steve shook his head. 'It's not just about money. Randerson's always fancied going up in the world, he wants a business with a classy lifestyle to go with it. And it sounds as if he's found what he's been looking for.'

'He hasn't got it yet though,' Gary added. 'It's early days, according to Josie. So we've got time to try to scupper the deal.'

Matthew was looking bewildered now. 'How can we do that?'

'We'll think of something,' Steve said, attempting to reassure him. 'He's not as clever as he thinks, Randerson.'

'No, he does most of his thinking with his balls,' sneered Gary. 'And he doesn't realise everyone knows that. I mean, look at this weekend.'

'What about this weekend?' was Matthew's innocent enquiry.

'Jackie told me she heard there's a little blonde he's wining and dining on the quiet.'

'Oh, heck, what if his wife finds out?' Matthew gasped.

'From what I've heard, Angela Bentham is no fool,' Gary said. 'She must know by now what kind of man she married, he's at it all the time, Randerson. If only we could all be as lucky,' he laughed.

Then Gary overstepped the mark.

He grinned and said to Steve, 'Talking of dirty weekends, did Carolyn enjoy hers?'

'Don't talk daft,' Steve snapped back, and was immediately annoyed with himself for over-reacting.

Gary, however, was too far into the joke to notice his friend's discomfort. He was looking for further entertainment from Matthew, who was always keen to be treated as a man of the world, even though secretly admitting to himself that he didn't qualify in that category.

'That boss man of hers, Ferris, drives a BMW,' Gary told his young workmate

'Does he?' said Matthew, very impressed.

Gary, who liked to think of himself as skilled in wordplay, pushed it a bit further.

'Yes, plenty of engine power Ferris's got, and he likes plenty of performance, from what I've heard.'

The other men were laughing, and Steve knew he should have put an end to it by laughing himself, but somehow he couldn't.

He wanted Gary to get off this topic, and resorted to a mocking rebuke.

'You hear too much, you. And you'll hear something else, from Randerson, if we don't shift these units a bit faster.'

The touch of 'management censure' in Steve's tone took Gary by surprise, and irritated him.

'Like what?' he said, giving Steve a hard look.

Steve tried to make his reply sound humorous.

'Like, 'Here's your cards, lads.''

But it wasn't the kind of joke they wanted to hear.

CHAPTER EIGHTEEN

As the day was a little cold, Alice Smith had promised herself at least two hours in Ellen Heywood's 'drawing room', which was always kept at a much higher temperature than Alice could afford to sustain in her own cold and shabby living room.

She had already prattled on for an hour, and her little jokes and pointed remarks were not what Ellen Heywood wanted to listen to, but even having Alice sitting opposite her, munching her way through a large slice of chocolate cake like an ecstatic hamster, was preferable to spending the afternoon alone.

They were sitting by the fire in the drawing room, which had a high ceiling and large square bay window. The interior of the house on Wellington Road was weighed down with the heavy velvet drapes and melancholy elegance of the home of a once well-to-do Edwardian family.

Like the rest of the house, the drawing room was furnished with the Buchanan family antiques which Ellen was very proud of. There was also a Chesterfield sofa in a deep red velvet of such richness that its quality seemed to defy anyone to remark that it bore the sheen of age.

The focal point of the room, however, was a baby grand piano on which stood silver framed photographs of Ellen's family, her parents in a straight-backed and joyless studio portrait, and her beloved son Richard, a handsome maverick with richly curled auburn hair, and gleaming eyes which demanded attention and homage. There was also a photograph of Carolyn Sheldon, when she was a young and very pretty schoolgirl.

Carolyn had been introduced to Ellen by her Nana, Sheila Stanworth, who had brought her granddaughter to the house as a child, initially to take the piano lessons kindly offered by her more wealthy friend. This had led, as Sheila had hoped, to a close relationship and generous patronage.

Ellen sat watchful and erect in her high backed winged chair close to the fire, a long narrow coffee table between her and Alice, who had perched herself daintily on the small sofa opposite her hostess. Ellen sipped tea from a china cup but ignored the chocolate cake, the small cream cakes and biscuits on the table. Her visitor, however, had for a while been helping herself, oh, so discreetly to several of these delicious confections, while chatting to Ellen with great animation.

In return for these treats Alice offered morsels of local gossip, or, as now, the programme of concerts which Ellen was now perusing.

'It was kind of you to bring me this, Alice. The Mozart Evening should be especially good.'

'Yes, and the Gilbert and Sullivan. Geoff loved Gilbert and Sullivan, didn't he?'

Ellen concurred but, as usual, didn't wish to talk about her late husband. Alice did, though.

'He would have been sad to see Dan handing over the bakery business to Atherton's.'

'He has not handed it over.'

Alice allowed herself to be corrected, she had a more titillating topic to introduce. Alice had had a stroke of luck on her travels around Milfield today. On the outskirts of the town the bus had passed by the Gateway Garage, and strolling among the second hand cars ranged on the forecourt Alice had spied a likely couple, Lynda Stanworth, and Dan Heywood. Alice had wriggled in her seat with excitement, here was a card she would enjoy playing.

'I saw Daniel earlier this afternoon. He was at the Gateway Garage, is he thinking of buying a new car?'

'I don't think so.'

'Oh, it must be Lynda who's looking for one. She was with him.'

'Lynda Stanworth?'

'Yes.'

Ellen saw Alice's eagerness, and decided she would not talk about her son in the context of that woman. 'You must have been mistaken. Would you like another cake?'

'Please.'

Alice took the hint, and the meringue she had been coveting, and then made a show of casting her eyes appreciatively around the room.

'It's such a pleasure to spend the afternoon in a room like this. You must love it in here, with all your memories around you. That's a lovely photo of Carolyn Stanworth, Sheldon now, of course. A beautiful girl.'

Ellen, sipping her tea, watched Alice and wondered what mischief the little minx would select next from her repertoire.

Alice knew she was about to step into dangerous territory now, but it was almost five o'clock and she knew there was little chance of her being invited to stay for supper, so she had nothing to lose.

Her voice dipped to a pitying sigh, as she echoed her favourite literature of frock coats, and lace trimmed bodices.

'I suppose you could say her beauty was her undoing. Getting herself with child in the sixth form, what a tragedy.'

155

Because she was feeling irritated by now, Ellen omitted to consider carefully enough the possible subsequent moves of the chess-like game Alice had set up, and was instinctively protective.

'We all make mistakes.'

Alice wanted to give a whoop of triumph, but was too skilled to lose control of the game like that. Instead she gave Ellen a searching look, and then composed her face into an expression intended to portray both knowledge and pity.

'Yes.' she said.

Ellen immediately struggled to her feet, her face contorted with frustration. How could she have allowed herself to be led into a trap like that?

Ellen Heywood had no doubt what secret suspicions had given rise to the malicious little smile which Alice was so keen for her to notice. But Ellen was confident that they were only suspicions.

Her parents had made sure that no-one had ever revealed their family secrets, and Ellen was practised in continuing that work. She refused even to glance at her tormentor, but stood up and turned off the gas fire.

Alice had seen Ellen's body stiffen with rage, and she lost her nerve a little. Ellen had always frightened her, right from that first meeting when Ellen, a prefect then, had towered over her in the shadows of the school corridor. Alice had, however, always been able to produce a little bravado to face such situations.

'Yes,' she said, 'I was getting a bit warm.'

Then, with the tendency towards recklessness which she had never learned to control, she continued on her way towards trouble.

With a hint of a stammer now, she said, 'I wonder how Carolyn will take it, her Mother coming back.'

Ellen did not return to her chair but picked up the leaflet Alice had brought, and began the dismissal of her guest.

'Thank you again for the concert brochure, she said with glacial politeness.

Alice reached into her bag.

'I've got another copy here, in case you wanted to pass it on to Carolyn. You'll be seeing her, won't you?'

'I expect so.'

Ellen remained standing.

For a moment or two Alice babbled on about Carolyn, suggesting that she might accompany them to one of the concerts. Ellen did not respond, and Alice, knowing she was going to get nothing more from her hostess, had to content herself with gabbling out the rest of her prepared script, tripping gaily along the path of insincerity.

'It's lovely the way Carolyn has kept coming to see you all these years. Of course, she's always loved coming here – like me,' she trilled. Then she gave a little laugh to indicate that she was aware of all the subtext under her next line.

'I think she must have spent more time with you than with her own Mother!'

There was no applause at the end of Alice's performance, only a stony silence which left Alice in no doubt that she had now outstayed her welcome. She picked up her bag and began to move backwards towards the door.

'Well, I must be going.'

She was bobbing up and down as she left, as if some servile gene was nudging her towards humility.

'Thank you for the tea, and the company of course.'

157

Ellen, shoulders back and looking down at her with eyes cleared of emotion, nodded briefly as if to a parlour maid.

Alice didn't want this to be her last visit to the Heywood residence and, in a more contrite manner, reminded Ellen, 'It's always good to have company, isn't it?'

But Ellen was not in the mood to concede anything; she walked past Alice and opened the door.

'Oh, please don't bother to show me out,' Alice pleaded, adding with another little trill of attempted laughter, 'I know my way! Cheerio, Ellen. Take care!'

Ellen stood in the doorway of the drawing room and watched Alice scamper along the hall. When she was satisfied that she had gone, she walked over to the bay window. The Westminster chime of the clock on the mantle-piece informed her that it was five thirty, and as she paused to look down over the town, Ellen wondered what time her son would come home.

It had been Lynda's idea to go to Alexandra Park after they'd bought the car. The sun was shining as she and Dan strolled along the paths through the Victorian shrubberies and across the lawns studded with beech and oak trees offering shady oases for picnics.

'I'm really pleased with the car, Dan, I've always fancied a Volkswagen Golf as a nifty little runabout. Thanks for pushing for a new gear box. You got a really good price.'

'You did, you mean. Fluttering your eyelashes at that salesman.'

She laughed, 'Amy taught me to do that.'

'Amy?'

'A girl I know who helps me with the wedding

business I told you about. But it was you who did the deal in the end. I was impressed.'

'I've learned not to be as soft as I used to be.'

'Except where your Mother's concerned. She doesn't deserve you.'

'I know.' He sighed, 'I thought when Richard died we might eventually get closer, but she doesn't seem capable of showing affection. Even when I was a kid, I used to notice that.'

He was silent for a while as he recalled a distant childhood memory of being pushed away as he tried to clamber on to his Mother's lap.

'She was so different with Richard. I never understood that.'

Lynda looked at him and wished she could explain. Instead she took hold of his hand to comfort him, and he held hers tightly, so that she couldn't easily let it go. Lynda found she didn't mind; the warmth and strength of his hand holding hers comforted her, too, and made her feel safe.

'It was a good job my Dad loved me,' Dan said. 'I still miss him. We used to have such a good laugh working together, and singing. I'll never forget when we sang for my Mother at her fiftieth birthday party. It was the only time I remember her looking at me and my Dad with affection. And we were so happy, him and me. Pathetic really.'

'No. You both wanted her to love you. That's only natural, nothing pathetic about it.'

Dan looked at her, with eyes full of gratitude. Lynda had always listened to him and helped him understand how he was feeling. And he had done the same for her, until 1985, when they'd had that heart-breaking row about her being married to his best friend, and the impossibility of their ever having a future together.

159

He instinctively understood how she was feeling now as she watched mothers and grandmothers with their children in the playground.

'Never tire of swings and slides, do they, kids? I used to bring Alex and Katie here when they were little.'

'Yeah, I used to bring Carolyn here. But never my grandchildren. I've missed all that, just as I missed a lot of Carolyn's childhood when I went out to work. I made a big mistake there, you know, Dan, letting Sheila Stanworth take over.'

'You needed the money.'

'I know, but it was still a mistake. That was when I started losing Carolyn. And it doesn't look as if I'll ever get her back.'

'You will. She's your daughter, you're her Mother. Nothing changes that.'

'We'll see what happens tomorrow. I wish you could be there to help me.'

Dan smiled ruefully to himself. Lynda didn't know that he, too, was dreading that meeting at Beechwood Avenue, and the prospect of Lynda being back in John Stanworth's arms.

When he had lost Lynda to John Stanworth, and then gone through the humiliation of a disastrous on-the-rebound marriage and divorce, Dan had made a decision.

He had decided that he would be happy, he would form his happiness in his head, and defend it from those who might enviously try to undermine that self-awarded state of mind. And that was what he had achieved for himself, what had made him the loveable man he was. But now that happiness was having to step aside and make way for hope.

CHAPTER NINETEEN

Jean had been a little annoyed that Lynda had invited Jenny Heywood round to her house that evening without her permission, even though she understood it was a spur of the moment invitation Lynda had issued via Katie. She was irritated now to see Lynda playing hostess, opening a bottle of Chardonnay with a flourish, while the lady of the house hunted for some suitable glasses.

'Cheers, Lynda, welcome home,' Jenny said as she raised her glass and beamed with delight at having her friend back.

Lynda smiled.

'Quite like old times, this, you and me sharing a bottle of wine.'

Jenny nodded and exchanged a look with Lynda that told her she, too, had a vivid memory of those dark days after Richard's death, when Lynda had been the only person she could really confide in.

'You're looking well, not put on weight like the rest of us!'

Jenny laughed. 'I get told off if I do. I'm at the stage of parenthood when your children tell you what to do, or try to.'

'I had that from day one nearly with our Carolyn.'

'Have you seen her yet?'

'Not properly.'

Lynda turned away from the surprised look on Jenny's face and noticed that Jean's glass was still empty.

'Oh, sorry, love, I didn't mean to forget you. I'm

just so excited to see Jenny again.'

'That's quite all right,' said Jean, making it plain that it wasn't.

'Expensive Chardonnay, this,' Jenny commented. 'You've got a taste for the good life while you've been away.'

Lynda paused, suddenly filled with thoughts of the man who had made that possible.

'Yes. Only wish it could have lasted a bit longer.'

Her hand shook a little as she filled Jean's glass, and she had to make an effort to steady her voice. 'Still, it's good to be home.'

Jenny, unaware of what undercurrents she was stirring, innocently enquired, 'Are you and John getting back together?'

'I haven't seen him yet, either. I'm seeing them all tomorrow night, round at Beechwood Avenue.'

'Oh, yes. I heard Carolyn and Steve bought the semi from John. I hear a lot about house buying at work,' she explained, not wanting to reveal that she gathered information about the Sheldon family whenever she could.

Jean took the opportunity to at last elbow her way into the conversation. 'Oh, yes. You work for Philip Lawson, don't you?'

'Yes, as his assistant, but I also deal with a lot of the conveyance related work. Reggie Broadbent brought me into the firm to do that when I needed a job, after Richard died.'

'Are you still living at Hadden Lea?' Jean enquired. 'It was a shame you had to sell that big detached house you had when you were married.'

Again, Lynda and Jenny exchanged a look which revealed the intimate knowledge which they shared.

'I love Hadden Lea, we've been so happy there, the girls and I. But the house is badly in need of some work at the moment.'

'Oh, what's wrong?'

'The kitchen mainly, it's falling apart, as these things do.'

'Oh, you'll have to get Steve to take a look at it,' Lynda offered immediately. 'He's the expert when it comes to kitchens.'

'Yes, he did mine,' Jean informed them, 'new cupboards and a new cooker. And John did the wiring for me. It's wonderful.'

Lynda, for reasons she had to keep secret, was interested in Philip Lawson. 'Do you like working for Philip?'

'Yes, he's lovely.'

'Calmed down a bit from when he and Steve used to drink whatever they could get their hands on at your Mum and Dad's parties?'

'A bit,' Jenny laughed.

'He was a good looking lad. Are you in with a chance there?'

'Lynda!' Jean protested, embarrassed by such forthright curiosity.

'It's all right, Jean,' Lynda countered, 'it's only natural that an attractive young widow like Jenny should be on the lookout for a man.'

Jenny was delighted to hear Lynda teasing her again just like she used to. 'I like the 'young'. I was forty last month. And Philip's married anyway.'

Lynda's reply was accompanied by a reproving glance in Jean's direction. 'That doesn't stop some people.'

Jenny didn't have any idea of the significance of that look, but was firm in the conviction of her own response.

'It stops me.'

Jenny and Lynda had been happily chatting and

reminiscing for over an hour when the doorbell rang. When Steve Sheldon walked into the room Jenny felt a schoolgirl blush warming her cheeks.

Her embarrassment grew, for Lynda, remembering what she'd told her greeted him with, 'Hiya, Steve, just the man we want for Jenny. She's got a kitchen needs doing, can you help? Friends and family rate, mind.'

'I expect so, when I've had a chance to get through the door, mother-in-law!' he teased, slipping straight back into the banter that he and Lynda used to share.

Lynda grinned at him. 'Less of your cheek, young Steven! You remember Jenny, don't you?'

'Of course, I do. But our paths don't often cross these days, do they?'

'No, except when dropping the kids off at school.'

'Oh, yes, of course, our Michael's at the same one as your daughters, now, isn't he?'

'Yes. I've seen you there, but you probably didn't recognise me. It's a long time since we were at my Mum and Dad's parties.'

'He had a crush on you, then, I seem to remember, but you thought he was just a kid,' Lynda laughed and didn't notice Jenny turning bright pink.

Jean, deciding it was time she asserted herself as hostess and close family friend, offered Steve a drink, and asked him if Carolyn had enjoyed the conference.

'I suppose so, but no thanks, Jean, I won't have a drink. I'm on my way to do a little job for somebody. I just came to let Lynda know what time tomorrow night. Will eight o'clock suit you?' he asked. Then, a little hesitantly, he added. 'I've arranged to pick John up about half past seven. I could come and pick you up after I've dropped him off at our place, if you want.'

'No, it's O.K. I've got a car,' Lynda said,

164

determined to sound casual about this vital reunion.

'Right.'

A small, anxious frown had formed on Steve's forehead, he was annoyed that Carolyn had set it up so that they would all be there.

'Are you O.K with this? We could change the arrangement if you'd rather make it more private, and meet John on your own?'

'No, it's fine. I'm looking forward to coming round to Beechwood Avenue,' Lynda stated, not sure if that were true.

'John's looking forward to seeing you,' Steve reassured her.

Jenny, sensing the tension about this arrangement, decided it was time to leave them to have a private chat.

'See you again, soon, Lynda,' she said, kissing her on the cheek.

'Yes, I'll give you a call. But don't go till you've arranged for Steve to come and see that kitchen. Have you got any time free this week?' she asked him.

'I could do Wednesday, about half past seven? Is that any good?'

'Fine,' Jenny replied, hardly able to believe this was happening. 'See you on Wednesday.'

As she watched Jenny leave, Lynda felt very pleased with her idea, which she thought would help out both of them. She didn't know then what the consequences would be.

Jenny couldn't think straight as she drove home from Jean Haworth's house, or rather she couldn't shut out the thoughts and feelings she was having about Steve Sheldon.

It seemed to her that all her life she'd been a fool, and made the wrong decisions, like marrying Richard Heywood because he had fascinated her, and because, to her shame, it had seemed the only way of achieving a different way of life.

Jenny had always wanted to belong to a highly respected, wealthy family like the Heywoods, instead of a haphazard household where paying the next bill was always a feat of ingenuity.

Marrying Richard had been the biggest mistake of Jenny's life, and as she parked her battered car in front of her home she reflected on what a fool she'd been at the age of twenty-one.

And now, as a forty year old woman who should know better, she told herself bitterly, she'd been a fool again, letting herself fall in love with a happily married man.

The houses on Beechwood Avenue were quiet and dark the following evening, except for cosy looking lamps in some of the front rooms. In the Sheldons' living room all the lights were on, filling the room with a blazing illumination which felt more hostile than welcoming.

Michael, sprawled on his stomach across the sofa, tried to ignore the tension which had started as soon as his Mother had walked in from work and begun a whirlwind of preparation.

Steve, putting on his coat, ready to go and collect his father-in-law brushed past Gemma who was standing at the mirror combing her hair with precision. He watched with amusement as she finished checking her immaculate appearance and then went to sit primly on the edge of a chair.

'You don't have to sit all formal like that,' he pointed out with a grin. 'It's not the Queen who's coming, it's your Grandma.'

'I know!' Gemma glared at him, and then looked at her Mother who was hurrying in from the kitchen with a vase of flowers which she placed in the centre of the dining table.

'Michael, take your feet off that sofa!'

Michael complied, but looked at his Dad, and Carolyn didn't like the quiet male empathy between them. Steve smiled to try to reassure her.

'I'll go and get your Dad. Will you be all right? She won't come early, will she?'

Carolyn's voice was tight with resentment of the ordeal about to be inflicted on her and her Father. 'Of course not. She likes to arrive late and make an entrance. Don't you remember?'

Steve did remember, and such memories were, for him, all full of affection for Lynda, which he now dared not show. He kissed Carolyn.

'I won't be long.'

As he closed the door Gemma looked anxiously at her Mother, but Michael ignored them both, he was looking forward to seeing his Grandma again.

Lynda had already had her shower and had brushed her hair into its natural curls. She was sitting at the dressing table now, in her black satin, lace-trimmed underskirt, trying to stop her hand from shaking as she put the finishing touches to her make-up.

Jean, sitting on the edge of the bed, was watching her, and trying to subdue her fear and jealousy as she saw Lynda making herself beautiful for John. She felt unreal, sitting there watching Lynda just as she had so many times in their teenage years, waiting for her to finish getting ready to go to the Saturday night dance together. Lynda turned to face her.

'Do you think he'll recognise me?' she joked.

Jean wasn't amused.

'You've hardly changed at all, you know you haven't.'

Lynda, thinking how small and scared her friend looked, sitting there with her hands clasped tightly on her lap, didn't want there to be this tension between them.

Trying to force some laughter into the room, she said, 'Liar! Hope Carolyn has the lights down low.'

She stood and hitched up her bra straps another half inch.

'Do you remember when all we had up top was what Marti Caine used to call 'two mince pies', and we used to stuff hankies in our bras?'

'You did,' Jean retorted, then looked away, ashamed of how spiteful she sounded.

Lynda was wiser and more tender-hearted now than she'd been as a teenager, and she could appreciate how hard it was for Jean to watch her preparing to go and meet John, and perhaps be reclaimed by the man Jean wanted for herself.

Getting up and walking over to the wardrobe, she took down the blue and white dress which was hanging on the wardrobe door next to a trouser suit.

'Do you think this or the trouser suit?'

Jean had had enough.

'I don't think you should be asking me,' she replied tartly.

'Oh, come on, Jean, I'm only going to say hello again.' She paused, and made her decision. 'I'll not wear the trouser suit, it's a bit formal.'

She slipped the dress over her head and asked Jean to zip it up for her. As she did so Lynda caught sight of the misery in Jean's face reflected in the mirror. She reached into the wardrobe and took out an elegant little green dress.

'This is a bit tight on me now, I kept it because I

168

thought it might fit you.'

That was a lie, she'd bought it for Jean but knew she might hesitate to accept an expensive gift. She saw immediately that it would have been better if she'd told the truth.

Jean brusquely moved away from her and stood with her head held high, defending the remnants of herself esteem.

'I don't need cast-offs. I'm not a charity case, you know.'

'I never said you were. Anyway, I'd better be going, got to be there on time. See you later.'

Lynda placed the dress on the bed, slipped her comb into her handbag and went downstairs to put on her coat.

Jean hesitated, but then couldn't resist picking up the dress and holding it against her. She admired her reflection in the mirror, until she saw how pale and lifeless her face seemed against the rich colour of the dress.

She heard the front door close, and then listened to the sound of Lynda driving off to Beechwood Avenue to be reunited with John. Jean put down the dress and walked towards the dressing table. She examined the array of pastel coloured containers, the selection of eye-shadow and lipsticks. She picked up a rose pink lipstick in a gold case twisted like barley sugar and slowly began to outline her colourless, dry lips.

John had moved Lynda's photograph to the centre of the sideboard, and placed their wedding photograph next to it. He looked at them and then at himself in the mirror over the fireplace. Running his hand across his cheek and the skin of his jaw line, he wished that he still looked as young as on his wedding day. He sighed, and then straightened his shoulders before going to start getting ready to meet his wife.

Steve, sitting in John's living room later that evening, kept looking at the clock. He'd hoped he'd be able to get John settled at Beechwood Avenue, with a beer in his hand to help him relax before Lynda arrived. He'd be lucky to get him there for eight o'clock at this rate.

When he'd arrived John had stood there, his shirt not yet buttoned, and with panic in his eyes. He'd held a tie in each hand, and asked nervously, 'Which one do you think?'

'They're both all right. But do you need to wear a tie?'

John had continued to look in bewilderment at the two slivers of silk, and then his eyes had met Steve's as he'd said with quiet resignation, 'I'll be lucky if she recognises me, won't I?'

'Don't be daft! Get in that bedroom, and finish getting ready.'

Steve was worried. He kept thinking of how Lynda was now even more beautiful, with a more delicate touch to her make-up and a more subtle colouring of her hair.

Lynda had style now, there was no doubt about that, and she wore her casual but elegant clothes with an ease and confidence many women would envy. She was a lot different from the young Milfield girl in that wedding photo.

Steve could have wept when John entered the room again. He was wearing his best jacket and had knotted his tie too tightly, trying to hide the signs of ageing on his neck.

He stood there stiffly, like a man waiting for his employer to hand him the brown envelope of redundancy.

'Very smart,' Steve commented, and hesitantly put his arm round John's shoulders as he walked with him to the door.

CHAPTER TWENTY

At Beechwood Avenue Lynda was already desperately aware that she was getting it all wrong. Anxious not to be late, she'd arrived fifteen minutes early, and she could tell that Carolyn wasn't pleased about it just by the look on her face as she opened the front door.

It had seemed wrong to Lynda, having to be let in to this house, instead of feeling she could use the key that was still in her purse, but she had to remember she was a guest here this evening. And obviously not a welcome one. Lynda couldn't stand the tense silence as she followed Carolyn through the hallway, and forgot to pause and stop herself saying what she was thinking.

'Strange, having to ring the doorbell to get into your own home.'

Carolyn had been rehearsing for this, and had a crisp and very defensive explanation ready.

'Dad insisted we should have the house. We didn't ask him. And it was his house, legally, and not yours.'

As she followed Carolyn into the living room, Lynda could have kicked herself for starting the evening exactly the way she'd vowed not to. Then Michael's wide, welcoming grin restored her courage. She greeted him and then turned to look with pride and wonder at the golden haired girl who sat resolutely on the edge of a chair.

Gemma had been trying to guess how her Mother wanted her to behave towards this beautiful, equally golden woman who moved in drifts of French perfume.

'And you must be Gemma,' Lynda said, and then announced with a boldness she did not feel. 'I'm your Grandma, or Nana if you'd prefer to call me that. I don't mind which.'

Gemma glanced at her Mother, and then very quietly said, 'Hello.'

Carolyn felt so numb she could hardly speak, but eventually turned to Lynda with icy politeness and invited her to sit down.

'Thought you'd never ask,' was the quick reply. It irritated Carolyn, and so did what seemed to her the great show Lynda made of sitting on the sofa next to Michael, and giving him a quick hug.

Carolyn, expecting him to flinch the way he did when she touched him, could not believe it when he seemed happy to accept the hug, and didn't even move along the sofa to put some physical space between him and his grandmother.

Lynda, not knowing that Carolyn would interpret the light of happiness in her eyes as one of triumph, smiled up at her daughter. Carolyn lost herself for a moment in that frank and open gaze, and then suddenly unable to cope, fled into the kitchen mumbling her intention to make coffee.

Lynda, feeling anxious now, settled back on the sofa, and looked round for inspiration, something to help her start talking to her grandchildren. It was provided by the small collection of cups and trophies which Michael had won for ten-pin bowling, and soon Lynda had arranged that Michael would go bowling with her one day soon. Gemma didn't like ten-pin bowling, she didn't like anything she wasn't good at, and quickly turned down Lynda's invitation to join them. She was glad she had said no when her mother returned with the coffee.

'Grandma wants to take me bowling,' Michael announced.

'Oh. Well, we'll have to see.'

Michael ignoring his Mother's resistance, said, 'We could take Grandad with us.'

'No.'

'He'd enjoy it,' Lynda said. Carolyn gave her a disapproving look as she saw her push back her hair in a familiar gesture of defiance. For this occasion Lynda had let her hair curl on to her shoulders, the way John had liked it, but now she wished she'd chosen a more elegant style. Carolyn, now coolly playing the part of the polite hostess, poured the coffee.

'Do you still take sugar?'

'Yes, please.'

'It's not good for you,' came the reprimand.

Lynda, who had seen from Carolyn's cold stare that no personal concern was motivating the remark, snapped back, 'Like a lot of other things that make life worth living.'

There was a silence. Lynda, scared that she was losing control, getting it all wrong, tried again.

'I hear you're doing very well at your job, and looking like getting a promotion.'

'Yes.'

'It would mean moving, though, Steve said.'

'Moving?' Gemma exclaimed. 'Where to?'

'Nowhere. Don't worry, Gemma.'

Carolyn glared at her Mother for broaching a subject they'd been trying not to discuss in front of the children yet.

Gemma was panicking. 'I don't want to move.'

'I don't blame you, Gemma. It's a nice place to live is Milfield. I've missed it.'

174

Carolyn's laugh was scornful. 'Obviously, that's why you didn't bother coming back for twelve years. And why you won't be planning to stay.'

Lynda took a deep breath and looked steadily at her daughter.

'I am staying, I hope. I've come home.'

Carolyn did not blink but stared at her with a cat-like dispassionate disdain. 'Oh, have you?'

Lynda was mesmerised by the coldness of Carolyn's gaze, but then the sound of the front door opening startled her to her feet.

Steve entered. Trying to disguise the apprehension he now shared with John, he announced loudly, 'Here he is, Lynda!'

John bowed his head a little as he stepped into the room, and as he lifted it again he caught the full force of the shock which whitened across Lynda's face.

He'd imagined that look so often as he'd stared at his sad reflection in the mirror, that his reaction was now automatic. He turned and strode swiftly back towards the front door.

'Take me home, Steve. Now!' he commanded, his voice harsh and almost choked away by emotion.

As he stepped past him, Steve saw that John's pride was about to be disintegrated by tears of despair, and he didn't want anyone to see that happen. He followed John and obeyed without question.

Lynda and Carolyn stood absolutely still until they heard the front door banged shut. Then Carolyn turned slowly to her Mother.

'Well done,' she sneered.

'John!' Lynda headed towards the door, but Carolyn stepped in front of her and grabbed her by the arm.

'Don't you dare go after him,' she cried, pushing

175

Lynda back into the room. 'Leave my Dad alone. He doesn't want you. Can't you see that?'

'Of course he wants me. I'm his wife.'

Lynda tried to pull herself free from Carolyn's grasp but she tightened her fingers on her arm, and pushed her face close to Lynda's.

'You've no right to call yourself that. Just as you've no right to come back. I'm not going to let you hurt him again.'

She began pulling Lynda towards the door now, opening it wide to push her through it.

'You can just clear off back where you came from. We don't want you. Do you hear me? We don't want you!'

Lynda couldn't move for a moment, caught in the glare of her daughter's hatred. Then she glanced back into the room and saw the horrified faces of her two grandchildren. She looked once more at Carolyn, shrugged herself free from her, and walked out of that house once again.

She got into the car and sat at the wheel, wondering where she could go. Not back to Jean's, that was for sure. Jean would want to know what had happened, and Lynda didn't want to tell her; she'd had as much humiliation as she could take at the moment.

She switched on the engine and drove away from Beechwood Avenue, not knowing where she was going at first, but eventually heading towards the one person who had never ever refused her comfort and sympathy.

They were not expecting visitors in the formidable house on Wellington Road. You could tell that by the way files and papers were scattered over the narrow Pembroke table which was serving as Dan's work space for the evening. There were papers on the desk front of the open bureau, too. Dan pulled a bundle of old cheque books from one of its pigeon holes, dumped them on the table and sat down to work his way through them.

Ellen, in her chair by the fire, leaned her chin on her hand to observe his frantic search, and made sure he heard her sighing at his incompetence. It did nothing to help him in his search for a record of the payment one of his suppliers had claimed not to have received.

Dan looked up when the doorbell rang, but it was Ellen who went to discover who was calling that evening. She had already decided that, having made her point, she would now retire to the quiet haven of her bedroom.

However, when she saw that the caller was Lynda Stanworth, and that she was obviously in some distress, Ellen changed her mind; here was the prospect of some entertainment.

Lynda made a huge effort to pretend that this was just a casual call, but Dan saw immediately how upset she was and offered her a brandy. As she accepted the drink Lynda silently cursed as she saw Ellen Heywood carefully scrutinising her tear-stained face, missing nothing. Declining to drink with them, Ellen embarked immediately on her probing.

'So, you've returned to your family, Mrs Stanworth.'

'Yes,' said Lynda forcing herself to calm down, and refusing to let herself be daunted by the formality and coldness of Ellen's tone. Ellen placed the next question like a card player flushing out the strength of her opponent's hand.

'And were you a welcome prodigal?'

Lynda, sipping the brandy, ignored the question,

177

and this gave Ellen the answer she wanted. Lynda saw her satisfied smile and decided to retaliate.

'Nothing seems to have changed here,' she commented, looking at the faded carpet and once expensive, but now well-worn sofa. 'Still as elegant as ever, I mean.'

Ellen, aware that the room was not up to standard, stiffened but held Lynda's gaze and took it across to the photograph of Carolyn. Lynda could not look at it, and Ellen smiled, feeling a sense of advantage to move forward with.

'No doubt you've found it was a mistake to leave your family as you did.'

'Mother!' Dan stepped forward to defend Lynda, but she already had her answer prepared.

'Yes, but we've all made that kind of mistake, haven't we, Mrs Heywood?' Lynda replied calmly. And this time it was Ellen who had to remember the history behind Lynda's confident statement, and lower her gaze.

'You won't be going away again, Lynda, love,' Dan said affectionately. 'Not if I can help it.'

Ellen looked at him disdainfully.

'You may not have any say in that, Daniel. You must realise that your friend will, no doubt, have formed 'personal connections' in the South of England. Is that not so?'

Lynda was more than ready to fight back now.

'One or two, but this is home. Any more questions?' she challenged.

Ellen picked up her book.

'I'm tired, so I must bid you goodnight.'

She walked slowly out of the room, and went upstairs, but did not immediately go to bed. She paused to listen for a while to the few fragments of conversation which were loud enough to reach the landing at the top of the stairs.

Lynda told Dan what had happened and, not wanting to go back until Jean had gone to bed, she stayed with Dan until almost midnight. He sat with his arm round her, and talked gently to her until he had soothed her battered spirit. As he had so many times in the past, Dan wished fervently that he did not live in his Mother's house, then Lynda could have stayed in his arms all night.

When Lynda eventually arrived back at Jean's, she closed her eyes in silent despair as she opened the door to the living room and saw Jean, in her thick woollen dressing gown, hunched by the fire clutching a mug of drinking chocolate. She turned slowly and looked at Lynda forlornly before summoning the courage to ask, 'How did it go?'

Lynda couldn't look at those frightened eyes, she looked instead at her own reflection in the mirror and brushed her hair back from her face as she replied, lying once more, 'Fine. It was wonderful to be back in my old home again.'

'You'd see a difference in John.'

'Yes.'

Jean wanted her to talk then, to have a hot drink and tell her everything, but Lynda couldn't stay another minute, could hardly say another word. She fled upstairs and shut the door to the bedroom firmly. She hurriedly undressed, got into bed and then waited. She heard Jean come up the stairs a few minutes later and pause outside the door.

Like a child afraid of the bogeyman Lynda lay still, holding her breath until Jean had gone into her own bedroom. After a few minutes she switched on the lamp on the bedside cabinet, quietly opened the drawer and took out Tom Meredith's photograph.

She stared into those loving eyes and stopped holding back the tears.

Did he know, as she did now, that she should never have come back to Milfield? How she wished she could hold that strong handsome face in her hands and kiss the man who had made her feel so safe, so loved. Still looking into those eyes, she silently wept until sleep gently pulled her away from her grief.

CHAPTER TWENTY-ONE

The next morning Jean, bringing Lynda a cup of tea before she left for work, saw Tom's photograph.

'Is that him? The man you were telling me about?'

Lynda sat up sleepily, 'Yes. Thank you for the tea.'

Jean stood there, not wanting to think about John and Lynda together, but that was all she could think about. She had decided last night that she should accept that she'd lost John, and should salvage her pride by being reasonable about it.

'Tell John, no hard feelings.'

'What do you mean?' Lynda asked.

Jean silently congratulated herself on managing to force a hollow laugh as she said, 'For dumping me.'

The laugh didn't fool Lynda, she saw Jean bowing her body in acceptance, just like she used to when teachers or the other kids were giving her a hard time at school. Now, as then, she couldn't stand to see that happen.

'Nobody's dumping you, love.' she reassured her, but Jean turned away, trying to hide the tears that filled her eyes.

Lynda didn't want this, she didn't want to see Jean losing again, as she had throughout her life. Gently she took hold of Jean's hand.

'He hasn't dumped you.'

With bitterness in her voice, Jean said, 'But he will. John will want, what he's always wanted, you.'

'He didn't want me last night.'

Jean stared, hope struggling into her consciousness.

'He took one look at me and walked out. And then our Carolyn told me to go to hell. So that was a nice welcome home, wasn't it?'

'Oh, I'm sorry,' Jean said, and meant it.

'John's changed, I've changed,' Lynda continued, 'but our Carolyn hasn't. It's a bloody mess. So just go to work and try to stop worrying for a bit.'

'What are you going to do?'

Lynda had been wondering that herself, but now the answer, when it came, was easy. 'I'm going round to see John, this morning.'

The post had come early at Beechwood Avenue, before either of them had gone to work. Carolyn's hands trembled as she opened the AFS envelope, but her heart leapt as she read the letter.

'Steve,' she called as he came down the stairs, 'Come into the front room for a minute.'

'What's up?' he asked.

'I don't want to talk about this in front of the kids, it was bad enough my Mother opening her big mouth and upsetting Gemma last night. I've been short-listed for the job in Leeds.'

'Oh.'

'Is that all you can say?'

'What do you want me to say?'

'Well done, would be a start!'

'Are you still going for it?'

'Of course I am.'

'Even though I don't want to move, the kids won't want to move, and your Dad will be heart-broken if we leave Milfield?'

Carolyn didn't hide her impatience. 'We've been through all that. Dad will be fine. We'll come and visit, and he'll have Jean to look after him.'

'He might not want that, especially now Lynda's

come back. I don't know why we're even talking about this.' Steve said, exasperated.

Carolyn's tone was determined. 'We're talking about it because it would be the best thing for all of us.'

'For you, you mean. Not us.'

Carolyn wished they weren't having this argument, especially this morning. But how could Steve know that it might be his last chance to stop her committing herself to an affair with Paul Ferris?

She'd arranged to see Paul that evening, using her visit to Ellen Heywood as an alibi. She'd been annoyed when Steve, having forgotten she was going to Ellen's, had told her he'd arranged to go out and assess a kitchen re-fit. She'd had to ask Jean to babysit, and therefore tell someone else the lie.

Carolyn wanted to beg Steve to see things her way, and to show her that he loved her. Instead she heard herself shouting at him.

'Doesn't it matter to you that I'm not happy, Steve? Can you not understand that I want more out of life than this?'

Steve had never seen Carolyn so determined. Looking at her angry and stubborn expression, he was suddenly reminded of a scene of unhappiness from the past. It was the last thing she wanted to hear, but he was going to say it anyway.

'You sound just like your Mother.'

Jenny Heywood wished there was less for her to do that Wednesday morning, she wanted to have time to daydream about seeing Steve Sheldon again. However, there was a lot of work making its way across from Philip's chaotic desk on to her neat and tidy one.

Philip Lawson was one of life's strollers. He had

183

decided many years ago that if he could spend his days doing mostly what he liked, and casually earning a comfortable living at the same time, he would be happy. He was well on the way to fulfilling this ambition.

His father, Edwin Lawson, had retired several years ago, but still endeavoured to keep a check on the successful firm his son had inherited. Edwin had been a solicitor who had hidden away from the world in an oak panelled office, and had achieved the utmost in terms of charcoal grey respectability.

He had also been a diligent, but not inspiring father to his only child. When Philip was small Edwin had read 'The Wind in the Willows' to him, dutifully, and with some pleasure but no funny voices. He had also played cricket with him on the extensive lawn at the back of their large house. But most of all he had been strict, and despairing of his son, who seemed incapable of adhering to his standards.

Philip's relationship with his father could not be described as close. Philip had decided at the age of eighteen that, although he had succumbed to his father's insistence that he would become a solicitor, he would reject him as a role model.

He had turned instead to Reggie Broadbent his father's partner in the practice. Reggie, a man with ties as loud as his voice, and an easy-going approach, had attracted the kind of clients Edwin Lawson did not, and so they had formed a successful business partnership. Reggie had retired early to play golf in Malaga, but his spirit was ever present in Philip's office.

Jenny had joined the firm as soon as she'd left the sixth form, and had become Reggie's assistant. When she was widowed and in need of an income, Reggie and Edwin had offered her employment with hours which fitted in well with her children's needs. It had been a wise appointment, especially as Philip was fond of Jenny and allowed her to moderate the more unsuitable aspects of his behaviour.

When he eventually became her boss, Philip was quick to point out to Jenny, that he was a bright fellow who was well aware that he had need of her conscientious and meticulous work ethic, and her unlimited patience. He was absolutely right, especially about the patience, but Jenny loved working for him.

She was amused by his weaknesses, especially his liking for gossip, but knew that, apart from confiding in her, and his wife, Philip was never less than absolutely discreet. Also she had to admit that Philip was not often wrong about people and that, like Reggie Broadbent before him, his amiability and interest in local 'goings on' often resulted in work for the practice.

He had been very interested to learn that Lynda Stanworth had returned to Milfield, and that morning he surprised Jenny when he talked about her again.

'I hope you gave Lynda my phone number when you saw her,' he said, only half jokingly. 'I wouldn't like anyone else handling the divorce.'

Jenny was taken aback. 'What divorce?'

'John wants to marry Jean Haworth, didn't you know?'

'No,' replied Jenny, suddenly comprehending the tension she had noticed between Jean and Lynda.

Philip, sticking his thumbs under the broad red braces which enlivened his white shirt, gave her a knowing look. 'Ah, you see, you don't keep up with the local gossip like I do.'

Jenny, who had been struggling to sort out some of his disorganized paperwork, closed the filing cabinet rather firmly.

185

'Unlike you,' she commented tartly, I don't have the time.'

Philip, not at all abashed by the implied criticism, just leaned far back in his chair, and put his feet up on the desk. Jenny looked pointedly at his expensive black patent leather shoes to signal, yet again, that this was a very inappropriate habit of his.

Philip blithely ignored her disapproval. He loved indulging in the unconventional, like having a red and white Milfield football club banner on the wall and his supporter's scarf draped over a filing cabinet.

He specialized in matrimonial disputes, and argued that such unexpected adornments helped his clients to relax, especially as for many of them seeking a divorce was their first visit to a solicitor's office.

He did, however, always hastily remove the scarf and banner on the rare occasions when his Father announced he would be calling in to see him. With some satisfaction, Philip now divulged more of his inside information.

'Carolyn told Tricia it was pretty definite.'

Philip's pretty and kind-hearted wife, Tricia, had been at school with Carolyn and, unlike the rest of her school-friends, had not shunned her when she'd disgraced herself by getting pregnant.

Jenny was shocked at the idea of John and Lynda getting divorced, and began to consider the effect it would have on the Sheldon family. She'd noticed the affection between Steve and Lynda the previous evening.

'Steve will be upset,' she commented, 'he's always liked Lynda.'

'Yes. How is Steve? I don't often see him at the match now I've got a seat in the directors' box.'

Jenny, wary of Philip's intuition, replied hastily,

186

'I don't really know, we'd lost touch, too, till the other night.'

Realising that it would look suspicious if she didn't tell Philip, she added, 'But he's coming round to see me this evening.'

Philip immediately seized upon the opportunity to tease her, and raised his eyebrows as accompaniment to a suggestive, 'Oh?'

Jenny scowled at him.

'It was Lynda's idea. I'd said I needed my kitchen re-fitting so she insisted Steve should have a look at it.'

Then, realising that she was blushing, she tried to distract him.

'Lynda reminded me that you and Steve used to be good friends at school.'

Philip gave a mischievous smile, 'Yes. But we were also rivals. Don't tell Tricia but I used to fancy Carolyn as well.'

Before she could stop herself Jenny remarked sharply, 'A lot of men do apparently.'

Philip took his feet off the desk and leaned forward eagerly.

'What have you heard?'

'Nothing.'

'Has Julia Ingham been spreading office gossip round your aerobics class again?'

Philip knew that Julia worked with Carolyn, and he also knew about Paul Ferris's reputation, which the drinking men among Philip's acquaintances often sniggered about, but also envied.

'Philip, stop it! Can we please get on with some work!'

CHAPTER TWENTY-TWO

John was listening to Elvis singing 'Wooden Heart' and didn't hear Lynda's brief tapping at his front door. Apprehensive again now, she hesitated before ringing the door bell. It seemed to jangle along with her nerves, and when John opened the door she found she was almost as speechless as he was.

'Hello, John,' she said quietly but he didn't respond.

'Can I come in?'

John was still numb with the shock of seeing her there but instinctively stepped aside to let her in. She seemed to fill the tiny room with colour and French perfume. He wanted to reach out and touch her, to make sure she was real, but instead he found himself faltering into the formal utterances of polite welcome.

'Sit down. Would you like a cup of tea?'

She stopped him there. 'Don't be polite, John. The last thing you should be with me is polite.'

They stood very still and looked at each other. The music seemed very loud between them, and reminded Lynda that John no longer belonged to her.

'Looks like you and Jean still share the same taste in music.'

He immediately turned off the stereo and again gazed at her in wonder. 'You look smashing, ' he said, and the words echoed between them, as if pulled back from the past.

'You don't look so bad yourself.' She paused, wondering how she could heal his pride. 'I'm sorry about last night.'

188

'No. I'm sorry. It was stupid of me to walk out like that.'

'Oh, John,' she gasped, and looked as if she was about to faint. He took her arm and guided her to the settee.

'Sit down, love. We'd better have that tea.'

As they drank, they talked, hesitantly and carefully. Lynda slowly tried to describe again how she had felt, what had made her walk out and leave them.

'Oh, John, these all sound such small, such petty reasons and perhaps they were, but every time I got contradicted or put down, it chipped away at me until I felt I was nothing, and nobody. I wasn't happy, John,' she said finally, 'I hadn't been happy for a long time.'

'I know,' he murmured.

'I wasn't leaving for good. I just needed to get away for a couple of days, or that's what I told myself. But I found another way of living, John, and somewhere I belonged. I felt happier than I ever had in the whole of my life. And I couldn't leave.'

'Till now. Why now?'

She stood up and walked to the window, not wanting him to see the pain she was feeling as she remembered why she'd come back now.

'I wanted to see you, and Carolyn, to ask you to forgive me. There were a lot of times I didn't listen, and I didn't make you happy, either of you.'

She looked at the good, kind man who had been, and still was, her husband, and wanted to cry as she imagined the pain she had caused him. John saw the tears in her eyes, and couldn't bear to see her humbled like this. He needed to make her laugh.

'Oh, hell, it wasn't all bad, was it?' he joked.

Lynda laughed with him, but then was serious again.

'No, but it wasn't going to get any better. We weren't going to be happy, any of us, not you, not Carolyn and Steve. And eventually my being there would have spoiled things for little Michael, too. I didn't want him to grow up listening to me and our Carolyn shouting at each other, and me causing trouble between her and Steve.'

John knew there was a lot of truth in what she was saying, but he also was aware that this might be his last chance to get Lynda back. He wanted more than anything to hold her in his arms.

'I always wanted you to come back, you know. I did want to go looking for you, but I didn't know where you were.'

Anger sparked in her eyes now. 'I sent you cards, John, and I left you Rose's letter, you must have found that. You did know where I was.'

'No, I didn't. My Mother took them and hid them from me, from all of us. We found them when she died.'

'What? Oh, my God!'

They stared at each other in silence as they acknowledged the enormity of that intervention in their lives.

John shook his head slowly.

'Till the day she died, she kept saying that we should never have got married. But she shouldn't have interfered like she did, and she'd no right to take those letters.'

'No. But she was right about me and you, we should never have got married.'

'Don't say that.'

'Let's not go on about the past. What I want to know is how you are, John. It was a shock to hear you'd had a heart attack, and you're having trouble getting over it.'

'What have they been telling you? I'm all right, I just have to think twice about what I get up to, that's all.'

Lynda, needing relief from the emotional pressure of this conversation, winked suggestively as she said, 'Oh? That must cramp your style.'

John paused, and was tempted to ignore the innuendo, but didn't. He'd done a lot of thinking since Lynda had left him, and knew that here was a chance to talk about something they'd never managed to face up to in the past. He, too, tried to laugh as he spoke, but shame dampened down the laughter.

'I never did have much 'style' in that department.'

Lynda's eyes moved away from his, she didn't want to hurt him more than she already had. She felt so sorry for this man who seemed to have lost so much of his pride and manhood.

She certainly didn't want to tell him now that his love-making had been another reason their marriage had been a failure. She also couldn't tell him that Tom Meredith had been the only man who had ever given her the passionate fulfilment she had dreamed of.

She made herself smile, and scold him mockingly.

'Hey, I haven't come here to listen to you running yourself down.'

John watched her as he enquired earnestly.

'What have you come for, Lynda?' It was his turn to chide her gently now, and he smiled as he asked. 'Do you know?'

'Like I said, I wanted to see you.'

'That makes two of us then,' he said softly, and she saw the love shining in his eyes.

A memory stirred, and she wondered for a moment if she could ever want John Stanworth's love

191

again. But it was only for a moment.

'I did what was right for me, John. In some ways it was selfish, I admit that, but I don't regret it.'

His sorrow leaned heavily on his shoulders again now.

'You can leave all the regretting to me. I've thought it all through, well, most of it anyway. We didn't give you much of a chance, did we, me and Carolyn? He paused. 'How are things between you and her?'

Unable to cope with the memory of the confrontation last night, Lynda lifted the heavy net curtains and looked out of the window.

'Bloody awful,' she replied. 'But I don't know what I can do about it.' She let the curtain fall again, and turned back to him. 'Anyway, never mind about her for now, what about you? Are you happy?'

'No,' was his forceful reply. 'But I could be, if you've come back to me. Have you, Lynda?'

Again she didn't want to hurt him, so she deflected the question, and asked 'What about Jean?'

John looked at her ruefully, but Lynda persisted.

'She loves you.'

John was embarrassed but didn't hesitate to be forthright.

'Yes, but she's not like you.'

He looked at Lynda, and remembered the magical sensation of making love to her. He stood up and took her in his arms.

'You're the one I've always wanted. There's never really been anyone else for me, Lynda. And you've come back, so I'm thinking it's the same for you. Is it?'

She pitied him as she saw his need of her, but she had to move her body away from his. He held his breath as he waited for her answer. It was given by her silence and the look in her eyes. He let go of her, as if she had pushed him away.

'I'm sorry John,' she said gently.

His mouth went dry, and he had to swallow hard before he could form the question. 'You found somebody else?'

'Yes.' Her voice faded to a whisper as she said, 'But I lost him. He died a few weeks ago.'

John's voice was rough now. 'Did you love him?'

'Oh, yes,' she confessed quietly, but with absolute certainty.

'But you've come back to me.'

'No. But I wanted to see how you are.'

'And how am I, do you think?' he challenged her.

'Could be better,' she said firmly.

'I've had a heart attack.'

'Yes, but you won't get over it doing nothing but sitting in this poky flat. You need to get back into the land of the living. Those net curtains are like a flaming shroud! Take them down, let the sunshine in!'

'It's raining,' he said sourly.

Lynda winced at this reminder of why John Stanworth had been the wrong husband. She forced herself to brighten her face with a smile. 'What you need is a good night out. Are Carolyn and Steve doing anything this Saturday, do you know?'

'No. If they're going out, they ask me and Jean to babysit,' he told her, a little embarrassed at talking about himself and Jean as a couple.

Lynda smiled and said, 'Right. How about you, me and Steve going for a Saturday night out, like we used to?'

'I'd love to, but I'm not sure I can cope with that yet.'

'Oh, come on John!'

'No. Our Carolyn would be worried.'

'What's it got to do with her?' Lynda argued. 'I can't bear to see you like this. Sitting in here waiting for nothing to happen. This isn't good for you, John. Come out with me on Saturday. Please.'

He was confused, trying to work out what should happen next in this strange reunion, but decided time with Lynda was what he needed, time to change the way she felt.

'O.K.'

'Right. I'll arrange it with Steve. The three musketeers out on the razzle, just like the old days, eh?'

'Carolyn won't like it.'

'No problem. We won't tell her.'

As soon as Lynda got back in the car, her mobile phone rang. Mark had decided to tell her about Suzanne removing items from the apartment, and her threat to contest Tom's will. He suggested he should come to see her soon, and bring some of the things which had belonged to her and his Dad, to prevent his Mother making any claim on them.

Suzanne's threat made her worry about Mark finding out that, legally, she was still married to John. Having to think quickly, Lynda told Mark she might not be staying in Milfield, so there was no point in bringing anything to her yet. He seemed to accept that, and she ended the call with a promise that she would phone him soon.

As she drove back to Jean's house, she felt guilty about lying to Tom's beloved son. Lynda knew she had already decided she would stay in Milfield; she wanted to get to know her grandchildren, and to make them love her as she already loved them.

CHAPTER TWENTY-THREE

That Wednesday evening Jenny waited impatiently for Katie and Alex to dawdle their way through the evening meal, and argue about whose turn it was to wash up.

As she changed into a smart pair of trousers and a wine coloured top which she knew she looked good in, Jenny again turned over in her mind the conversations she'd overheard between Julia and her friend Jackie Pearson on the subject of Carolyn Sheldon.

It seemed that Carolyn was no longer playing so hard to get, but was now showing signs of having been beguiled by Paul Ferris. Julia had had no doubt what Paul's intentions had been when he'd arranged for Carolyn to go with him to the conference, but she wasn't sure whether Paul had slept with her yet. If he hadn't, it wouldn't be long before he did. Julia knew to her cost that Paul always got what he wanted.

Jenny wondered if Julia was right, and tried to stop herself hoping that she might be. She was still allowing these thoughts to undermine her conscience when she went back into the living room.

The television programme Alex had been watching had finished, and she was struggling to summon the energy and the will to go up to her room and begin her essay. She was ready to be distracted and was quick to notice her Mother's clothes, and that she'd put on fresh make-up and re-styled her hair a little.

'Look at you!' she mocked.

Jenny knew that her embarrassment was clearly

visible in her cheeks, and was glad that Katie chose that moment to charge through the room on her way out.

'Have you tidied the kitchen like I said?' Jenny demanded.

Katie, still in a bad mood for some reason, yelled, 'Yes!' and made a door banging exit. Alex, like her Grandmother, was shrewdly observant, and ignored the distraction.

'You seem to be making a lot of fuss. Is this Steve Sheldon good-looking or something?'

Jenny was startled by this dart into her secret thoughts, and blustered into denial.

'I am not making a lot of fuss, I just want the place decent. And Steve's married.'

Alex was intrigued.

'Then why are you so keen to make a good impression?'

'I'm not!' Jenny insisted. 'I thought you had an essay to write,' she said, wanting to end this conversation. Alex saw that her Mother was rattled and decided to back off. She went up to her room to make a start on her task, but wondered about the reason for her Mother's agitation.

Alex's Grandmother was also observing someone's behaviour that evening. Ellen was delighted to be entertaining her protégée, but saw that Carolyn seemed a little preoccupied.

'You are to be congratulated, Carolyn, on being short-listed for the promotion. I would, of course, miss you if you left Milfield, but Leeds would be a wonderful opportunity.'

'Steve doesn't think so.'

'That doesn't surprise me.'

Many times Ellen had wished that Carolyn had not

196

married Steven Sheldon, the man who had destroyed all the dreams she and Carolyn had created together.

Carolyn was glad to confide in someone who was sympathetic.

'I wish Steve would see that there's nothing for him here. He hates working for Tony Randerson, but we'll never have the money for him to set up on his own.'

'And if you did, there's no guarantee your husband would make a success of it. You are the one with ability and prospects, Carolyn, and you should be allowed to pursue your career.'

Carolyn sipped her glass of sherry and considered again how much her marriage to Steve had limited her.

Ellen interrupted those thoughts with an invitation. 'I wonder if you would like to accompany me to a concert in Manchester on the Saturday of the Bank Holiday weekend, Carolyn?'

When Carolyn hesitated to accept the offer, Ellen continued, 'I shall buy two tickets in any case, and you may let me know later if you wish to come.'

Carolyn was used to this kind of tactic from Ellen, and had learned the art of seeming enthusiastic without making any firm commitment, but the negotiations were interrupted by a phone call. Ellen picked up the receiver and then, with an expression of distaste, placed it on the table beside her.

'Daniel is in his bedroom. Would you go and tell him he has a phone call.' She lowered her voice to a hiss, 'From your Mother.'

She was pleased to see the animosity which clouded Carolyn's face at the mention of her Mother, but she was less pleased at Dan's eager acceptance of Lynda's invitation.

'Lynda's invited me round for a drink,' he

announced with a broad smile on his face.

'Indeed? Well, it's fortunate that I shall have you for company this evening, my dear, as Daniel is deserting me.'

Carolyn, glancing at the clock, cursed her Mother for making it even more difficult to leave in time to meet Paul.

'Oh, I'm so sorry, Ellen, but I won't be able to stay much longer.'

It was obvious that Ellen was extremely disappointed and Carolyn was upset that she was having to deny her old friend the evening she had expected.

'But you always stay for supper.'

'I know, and I would love to, but Steve annoyingly has arranged to go out to give an estimate for some work, so I have to get back.'

'How very inconsiderate of him,' fumed Ellen.

Carolyn worked hard for the next half hour, trying to ensure that the visit was as satisfying as possible for Ellen, but at twenty past eight she announced that she really had to leave.

Ellen suspected that there was more occupying her visitor's mind than she was being made party to, but knew that Carolyn would confide in her eventually, as she always had in the past. With an effort she stood up and clasped Carolyn's hands within her bony but still strong fingers.

'You know I'm here if you need me. Always.'

Carolyn looked into those eyes which had always seemed capable of searching into her soul, and was ashamed at having to deceive her.

'I'll see you again soon.'

Ellen nodded. Not wanting to betray her need too much, she hesitated before adding a plea.

'Don't let your Mother, spoil things.'

Carolyn kissed her on the cheek.

'I won't.'

When she had closed the door, Ellen turned and faced the prospect of another long evening. She went to the window to draw the curtains, and paused to watch Carolyn, her dear child, hurrying along the pavement. A silver grey car moved slowly towards her.

Ellen could see that the driver was a handsome young man, and she caught her breath in alarm as he stopped the car. But then she saw that Carolyn knew him, for she smiled, and hesitated only long enough to glance along the street before quickly getting into the passenger seat.

Instinctively realising that she was not supposed to witness this scene, Ellen drew back from the window. She listened until the car had been driven away before closing the curtains. In her breast the small clawing sensation of pain which insisted on reminding her of her mortality, stirred again but Ellen impatiently attempted to massage it away.

She had immediately realised the reason for the air of preoccupation she had sensed in Carolyn that evening, and was disturbed by what she had seen. However, as she sat alone by her fireside that evening, she hesitated to condemn Carolyn for seeking a little excitement outside her imperfect marriage. Ellen herself knew the temptation of excitement, indeed, she could not help but contemplate, with a certain frisson, the possible consequences of Carolyn's behaviour.

Dan was delighted that he was spending the evening in Lynda's company instead of being at home in the service of his Mother and her guest.

He had come home from work to find Ellen

making herself breathless by trying to tidy up some books he'd left on a shelf. He'd made a mental note to persuade her to see the doctor again, to ask if he could improve the medication which was supposed to be keeping her heart problem under control.

Annoyed at her inability to carry out a simple task, she'd spoken to him as if he were not her son but a servant. Usually he tried to ignore it when she did that, but suddenly he'd found himself resenting that she was making all this fuss just because Carolyn Sheldon was coming to see her.

He'd been glad to leave the house, glad that he would not once more have to see his Mother fawning over her 'adopted daughter', just as she had fawned over her favourite son.

Lynda poured him a whisky and topped up her own vodka and blackcurrant. She studied the contents of her glass.

'It's ages since I've drunk vodka. I bought it when I was stocking up Jean's drinks cupboard, but I don't know why. I only like it with loads of blackcurrant. It's what I used to drink when I got really angry and upset, when John and Carolyn drove me to it.'

'Are you angry about something now?'

'Yeah. Jean babysitting for my grandchildren when it should be me.'

Dan nodded. 'I can see why that would upset you. But I was really happy when you phoned to ask me round. And, for once, my Mother didn't raise any objection to my going out because she had Carolyn for company, or thought she had.'

'Was it Carolyn who was with her when I phoned?'

'Yes, she still comes to visit fairly regularly,' Dan said, not realising that he was causing a host of memories to crowd forward to taunt Lynda.

'She stole my daughter from me, you know, your damned Mother.'

Dan had heard this accusation before, and didn't want it to be true.

'Don't exaggerate, Lynda, it wasn't that bad.'

'Carolyn got a lot of her fancy ideas from Ellen, including the idea that I was a load of rubbish. Mind you, Sheila Stanworth had already told her that. Our Carolyn has always thought your Mother was something special, though.'

Dan didn't want to talk about his Mother and Carolyn, and was relieved, although also a little apprehensive, when Lynda informed him that his mission for the evening was to cheer her up.

It was easier than he thought, as all Lynda wanted was to play music and dance. It meant that they risked wearing some more holes in Jean's faded carpet, and Dan felt a little foolish dancing around and banging into the furniture, but if it made Lynda happy it was worth it.

He didn't have the stamina to keep going for long, though, and was glad when Lynda agreed that they should sit down at last and just have a chat.

The subject of Ellen couldn't be avoided completely, and Lynda, never afraid to ask awkward questions, soon learned that Dan was paying most of the bills at Kirkwood House.

'Has she spent all her parents' money, then?'

'It seems like it. We manage all right, though. What about you, are you all right financially?'

Lynda smiled. 'Oh, yes, thanks to Tom and Loveday.'

'Tell me about that,' he urged, curious about Lynda's life at Loveday Manor. She happily began to talk about the work she'd done and the happy times she'd had there.

Previously when she'd talked about it, she'd always being very careful what she said, but this evening she was feeling lonely, and was being encouraged by the glass of vodka clasped in her hands. Sitting on the settee next to Dan, she allowed herself to talk more freely than she had before.

She described the experiences she and Tom Meredith had had, and the lovely mementos they'd bought. As she talked about their life together Dan, who hadn't wanted to think of Lynda with another man, finally recognised how close the relationship had been.

'I didn't realise that you and Tom had set up home together.'

Lynda smiled, a little tearfully.

'Yeah. We used to laugh about having a chair for the master of the house on one side of the hearth and a rocking chair for me on the other.'

Dan laughed, 'Just like an old married couple, eh?'

Lynda stared at him intently, deciding that she needed to share her secret, and that Dan Heywood was the one person in the world she knew she could trust.

'Yes,' said quietly. 'In fact, exactly like a married couple.' She paused. 'I married him, Dan.'

He blinked and then stared at her.

'You can't have!' he gasped.

'I did.'

'But that's . . . .'

'Bigamy. I know. Funny sounding word, isn't it?' she tried to joke as she got up and poured herself another drink, but Dan wasn't going to laugh. He was frightened for her, she could see that.

She refilled his glass with whisky and together they faced the possibility that she could go to jail, and that Suzanne Meredith could find out the truth and challenge Lynda's claim on Tom's estate.

Dan couldn't sit still he was so agitated. He got up and stood looking down at her.

'What are you going to do about it?' he asked.

'I don't know.'

'You must see a solicitor, get some advice.'

'Yes, I've been telling myself that ever since I found out I was still married to John. But I'm scared of what a solicitor will say.'

'Go and see Philip Lawson, he's a good-hearted young man. He'll help you.'

'I'd wondered about him.' She tried to smile. 'He used to be a bit of a tearaway on the quiet, he'd be sympathetic to a sinner like me.'

CHAPTER TWENTY-FOUR

Steve was glad to be going to Jenny Heywood's house that evening, it was a chance to think about something other than his worries about the future.

He and Gary had stayed on for a few minutes after the others had gone home, and had tried to work out exactly what Randerson was up to. He was very unwilling to order more materials and that had really caused alarm bells to ring for Steve and Gary. Was Randerson's cash-flow really that tight, or was he playing with the book-keeping to make the company look more profitable than it was?

They couldn't decide but they knew whatever Randerson was doing would mean bad news for them and the rest of the employees. Steve was worried sick, and wished he could talk it over with Carolyn. She was always able to be rational and analytical about things like that, but he'd had to stop talking to her about work, it had already led to too many rows.

It seemed difficult for him and Carolyn to avoid arguments at the moment, and he knew she was having to edit her conversations just as he was, to side-step potential causes of conflict between them. It made him feel tense and the tension made him weary and sometimes depressed.

He felt his spirits lift now, though, as he parked outside Jenny Heywood's house and looked up to see the warm, rosy glow of a lamp in the square bay window. Instinctively he knew that here was a home that offered warmth, and welcome, and a quiet fireside. And he felt very much in need of that.

Alex, who had come downstairs to take a look at her Mother's visitor, noticed the weariness in Steve Sheldon's eyes, and that he did not have the look of a romantic hero. She helped herself to a cup of the coffee Jenny had made, and went back to her room to complete the work which was proving more arduous than she'd expected.

She might have changed her assessment of Steve Sheldon if she'd seen him a short while later, sitting in an armchair with a large mug of coffee in his hand, and looking more youthful as he let his whole body relax.

He'd pushed the grubby politics of the workshop out of his mind, and allowed his artistic spirit to take precedence as he looked round Jenny Heywood's living room. He was impressed. The walls were the pale gold of the edge of a sunset, and the two well-worn but comfortable sofas had been re-covered in a rich modern tapestry of bronze, gold and green.

A log fire glowed in the fireplace with its antique polished tiles and wooden mantel-shelf. There was a feeling of warmth and serene comfort, but the room was also enlivened with vivid touches of colour like the bright yellow of the tulips and daffodils in the earthenware jug in the centre of the dining table.

'I recognise that jug,' he said with a smile. 'It used to be in the kitchen at your Mum and Dad's.'

Jenny was delighted that he remembered. 'Yes, they didn't leave any valuable ornaments, but things like that are rich in memories.'

'Yes, they never had much money, but what they had they shared. I'll always be grateful for them taking me in, when my Mum died.'

She noticed the catch in his voice which he could never quite suppress when he talked about that tragedy, but Steve had never been someone who wanted pity, and moved on quickly.

'I still miss your Mum and Dad.'

'So do I.'

'They'd be pleased you'd got a nice home for yourself here,' he commented, and felt stupid, stumbling along with polite remarks like that, even though he meant them.

'Yes, I was glad to find it and move out of my other house.'

'I remember Lynda talking about your wanting to move after your husband died. It must have been a tough time.'

'I'd never have got through it without Lynda. I'm so glad she's come back.'

'So am I,' Steve agreed, unwillingly recalling how Carolyn had resented her Mother spending time with Jenny instead of being at home with her and their baby son.

'Anyway, that was a long time ago,' Jenny said, not wanting to talk about those terrible days. 'As you can see, this place needs some money spending on it now, but it's home.'

'I love the way you link colours, and how you add interest and humour with small details.'

She was surprised and delighted at his analysis.

'Thank you, it's what I love doing, designing rooms. But of course I've never had the money to do it properly.'

'You'd never guess. Rich people pay a lot of money for what you've got, it's called 'style'.

She laughed. 'Well, I hope you can help me create style on a budget when it comes to re-designing my kitchen. I can only do it now because Philip and I had a win on the pools a few weeks ago.'

'The football pools? Do you still bet on those?'

'Only because Philip insists we do them every

week. He's football mad.'

'Yeah, I see him at matches sometimes.' He smiled again as he shared a fond memory, 'I used to go with your Dad.'

'Yes.'

Thinking about those days, he looked at her and remembered how, as an eleven year old boy, he had dreamed about Jennifer Kelly who, at seventeen, had been too grown-up, and too beautiful, to pay him any attention.

As they chatted over their coffee, and shared tales of her parents and the community on Bennett Street, Steve found himself wanting to know all he could about Lynda's friend Jenny and her family.

Lynda had told him in confidence that, when her husband had been killed, it had been difficult for Jenny to mourn a man who had been so violent towards her.

At that time Steve had been fully occupied with his own problems as a new father with a low income, but he understood now how hard it must have been for Jenny to bring up her daughters on her own, especially, as Lynda had commented, with Ellen Heywood as a demanding mother-in-law.

As she talked, Jenny didn't indulge in self-pity, but Steve was astute enough to hear a great deal in what she didn't say, and when she had sometimes to turn away suddenly and stare into the flames, he understood.

He found himself watching this vulnerable woman with great concentration, and then with an awareness of the gentle curves of her body and the way the light moved through her chestnut brown hair. This awareness soon became a pleasure.

For so long Carolyn had been the only woman he had desired, and he was shocked to discover that

Jenny Heywood, too, could reach him in that way. He disciplined his body and shut out those thoughts, but it made him realise that perhaps he needed to do some hard thinking about the state of his marriage.

Jenny could only think about how wonderful he looked, leaning against the cushions, and looking so relaxed, so at home. She found that with Steve she could talk with ease about herself and the things she loved, and she was thrilled with the way he appreciated what she had achieved with little money.

When they eventually began to discuss the kitchen, it was Jenny's turn to be impressed. Steve immediately had radical suggestions to make about changing the layout of the kitchen, starting by moving the sink so that it was by the window.

'I've always wanted to do that,' she told him. 'But it will cost too much.'

'Not the way I'll do it,' Steve said quickly. He was always willing to sacrifice profit for satisfaction in his work, and for people he liked.

'I'll get John to do the wiring, so that will be at 'family and friends rate' too.

'Are you sure?'

'Yes. He's desperate to do some work instead of sitting at home like an old man.'

They went back into the living room and Steve placed a large square of paper on the table. Jenny stood at his side and watched as he began to sketch out a plan.

It was the first time she had been so close to him, and Jenny found it hard to concentrate on what he was saying as she watched his craftsman's hands deftly drawing the outlines of cupboards and work surfaces.

She kept being distracted by the movement of the

muscles in his strong shoulders and the way his hair fell softly on to his forehead. She could feel the warmth of him, and longed to hold him close. Jenny was certain now that she wanted this man, but she had to close her eyes against her desire because she knew she could not have him.

Steve was holding back his strong awareness of her, too, and keeping his voice calm and matter of fact, taking refuge in the practicalities of the task before him. Then came the moment when they both leaned forward together and brushed against each other. They both knew that they were close enough to kiss.

The seconds of stillness before they moved apart told them that they had both felt the power of the attraction between them, and when they straightened up and looked at each other, their eyes held for a moment, long enough to betray their need of what was forbidden to them.

The relaxed companionship was gone, and though they both tried, they couldn't recover the light tone of their conversations earlier that evening. Steve left soon after that, in haste to clear his head of the thoughts and feelings which were clamouring to be listened to.

Jenny watched Steve as he hurried down the steps to the road and got into his car. She closed the front door and leaned against it, fighting back tears, and trying to be determined that she would never again torment herself with dreams of Steve Sheldon.

In a softly lit, discreet corner of the lounge of the Weston Grange Hotel Carolyn leaned back against the burgundy velvet of the deep sofa and sighed with pleasure as Paul refilled her glass. She loved the way he took control of everything, quietly instructing the waiter to leave the bottle of Chablis on the table, making it clear that he should not disturb their intimacy again.

Paul was such good company, he listened with amusement, but also with understanding, as she told him about Ellen Heywood and the future they had imagined for her.

Paul made her laugh, admired her and told her how much he cared. Paul was the kind of man Ellen had predicted she would marry; a successful man, ambitious, charming and attractive. Ellen would have been so proud to see her marry a man like Paul Ferris. But she had married Steve.

Carolyn drank more wine, she wasn't going to think about Steve this evening. She just wanted to enjoy being with this man who made her feel cherished and protected. She saw him caressing her again with his eyes, and had to look away, drinking deeply and wishing she could give way to the warm sense of well-being the wine was coaxing into her body.

Paul glanced at his watch. There was still time to take her back to his flat. 'Perhaps we should be going soon.'

Carolyn was a little startled. 'I can stay a bit longer,' she said.

'Long enough to come home with me?'

'No,' she said, immediately flustered.

Paul looked at her with an air of regret.

'You can't offer me what I want, beautiful girl, can you?'

'What do you mean?' she whispered.

'You. All of you,' he murmured. 'I want you so much, but I can't have you.' He sighed. 'We have to accept, my darling, that this can't go on.'

He stood up and went to get their coats.

Carolyn felt the warmth fading from her cheeks as she stood up and waited for him to return. Helping her to put on her jacket, he brushed his lips against the nape of her neck and smiled as he felt her shiver of pleasure.

Confident now, he held her tightly against him as he escorted her across the room, and Carolyn knew that this was what she had always dreamed of, to walk beside a man whom people looked at with admiration, a man who was self assured, who could take care of her.

As they got into the car there was a heavy shower of rain. Paul started the engine but didn't put it into gear, he just sat and waited, giving Carolyn time to think. He watched her staring at the rivulets of water running down the windscreen.

Carolyn tried to accept that the affair was over, and tried to tell herself that she felt relieved. She would go back home to Steve and her children, and it would be as if nothing had happened.

Life would go on as usual, day after day, night after night. There would be no change, except that Paul would no longer make her feel special, he would no longer try to make love to her.

She felt cold and despondent, a drab little creature sinking back into a dark and dreary existence. Paul reached across and stroked her hair.

'What are we going to do, Carolyn?'

'I don't know,' she whispered.

He brushed his fingers through her hair, turning her face gently towards him. He kissed her and she was so thankful to have regained what she thought she had lost that she returned his kisses more passionately than she ever had before.

She was breathless with her need of him, and he kissed her and caressed her breasts until he felt her body yield towards him.

'There's still time for us to go to my place,' he murmured.

She pulled away, 'No. I can't. I told you.'

Paul wasn't disappointed, it was what he had expected, but he put on a show of anger.

'What's going on here, Carolyn? Is this some sort of game to torment me?'

'No.'

'Then come home with me.'

'It's too late. They'll be expecting me back. I'm sorry.'

Paul made sure his voice was icy cold.

'So am I. Are you making a fool of me? I thought you loved me, but now it looks as if you're just a bored wife looking for a good time.'

He could not have known what impact that phrase 'a good time' would have.

'No! No! I do love you,' she cried.

He leaned over and took hold of her again.

'Then show me. I want that commitment, Carolyn. O.K. not tonight, but I want you to find a way for us to be together. Will you promise me that, or do we end this now?'

Carolyn looked at this strong, passionate man who wanted her so much, and decided that it was true what she'd said, she did love him. 'I'll find a way,' she said softly, and kissed him again.

He had to be sure.

Before setting out this evening he had constructed a whole strategy in his head. He was quite enjoying the campaign, and had even begun to believe some of the things he'd said to Carolyn about wanting a more satisfying, more enduring relationship.

Paul Ferris could get sex any time he wanted, there were plenty of women who would welcome him into their bed, but Carolyn was a bit special.

'Soon. Promise?' he persisted.

'Yes.' Calm and certain now, she looked at him, and they both knew that she would keep her promise.

Paul Ferris drove back triumphantly at speed through the centre of Milfield, and the car braking hard at the traffic lights caught the eye of a group of women teetering drunkenly on the kerb.

He felt Carolyn gazing at him adoringly and reached across to squeeze her hand. He didn't see the women, but before he drove off they saw him, and his passenger.

'Was that who I think it was?' squealed Jackie Pearson, still holding her skirt up on her hip as she pretended to hitch a lift.

Julia smiled slowly, 'Yes.'

Jackie leered back at her, gaping in amazement, 'Bloody hell!'

CHAPTER TWENTY-FIVE

Lynda hadn't slept very well, but had done a lot of thinking as she lay awake, and by the time she went downstairs on Thursday morning she was feeling calmer.

'Do you want a cuppa, Jean?'

'I haven't got time, I'll miss my bus,' Jean said irritably, as she finished packing her sandwiches.

'You've plenty of time. Are you annoyed with me because I took the hire car back too soon?'

'No. I managed all right on the bus before you came back.'

'Yeah, but it's nice to have a lift. Normal service will be resumed tomorrow,' Lynda quipped. 'I'm picking my car up but not till this evening. Steve's insisted on taking me to get it. I think he wants a chance to talk to me.'

'Oh? Nice to be popular,' was Jean's peevish comment.

Lynda stepped in front of her. 'What's the matter, Jean?'

'What do you think?'

Jean pushed past her and stuffed her sandwiches and umbrella into her shopping bag with more force than was necessary. Then she stood and glared at Lynda.

'When are you going to tell me what John said when you saw him?'

'There wasn't time last night, with you going out babysitting my grandchildren.'

'Oh, still mad about that, are you? It wasn't my fault Carolyn asked me and not you.'

'I know. I'm sorry. Have you got time to talk now?'

'Not really, but I need to know.'

'He was so glad to see me, I could have cried. I felt so sorry for him.'

Jean drew a sharp breath. 'Feeling sorry for him isn't the same as loving him.'

'No.'

'Do you love him?'

Lynda took a moment to control her feelings, and then said slowly, 'I can't love any man now. I gave Tom Meredith all my love, my heart and soul. And that hasn't changed, even though he's not here.'

'Oh, Lynda.' Jean put her arm round her friend. 'I'm so sorry, love.'

Lynda steadied her voice, 'He was so special. And he helped me to become a better person.' She tried to laugh, 'Still a work in progress though, that!'

Jean felt it was wrong to persist, but she had to know.

'So you can't love John?'

'No,' Lynda replied gently, 'but you do, don't you?'

'I always have. Like he's always loved you.'

'Wanted me. It's not the same thing, I've learned that.'

'He won't want me, now that you're back.'

'Don't say that, Jean. He loves you, I'm sure. He just doesn't realize it. And he can't have me, but he wasn't ready to accept that yesterday. And I don't want to tell him yet, it would be cruel, the way he feels about himself at the moment.'

'So you are going to divorce him?'

Lynda looked away, aware that what she was going to say wasn't a straightforward answer.

'I'm going to make an appointment with Philip Lawson today.'

Alice Smith was bored that morning, and so had decided that it was time to enjoy another part of the drama of the return of Lynda Collins. Although she was Jean Haworth's cousin, they were not at all close, partly because Alice was so much older, but also because Alice's parents had looked down on 'the rough end of the family' to which Jean had belonged.

When she walked into the dress shop Alice found Jean on her hands and knees, brushing the carpet underneath the racks of dresses.

'Oh, dear. That looks like hard work. Can't you get Frances Horton to get you a Hoover?'

Jean straightened up, and was annoyed to see Alice's pitying expression.

'Some of our fabrics are very fine,' she explained in a proud and patronising tone, 'you can't risk them being caught in a Hoover.'

'Oh, of course.'

'Did you want something, Alice?'

'A dress, actually.'

Alice had always had a nimble talent in the art of inventing a pretext, but the real reason for her visit, the prospect of a little Schadenfreude, soon became apparent.

'I was so sorry to hear about you and John,' she simpered.

Jean, knowing Alice only too well, was immediately alert to her mission.

'What about me and John?'

'Lynda coming back.' Alice watched for Jean's reaction, then added, with a sigh. 'Such a pity, it's a long time since I've been to a wedding, I was hoping

I'd be going to yours soon. I was looking forward to it.'

Ignoring that, Jean set aside the dustpan and brush and asked briskly, 'What kind of a dress, Alice?'

'Quite a smart one. Ellen Heywood's begging me to accompany her to the new season of concerts.'

'Oh, really?. Well, we have a lovely selection. We might find one suitable for you, though some of them are rather expensive.'

'Of course, I'd hoped that I'd be buying this dress to be worn at your wedding,' Alice twittered. 'I am sorry, Jean,' she repeated, now in a voice heavy with sorrow and empathy, 'I know what it's like to be jilted. You have my full sympathy.'

Jean smiled, hugging to herself the secret of what Lynda had told her this morning.

'Thank you, Alice,' she responded calmly, 'but your condolences might be a little premature.'

Alice tried to work out this puzzle as Jean flicked purposefully through the dresses in the 'petite' section. With a glance of professional assessment, she pondered elaborately, 'Now let's see if we can find something that would be suitable for a concert as well as a wedding.'

Alice enjoyed the charade of trying on dresses, and coming out of the cubicle several times to twirl for Jean's approval. She kept pausing to ask probing questions, but Jean would give no answers, so Alice left the shop, without answers, and without a new dress, of course.

Jean was glad to close the door behind Alice, and even more glad that she was having lunch with Carolyn, who last night had invited her to the Vienna Cafe.

This was a new addition to the cafés in Milfield,

and its owners had taken care to create a more genteel ambiance, to contrast with the other more chip oriented establishments in town. Carolyn and Jean loved the café, with its deep red carpet, brocade curtains and elegant little tables and chairs.

The distant echo of Chris de Burgh worshipping his 'Lady in Red' accompanied the waitress performing the ceremony of arranging the china cups, and noting down their order.

As soon as she'd gone Carolyn apologised that it had been so long since she'd had lunch with Jean.

'It's very kind of you to ask me, Carolyn. I know you're always very busy at work, I expect you hardly get time to have lunch most days.'

'It is a very demanding job,' Carolyn agreed, guiltily aware that Paul Ferris was usually the reason her lunch-hour was occupied. She disciplined herself to erase Paul from her thoughts for a while.

'But I hear you're looking for something even more demanding.'

'Yes, I've been short-listed for a job at head office. I didn't think I'd told anyone about it, except Steve. I don't want Dad to know.'

'I won't say anything,' Jean assured her. 'I'm sorry if I'm not supposed to know about it, but Steve mentioned it when he came round the other night.'

'Oh, yes. To see her.'

Jean noticed the scornful tone, and didn't like it. 'Your Mother.'

Carolyn couldn't suppress her anger.

'I don't know why she's come back.'

'It's her home. And you're her family. You can't blame her for wanting to come home.'

'It's too late for that.'

'She's changed, Carolyn, she's learned a lot. Did you not see she's a different woman now?'

218

'Wearing smart clothes and less make-up, doesn't mean she's changed.'

Jean shook her head, 'I think she has, in a lot of ways. For a start, she doesn't lose her temper like she used to.'

Carolyn winced as she remembered their confrontation in the street.

'She does with me.'

Jean wondered if she should ever have started this conversation, but she felt she owed Lynda this support, so she persevered.

'Give her a chance, Carolyn. Your Mother's not perfect, nobody is, but she's good-hearted. She had a tough time in her younger days, especially from Sheila Stanworth when she married your Dad.'

'On the rebound!'

'Yes, all right, on the rebound. But also to please her Grandma. Madge Collins wanted to see her granddaughter married before she died. Lynda was only seventeen and Madge didn't want her to be on her own. They had nothing after The Black Bull burned down, Madge was frightened for her, and Lynda was scared too, I think.'

'She didn't love my Dad, though.'

'She did, but lots of things got in the way,' Jean tried to give a little laugh, 'including you. You took over your Daddy, you know, when you arrived.'

Carolyn didn't respond, but a childhood memory pushed its way into her mind. A Sunday walk, running ahead and then turning round to see her Dad with his arm round her Mother's waist. Another vivid image of struggling to clamber up and push in between her parents as they sat on a bench, and being annoyed as they kissed over her head.

She was glad the waitress arrived with the silver teapot and hot water jug, giving her chance to move

219

the conversation away from sympathy for her Mother.

Jean, who knew that she wasn't particularly gifted in persuasion, watched Carolyn, and tried again.

'She was a wonderful friend, she looked after me.'

'And married the man you were in love with,' retorted Carolyn sarcastically.

Jean smiled ruefully. 'Yes, it took me a long time to forgive her for that. And now it's her turn to forgive me, for trying to steal her husband.'

Carolyn was indignant now.

'She'd left him, she didn't want him any more.'

'No,' Jean conceded, 'but I didn't know that at the time.'

She paused as the waitress brought their asparagus quiche and salad, and then continued her mission of persuasion.

'I've always been able to talk to Lynda about anything,' she said fondly. 'I've missed her.' She gave Carolyn a perceptive look. 'And so have you.'

Carolyn's heart was quite still for a moment as she acknowledged to herself that this was true, but she felt there was no justice in that, so she carried on her campaign.

'And what's going to happen now? Is she going to try to take my Dad away from you again?'

Jean didn't want to answer that and so concentrated on her lunch, but Carolyn continued to make the case against her Mother.

'Don't worry about her, Jean, she'll have found somebody else, anyway.'

Without thinking, Jean confirmed Carolyn's assumption.

'Yes, she did, but he died.'

She knew she'd already said more than she should, but the old devil of envy nudged her again, 'And left her a lot of money.'

Carolyn relaxed, now she could feel vindicated once more.

'Good, then she'll be able to move on somewhere else.'

'She doesn't want to.'

Carolyn was sure she could win now.

'My Dad won't want her back when he finds out she's been with another man.'

'She's already told him. She went to see him yesterday.' Jean paused, it was painful to have to say this. 'And he does want her back.'

'He can't!'

'Don't worry, it's not going to happen.'

'She's going to divorce him?'

'I think so. But don't say anything, Carolyn. Promise. Give her time to break it to him, when she's ready.'

Carolyn smiled at last.

'I'm so glad. He'll be much happier with you, Aunty Jean. You look after him a lot better than she ever did.'

'Don't be hard on her,' Jean pleaded. 'She needs you, Carolyn, she needs her family. You have to forgive her.'

Carolyn sat back in her chair and scowled. 'You're as bad as Steve.'

'What do you mean?'

'He thinks she's wonderful. He keeps phoning her, he talks to her more than me at the moment.'

'You should talk to her as well.'

Carolyn was beginning to get annoyed now.

'Whose side are you on, Aunty Jean?'

Jean put her knife and fork neatly in the centre of her empty plate, and said wearily, 'It's not a case of 'sides', Carolyn. It's a question of people being happy.'

On her way back to the office Carolyn thought hard about everything Jean had said, but once she returned to her desk there were other things which monopolised her attention, her work of course, but mainly Paul.

She'd been waiting all morning for an opportunity to tell him of her plan, but they had both been busy with calls from clients, and then after lunch their boss, Gerald Critchley, called Paul into his office.

Julia Ingham, always alert to male complicity, had noticed a little excitement in Paul Ferris, and she was curious about a document he had left on his desk in his hurry to obey Critchley's summons.

Pulling her tight sweater down over her well-supported attributes, Julia walked over to Paul's desk, picked up a stapler, and then stood there for a moment as she read the document which had caught her eye. Returning to her own desk she spoke to her wispy-haired junior colleague, Michelle Marsden, making sure that Carolyn would also hear what she said.

'I didn't know there was an executive account manager job coming up at head office, did you?'

Michelle, a clever and eager girl, was immediately attentive.

'No. Where have you heard that?'

'I've just seen the job description on Paul's desk.'

Carolyn glared at her, but Julia, unrepentant, just stared back.

'I just happened to glance at it, Carolyn. Looks like he's applying. It'd be a helluva step-up for him.'

Michelle, who liked to try to emulate Julia's boldness, asked, 'That's not the job you're after, is it, Carolyn?'

'No. It's a lower grade, senior account manager, I've applied for.'

'You ought to have been told about this one Paul's fancying,' Julia commented, as if this were a matter of female solidarity, but in truth she was more motivated by a need for revenge. 'You're much better qualified than he is.'

Carolyn wasn't sure that was the case, but she did wonder why Paul hadn't told her about it.

'When's your interview for the other one?' Julia enquired.

'A week next Wednesday.'

Julia raised her eyebrows, and speculated archly, 'You could both end up in Leeds together. That'd be nice, wouldn't it?'

Carolyn bent her head to signal that she, unlike them, was getting on with her work, but she didn't miss seeing Julia wink at Michelle, who responded with a smirk.

Carolyn wasn't sure how she felt about Paul also applying for a job at head office, but had to forget about it as she needed to concentrate on completing a resources forecast for one of her clients.

Later that afternoon Paul gave her a discreet nod as he left the office and headed for the 'oasis'. She waited a few minutes and then followed him.

The 'oasis' was what Julia had nicknamed the area at the top of the stairs where potted palms stood guard by the cloakroom doors and coffee machine, and provided the privacy Carolyn needed for her talk with Paul.

He was at first a little wary when she told him Julia had noticed the document about the post at head office. He relaxed, however, when he realised that Carolyn's thoughts were focused on the possibility of their both moving to Leeds.

'Why didn't you tell me you were applying for a job at head office?'

'I've only just decided really,' he lied.

'Because of me?'

'Could be,' he said teasingly. 'I had a chat with Critchley about my future and he told me about the job.'

'Do you think they'd promote both of us?'

'I don't see why not. I think you're in with a good chance for the one you've applied for. Apparently you made quite an impression on the chief executive when he came over.'

Carolyn was delighted. 'Did I?'

Paul, sliding his hands appreciatively over her body, murmured, 'Well, you would, wouldn't you?'

Carolyn's thoughts were still focused on the news of an unexpected possibility. 'So, we could both be going to Leeds.'

He pulled her close and kissed her fiercely on the mouth.

'Isn't that what you want, you and me together?' He stroked her and kissed her again, giving her no choice but to respond to his touch.

'Now, have you made 'a cunning plan' yet?' he asked with a husky laugh. Then his voice deepened sexily, 'We can't wait much longer, can we?'

'No,' Carolyn whispered, 'And yes, I have a plan. I'm telling him I'm going to a special concert in Manchester, the Saturday of the Bank Holiday weekend. We'll have the afternoon as well as the evening.'

Paul laughed softly, 'Wonderful.'

He pushed her gently but firmly against the wall and, in excited anticipation, he kissed her and ran his hands over her body. Then a door opened and they hastily moved apart as Julia approached them.

'Don't mind me,' she said sourly, as she walked past on the pretext of a visit to the Ladies. 'But I'd be careful if I were you, Carolyn. He's a heart-breaker. Aren't you, Paul?' she drawled as she disappeared through the cloakroom door, pausing only to give a wintry smile of experience to underwrite her claim.

CHAPTER TWENTY-SIX

The workshop was silent apart from the swish of the hard bristled broom Steve was using to sweep up a small pile of wood-shavings Matthew had overlooked. The rest of the workers had gone home but Gary had waited to have a private conversation.

'So what do you reckon, Steve? Has Randerson got what they call 'a temporary cash-flow problem' or what?'

Steve put the broom away in the cupboard. 'Like I said, I think he's holding on to money to make the books look good to a possible buyer.'

Gary lit a cigarette.

'Or he's going bankrupt. Whatever's he's up to, you can bet it won't be good news for us.'

'No,' Steve said with a heavy sigh. He usually kept family business to himself, but today he was worried enough to need to talk, so he added, 'It might be for Carolyn, though.'

'What do you mean?'

'If I end up without a job and she gets this promotion, I'll have to do what she wants and move to Leeds.'

Gary was silent for a moment, but keeping quiet had never been one of his strong points.

'Is it true her boss is moving to head office as well?'

'I don't know. Why?'

'I just wondered.' Gary hesitated, but decided Steve needed to know. 'Jackie says she saw Carolyn with Ferris in his car last night.'

'She couldn't have,' Steve said firmly, but even as he spoke the words he wondered if that was true.

'She's absolutely sure it was her, and so is Julia Ingham, who was with Jackie. She works with Ferris as well.'

'I know she does. And I also know she practically threw herself at Ferris when she got divorced. She just wants to make trouble for him because he dumped her.'

'Was Carolyn out last night?'

'Yes, at Ellen Heywood's.'

'Oh, perhaps Ferris was giving her a lift home then, if you had the car.'

'That's not very likely. I told you, it wouldn't have been Carolyn Jackie saw.'

'Are you sure?'

'Yes, I'm bloody sure,' Steve declared, clenching his fists. 'Now go home and tell Jackie to stop spreading dirty rumours about my wife!'

Gary had never seen Steve so angry.

'O.K. O.K. Cool it, Steve. I just thought you should know. I didn't mean any harm.'

Steve, grim-faced, turned his back on him, and walked out into the yard. His mind was so blurred with fury that he stared blankly at Lynda as she walked towards him, her stiletto heels striking the well-worn stone flags.

Lynda hadn't wanted to come to Steve's place of work, but she couldn't explain why not when he'd suggested she meet him there. He'd been so keen to take her to pick up her car, and to have the chance of a confidential chat.

'Hiya, Steve. I'm not late, am I?'

'No.'

Lynda noticed Gary walking past, and greeted him, but he didn't seem to see her.

'That is Gary Pearson, isn't it?'

'Yeah. The car's over there.'

As they walked across the yard Tony Randerson came out of the office, carrying the keys to lock up the workshop, a job he usually delegated to Steve or Josie. He'd surprised his P.A. by encouraging her to go home early, and he'd then spent an hour going through the files to check that he could manage to substantiate the claims he was going to make to his buyer, a golf club acquaintance, Neil Spencer.

Randerson was smiling as he strode jauntily across the yard. He was musing to himself that Spencer might have inherited most of his father's money, but not, it seemed, much of his business acumen. He stopped smiling when he saw Lynda.

Unable to hold back his instinct, he marvelled at how little she had changed, the same blonde hair, the same eye-catching figure, albeit a little more generous than he remembered. Then she turned towards him and he saw at first a flicker of fear in her eyes, but it was soon replaced with a look of hatred.

It must be almost twenty years ago, he thought to himself, but she obviously hadn't forgotten what he'd done to her that night.

Lynda began to hurry, almost running towards Steve's car. Steve was surprised by her change of pace, but let her go on ahead as his employer came towards him.

'Goodnight, Mr Randerson.'

His words were ignored as he saw his boss staring at Lynda, who had her back turned and was gripping the handle of the car door as if desperate to get in. Steve caught up with her.

'What's up?'

'Nothing. We're running a bit late, that's all.'

She quickly got into the car and drew her coat

closer around her, feeling the chill of a bad experience. As they drove out of the yard they both saw that Randerson was still standing by the door of the workshop, weighing his bunch of keys in his hand. As they drove past him, Steve noticed that Lynda, no longer in a panic, stared at him, with cat-like malevolence.

'Do you know Randerson?'

There was deep bitterness in her voice. 'I met him once, unfortunately.'

'John doesn't like him either.'

'No.'

'Neither do I, but it's a job. For how much longer, though, is anybody's guess.'

'You still think he's going to sell up?'

'If he can get the money he needs to get a share of Nigel Kavanagh's business.'

'But has Randerson got a buyer lined up? It doesn't look much of an investment prospect to me,' Lynda commented, feeling the business knowledge she'd acquired starting to click over in her brain.

'I'd buy it, if I had the money,' Steve said with a sigh.

'Would you?'

'Oh, yes. It could be a fantastic business with investment and the right ideas and designs.'

'Like yours, you mean?'

'Yeah.'

'We'll have to have a talk about that, Steve, but perhaps not this evening. I've promised to take Jean for a run-out in the new car.'

Steve looked at his watch. 'Oh, hell, and I've promised to pick Carolyn up from work. We'll have to go there first. Do you mind?'

'No, but she won't like it. She won't like what I'm going to ask you to do, either.'

'What's that?'

'Come with me when I take John for a night out on Saturday.'

'A night out?'

'Just a few drinks, a bit of life. It's what he needs, Steve, he's turning into a candidate for an old people's home, stuck in that flat the way he is.'

'I know. But a boozy night out? Carolyn won't allow that.'

'Carolyn doesn't need to know. Tell her you're just going to the pub with some mates. That won't be a lie. Come on, Steve, come with me. It'd be just like old times, the three of us out together.'

'Yeah,' he laughed dryly, 'and remember what that used to lead to.'

'All right. You don't have to come.'

'I think I do, if only to keep an eye on you.'

Lynda reached across and gave him a smacking kiss.'

'Get off, I'm driving,' he said, laughing.

'Oh, it'll be great,' Lynda declared. 'And Jenny Heywood says she'll come as well, to make up the foursome if Carolyn can't come.'

Steve's hands tensed on the steering wheel. He didn't know whether that was good news, but he couldn't object to the idea without causing Lynda to wonder what the problem was.

Instead he asked, 'When did you speak to Jenny about it?'

'I called in at Lawsons' and saw her,' Lynda told him, and then, not wanting to give the real reason she'd gone to the solicitor's, added, 'She's told me her Mum and Dad's old house is coming on the market.'

'Oh, does she want to move back there?'

'No, she couldn't afford it. But I can.'

'Do you want to buy it?

'I fancy taking a look, once it's up for sale.'

They pulled into the AFS car park and waited for Carolyn. Steve knew that Lynda was right, she would not be pleased to have her Mother as a travelling companion on her way home from work. 'But,' Steve said to himself, 'she'd just have to put up with it.' He wasn't in the mood for taking any hassle from Carolyn, he was still shaken by what Gary had told him.

He'd refused to believe it, there was no way Carolyn would volunteer to be Ferris's next victim. But doubt had taken hold when Gary had asked him quietly if he was sure. Steve couldn't get it out of his mind, or get rid of the fear which had tightened in his chest since that moment.

In the empty office Paul Ferris was holding Carolyn in his arms when they heard the sound of the car horn.

'That'll be Steve,' Carolyn said as she hastily pulled away from him. Paul picked up her coat and clasped her against him as he helped her put it on. He followed her out of the office.

'No,' she protested. 'Wait till I've gone.'

'Why? Come on, Carolyn, let's live dangerously.'

As they stepped through the exit into the car park Ferris held the door open only a little way, thus forcing Carolyn's body to brush against his on her way out.

Lynda had intended to be tactful and move into the back seat, but as she opened the door she was distracted for a minute when she saw that Carolyn wasn't leaving the office alone. She glanced at Steve, who had also observed the body language between the two of them.

As Steve had expected, Carolyn was livid when she

saw that her Mother was with him. She slammed the door as she got into the front seat. She'd seen the sharp look Lynda gave her, and knew that her Mother had noticed Paul's intimacy; she always had been quick to recognise signs of sexual attraction.

Direct as ever, Lynda said, 'That was your boss, was it?'

'Yes,' Carolyn said, and looked straight ahead, making it clear she didn't want to talk to the unwelcome passenger. Lynda still decided to pursue the conversation.

'Good looking fella.'

Carolyn ignored the comment, but Lynda wasn't going to let her get away with that, and challenged her daughter's silence.

'Don't tell me you haven't noticed. Is he married?'

'No,' Carolyn replied tersely, noticing Steve's sideways glance and wishing her Mother would shut up. Lynda, however, was worried, and wanted her daughter to know, so she carried on, and leaned forward to scrutinise Carolyn's face for a reaction.

'No, he didn't look the sort to be married.'

Carolyn decided this would end now, and turned away to silently stare out of the window for the rest of the journey.

CHAPTER TWENTY-SEVEN

At ten o'clock Lynda and Jenny giggled as they snuggled up to John in the back seat of a taxi. Steve, in the front, asked the driver to take them to The Madison.

'Where's that?' Lynda asked him.

'Not far. It's the only pub I know of with a dance floor, and you said you wanted to dance, didn't you?'

'Oh, yes,' squealed Lynda, 'got to have a dance, haven't we, Johnny Boy?'

'Yes, definitely,' John said, with the strength of conviction endowed by several pints of beer. He beamed at Lynda and his eyes sparkled at the thought of dancing with her, holding her in his arms again.

The pleasure was replaced by horror when he and Lynda stood outside The Madison and realised where they were. They stood there together, not moving, just staring up at the front of the building, now decorated with neon stars and American Flags, but still very recognisable to them as what had been, in the 1970s and '80s, a club called the Star and Garter.

Steve had gone ahead to pay the entrance fee, and Jenny was following him, till she looked back and saw the couple standing there.

'Come on, you two,' she urged.

'No, we've changed our minds,' Lynda said. 'we're ready for home now, aren't we, John?'

Jenny, who had been thrilled at the thought of dancing with Steve, was very disappointed. 'Oh, are you sure? I thought we were all looking forward to a dance.'

John realised what he, too, would be missing, and hesitated.

'It's changed a lot, it might be all right,' he said quietly to Lynda. 'And it was a long time ago.'

'I'll go and see if Steve's already paid for the tickets,' Jenny said and left them standing there looking at each other.

'I can't go in there,' Lynda whispered. 'I haven't been in there since that night, and I don't want to be reminded of being here, with him. I saw the bastard the other day when I went to meet Steve, and it was horrible. It made my flesh creep.'

'You need to forget it, Lynda,' John said quietly, 'and so do I.'

He looked at her with so much anguish in his eyes that she took hold of his hand.

'Don't get upset, John. It wasn't your fault.'

'I should have forgiven you, and I should have forgotten about it.'

Lynda felt a tear making its way down her cheek. 'I never have,' she said, 'and I don't think I ever will.'

'Perhaps we should go in, then,' John suggested, 'lay a few ghosts.'

Lynda drew her coat tightly round her body, and remembered another coat, the one she'd worn that night, and which had been one of the things that had made her act so recklessly. Steve came hurrying towards them, waving some tickets.

'What's up? Jenny says you don't want to come. I've bought the tickets. It's great in there, they're playing sixties music, you'll love it.'

John made the decision for his wife.

'O.K. we'll come in for a dance,' he said, turning to Lynda and failing, as he had so many times in their married life, to understand what she was feeling.

He and Steve walked either side of her as they

entered the main room. Round the sides were tables with small red-shaded lamps in the centre, and a glitter ball, turning slowly, was sending flashes of light across the dance floor. Jenny had found a table, and Lynda, released from the support of John and Steve's arms, sank down on to a chair and felt sick.

John insisted it was his turn to buy the drinks and headed towards the crowded bar. Steve gave in to the longing in Jenny's eyes, and asked her and Lynda to dance. Lynda shook her head but Jenny sprang up and moved quickly to join the other dancers.

It wasn't until much later, when the DJ played one of John's favourite rock and roll records, Gene Vincent's 'Be-Bop-A-Lula', that Lynda also gave in and walked towards the dance floor with her husband.

'I always used to feel sexy, dancing to this,' John grinned as they began to jive slowly.

Lynda who'd had a couple of vodka and blackcurrants to block out the bad memories for a while, laughed. 'You always looked sexy, too, it used to frighten me to death.'

'Doesn't frighten you now, does it?'

'No. Very little frightens me now. I've learned not to be scared, most of the time.'

'You shouldn't ever be scared, I'll look after you, Lynda,' John assured her, his words slurring together.

He pulled her close, leaning on her a little for support as he felt the impact of too many pints of beer. 'I'm having a wonderful time tonight, Lynda, and it's all thanks to you.'

'And Steve,' she nodded towards her son-in-law who was dancing with Jenny.

'They're having a good time too,' John said, smiling benignly at the couple who seemed unaware of them, or anyone else on the dance floor.

To Jenny, dancing with Steve was one of her dreams turning into reality, and she didn't want it to end, but as the track finished she saw her partner was looking at his watch.

'What time's Carolyn expecting you home?' Jenny asked, reluctantly speaking his wife's name.

'I didn't say when I'd be back. She doesn't know I'm out with John, nobody does, except Jean, and Lynda persuaded her to keep quiet about it.'

'Not to tell Carolyn, you mean.'

'Yeah. I hope she doesn't wait up for me.'

Steve was annoyed with himself for sounding as if he were afraid of his wife, but he knew that, in a way, he was. He was afraid she had stopped loving him.

How else could he explain why Carolyn behaved the way she did, making him feel as if he and his opinions were unimportant? It had been so relaxing tonight, to be with people who told him he was a great guy, who laughed at his jokes, who loved him.

The thought made him look at Jenny, standing so close to him and he found himself wondering if she could love him. There was a tenderness in her eyes which filled him with pleasure. He knew he'd had enough to drink to make him reckless, but tonight he felt like being admired for once, and loved.

As the music changed to a slow, romantic ballad, he drew Jenny closer, and she knew that this might be her only chance to hold him tight. She put her arms round his neck, placing her cheek on his. Steve closed his eyes and let himself drown in the scent and silky softness of her hair.

They weren't aware that Lynda and John were dancing not far away from them. Lynda had her arms round John, but her eyes weren't closed. She saw Steve and Jenny holding each other close and moving very slowly to the music. For a moment she wondered if she'd done the right thing, inviting Jenny, but immediately shrugged away any worrying thoughts. They'd all had a lot to drink, they were just having a good time, where was the harm in that?

Carolyn knew exactly where the harm was, and told them so, as soon as they'd staggered into her living room and dumped John on the sofa where he immediately passed out.

Lynda was finding it hard to stop herself swaying about as she tried to reassure Carolyn that John was alright. They'd brought him back to Beechwood Avenue because Steve wanted to make sure he was all right. He could see that John certainly wasn't in a fit state to be left in his flat and cared for by Lynda, as she had suggested.

Lynda, sobering up a little, was glad they'd got the taxi driver to drop Jenny off first; she could see from the look on Carolyn's face that this was going to be the kind of row that should be kept within four walls and the family.

Carolyn knelt beside her Father and shouted at Steve to phone for the doctor, and then turned to yell at Lynda.

'What the hell have you been doing?'

Steve, as he'd always done in the past, stepped forward to defend his mother-in-law.

'John wanted a night out, so we took him for a few drinks.'

Carolyn began to panic.

'He's not breathing properly. Phone for an ambulance, Steve!'

He didn't obey. 'No, there's no need for that.'

Lynda, holding on to the back of the sofa, waved an arm discouragingly. 'He's only asleep. I told you,

Steve, we should have taken him back to his flat. I'd have stayed and looked after him.'

'You're not capable of looking after anybody,' her daughter snapped at her. 'Can't you see what you've done to him?'

'Given him a good time, that's all,' Lynda declared. 'It was what he needed.'

'If you won't phone the doctor, Steve, I will!' Carolyn said, glaring at her husband, but John stirred and pushed himself up on one elbow.

'No, don't. I'm all right. I just need a drink of water.'

Steve, greatly relieved, put down the phone and walked unsteadily into the kitchen to get the water. As soon as he'd left the room he heard Carolyn shout at her Mother.

'Get out, you. Get out of my sight! Just go home, will you!'

The half bottle of brandy which Lynda had been sucking at in the taxi delivered a strong surge of passion and defiance.

'I am home!' she cried.

Carolyn, taking the water from Steve and helping John to drink it, snapped out an order.

'Phone for a taxi, Steve. I want her out of here. Now!'

Steve saw Lynda nod to him, and started hunting in the phone book for a taxi firm. John, looking up at Lynda, expressed his disgust at the taste of the water, and he and his partner in trouble began giggling.

'We had a good time, didn't we, Johnny boy?' Lynda chuckled.

That phrase again, it had echoed in that room throughout Carolyn's teenage years, and hearing her Mother use it again unleashed some of the fury which had seethed for so long in Carolyn's heart.

'A good time!' she almost spat out the words. 'That's all you think about, all you've ever thought about.'

Lynda stood up tall and spoke to her daughter with disdain.

'You haven't changed, have you? Little Miss Killjoy.'

She smiled down at John.

'Your Dad's all right. He's enjoyed himself, haven't you, love?'

John grinned in agreement, and Lynda felt encouraged enough to let loose some home truths.

'He's back in the land of the living, Carolyn. Where he belongs, not shut away in that pokey little flat you thought was a good idea.'

John joined in now, his voice slow and heavy with drink as he said sombrely, 'No room to swing a bloody cat.'

Again he and Lynda giggled together like naughty children, and Carolyn couldn't stand it. She turned on Lynda, taking her arm in a steely grip.

'This is what you've come back for, isn't it, to cause trouble.'

John, trying to prop himself up against the sofa cushions, proudly contradicted this.

'No, she's come back to be with me.'

Carolyn stared at him, and then at her Mother, and there was a look of triumph in her eyes now.

'No, she hasn't,' she announced. 'She's come back for a divorce. She's already been to the solicitor's, she's divorcing you, Dad.'

'Over my dead body!' John shouted as he struggled to sit fully upright, and to speak out as he'd never done before.

'Shut up, Carolyn,' he began, but the rest of the magnificent speech, which he'd been trying to put together for the last few days, dissolved into the alcoholic haze, and he could only add firmly 'She's my wife.'

Carolyn's response was quick and confident. She dragged Lynda to face John.

'The wife who walked out on you. The wife who went with other men!'

'No! You've got it all wrong,' John groaned. 'It wasn't your Mother's fault, any of it.'

But he couldn't continue, the effort was too much and he passed out again. Lynda looked down at the man who, after all those years, had at last tried to defend her, and she wanted to weep, but she wasn't given the chance.

Carolyn glared at her again, the full force of her contempt blazing in her eyes. Then she turned Steve who was watching the two women in stunned silence.

'Is the taxi coming?' Carolyn demanded.

'Yeah. It'll be here in about five minutes,' Steve replied, finding that his voice was hoarse. Carolyn tightened her grip on Lynda's arm and began to propel her towards the door.

'Right. You can wait for it outside, on the street, where you belong!'

Lynda had been mesmerised by the look of hatred in her daughter's eyes, but now she was back, fighting her again, like in the old days.

'Get your hands off me!' she shouted, shaking herself free, and storming out of the house.

Carolyn smiled in triumph at Steve, but was shocked to see him staring at her as if she were an unwelcome stranger. He turned away, and walked out of the house to stand on the street at Lynda's side.

CHAPTER TWENTY-EIGHT

The following Tuesday was a very good day for Paul Ferris, it was the day his boss, Gerald Critchley, invited him into his office for a coffee. Paul accepted the offer eagerly, for he knew from past experience that such a tête à tête would bring him some advantage.

Critchley, a sixty year old man, was small in both mind and body, and had a bald and slightly bulging head. He preferred old hierarchies to new equalities, and waited until Michelle had completed her duties as waitress before he began this private conversation.

'As you know, Paul, I forwarded your application to head office, with a very favourable reference.'

'Yes. Thank you, Mr Critchley.'

Critchley clasped his hands in front of him, and peered over the top of his glasses as he continued with the purpose of the meeting.

'However, I think you should know that I have, just this morning, been given some confidential information. Apparently, the Chief Executive has now decided that there is to be a re-structuring, which will result in a layer of management being removed, namely that of executive account managers.'

Paul was annoyed he'd wasted his time, so there was a peevish note in his voice as he said, 'Oh, so the job I've just applied for will no longer exist.'

'I'm afraid that is the case.'

Here Critchley paused and leaned back in his chair, his fingers forming a steeple on which he rested his thin lips.

'There will, however, still be at least one senior account manager post available.'

He smiled to himself as he watched the young man he had recruited lean towards him, like a pet anxious not to miss any treat his master was ready to hold out.

Paul took care to keep his voice steady.

'Would it now be possible, may I ask, for me to apply for one of those positions?'

'Undoubtedly. But you will have competition. As you know, one of your colleagues has already applied and,' he paused, to consider how best to signal his partisan support, 'and, somewhat surprisingly in my view, has been short-listed.'

It vexed Critchley to see how young women like Carolyn Sheldon were allowed career paths unheard of when he was an ambitious young man. His progress to the post of manager of the Milfield office had been slow, and never a foregone conclusion. Critchley had known since his early forties that his career would be limited to small town rather than head office opportunities.

He had played golf on several occasions with Paul and his father, a friend of his, and had decided that, as he could never be king, he would at least have the satisfaction of being a king-maker. And no-one was going to get in the way of that ambition, especially a woman with blonde hair and a shapely figure. Gerald Critchley had never denied himself the pleasure of looking at attractive young women, but he had learned many years ago that there was no advantage for him in furthering the career of such female employees.

He knew Paul's reputation as a ladies' man but he hoped that such pursuits would take second place where his career prospects were involved. He was not to be disappointed.

'Would you, therefore, like me to arrange the transfer of your application from the vacancy which no longer exists to the one which is still on offer, that of senior account manager?'

With no hesitation, Paul replied, 'I would be extremely grateful if you could do that, Sir.'

Critchley, enjoying playing benefactor, was prepared to extend his male patronage to the limits of discretion. He allowed himself the drama of a small silence before answering.

'I can, and I shall. And I assume that, if it were possible at this late stage, you would also like your name to be added to the shortlist.'

Paul again leaned forward eagerly. He was in no doubt who could achieve that possibility for him, and drenched his face and voice in adoring gratitude as he said, 'Oh, yes, please. I'd like that very much.'

'Good, that's settled then,' Critchley declared, thus drawing the meeting to a very satisfactory close. Paul stood up and shook his hand, thanking him in hushed tones, before preparing to leave.

Critchley, enjoying this little intrigue, added sotto voce, 'You will keep this matter under wraps, though, for the time being. I think it would be wise.'

The two men exchanged a look of complete understanding.

'Oh, certainly. Yes, indeed, Mr Critchley.'

Paul went back to his desk, taking care not to look at Carolyn as he walked across the office.

Philip Lawson was impressed when Lynda walked into his office that same morning. His teenage memories of her, as a straight-talking, provocatively dressed curvaceous blonde, hadn't led him to expect that she would have turned into a sophisticated lady with expensive taste in clothes and accessories.

Lynda was pleased to see his reaction, for she had dressed to impress, in a black trouser suit, pale gold silk shirt, and Cartier gold earrings and wrist watch, and she spoke at first in an accent carefully adjusted to match her new image.

Then her gaze moved from the bookshelves and oak panelled walls to the football banner and Philip's red braces, and she laughed. And he knew she understood, all too well, what he'd had to allow his life to become.

They began to chat and Philip found that Lynda was still as fascinating to him as she'd always been. It had been Lynda who, in her younger days, had taught Philip that you could get away with being a rebel. He'd realised, though, that he was, and always would be, an amateur in that role compared to Lynda.

Philip recognised, however, that she'd been changed by the experiences of the past twelve years, and not just in her appearance. He also noticed the anxiety in her eyes, and the way she clutched at her gold pendant in the shape of a horse shoe. He could see that Lynda needed to get on with the purpose of her visit.

'How can I help you, Lynda?'

He saw her confidence slip away, and heard her Milfield accent emerge again as she confessed, 'I don't know where to start.'

'Let me make it easy. I assume that, in the circumstances, you've come to see me about a divorce. It's very sad when a marriage like yours and John's has to come to an end, but these things happen. People grow apart.'

Philip had a sign on his desk, a present from his old mentor Reggie Broadbent, advising him to 'Assume Nothing' and he wished he'd read it again before starting this conversation.

'It's a marriage I need to talk to you about,' Lynda told him.

'A marriage?' Philip sat up to concentrate properly on what she was saying.

'I got married again.'

'Oh, I didn't think you and John had got divorced.' He stopped as he saw the look on her face, and sensed that he was in a different game.

'We haven't,' Lynda said, trying to sound matter-of-fact. 'I've committed bigamy. Is that the legal term for it?'

'Yes,' Philip said with what little breath had not been taken away, and then managed to hold his mind on a steady course as Lynda told him her story.

Straight-talking as ever, she discussed her fear of being prosecuted, and also of losing her inheritance, or at the very least having it threatened by legal proceedings. Although bigamy was not an aspect of the law that he was familiar with, Philip assured Lynda that he'd do his best to help her, and would consult a friend who might be able to offer expert advice.

She thanked him, and then, trying to keep calm, she said, 'And we'd better also talk about my divorcing John.'

'You're sure that's what you want to do?'

'Yes. I agree, it is very sad to have to end a marriage, but it's the right thing to do, for both me and John.'

When she left Philip's office, Lynda was still very worried; not about having enough money for her own needs, which could be scaled down if necessary, her real concern was having the extra resources available now, to help those she loved.

She was glad to have something more positive to focus on, she was hoping to view the Kellys' old house. Jenny took her round to the estate agents and introduced her. She hid a smile as Lynda played it cool, pretending to be interested in other houses too.

Excited at the prospect of seeing 21 Bennett Street again, Lynda called at the café to tell Dan, and also to have a quiet chat with him about her meeting with Philip.

'What did he say? Are you in trouble?'

'He said, as you can imagine, that bigamy is not one of his areas of expertise, but he's going to look into it for me. So fingers crossed.'

'Yes,' he said, and tried not to look too worried.

'In the meantime, what about this?' Lynda said as she placed the estate agents' information sheet on the table in front of him. With a big smile on her face she watched him reading the details.

He looked up at her, 'Isn't this Jenny's Mum and Dad's old house?'

'Yes,' she said, beaming.

'Looks like it will need a lot of work.'

'No problem,' she stated confidently.

Katie, who had come over to ask if they wanted another cup of coffee, saw what they were discussing.

'Are you buying a house, Lynda?'

'I could be. And not just any house either, it's the one your grandparents used to live in.'

'Bennett Street? I don't remember it, but my Mum took me and Alex to see it once, only from the outside though, because it had been sold then.'

'I'm going to view it tomorrow afternoon.'

'That'll bring back a lot of memories,' said Dan.

'Could I come with you?' asked Katie, 'I'd love to see where they lived.'

'Of course you can, if Dan can let you have the

246

time off.'

'Yes, I can manage on my own for a bit.'

'Right then, Katie, I'll come here after I've picked up the keys, and we'll go straight there. We can have a good look round. The agents said I could view it without them as they know your Mum.'

Dan swallowed hard before enquiring, 'For you and John, is it, this house?'

Lynda knew how weighty that question was.

'No, just me,' she said quietly and saw hope light up Dan's eyes.

'It's a big house for one person,' was Katie's comment.

'I can always take in a lodger,' Lynda joked.

'Put my name down,' quipped Dan.

Katie was taken aback. 'Who'd live with "Grandmama"?'

Dan laughed. 'Exactly!'

CHAPTER TWENTY-NINE

The following afternoon Lynda was excited as she opened the gate of the tiny garden in front of the large, Victorian stone terraced house on Bennett Street. She paused and looked at the thick sandstone pillars which framed the deep bay window, below which was a smaller cracked window which peered up from the cellar.

Katie, standing behind her, was impatiently waiting to go into this house which was part of her family's past. It was part of Lynda's past, too, and that was what made her halt in its gateway.

'What's wrong?' asked Katie.

'Nothing.'

Then those damned tears, which had got into the habit of never being far away, threatened to arrive again as Lynda thought of Kathleen Kelly, with her laughing face and motherly figure, the understanding friend who used to open the door and stand there with her arms open wide. Kath would never have allowed her to feel as lonely as she did now.

'I just wish your Grandma was here to open that door and welcome me like she used to.'

Then she was startled for a moment as Katie, unknowingly copying her dead Grandmother, linked her arm through Lynda's and pulled her close, so that she no longer felt lonely. Together they went up the three well-worn steps to the front door.

Lynda was amazed at how little the house had changed. The previous owners had installed central heating and to some extent modernised the kitchen and bathroom, but the character of the house remained intact.

They explored every room, grimacing at the garish taste which had been inflicted on some of them, and then came back downstairs. Lynda stood in the centre of the spacious front room and was filled with pleasure as she looked around it, gazing once more at the old fireplace with its decorative dark green tiles and polished wooden mantel, and remembered how the blazing coal fires had lit up the room.

They sat on the old sofa the previous owners had left, and shared the Eccles cakes and the thermos of coffee Katie had brought.

'What do you think?' she asked.

Lynda's eyes sparkled. 'I can hear your Grandma talking to me. Does that sound crazy?'

'It does a bit.'

'She's telling me I have to buy this house. There are so many happy memories in these walls, and I can feel the house is welcoming me.'

'I know what you mean, I feel it, too.'

Lynda held out her cup for a toast.

'Welcome to my new home, Katie!'

They both jumped when Lynda's mobile phone rang a few minutes later. It was Mark.

'Hi, Lynda. Just phoning to see how you are.'

'Hello, love. I'm fine, thank you. How are things with you?'

'O.K. but I'm missing you, and so is Loveday.'

Lynda felt a tightness in her throat as she thought of Loveday Manor and all it meant to her.

'Are you still there?' asked Mark.

'Yes.'

'Lynda, I don't want to upset you but my Mother is still trying to get me to agree to empty the apartment. I'm worried that I'll come home one day and find she's had all your things taken out. You need to come back and let her know you still live there.'

'I can't come back, not yet. Can you not put my things in storage, somewhere Suzanne can't get hold of them?'

'No, I've had a better idea. I need to see you, Lynda, and I think the safest thing I can do is pack a lot of your personal stuff in boxes and bring it to you.'

'No!' Lynda was horrified at the thought of Mark coming to Milfield and finding out the truth of her situation.

'Why not? I'm coming to a conference in Edinburgh, I can load your things into the Range Rover and drop them off for you on the way. I don't need to stay. I can just call in.' He paused, making an effort to hide his emotion. 'I'd really like to see you, Lynda.'

She heard the need in the voice of this young man who was Tom Meredith's son, and decided to take the risk.

'And I'd love to see you. When were you thinking of coming?'

'The Wednesday after the Bank Holiday. That's settled then,' he said, sounding decisive like his Father used to. 'Text me the address and I'll let you know what time to expect me. It will be great to see you again, and to persuade you to come home.'

'Mark, I've got something to tell you.'

'Wait till I come up. See you soon.' He paused, then blurted out, 'Lots of love,' and rang off quickly.

Katie was a little puzzled. 'Who was that?'

'Mark, the son of the man I, worked with.'

'I thought you'd decided you were buying this place, that you were staying in Milfield.'

'I am.'

'Why didn't you tell him?'

'Lots of reasons.'

Katie gave a sigh. 'Oh, I see, things that can't be talked about. Just like loads of stuff in our family.' She poured the last of the coffee into their cups, and looked at her.

'Will you talk to me, Lynda?'

Lynda had guessed that this was one of the reasons Katie had been so keen to come with her today.

'Yes, of course I will.'

They sat there and Katie was fascinated as Lynda told her tales about her grandmother, about the parties and the sing-songs round the old beer-stained upright piano her Grandad had bought for a few pounds from a local pub.

'My Granny sounds like the kind of person everyone would like for a Mother, easy-going, someone you could have a proper chat with. I can't talk to my Mum.'

'My daughter couldn't talk to me when she was your age.'

Lynda wanted to add that Carolyn still couldn't, but had learned that sometimes you had to keep things to yourself. She thought carefully before saying to Katie, 'It was very hard for your Mum, you know, when your Grandma died.'

'And then my Dad.'

Katie turned to face her now. She and Alex had had a discussion about their Mother's old friend, and Lynda had guessed right, Katie had come with her, not only to see the house but also with another purpose. She and Alex hoped that Lynda might be willing to tell them the truth about their father, the things which others were obviously trying to keep from them. And so she began her quest.

'You knew my Dad, didn't you?'

Lynda stiffened, sensing where Katie might be leading her.

'Yes, I knew him.'

Katie didn't hesitate but asked, with a directness inherited from Kath Kelly, 'But you didn't like him?'

Lynda walked across the room and sat down on the broad window ledge as she had so often with Kath Kelly. She looked across at Katie and thought how much this young woman reminded her of her old friend and mentor.

Katie was calm but determined, 'Will you tell me about him? The truth. Alex and I aren't stupid. We know there are things being kept from us.'

Lynda sighed, but knew that Kath would want her to be honest.

'How much do you know?'

'That he died in a car crash and that, apart from Grandmother Heywood, nobody seems to want to talk about him.'

'Well, perhaps it's best that way.'

Katie came to sit in the opposite corner of the window, clasping her hands tightly together in her lap.

'No, it isn't. Alex and I need to know. Alex thinks she remembers him hitting Mum, but she was only five or six, so she isn't sure if it's just bad dreams she remembers. Is it?'

Lynda knew the answer, but wasn't sure it was hers to give.

'You need to talk to your Mother, not me.'

'We've tried, she's not telling.'

'If she doesn't want you to know, I've no right to tell you.'

Katie saw the closed expression on Lynda's face, and knew she'd made her decision.

'All right. Will you answer one question then? Yes or no? Was it just bad dreams?'

Lynda saw the anguish of the girl who was trying so hard to look grown up and dispassionate, and couldn't lie to her.

'No.'

Neither Katie nor Alex were at home that evening when Steve Sheldon went to do some more work on the kitchen. He thought he'd been coping well with his visits, laughing and joking with Jenny as she helped him fit cupboards and shelves.

He'd managed to keep the mood light and free of sexual tension that evening, too, until one of her cheeky remarks provoked him to playfully grab hold of her to keep her in order. He looked down at her sweet face and suddenly a kiss was only a breath away. He stepped back hastily.

'I'll come back on Saturday morning to do the rest,' he told her, trying to sound business-like, but he couldn't take his eyes off Jenny, and he saw that she had wanted that kiss.

She knew she was about to risk humiliation by revealing her need of him, but she might never have another chance.

'You'll soon have the kitchen finished at this rate.'

'Yes.'

Steve knew her thoughts matched his, that there would soon be no more time together.

'I suppose I should be glad,' Jenny said, and then gathered all her courage and added slowly, 'but I'm not.'

Steve reached out to touch her cheek, but stopped himself and instead collected his things together and went into the living room, preparing to leave.

Jenny, who had for so long lived her life

cautiously, felt a surge of recklessness as she followed him.

'Don't go, Steve. Please stay. Be with me, even if it's only for a little while.'

He heard the tremor in her voice as she looked up at him, like a child making a wish, and he could not refuse. His arms reached out to hold her as Alex, home early, paused in the doorway.

Steve met her cool gaze and stepped away from Jenny as he greeted her daughter briefly before saying goodbye and swiftly leaving the house.

Alex looked searchingly at her Mother. 'What's going on?'

'What do you mean?' Jenny responded, with a touch of the defiance she experienced so often from her daughters.

Alex saw that she was wishing that moment with Steve had not been snatched away from her, and there rose in Alex a self-righteous anger worthy of her Grandmother. Jenny almost laughed as she heard her daughter speak in a tone so like Ellen's.

'You and him, Mum. He had his arms round you, and I saw the way you were looking at each other.'

Denial seemed the surest way to deal with her daughter's disapproving scowl.

'Don't be silly. Steve's married. He's got two kids. There's nothing 'going on' between me and him.'

'But you wish there was.'

'No.'

'Liar.'

Jenny was suddenly angry, crying out against the unfairness of her solitary fate.

'Yes, O.K.,' she cried out, 'I do!'

Alex was shaking her head in disbelief now.

'For heaven's sake, Mum! I know we said we want you to find another husband, but we didn't mean

254

somebody else's.'

Jenny was silent for a moment, filled with longing for the warmth of Steve's arms.

'I can't help how I feel about him,' she said piteously, but Alex was too young to know the dangers of judgement, and her response was harsh.

'You're just being stupid. And if I were you, I'd stop right now.'

Jenny recoiled before her daughter's unflinching certainty, but then struck back.

'Yes, you probably would. It must be great to be like you, Alex, cool and rational and on your way to university.'

'Wrong on both of those, Mother,' Alex declared, A – it's not great to be me and B – I'm not going to university.'

And so Alex began the speech she'd been working on for so long in her head, and Jenny had no choice but to sit down on the sofa and listen.

Alex had done the calculations and she knew what it would cost her Mother in terms of money and self-sacrifice to send her to Cambridge.

'There is no financial problem, Alex,' Jenny argued back. 'Your Grandmother told you, she has set aside the money for your university education, and she'd be heart-broken if you didn't go to Cambridge.'

'And you, and I, would be having to grovel to her all the time for her handouts. I don't want to do that, and I certainly don't want to see you doing it!'

Jenny blinked back tears as she saw her daughter trying to protect her. 'I want you to take this opportunity, Alex, and you'll always regret it if you don't. Please change your mind.'

Alex knew she was right, but there was another issue.

'And what about Katie? What about the money for

her education? Grandmother never mentions that.'

Jenny, well aware that Ellen had a low opinion of Katie's academic capabilities, knew she was not sure of her ground now.

'Katie will have just the same support as you, whatever she chooses to do.'

'Well, if that's true, it's time you told her that. It's time you talked to her, gave her more attention.'

'I didn't realise I'd been neglecting Katie. It's just that I've been so busy.'

'Yes,' Alex jeered, 'too busy with Steve Sheldon!'

CHAPTER THIRTY

Frances Horton had arranged to have lunch with some of her friends on Friday April 25th, and then take them to her shop for a private viewing of her new fashion collection. She'd therefore told Jean that she would take over from her at one-thirty, and give her the afternoon off. Jean had been pleased to hear of this arrangement, it gave her a chance to arrange a much needed meeting with John Stanworth.

Love was an experience which seemed to have eluded Jean Haworth all her life; even in her marriage it had not been truly vouchsafed for her. Yet she had love to give, and had prayed that God would bestow that happiness in the remaining years of her life, by allowing her to marry John Stanworth.

She wasn't sure it was right to pray for that kind of thing, but she felt the Almighty would understand and forgive her. And perhaps it wasn't appropriate for such a modest and secular campaign, but the words 'Fight the Good Fight' kept sounding in her head as she walked into The Vienna Café that Friday lunch time.

She'd been proud of how coolly she had phoned and invited John to meet her there, but now, as she picked up her cup of tea, she found her hand was shaking so much she had to quickly replace the cup in its saucer.

John Stanworth wasn't a good fit for The Vienna Café, everything seemed too small for him, the small round table, the spindly chair, the dainty china cups.

He didn't look or feel comfortable in those surroundings.

His discomfort, however, was not entirely to be blamed on the designer of 'The Vienna', it had more to do with the fact that he had been avoiding Jean Haworth ever since he'd seen Lynda again. He'd been surprised when Jean had phoned and invited him to meet her here, but had felt guilty enough to accept the invitation.

Jean kept telling herself that she must keep calm, take this slowly and gently, but it was hard. After ridiculously banal enquiries about each other's health, they began to talk first about Carolyn. John was glad to be able to confide in Jean, and he was grateful for the comfort of her understanding.

He had been grateful to Jean for so much over the last few years, and including her in his life had been such a natural thing to do. But, it seemed to Jean, that he appeared to have now forgotten about the relationship which had developed between them.

'Carolyn has to give Lynda a second chance,' he said. 'She has to understand, Jean, that Lynda's still her Mother. And she's still my wife.'

His firm statement of this fact confirmed what Jean had suspected, that he hadn't believed Carolyn when she'd told him that Lynda was going to divorce him.

Jean took a deep breath, and there was anger as well as fear in her eyes, as she asked the question she had to have answered.

'Yes. And where does that leave us, John?'

She could see she had startled him, but it had to be now, she couldn't carry on not knowing.

'I don't know,' he stuttered. 'All I know is that Lynda's come back.'

'But has she come back to you?'

258

John's face took on a familiar stubborn expression.

'We've been talking about how things were between us, and how we both made mistakes.'

Jean knew it wasn't for her to talk about Lynda seeking a divorce, but felt the need to push John towards reality.

'Has she said she wants to come back and live with you?'

John was disconcerted by the directness of the question and could only say, 'No.'

Jean felt her heart begin to beat like tiny fists against her chest but she held on to her courage.

'Has she said she loves you?'

John wanted so much to say that Lynda loved him, and tried to answer 'yes', but could not.

Jean fought back the emotion which threatened to weaken her, but her hand trembled as she took hold of his. Facing him with no doubt in her mind, she said quietly, 'I do.'

The sound of teaspoons on china, daintily flowered cups replaced in saucers by ladies at the other tables suddenly seemed deafening. Jean lost her nerve and broke the tension which had set itself between her and John.

'Do you want more tea?' she asked, picking up the china teapot.

'No. Thank you.'

Jean poured more tea into her cup and took her time as she stirred in a little cloud of milk. John, by contrast, wanted to move swiftly now, he'd had enough of being perched on a chair too small for him, and being made to answer awkward questions.

'I've got to be going. I've some shopping to do.'

'Oh.'

John couldn't bear to see the disappointment in her eyes, but he'd been doing a lot of thinking, and there were things he needed to say.

'I've been very grateful, Jean, for the way you and Carolyn have looked after me since my heart attack. But I'm better now, and things have changed.'

'Because Lynda's come back?'

'Yes. She's put life into me again.'

'That's nice,' Jean said, managing to maintain an unperturbed tone.

His sigh was one of exasperation.

'Like I said, things are different now.'

'Are they?'

'Yes. And I know Carolyn will have told you that Lynda wants a divorce, but it's not true.'

'Isn't it?' Jean said boldly.

John stood up, and thrust his chair back under the table.

'No. She won't want a divorce. And so I think it'd be a good idea if you gave me back my key.'

He had hurt her now, he could see that, but he stood his ground as she fumbled in her bag and then, looking up at him like a child wrongly chastised, placed the key in his outstretched hand.

Ellen Heywood's drawing room at Kirkwood House faced the main road, but was kept out of reach of the curiosity of strangers by virtue of its steep driveway and lichen clad stone balustrade.

Sometimes when she stood at the window Ellen felt like an eagle in its eyrie, and the image pleased her. She liked to think of herself as a strong, proud individual, and of her house as a stronghold against the outside world.

She had not, however, been born to be a solitary creature. What Ellen Heywood had always craved was to be the centre of a glittering social milieu, but life had conspired against her, and Ellen's anger against her fate had long ago become lodged deep within her, and become part of her being.

Ellen did not like being alone in the house and was glad that she was not alone this Friday lunchtime, though she gave no sign of that to her visitor.

Jenny had come to deliver the tablets which Dan, busy serving his customers at The Copper Kettle, had asked her to collect from the pharmacist's in her lunch break, and take to her mother-in-law.

'Thank you, Jennifer,' Ellen said politely as she took the package from her. 'But there was no rush, Daniel could have brought them this evening.'

'He's worried about you.'

'There is no need. However, since you are here, perhaps you could make us some coffee?'

'Yes, of course,' Jenny said, and went off to the kitchen.

Jenny knew that the reason for this demand for her company was that Ellen was lonely, and so was willing to sacrifice her precious free time. It was not long, however, before she wished she had been more selfish.

Ellen began their conversation with a criticism.

'You've altered your hairstyle, Jennifer. Is there a reason for that?'

'I just thought it would be nice to have a change.'

'And to look younger?' Ellen said mockingly.

The remark delivered an extra sting, for Jenny had made the mistake of looking in the unflattering mirror in the hallway that morning, and had despaired at the signs of ageing on her face.

'I'm only forty. I'm still young enough to ...'

Ellen, who had noticed a difference in Jenny lately, and had wondered about the cause, swiftly cut in.

'And young enough to marry again? Is that what

261

you were going to say?'

'No, but it's true.'

Ellen gripped the arms of her chair, and leaned forward.

'Does my son's memory mean nothing to you?' she hissed, and her face took on an expression of disgust as she continued, 'And you have two daughters. You need to set them an example of morality, not to mention loyalty to the memory of their dear Father.'

Jenny had been giving a lot of thought to her circumstances, and whether she had any chance of a happy future. And Ellen was once more denying her the right to any such hope.

'My daughters are almost old enough to leave home. I'm not looking forward to being on my own, Ellen.'

There was a silence as Jenny realised the pertinence of the statement. Ellen, silently acknowledging that loneliness was not something she should wish on anyone, changed the subject.

'Will lunch be here again on Sunday, or is your kitchen in working order now?'

'No. I'm sorry.' Jenny was annoyed that she felt she needed to apologise. 'Steve won't have it finished for a few days yet.'

Ellen, always ready to criticise Steve Sheldon, said, 'He seems to be taking his time.'

To her surprise she saw Jenny blush at this, and a suspicion suddenly planted itself in her mind. Her next comment was calculated to probe further.

'I expect you'll be glad when it's finished, one doesn't like having strangers in the house.'

'I wouldn't call Steve a stranger,' Jenny replied guilelessly, and then recoiled as Ellen pounced.

'Wouldn't you?'

The question was simple but Jenny realised immediately, from the tone and the look in Ellen's eyes, that it was not harmless. She decided that the best thing to do was to ignore the question, put on her coat and quickly head for the door.

'I have to go now, Ellen, I have to get back to the office.'

Ellen, taken by surprise, didn't try to stop her, but did go and stand at the window to watch her departure.

The sunlight caught hold of Jenny's hair and threaded it with dark gold as she moved swiftly down the driveway. Ellen saw that Jenny was indeed still a young woman, and an attractive one. But not free to love again. She was Richard's wife, still a close link to her son, and Ellen would not allow that to change.

Had she known about the suspicions Gary and his wife were planting in her husband's mind, Carolyn would have cancelled the secret arrangement she had made with Paul Ferris, and would have been glad of the excuse.

She couldn't cope with the lies she was being forced to tell. Lying to Steve, to Ellen Heywood, to Jean Haworth, and this evening, to her own innocent young daughter.

They'd been discussing plans for the May Bank Holiday weekend, and Carolyn had told her daughter that she'd be away most of the Saturday as she was going to a special concert in Manchester, as a favour to Ellen Heywood. Gemma, thinking that her Mum was being kind to an old lady, had accepted the lie without question.

But that lie had caused Carolyn to stop and think, and panic about what she was planning to do.

She was no fool, and had confronted all the reasons against getting involved with Paul; she knew the danger, but the truth was that the danger was part of the attraction. Paul Ferris offered more excitement, more glamour, more sexual magnetism than she had ever experienced in the whole of her life.

But now, getting ready for bed, she thought again of Gemma's trusting acceptance of her lies, and knew that she must end this madness. She looked at Steve lying in bed with his hands clasped behind his head, and staring at nothing.

He looked so tired and careworn, so different from the young man she'd fallen in love with so passionately that nothing else had seemed to matter. There was no passion in his eyes now, only anxiety.

She got into bed and curved her body towards him. He was startled by this physical contact, now so rare between him and his wife. He also felt guilty, because he'd been thinking, yet again, about Jenny Heywood.

'What is it, Steve? What are you worrying about? Randerson?'

Steve didn't want to deceive her, but he didn't want to talk about his fear of redundancy either, so he shrugged away the subject swiftly.

'Yeah, but it's all right, I can handle him.'

'Of course you can,' she murmured, wrapping her arms round him and pressing her body against his. 'I'm sorry I've been so rotten to you lately. I hate having rows. I want us to be happy. You're all that matters to me, Steve, you and the kids.

Steve held her, stroking her hair. 'That's what's important to me, too. It's what I've always wanted, a good marriage and a happy family.'

'I know.'

She kissed him gently.

264

Steve looked at his wife and remembered why he had married her.

'I can cope with anything, as long as I've got you to cuddle,' he murmured, looking at her lovingly.

She began to caress him, and the warmth and softness of her was easing all the pain from his body.

'You look so tired,' she said gently.

'Well, I'm not,' he said.

And he smiled at her, that cheeky, sideways grin that had always sparked excitement in her, and which made her want him now.

She knew it was crazy to have another man seducing her, and yet wanting to make love to her husband. But Steve needed her, and that felt wonderful.

He kissed her, and they touched with all the tenderness and awareness of each other's needs nurtured by years of making love together. They gave themselves into the freedom of their senses, and for a while all turmoil was stilled and only love was there.

CHAPTER THIRTY-ONE

On Friday 2nd May it was announced that the New Labour Party, led by Tony Blair, had won a landslide victory in the General Election. Many of the inhabitants of Milfield watched the television pictures of the new Prime Minister and his adoring wife standing exultantly at the door of Number 10 Downing Street, and were filled with hope.

Steve had gone with his workmates for a celebratory pint after work, but found it hard to fully share the optimism singing out from the crowds in London. Tony Randerson still had the power to put them out of work.

The next day life in Milfield quickly returned to normal, and in the Sheldon household there was a lot of tension. Steve couldn't stop worrying about Randerson's threats and also about having to go and finish the work at Jenny Heywood's that morning.

He knew the dangers there, and decided it would be a good idea if he took his children with him. Both Michael and Gemma were bored with watching television and went quite willingly upstairs to get ready. It was fortunate that they had left the room, because their parents embarked on yet another row.

In the last week there had not been the fresh start Steve and Carolyn had both hoped for after they'd made love that Friday night. In fact nothing had changed, they'd just carried on with their daily lives, aware that they still couldn't talk to each other.

None of their differences seemed capable of being resolved. And at the office Carolyn couldn't free herself from the attraction she felt for Paul Ferris, and the awareness that they were both sharing an excited anticipation of what was to come.

But when Carolyn had woken up that Saturday morning her first thought had been that this was the day she was going to commit adultery. And she knew she couldn't go through with it, she couldn't hurt Steve.

Unaware of her panic, he asked, 'What time will you be getting home from the concert tonight? I'll come and pick you up from Ellen's.'

'No, it's all right, I've arranged a lift. And actually, I'm not sure I want to go. I'd rather have a night in with you.'

She almost laughed at the irony as Steve insisted that she mustn't even think about changing the arrangement.

'You'll really enjoy it, and you can't let Mrs Heywood down after she's got you the ticket.'

'O.K.' she said, deciding that she'd ring Ellen and tell her that she could go to the concert with her after all, if the ticket was still available. 'I'll get a lasagne out of the freezer for you and the kids tonight.'

'No, don't do that,' Steve said, and realised that she would have to be told. He braced himself for the row which he knew couldn't be avoided.

'Why not?' Carolyn asked.

'We won't be back for tea. We're eating at the burger bar after the match. Lynda's treat.' He hesitated but he was sick of pretending, and a need for honesty drove him to continue. 'You might as well know, Lynda's coming to the match with us, and so is your Dad.'

Carolyn stared at him, a sense of betrayal beginning to course its way through her soul.

'When was this arranged?'

267

'Yesterday.'

'Why are you doing this, Steve? You know I don't want her near my kids.'

He had known she would be angry, but he'd had enough of Carolyn dictating what 'was good' for everybody.

'Our kids,' he corrected her. 'And she's their Grandma, Carolyn.'

It infuriated her to see him standing there, calmly ignoring her wishes as he so often did, as if what she thought was of little consequence in his great male scheme of things.

'And I'm their Mother,' she snapped at him. 'But it doesn't seem to matter what I say, or think. You just go ahead and do what you want, what you decide.'

Steve knew this was true sometimes, but had to defend himself.

'Only if you're wrong.'

'And who decides that? You.'

Carolyn clenched hold of her anger and struck into the brittle core of their relationship.

'There's a basic problem here, Steve. You don't care what I think. And why not? Because you don't really care about me.'

'Of course I do.'

'No, you don't. And sometimes I don't think you know me any more, or even want to know me.'

He hadn't a clue what she was talking about now. To him, she'd left the realm of reason and rational thought.

'That's a stupid thing to say.'

'You're the one who's being stupid!' Carolyn cried out. 'Welcoming that woman back with open arms. You've always taken her side against me. Who do you love, Steve, her or me?'

More than anything else that morning, Carolyn

needed him to answer that question, to take her in his arms and reassure her that she was the one he loved.

But it was not to be. The phone rang, and Steve paused only momentarily before he turned his back on her and went to answer it.

It was a helluva shock that phone call from Gary. Later that morning Steve was still trying to think what to do about it as he walked up to Jenny's house and rang the bell.

With her eyes sparkling and her cheeks glowing with her love for him Jenny opened the door. She smiled at him, but the smile faltered a little when she saw he had his children standing guard at either side of him.

'Hello. Michael and Gemma isn't it? How lovely that you've come to my house,' Jenny said, making sure they had no doubt that they were very welcome here. But the quick glance she gave Steve told him that she had realised what he was signalling to her by bringing his children with him. Alex understood the significance too, and was pleased.

She and Gemma, who knew each other from the ballet school where Alex sometimes acted as accompanist, soon went over to the piano so that Gemma could try out some new ballet steps. Michael, who was mad about dogs, immediately made friends with Tigger. The dog was, in fact, the reason he'd volunteered to accompany his Dad on this visit.

'Can I take him for a walk?' he asked.

'Yes, of course,' Jenny replied, 'would you like me to come with you?'

'I'd rather take him on my own, if you don't mind? No offence.'

'None taken,' Jenny laughed.

Steve got on with the work in the kitchen and

Jenny kept out of his way, though not, he soon found, out of his thoughts. He could barely concentrate on what he was doing, for if he wasn't thinking of Jenny, he was going over Gary's phone call in his mind.

Ever since they were lads and he'd hidden round a corner watching Gary harvesting apples from forbidden trees, Steve had known that Gary Pearson walked close to the edge when it came to crime. But breaking into Randerson's office was no childhood act of mischief.

As he worked, Steve ran the conversation again in his head.

'I didn't break in. I had a key. And I didn't pinch anything, all I did was copy a few documents. And when you see what's in them, you'll be damned glad I took the risk.'

He'd arranged to meet Steve at the burger bar after the match. Steve now tried to forget about Gary's phone call, and instead look forward to being at a football match with Lynda and John again.

When Michael got back from his walk with Tigger, he announced proudly that he was going to the match with his Grandma and Grandad today.

'How lovely,' Jenny said. 'And Milfield could win today, they're on good form.'

'Do you go to watch Milfield?' asked Michael.

'No, but my Dad used to go with your Grandad. And I used to wish I'd gone with them sometimes.'

Michael caught the wistfulness in her voice. 'You can come with us if you want. Can't she Dad?'

There was a silence, which seemed to freeze the air in the room. Jenny saw Alex tense as she awaited her Mother's response, her look defying her to accept the invitation.

Jenny felt like being defiant, and she wanted to be with Steve, but saw the shock and doubt on his face.

Then Michael made it easy for her.

Remembering a snatch of overheard conversation he said, 'You're a friend of my Grandma's, aren't you? She'll be glad if you come as well, otherwise it'll be all blokes.'

Steve suppressed a grin, thinking how that sort of situation had never presented a challenge to Lynda in the past. Jenny, sharing the same thought, also laughed. Then she looked at Steve's son, this young man who was shyly offering this token of instinctive friendship, and she was suddenly filled with hope.

'O.K. I'll come. Thank you for asking me,' she said brightly, avoiding looking at Alex, but knowing that her face was tight with disapproval.

'Where shall I meet you?' she asked Steve.

She saw that he, too, was relaxed now, accepting that fate seemed intent on undermining their resistance.

Milfield always felt different on a Saturday when the football team was playing at home. On such days its inhabitants melded themselves into a community, and there was an echo in the streets of the bustling energy of the days when it was a prosperous cotton town.

That energy was at its most vibrant in the crowd at the match, and John Stanworth's eyes sparkled as he felt a share of it running through him. It was as if he was learning to breathe properly again, and he knew who he had to thank for that, the woman sitting beside him in the stand, Lynda.

They were occupying the best seats in the ground, courtesy of Philip Lawson, who had spotted them in the queue at the turnstile, and immediately invited them all to be his guests. Steve's instinct had been to refuse the offer, but Lynda, knowing Philip intended friendship not patronage, had immediately accepted

271

the invitation for all of them.

'Great seats, Phil,' she said as they settled down to watch the match. 'Though it's a bit much, seeing you twice in the same week,' she teased.

John heard this, and began to worry that what Carolyn had said might be true. Fortunately for Lynda the referee blew his whistle, and for the next ninety minutes everything had to take second place to the football.

Milfield worked hard, but their opponents were the more experienced team, and three minutes from the final whistle Milfield were doing well to hang on to a draw. Michael's fists were clenched tightly, a draw was no good, Milfield needed to win if they were to stay in the race for promotion.

Then his hero, Layton, intercepted a pass in centre field and the crowd gave full voice to their hope. Adrenalin and ambition suddenly gave Layton a determination that could not be defeated, and he flashed past his opponents and scored.

It was as if the whole of Milfield had jumped three feet in the air, and the shouts of joy were deafening as the Milfield supporters hugged each other. Steve turned to grab hold of Michael, but he had already pinned himself on to his Grandad's chest. Steve turned to the other side and hugged Jenny instead.

She held on to him tightly, and they looked at each other, at last acknowledging their need. Steve didn't kiss her, but Jenny had no doubt he wanted to, just as she knew that he was reluctant to move his body away from hers. It was the moment which gave Jenny real hope, but it was a moment observed by Lynda, too, and she didn't like what she saw.

As they left the stand they thanked Philip again for giving them the special seats. He gave Lynda a hug. 'Great to see you here again, Lynda. See you next week. Your appointment, remember?'

'Oh, yes,' Lynda said, and looked round to see if John had heard this. He had.

'You've been to see Philip, then?' he said as they made their way out of the ground.

'Yeah.'

'You're not divorcing me, are you?' he asked anxiously.

Lynda saw the pain in his eyes. She didn't want to hurt him, but knew she would have to. But not yet.

'Not here, John. We'll talk about it later.'

'No!'

'Come on, we're losing Steve and Michael,' she said and followed them through the gate.

John grabbed hold of his wife's arm.

'Lynda! We're not getting divorced. You've only just come back. You've got to give me a chance.'

'John, please.'

'Lynda, you can't do this to me.'

She looked down at his hand gripping her arm, and hurting her. It made her think of all the pain of their marriage.

She spoke quietly, but with certainty.

'I'm sorry, but I am going to divorce you, John. Now, please let go of me.'

She pulled away from him and his fingers released their hold on her.

'Come on, you two,' Steve called out, and then saw John beginning to walk away.

'John, aren't you coming?'

'No, I'm not. I'm going home!' he shouted angrily, and strode away, his face clenched tight against the tears he would never allow anyone to see.

CHAPTER THIRTY-TWO

The shouts and roars and bright colours of the crowd at the Milfield football ground could not have been a greater contrast to the stillness, and the dusky blue and palest shimmering grey tones of Paul Ferris's flat. The curtains were patterned with streaks of different shades of blue, echoing the swimming pools of the David Hockney paintings on the wall.

In the centre of the window recess stood a small, elegant chrome and glass table and chairs, and in the centre of the table a bottle of champagne reclined against a bed of ice.

There were vases of white roses and freesias perfuming the room, reminding Carolyn of the elegant floral decorations featured in glossy magazines. A small dining table glittered with silver and crystal set against luxurious white table linen, all elegantly prepared for a supper which they would share that evening.

Carolyn was relieved that Paul had taken such care to make everything perfect. She knew that the scene had been set with style and finesse; this would not be a careless, hasty seduction it would be a wonderful fantasy.

Walking closely behind her, and running his hands slowly down her body, Paul ushered Carolyn gently into the room. She again felt a tremor of fear at the thought of what was to happen now.

He kissed her as he took her coat, and invited her to sit on one of the large dove-grey velvet sofas placed at either side of a white marble Georgian style fireplace. He was wearing blue chinos and a dark blue silk shirt, unbuttoned just enough to give her a glimpse of his suntanned chest.

He watched her looking round the room, and congratulated himself on having judged precisely what she would want. She would not refuse him this time.

Waiting while Paul opened the champagne Carolyn admired the large porcelain vase which stood in the centre of the hearth, and which was filled with white roses.

Paul knew her, she thought, he understood what she wanted from life in a way that Steve never would. But she immediately blanked out any thoughts of her husband and children, that had got in the way before. This was about her, what she wanted. She still had some doubts but the row with Steve that morning had confirmed her decision to go through with this. She was thirty, she knew her life had to change, and she needed to know if her future was to be with Paul.

Watching him pour the champagne and hand her a crystal glass as if she were a princess, Carolyn felt she had made the right choice. And she was already physically aroused, just having him sit beside her, his arm stretched along the back of the sofa as he gazed at her in that admiring way of his which told her she was very, very special.

'It's wonderful to have you here at last,' he murmured, and as she sipped her champagne he began to stroke her hair and then her body with deft, sensitive caresses. He put down his glass and, kneeling before her, he took off her shoes and gently lifted her legs up on to the sofa.

He slid his hand beneath the soft fabric of her dress, slowly stroking the inside of her thighs. He paused and gently took her glass from her, kissing her as he returned to the sofa and eased his body on top of hers. She thought for a moment that he was about to take her there and then, but this moving of his body firmly against hers was only the beginning. Paul didn't want to hurry this seduction, he wanted to enjoy every sensation.

He kissed her and moved his hands expertly over her body. He waited until his every touch threatened to overwhelm her, and then he moved away and stood looking down at her. He held out his hands, lifted her to stand before him and then, pulling her tightly against him, kissed her again, long and hard, before leading her into the softly lit bedroom where the curtains were already drawn.

Carolyn stood looking at the white covers which rested like a cloud on the bed, and Paul saw that she suddenly felt very gauche and foolish. He kissed her gently on the lips, and then stood submissively before her, inviting her to unbutton his shirt, before he swiftly took it off. He kissed her again, moving his naked flesh against hers as he skilfully slipped off her dress, removed her bra, and bent to caress her breasts with his lips before leading her slowly towards the bed.

With speed but elegant control he stripped off the rest of his clothes and, pushing aside the duvet which she'd begun to wrap round her, he slid up against her, moving his hands and mouth gently but expertly all over her body until he felt her not only lose all resistance, but move breathlessly towards him.

Carolyn looked at the handsome man making love to her in this luxurious room and told herself that this was what she wanted. She made herself respond to him, anxious to be the woman he thought she was. She didn't want to disappoint Paul and made her body move in harmony with his. He raised himself up, and she glimpsed the sense of triumph that overwhelmed him.

He wanted her too much to hold back any longer, and he became more forceful, holding her down, as he lost control and became aware of nothing but the final gratification of his lust.

Then he slid away from her and lay on his back with his eyes closed and his lips slightly parted as he breathed out diminishing sighs of satisfaction. Carolyn's eyes weren't closed. She stared at the ceiling, feeling the sensations melt away from her body, and realising that she hadn't really meant this to happen, but that it was too late now.

She pulled the soft white linen up to her chin as she had as a child when dark shadows had invaded her bedroom. She felt the warmth of tears in her eyes but blinked them away, she would not cry, she would look stupid to Paul if she cried.

Paul had one of his fluffy cotton bathrobes ready for her to wear when they eventually left the bedroom. He put on a short silk wrap which he fastened only loosely at the waist so that she could not be unaware that he was still naked.

Quickly, he moved on to the next part of the evening he had planned with meticulous precision. He placed dishes of prawns, smoked salmon and Waldorf salad on the table, together with more champagne. They ate almost in silence, Paul simply wanted to sit and look at her, as if admiring a newly purchased valuable work of art. Carolyn ate slowly but without enjoyment. Paul noticed how listless she seemed and leaned across the table to take hold of her hand.

'What is it? Haven't I made you happy?'

She heard the edgy tone beneath the question, and knew his ego couldn't handle the truth. She smiled and then lied, for she knew that if he suspected she wasn't satisfied he would see the fault as hers, and want to take her back to bed. She despised herself as she murmured reassurances that he had given her the ultimate sexual experience.

She began to panic as she started to wonder how she would cope if Paul did reject her now he had won. She couldn't just walk out of this flat and back into her marriage to Steve. She needed to talk to Paul about the future.

'What happens now, Paul?' she asked, carefully avoiding any nuance of pleading but nevertheless sounding pitiful to her ears.

He looked at her blankly, and then answered, 'Whatever you want.'

'I can't leave them. I can't walk out.'

It took a few seconds before he understood that she was talking about her family. He hadn't even considered the possibility she might leave them, and it was certainly not what he wanted, but he was careful to conceal his alarm at the idea.

'Of course not,' he said, looking at her dolefully as he kissed her hand. 'I could never ask you to do that for me.'

Paul knew he must stop this conversation as soon as possible, but he didn't want the affair to end, not yet, he would feel cheated if this were to be the only time he would possess this woman he had pursued for so long.

No, he was determined to have more from her than this, in fact he wanted her again, now. He pushed back his chair and stood in front of her. He pulled her up into his arms and pleaded softly as he kissed her face and neck, 'Let's just keep it simple, the simple pleasures of a passionate relationship.'

'An affair,' she said, with a touch of accusation in her tone.

He moved behind her and, pulling her robe aside,

278

he stroked his hands over her again and pressed his lips against her neck and shoulders.

'No,' he breathed, 'not an affair, but our wonderful and exciting secret.'

He turned her towards him again, his arms round her waist, his eyes full of certainty.

'You have to take what you want from life, Carolyn.'

She stared at him as she tried to weigh this philosophy in her mind. As she stood there, letting him kiss and touch her, taking over her body once more, she went through all the reasons she had assembled in order to justify what she had committed herself to today. She'd slept with Paul because she had fallen in love with him, she reminded herself, and because he really cared about her.

Steve loved her, but not enough to give her what she wanted. She knew what the future with Steve would hold, for her and also for her children, and she wanted more for them than that. She wanted them to have the kind of life she had always dreamed of, the kind of future she knew that Paul Ferris could provide.

He was holding her tightly now and half pushing, half carrying her towards the bedroom. She looked at Paul's face, his open mouth and his eyes alight with lust, and suddenly the golden image she had created so carefully in her mind vanished, and all she now saw was the truth. Paul Ferris was just a man who wanted to possess her, and he was not the man she loved. Carolyn knew for certain that she didn't want to have sex with him again, she wanted to go home.

She wriggled out of his arms, 'No, I have to go, Paul.'

'Not yet' he said, smiling confidently. 'We can have just a little more time to enjoy each other.'

'No,' she insisted, pulling the thick white robe defensively across her body, 'I need to have a shower before I go.'

Paul was displeased, but wouldn't give her the satisfaction of disappointing him. Instead he walked ahead of her, stretched himself lazily on the bed, like a tomcat in the sun, and watched her as she walked self-consciously across to the en-suite shower room.

'I suppose I can wait.' he drawled, and then, tilting the balance of power, he added, 'As long as I don't have to wait too long.'

Carolyn fled into the bathroom, forgetting her clothes in her haste to escape. Paul felt tempted to follow her and take her again in the shower, but then heard her lock the door. This annoyed him, but he soothed his frustration away with the satisfaction of anticipating the many other times when he would have her.

CHAPTER THIRTY-THREE

Lynda had hoped that she might be invited back to Beechwood Avenue after their visit to the burger bar, but it was a wonderful surprise when it was Gemma who cast off her diffidence and invited her to go home with them.

'It's the Eurovision Song Contest, tonight, Grandma,' she announced, giving the word Grandma extra emphasis. 'Do you watch it?'

'Oh, yes. I've always loved it.'

'I'm going to put my best dress on to watch it, so I can dance properly.'

'Are you now?' said Steve. 'I think it had better be your pyjamas you change into when we get home, because you'll be going to bed after you've seen Katrina and the Waves.'

'Aw, can't we stay up and watch the results?'

'No, you can't. You've had a busy time at your friend's, and now a meal out. You need an early night, or you'll be shattered tomorrow, not to mention bad-tempered.'

He grinned at Lynda who, he could see, was delighted that her grandchildren wanted to spend the evening with her.

'Love Shine a Light' had them all dancing around and cheering after its wonderful performance.

'We're bound to win, aren't we, Grandma?' cried Gemma.

'We're certainly in with a good chance.'

'Can we stay up and watch the results, please,' Gemma begged.

'No. Up to bed now,' her Dad insisted.

She began to plead again, but then started giggling as he chased her towards the door. Then, to everyone's surprise, she doubled back to give Lynda a goodnight kiss before charging out of the room and up the stairs, not knowing that she had caused a tear to join her kiss on her Grandmother's cheek.

Michael had watched this and wondered if he should follow his sister's example, but Lynda saw his embarrassment and blew him a kiss. He grinned at her, and loved her even more for understanding.

After he'd settled the children into their beds Steve poured Lynda a glass of the wine she'd brought, and himself a beer. He sat down opposite her, wondering if he'd be able to ask the favour he needed so desperately, and whether she would, in fact, have enough money to be able to help him.

He needn't have worried, it was soon clear that Lynda had already been thinking about how she could make it possible for Steve to take over the company.

He showed her the documents Gary had photocopied, but didn't tell her how he'd come by them. Lynda had noticed the short, furtive meeting he'd had with his workmate, and decided it was best not to ask. She listened carefully as he explained the situation.

'Randerson's selling the company to Neil Spencer but the sale seems to depend on Randerson getting the contract for Bob Horton's new housing development. And, here's the important bit, this letter from Horton, specifying that he wants me to do all the design work, and be project manager.'

Steve paused and looked at Lynda, hoping that she would see what he needed without his having to ask.

Glancing through the documents again, she said, 'In other words, that contract depends on your skills and reputation.'

'Looks like it.'

She smiled at him. 'You could set up your own business if you could get that contract for yourself.'

'Yes.'

'But you need money to do that.'

'Yeah. We've been trying to save up, but we're still paying John for this place.' He stopped and looked at her, again feeling guilty that they'd bought her home without her consent.

'It's all right, Steve, I told you, I'm buying Kath's house.' Then, thinking about the tensions she had observed between him and Carolyn, and the way Jenny Heywood had thrown her arms round him that afternoon, she added, 'I'm just glad you and Carolyn are happy here.'

Watching for his reaction, she saw him wince.

'You are happy, aren't you?' she probed.

'Carolyn isn't,' was Steve's blunt reply, and she understood what his eyes were saying about her daughter.

'But she might be if you could have your own successful company, and eventually give her the lifestyle she wants.'

'That's what I'm hoping.'

They were both silent, thinking their own thoughts for a while. Then Lynda, looking round the room, said, 'There's a lot of bad memories here.'

Steve nodded, thinking he knew what she meant.

'Sheila, and you and Carolyn.'

'And me and John,' Lynda said, deciding to tell Steve the secret she and John had kept for so long, especially as it had a bearing on what they were about to discuss.

She paused, still feeling the pain of these particular memories.

'It was never the happiest of marriages, as you know, but it might have survived if it hadn't been for Tony Randerson.'

Steve was puzzled now. 'Randerson?'

She looked down at her glass of wine, and spoke very slowly.

'You know how I've always loved a night out, a bit of fun, but John would never want to go with me. He always preferred to stay in and watch television.

'Yes,' Steve said, wondering what was the cause of the anguish on Lynda's face. She was struggling to talk now.

'When Carolyn was a teenager, I used to go out with my friends and have what I considered a good time. Carolyn and her Nana used to think it was disgusting. And one night it was.'

Her voice shook as she continued to make this confession, just as she had all those years ago in this same room.

'I went to The Star and Garter, the pub that's The Madison now, to meet up with a girlfriend who'd decided to get divorced. When I got there she was already chatting up some good-looking fellas, and she pushed me into drinking with them.'

'Is this why you didn't want to go there the other night?'

'Yeah. To cut a horrible story short, we all had too much to drink, she went off with the guy she fancied, and I let Randerson give me a lift home.'

'Tony Randerson?' repeated Steve, trying to relate the image of his now middle-aged, overweight boss with that of a young man chatting up Lynda in a pub.

'Yes.'

Her hand was shaking so much now, she had to

put down the glass.

'Only Randerson didn't take me home, he took me back to his place, his wife was away. And he.'

She stopped again, and Steve saw tears running down her cheeks. He moved across and put his arm round her shoulders.

'He raped me, Steve.'

She put her head in her hands and her body shook as she sobbed, just as she had before in this room, on that terrible night. There was a difference though. This time there was someone here to comfort her. Steve held her close till she could manage to stop crying.

'I'll never forget the look on John's face when I told him,' she whispered. 'Well, I didn't have to tell him, he could see from the state of me, and my dress.'

'Bloody hell,' Steve gasped.

'We decided nobody should ever find out. We told no-one.'

'And what did John do about it?' Steve wanted to know.

'Nothing. Randerson would have made sure John lost his job if he'd gone to sort him out.'

'So what happened?'

'Like I said, we kept quiet about it. But it was always there. John thought it was my fault, and it was, partly. I got drunk and was stupid, but I didn't deserve what Randerson did to me.'

There was no doubt in Steve's mind. 'Of course you didn't.'

'It was the end of our marriage, though, Steve. John and I could never be happy together after that. I had to leave. Because of that, and because of Sheila, and our Carolyn, as you know.'

'Yeah.'

Lynda sat up straight, took another tissue from her handbag, and brushed her hair back from her forehead.

'Would you pour me a drop more wine, love?'

Lynda took a few steadying breaths as he poured the wine.

'And Steve, promise me you won't tell anyone what I've just told you.'

He handed her the wine, 'Not even Carolyn? It would help her understand.'

'No, it wouldn't. Sheila, and Ellen Heywood, had too much influence on Carolyn and the way she thinks, she'd judge it was my fault.'

Steve wished he could contradict Lynda, but he knew that, in all honesty, he couldn't.

'Steve, you won't tell.'

'No I promise.'

They sipped their drinks silently for a few moments, then Lynda spoke in a voice that was now steady, and strengthened by anger.

'So, going back to the reason I had to tell you this sordid tale, I've seen an opportunity here, for both of us. I'm going to lend you enough money for you to take this contract off Tony Randerson, and with any luck, take over his business.'

'Are you sure you can do that, Lynda? It'd be a lot of money. I'd be asking you to gamble on me.'

Lynda hesitated, she was no longer confident about having enough money for Steve and for her own needs; she couldn't ignore the threat that Suzanne might try to take a good part of her wealth away from her.

Then she looked at Steve's honest face, and saw how hard it was for him to pretend he could turn down this chance to achieve his dream. She remembered the same look in Tom Meredith's eyes when she'd offered to work for nothing, and to invest all the money she had in helping him make a success of Loveday Manor.

She stood up, squared her shoulders, and heard her voice change as she felt herself becoming a business woman once more.

'You'll have to draw up a business plan. Work out some estimates, and we'll talk about it.' Then a happy memory lightened her tone and, fingering her horseshoe pendant, she imagined the twinkle in Tom's eyes. 'Me and Tom could always recognise a good bet.'

Steve gave her a hug of gratitude, and then they sat and talked about the business. Lynda also told him a lot, or as much as she wanted him to know, about her and Tom Meredith. Steve realised that Lynda had loved him very much, but couldn't help asking, 'What about John?'

There was deep sadness in her voice as she answered that question.

'I'm sorry, Steve, but Carolyn was right, I am going to divorce him. And he made me tell him this afternoon. That's why he was upset, and didn't come with us after the match.'

'I wondered what was wrong.'

'Our marriage was over before I went away, but I wasn't looking for anyone else, Steve. I promise you I wasn't. But then Tom Meredith came into my life, and he was very special. With Tom I was me, Lynda Collins. No holding back, no pretence, just me, the woman he loved.'

Paul Ferris had wanted to drive Carolyn to her home, but she insisted on getting out of the car on the main road. Paul was amused that she was so afraid of being found out, whereas he would have loved the danger of being seen by Carolyn's husband.

He still felt elated at his conquest and wished he could display his triumph to someone. It was very satisfying to feel so sure of her now, and he had taken pleasure in watching her dress after her shower; there was something about Carolyn Sheldon, an untamed creature beneath the cool façade, and it fascinated him.

Carolyn had hated the way Paul had watched her put on her clothes, as if she were a prostitute and he'd paid for the right to look at her like that. She felt that same anger and shame now, when he leaned across, sliding his hand beneath her dress and up between her thighs, as he kissed her goodnight. She got out of the car quickly slamming the door and running across the road, scarcely pausing to see if there were any cars coming.

With tears in her eyes Carolyn walked slowly down the hill towards Beechwood Avenue, and resolved she would end the madness of this affair with Paul.

Her plan was to get the job in Leeds and make their financial future secure, so that Steve would be free to look for the kind of satisfying, creative work he really wanted.

She had realised today that there could be no other man in her life, that Steve was the one and only love for her, and always would be. That love, and the hope she had for the future lifted her spirits as she walked towards her home.

Lynda's glass was empty, and she was about to reach for the bottle of Chardonnay when she saw Steve look at the clock. She knew why he was anxious, he wouldn't want Carolyn to come home and find her here. It had been a lovely evening, being with him and the kids, but she didn't want to spoil it, so she put down her glass and made ready to leave.

'I'd better be going. I don't think Carolyn's ready to kiss and make up yet. Perhaps she never will be.'

Steve wanted to reassure her, but knew he wouldn't sound convincing, so he went to get her coat. Lynda, suddenly feeling lonely again, was glad to wrap its softness around her. Then they were both startled to hear the front door open.

'Looks like she's back early,' Lynda said, wishing Steve didn't look so worried.

Carolyn had been too preoccupied to notice that Lynda's car was parked on the other side of the road. Walking up to the front door her vision had suddenly become blurred by an intense memory of Paul Ferris taking full possession of her body. She looked at the door and wondered how she could walk back into that house, how she could look into Steve's eyes and not betray her guilt.

But she had to do it, had to act as if nothing had changed. She'd have to tell just a few more lies, and then it would be over. She took off her coat, breathed deeply and made herself relax as she opened the door into the living room. But it wasn't just Steve she had to face, her Mother was standing beside him.

Lynda fixed a smile on her face, as if it were the most natural thing in the world for her to be there, and it was, in her opinion.

'Hiya,' she greeted her daughter in a manner which was a little heartier than she'd intended. 'Was it good?'

Carolyn looked at her blankly, her guilty mind transforming the polite enquiry into something sinister.

'The concert,' Lynda said, moving closer to her daughter and looking at her pale face, and startled eyes. Then she noticed the streaks in Carolyn's make-up and a small tear which still lingered on her cheek.

'Is it raining?' she asked, reaching out to wipe away the tear. For a second they were mother and child again, but then Carolyn moved out of reach.

'No,' she said, quickly brushing her hand across her cheek. She didn't want this, she wanted to talk to Steve, to hold him and tell him she loved him. But her Mother was there, standing between them, with an inquisitive look in her eyes.

'What are you doing here?' Carolyn demanded rudely.

Lynda trying not to feel hurt, responded with a pretended nonchalance.

'Going home. See you.'

She closed the door behind her, leaving Carolyn wondering once more whether she could hide her adultery from Steve.

'Hello, love,' he said, his guilt almost matching hers. 'Have you had a good time?'

CHAPTER THIRTY-FOUR

Jenny Heywood was dreading taking her daughters to Sunday lunch at Kirkwood House that Bank Holiday weekend. Jenny was making a last attempt to change her daughter's mind, but Alex was determined that she would not share her birthday with her Grandmother.

'It's my eighteenth birthday party! I don't want to have it at Kirkwood House, and I certainly don't want it full of my Grandmother's old cronies! None of my friends will want to come!'

'I know it's not what you wanted, Alex, but Ellen is desperate to have a party for you and her at the family home. I think she's got a feeling that it will be the last birthday celebration she'll hold there.'

'That's ridiculous, she can't know that.'

'Sounds like emotional blackmail to me,' Katie said, firmly supporting her sister. 'And like Alex says, her friends won't want to party with a load of stuck up old biddies.'

Jenny repeated some more of the conversation she and Dan had had about the party.

'There won't be many of Ellen's friends there. That's part of the problem, so many of them have died recently that she has very few people she can invite.'

'That's not my fault, and it's still no reason to spoil my birthday party,' Alex argued.

Jenny shook her head. 'I'm sorry, but Uncle Dan and I don't see how we can refuse her. And there will be compensation, we'll be giving you money to take your friends out on the town afterwards, so it'll be just an hour or two with 'the oldies' and then you can go and have the celebration you want.'

'She'll need a lot of money to do that,' Katie commented, looking at her mother doubtfully.

'It's O.K.' Jenny reassured her, 'Uncle Dan and I have saved up, and Lynda Stanworth's given us some money towards it as well.'

Katie was astonished. 'Has she? That was kind of her. Don't tell Grandmama, though, she'll blow her top!'

'Why would Lynda Stanworth want to do that?' Alex asked, 'she doesn't think I'm a charity case, does she?'

'No. She wants to do it as a thank you for all the parties she went to at Grandma and Grandad Kellys' house.'

'Oh, that's all right, then,' Alex said, thinking Lynda was a lady who knew how to make up a good excuse for being generous.

'So will you do this, Alex? Please,' Jenny begged. 'I know it's not what you want, but it would be so kind.'

'If you promise we won't have to stay long before we escape into town?'

'It's a deal.'

In spite of all this diplomatic preparation, the Sunday lunch still had moments of tension and exasperation, not to mention confrontation. It began well, with Alex thanking her Grandmother for hosting her birthday party, and Katie managing to keep a straight face as she listened to her sister's seemingly very sincere expression of gratitude.

Ellen was pleased, but could not resist adding a criticism aimed at reminding her daughter-in-law of the decision she had opposed many years ago.

'Your Mother's house is entirely inadequate for such functions. Even a Sunday lunch seems to be beyond its capabilities these days. I hope Steven Sheldon did finally manage to complete his work on your kitchen yesterday?'

'Not quite,' Jenny replied carefully. Then, feeling she had to defend Steve, she explained, 'He had to take Michael to the football match.'

'And you,' said Katie teasingly trying to lighten the atmosphere, but immediately realising she had blundered again, as Ellen turned to Jenny, her eyes glinting.

'You went out with him again?'

Jenny wondered how on earth Ellen knew she'd been out with Steve, and guessed that Carolyn must have told her. Katie tried to distract Ellen by asking if she'd like more gravy.

'No I would not,' Ellen replied curtly. 'But I would like an explanation.'

Jenny was furious that Ellen was once more assuming she had a right to police her social life. As Alex and Katie had been saying for months, it was time to stop letting her get away with such bullying.

'I am allowed to go out, you know,' she replied in a tone which made Ellen withdraw back in her chair, but only for a few seconds.

'It depends who with,' she retorted, but then was shaken again as Katie pitched in.

'She's forty, you know, not fourteen!'

'Do not address me in such a manner, young lady,' Ellen reprimanded her granddaughter. 'I have no objection to your Mother going out,' she continued condescendingly, and then added the caveat, 'when appropriate.'

'And when would that be?' Katie demanded.

There was a complete silence which seemed to go

on for ever, until Jenny rescued her daughter by changing the subject, asking politely.

'Did you and Carolyn enjoy the concert last night, Ellen?'

'Yes, it was superb, but I went with Alice in the end, not Carolyn.'

Jenny's eyes opened wide at this contradiction of what Steve had told her, but she had no time to speculate what it might mean, as Ellen was intent on discussing the guest list for the party in June.

With a glance at Jenny, Ellen announced, 'Carolyn will, of course, be coming to my birthday party, together with her husband on this occasion.'

Ellen, unaware that Carolyn had decided to make every effort to save her marriage, had been surprised when she had, unusually, asked if her husband could accompany her to the party. Jenny was pleased that Steve was invited but wondered how she would cope with seeing him with his wife.

'I have also invited Edwin Lawson and his wife,' Ellen continued, 'and a select few of my friends from church.'

Dan knew that his Mother wouldn't have wanted to invite Steve, and he knew that the guest list also included another person of whom she would definitely not approve.

He couldn't find the courage to mention the name yet, so talked instead about the cakes he was making for the occasion, and another possible guest.

'Alice Smith is decorating the cakes, so it would be nice if we could ask her along as well,' he suggested.

'I see no need,' was Ellen's swiftly voiced opinion. 'I'm becoming a little concerned about the length of the guest list as it is. How many of your friends will be coming, Alex? Not too many, I hope.'

'It is my eighteenth birthday,' Alex reminded her

Grandmother, 'so there will be a fair number.'

Dan could see Ellen wasn't pleased and, deciding that it might be easier to deal with all the problems together, said, 'And Alex has kindly allowed me and Jenny to invite some of our friends, too.'

'And who might they be?' asked Ellen, her eyebrows anticipating her disapproval.

Dan took a deep breath, 'Lynda Stanworth for one.'

His Mother drew herself up, and the way she looked at him told him she recognised this as the full rebellion it was.

'Indeed.' She paused as she thought of a retaliation. 'And I assume you are also inviting John Stanworth, as your best friend.'

He winced but managed to turn it into a smile. 'Yes, of course.'

Ellen hadn't finished with him yet,

'It would be charitable also to invite Jean Haworth, that widow who is a friend of theirs.

'Yes, if you like,' Dan conceded, thinking that his Mother's talent for making mischief sometimes rivalled that of Alice Smith

Ellen decided she'd had enough of this discussion.

'That's all settled then,' she concluded, and then indulged in a final assertion of opinion. 'I've always thought John Stanworth would have done better to have married Jean Haworth rather than Lynda Collins.'

Dan couldn't resist challenging his Mother's judgement which was, as ever in her opinion, indisputable.

'Not financially,' he said cockily. 'Lynda's got a bit of money now.'

'Has she indeed?' said Ellen, the tone of her voice and the look on her face fully justifying Lynda's nickname for her, 'Lady Disdain'. Watching his Mother, Dan added jauntily, but with an undercurrent of intent, 'I've always fancied marrying into money.'

Ellen, having had quite enough of this bad behaviour, glared at him, and considered making some sharp remark about his past mistakes where women were concerned. Then she reminded herself that she had resolved to be kinder to Daniel.

'I feel rather tired,' she said, pushing back her chair. 'I shall go to my room and leave you to enjoy yourselves without me.'

Ellen's heart had been persistent lately in drumming into her that one's life could not continue indefinitely, and she had spent many hours reflecting on the past.

Ellen Heywood desired the immortality of being remembered, but she knew that such true and precious remembrance was granted only to those who are loved.

On the morning of Bank Holiday Monday Lynda, wearing old jeans and a baggy T shirt, was in Jean's living room on her hands and knees, smoothing filler into the cracks above the skirting board. When Jean came downstairs and saw her she felt a little guilty.

'You've made an early start,' she said.

Lynda noted that Jean was wearing a pretty cotton blouse and a very respectable pair of trousers.

'I want to get the filling done before John arrives.'

'He won't come,' Jean predicted, but was pleased when Lynda contradicted her, as she'd hoped.

'He will, he promised me last week. He knows I can't paper the ceiling on my own.'

'He won't want to come here, not after our row in the Vienna, and what you told him on Saturday.'

'He will. You should know by now that he's like a

big kid, likes to sulk a bit, but he'll get over it.'

'He asked me for his key back.'

'Forget about that. When he comes, just give him a big smile and a piece of that chocolate cake you've made for him, and he'll be fine.'

'I didn't make the chocolate cake for John.'

'Oh, no? And you've not dressed to look nice for him either.'

'No, I haven't.'

'Well, all I can say is, you look a bit glamorous for just decorating.'

'I'll go and change.'

'Don't be daft. Put the kettle on and get some breakfast before you do anything. I could murder a cup of coffee and a bacon sandwich.'

The doorbell rang.

'Make that three bacon sandwiches, I think John's just arrived.'

She was right. Jean let John in and made him welcome, and he seemed to have forgotten there was a problem between them. Jean was amazed at how Lynda's predictions about John's behaviour always proved to be accurate. She tried to tell herself it was only to be expected, after all they had been married for over twenty years before Lynda had left.

She watched them falling into their old way of working together, as if they'd never stopped being a married couple. Jean had worried that John might not be fit enough to do such strenuous work, but he rejoiced in the physical effort and found skills and reserves of energy he'd thought he had lost. It was just like old times, John and Lynda decorating, and cursing and laughing as they wrestled with strips of wallpaper which offered maximum resistance to taking their place on the ceiling.

'It's going to look good,' he said, looking round the room as they took a tea break.

'This is the wallpaper I've chosen,' Jean said, holding out a roll of pale green embossed paper for his approval.

'Yeah, that should look nice. It's a lot lighter in here already,' he commented.

'I made her take her net curtains down,' Lynda said. 'That made a difference. Have you got rid of yours yet?'

John looked at her, and nodded. 'Yes, when I got home from the match on Saturday. I was in a bad mood and yanked them down.'

'Oh.' Lynda concentrated on drinking her tea.

Jean knew John had been upset by Lynda's talk of divorce, and didn't want that to be discussed now. She made a sound which attempted, with little success, to be a laugh.

'Lynda's always had a thing about net curtains, haven't you, Lynda?'

'Yes, they're old fashioned, and depressing to me.'

'Me and Carolyn put them up for John, to give him a bit or privacy, with it being a ground floor flat,' Jean said defensively.

'Something else my daughter and I don't agree on,' Lynda sighed. 'Did you see her yesterday, John?'

'Yes, she asked me round to tea after she and Steve had taken the kids to that new theme park place that's opened.'

'Did they not invite you to go there with them?' Jean asked.

'No. They know I don't like fairground rides.'

Lynda laughed, 'Yes, I remember you being sick after I made you go on that roller-coaster at Blackpool when we were first married.'

'Yes, so do I.' John looked at her, his eyes full of

298

regret. 'We had some good laughs, didn't we, love. I wish I'd appreciated it more, the way you used to make me laugh and enjoy life.'

Lynda sighed. 'I wish our Carolyn had appreciated it more as well, she just thought I was being stupid, not to mention 'common' whenever I tried to have a bit of fun.'

'It wasn't all her fault, my Mother didn't help either.'

Lynda got up and began to move the pasting table to the other side of the room.

'Yeah. What was it Princess Diana said? Three people in her marriage? Well, there were four in ours. And your Mother and our Carolyn between them didn't give me much of a chance.'

John got up and took hold of the other end of the table to help manoeuvre it into position.

'You can't blame Carolyn.'

'Can't I?'

'No,' Jean joined in at last. 'She was just a child, Lynda. You can't say she came between you.'

'Not on purpose, but you have to admit, John, that it was you and her against me a lot of the time. You always took her side.'

John stood very still for a moment.

'Yes, I suppose I did,' he said quietly. 'I won't make that mistake this time, Lynda. I'll tell her she has to give you a chance.'

'No, I don't want to cause trouble between you and her. That was part of the reason I went away, remember?'

'And now you've come back.'

Lynda ignored the hope in John's eyes. 'Yes.'

'And she's buying a house,' Jean informed him, hoping to add something positive to this conversation.

'Yes, so I've heard. Kath and Bernie's place. I can see why you'd want to live there.' There was a wistful look in his eyes as he remembered, 'We had some good times in that house.'

Lynda smiled gently at him, and Jean was jealous of the memories they were sharing.

'When will you move in?' John asked.

'I don't know, I've only just had the offer accepted, but I'm hoping to be in at the beginning of June. It should be possible, as I'm paying cash.'

Jean smiled wryly to herself as she saw John's eyebrows move upwards in astonishment. She picked up their empty beakers and walked towards the kitchen.

'It's the sort of house I've always wanted to buy,' John told Lynda.

Jean paused to challenge that statement.

'I thought you fancied a bungalow?' she said, her look reminding John of all those conversations they'd had about possibilities for the future.

John knew what she was thinking, but still said, 'Lynda doesn't like bungalows, do you?'

'No,' Lynda, unaware of the significance of this conversation, agreed with him.

'I don't like them either,' John stated firmly.

'Oh? Well, in that case, I hope you two will be very happy together,' Jean cried as she flounced into the kitchen.

There was a moment's stillness before John, looking hopefully at Lynda, said quietly, 'We could be, you know.'

'What?'

'Very happy together.'

'No, John. I told you, I am asking you for a divorce. I have to. You'll be getting a letter from Philip Lawson, very soon.'

300

John couldn't move, anxiety invaded his whole body. He wasn't ready for this. He wasn't sure if he ever would be.

'There's no hurry for this divorce, is there?'

She couldn't answer that, but instead said gently, 'Let's stay friends, John. For the sake of our grandchildren, if nothing else. There's too much between us for us not to be friends.'

CHAPTER THIRTY-FIVE

Steve was glad to get back to work on Tuesday morning, he'd had enough of Carolyn and her constant changes of mood. He could understand her being upset when she arrived home on Saturday night to find he'd invited Lynda round. He'd tried to explain that it was Gemma's idea, but of course that had made it worse. Carolyn didn't want Lynda near her children, which was ridiculous, but Carolyn was too knotted up in the past to allow herself to see that.

She'd seemed to have got over it on Sunday, though, and had snuggled up close to him in bed when they woke up. But they'd ended up arguing again yesterday.

Steve hated keeping secrets from Carolyn, and remembered how he used to tell her his fears, and listen to her advice. Now, however, she had embraced the AFS world of bean-counters, where employees were no longer people, but 'human resources'. He knew what solution to his problems she would offer this time, and it wasn't one he was willing to accept.

He also knew what her reaction would be if she found out that he'd asked Lynda to lend him the money to 'buy-in' to a self-employed future. He'd have to tell her soon, but he wanted everything to be under control, and to look like a good prospect, so that she'd see that he would deliver success.

Lynda had warned him to be careful what he said to Gary; she couldn't promise yet that she'd be able to offer all the money Steve would need.

That morning, he and Gary found a few minutes

to have a private conversation in a corner of the yard well away from anyone. Steve found that Gary wasn't ready to be cautious; he was determined to embark on this adventure, even if it did turn out to be foolhardy.

'We'll have to get a bank loan if Lynda hasn't got enough to lend us,' he said when Steve warned him that nothing was certain yet.

Steve felt his hopes become vulnerable as he thought what that would mean.

'The bank will want not just the business plan, they'll want some security as well. I've got nothing except the house.'

'Same here,' Gary muttered as they looked at each other and thought about the risk.

'Jackie won't be keen,' Gary confessed, marvelling at his own understatement, 'What about Carolyn?'

Steve stared at the grimy windows of the mill, and finally voiced his fear.

'All she can talk about is this interview she's got.'

'Julie told Jackie she thinks it's going to be cancelled.'

'No, they've just postponed it for some reason. It'll be next month now. If she gets that job,' he said slowly, 'she'll go to Leeds, with or without me.'

Gary drew in his breath sharply. 'Oh. That bad, eh?'

'Getting that way.'

Gary couldn't bear to see Steve, or any man, bow his head like that. He tried to demolish Steve's doubts about himself, bring him back into the realm of macho belief.

'Not to worry,' he said jauntily, slapping Steve on the back, 'From the way Jenny Heywood was looking at you on Saturday, she'd give you a bed to sleep in.'

Gary hadn't really expected Steve to laugh, just to lighten up a little, but he was staggered by the vehemence of Steve's reply.

'Stop talking like that, Gary!' he shouted. Then, looking round, he lowered his voice, speaking through gritted teeth. 'I've got two kids to think about. And anyway,' he added, unaware that he sounded as if he were trying to convince himself, 'I love Carolyn.'

Gary, who never liked to be shouted at, or be in the wrong, tilted his head on one side and asked, 'Do you?'

Gary didn't get an answer.

On Wednesday afternoon Mark Meredith's Range Rover parked on Bridge Street and made Jean's little terraced house look tiny. Lynda, too, felt smaller as she stood at the front door and watched this young man she loved jump down on to the pavement. She also felt all her strength leave her, as seeing Tom's son caused her grief to sweep through her once more.

Mark was not quite as tall as his father, but he had the same tousled dark brown hair, and the same magnetic energy. He opened his arms wide as he strode up to Lynda and lifted her off her feet. He blinked back tears before he released her, for his grief made him feel a need for her to hold and comfort him again, just as she had when he was a boy.

'How are you, love?' she asked quietly, and he heard that warmth of her Northern accent which always came back into her voice when she was vulnerable.

'Fine,' he said firmly. 'How are you?'

'Fine,' she lied, and then they both shook their heads as the tears filled their eyes again.

'We'd better go in, before we show ourselves up in the street,' Lynda said, trying to smile.

He followed her into the house, which made him feel he needed to bend his head before going through the door into the living room.

'Sorry about the mess. I'm in the middle of decorating.'

'As usual,' he grinned.

'Yeah. I'm doing this as a thank you to my friend Jean Haworth, for having me to stay.'

'You said you were with your family.'

She blushed at the lie she'd told. 'They haven't really got the room, with my two grandchildren, so I moved in here, but I'll be moving again soon. I've bought a house.'

'Oh. So you're staying in Milfield?'

'Yes, love. I think I have to, for a while at least. Sit down, you make the place look untidy,' she joked, patting the seat next to her on the settee.

'But you will come back to Loveday?'

'When the time is right. How is everyone? Have you been busy over the Bank Holiday?'

'Oh, yes, it's been crazy as usual. We had that wedding booked in on Saturday, remember?'

'Oh, yes. Quite a big one.'

'Yeah, so there were all the guests to accommodate, and our usual Bank Holiday bookings as well.'

'But you're coping without me?'

'Sort of. But it's not the same, the whole place doesn't feel the same without you, and without my Dad.'

They were silent, knowing there was nothing they could say, nothing they could do to restore the happiness they had shared.

'I'll make you a cup of tea,' Lynda said, taking refuge in simple hospitality. Mark followed her lead, to try to ease the pain.

'A proper cup of tea,' he said. 'You always claimed you couldn't make 'a proper cup of tea' with the water down South.'

'You'll taste the difference, I guarantee.'

'I'll bring your things in while you do that,' he said and went to unload the boxes he had packed carefully in the Range Rover.

'Would you put them in the front room, love?' Lynda called after him. 'I'll bring the tea in there. And I've made you roast beef sandwiches, just as you like them, salt but no pickle.'

'And plenty of butter,' he reminded her, knowing she wouldn't have forgotten.

It was strange to see her belongings packed away neatly in boxes, and it was heartbreaking to see the small antique rocking chair standing in Jean's tiny front room.

'I didn't know you were bringing furniture as well,' Lynda said, finding it a little hard to speak.

'Just your rocking chair. My Mother took it to an antique dealer, I was lucky to get there before he sold it,' he told her, angry and embarrassed at Suzanne's behaviour.

'Oh.'

'I've had a new lock put on the apartment so she can't get in there now. I'll hire a van and bring the rest of your stuff, and any other pieces of furniture you want, when you've moved into your house. Unless you want to leave them for when you come back?' he said hopefully.

'It might be as well to bring them. Thank you.'

Lynda sat on the rocking chair and closed her eyes, letting its gentle rhythm calm her as it had so many times. When she opened her eyes again, she was startled as she found herself looking into Mark's, which were almost as blue as Tom's, but not as ready

306

to spark with laughter. He saw that she was picturing his Dad sitting opposite her.

'It's hard, isn't it?' he said softly.

'Yes.'

He looked uncomfortable perched on the neat, dove grey sofa which Jean had coveted so much that Gordon Haworth had bought it, even though it had not been an item in the Co-op sale.

They talked for about an hour, trying to deal with practicalities like business he needed to discuss with her, but also needing to talk about Tom, in a way which only the two of them could share.

But there were things like Suzanne's determination to contest the will, and her future at Loveday Manor, which they didn't want to talk about, but had to. They were both a little relieved when it was time for Mark to go.

'It'll take you a couple of hours to get to the Lake District from here.'

'Yes.'

'And you're not going to call in on your way back?' Lynda asked, needing to check; it had been tricky to arrange a time when Mark would not meet people like Jean, who might let him know the true situation Lynda was facing.

'No, I'm treating myself to a couple of days walking after the conference as we're quieter next weekend. I'll need to drive straight back down on Sunday night.'

She stood up and kissed him on the cheek.

'Give my love to Patrick and Amy and the kids.'

'I will. And I'll come back when you're ready for me to bring whatever else you need from Loveday. But remember, it's still your home, and always will be.'

When Jean came home from work she was shocked to find her front room full of boxes.

'There isn't room to sit down in there. You'll have to find somewhere else to put it. You might not be moving into Bennett Street for ages yet.'

'You never sit in the front room anyway,' Lynda said sharply, still feeling upset after Mark's visit. 'You're as bad as Sheila Stanworth. What's the point of having a room if you never use it?'

Jean didn't like being compared to John's late Mother, and repeated, 'Well, all those boxes can't stay in there.'

'Don't worry, I'll phone Dan and ask if he can look after them for me. There's plenty of room at Kirkwood House. He'll be happy to help me out.'

'His Mother won't.'

Lynda knew Jean was right, and was relieved when Dan, eager for anything which would give him contact with the woman he loved, agreed to bring his van round tomorrow.

Lynda and Jean had their evening meal together, with little pleasant conversation to accompany it. Lynda spent the rest of the evening alone in Jean's 'best room' looking through the contents of the boxes, and allowing herself to cry. Later, she would wish that she had paused to consider in whose house she would be placing such personal possessions.

Jean had been in a bad mood since Monday. She'd seen that John was still hoping Lynda would change her mind about a divorce. It seemed to Jean now that she would never have John Stanworth and that chance of happiness she'd always craved.

When she came home from work on Thursday, after a day spent with customers who thought having money gave them the right to be rude, she didn't want to listen to Lynda talking about Loveday Manor as she looked at some of the things which were so precious to her. Jean didn't want to see the lovely vases and small works of art which Lynda and Tom had brought home as mementos of their holidays together.

'It must be nice to have money,' she commented. 'I've never been able to buy myself things like that.'

Lynda was getting tired of Jean's envy. 'I've had to work hard for the money I've had.'

'So have I, but I've never had your luck. Especially with men,' she laughed a little hysterically.

'I was lucky, finding Tom Meredith,' Lynda conceded carefully.

'And John. You got him as well, don't forget.' Overwhelmed by her resentment and her misery, Jean cried out, 'It's not fair, you always getting what I'm only allowed to dream about. Even now when, by rights, you should have come back in disgrace, you turn up with a load of money – from your fancy man!'

'Don't you dare call Tom that.'

Jean's eyes blazed with self-righteousness. 'Well, what else was he?'

The truth came loud with pain and pride, 'My husband, that's what!'

Lynda felt the cold grasp of fear at her throat as soon as she'd said the words.

'Your husband?' Jean gasped.

The doorbell rang and Lynda, still white-faced, went to let Dan in.

'Good evening, ladies,' he greeted them jovially, but then stopped as he saw the expressions on their faces.

'What's happened?'

'I've just told Jean that I married Tom Meredith.'

'Oh.'

'Do you know about this, Dan?'

309

'Yes, Lynda told me a while ago.'

Jean turned to stare at Lynda.

'How could you marry him, Lynda? You're married to John.'

With tears in her eyes, Lynda described how Tom had pleaded with her to become his wife, and how she had wanted to make that eternal commitment to the man she loved so much. She also told them that Tom Meredith's ex-wife would do anything to take Loveday from her.

'She sees it as hers, and also she doesn't want to let go of any connection to Tom, and I understand that. But I invested both money and a big part of my life into making Loveday Manor the success it's become.

And now I need the money to help Steve set up his own business. I want to do that for him and Carolyn, and my grandchildren. But if Suzanne, or anyone at Loveday, finds out I wasn't legally married to Tom it would lead to, to all kinds of trouble.' She stopped there, not wanting to give voice to her fears.

'Oh, hell,' Dan said as he thought of the possible consequences. 'You could lose the lot.'

'Yeah,' Lynda agreed quietly.

'If anyone finds out,' said Dan pointedly looking very hard at Jean, who hesitated too long, and then faltered as she spoke.

'I won't tell anyone,' she said, but then worried that it sounded too firm a promise, she added, 'unless I have to.'

Dan and Lynda sat back and looked at each other, silently acknowledging that Lynda would have to make do with that conditional reassurance.

They were all glad of the distraction of clearing Lynda's boxes out of Jean's front room and loading them into Dan's van, ready to be transported to Kirkwood House. Jean was feeling ashamed of her behaviour this last couple of days and, hoping to make amends, invited Dan to stay for some supper.

'Thank you, Jean, I've love to but I can't. I'm still in the dog-house for coming home late last time I came round here. And I only got let out then because she had Carolyn for company.'

'Your Mother gets more of my daughter's company than I do,' Lynda complained.

'She didn't get it for long that night. Apparently Carolyn left very soon after I went out. Mother was very disappointed.'

Lynda turned to Jean, 'But you were babysitting round at Beechwood Avenue till eleven, weren't you? Or was it Carolyn wanting to have a private chat with 'Aunty Jean' that kept you?'

Jean, feeling guilty about keeping secret from Lynda many of her conversations with Carolyn, denied this indignantly.

'No, Steve brought me home as soon as Carolyn got back.'

The three of them were silent for a moment, and then looked at each other, with one question in mind, 'Where had Carolyn been for the rest of that evening?'

CHAPTER THIRTY-SIX

The next day was Carolyn's thirty-first birthday, and she and Steve were going out for a meal. Normally Carolyn would have asked Jean Haworth to babysit with John, but he had made it clear that if she wouldn't ask her Mother to babysit with him, then he would prefer to do it on his own.

Carolyn had booked the afternoon off so that she could have her hair done, pick up her Dad and the children and cook them a birthday tea before she and Steve went out. Normally John would have looked forward to such an occasion, but all he could think about was the letter he'd received that morning from Philip Lawson, and the divorce he didn't want.

Gemma and Michael, eager not to miss their television programmes, dashed into the house as soon as Carolyn had parked the car, but John took his time following her through the garden.

He stopped to admire the trailing golden alyssum, and the dainty pale pink flowers of the clematis which Lynda had planted to grow up the old apple tree, which had been there when he and Lynda had bought the house.

'Your Mother planted most of the things in this garden,' he said. 'In the spring she'd watch out for every plant and bulb flowering again. That was one of the things I loved about her, her pleasure in things that others would take for granted.'

He saw Carolyn stiffen, she obviously didn't want to hear this, but he'd made up his mind that it was time he talked to her about Lynda, and he wasn't going to allow his daughter's scornful look to deter him.

'Come on, Dad, I need to see to the dinner.'

John stood his ground. 'We didn't give her much of a chance, you know. She just wanted us to get out and enjoy life. But I was too lazy to join in, and selfish.'

Carolyn looked at him, then turned and walked into the house, not willing to wait any longer for him to follow her.

John enjoyed the meal with his lively grandchildren and Steve, who'd decided he needed a small portion to stop him being ravenous. Carolyn was a very good cook and, though no-one seemed aware, preparing a lovely meal was one of the ways she showed her love for them all.

As they sang 'Happy Birthday' round the cake Carolyn had made for herself, John looked round the table with pride; this was a good, strong family and his grandchildren loved their parents, even though they might not always show it. They took it for granted that their parents loved them and loved each other, and John was glad.

When the children had disappeared into the front room to continue watching their television programmes, John sat back and looked at Steve and Carolyn who were enjoying a cup of coffee with him.

'Those kids have a much better family life than I ever had, you know. It's great to see you all relaxed when you sit round the table together. Meals were often a nightmare when I was growing up, with my Mother and her criticisms.'

'You shouldn't talk about Nana like that,' Carolyn reprimanded him, sounding a little like the woman she was always ready to defend.

'And you shouldn't talk as if your Mother wasn't a

313

nice person either.'

'Dad, will you stop this? I don't want an argument with you, especially on my birthday!'

Carolyn went into the kitchen to do the washing up, leaving John to exchange a sympathetic look with his son-in-law.

Later, while Steve was persuading the children to go to bed and Carolyn was getting ready for what she hoped would be a romantic evening with her husband, John sat by the fire, reading the evening paper. Then he saw some holiday brochures in the magazine rack, and showed the Norfolk Broads one to Steve as he came back into the living room.

'Planning a holiday?' John asked.

'Nothing definite,' Steve replied quickly, making an immediate connection between affording a holiday and the unpredictable future he had at the moment. He was finding it hard to think about anything except his hope that he would be able to pull together a deal and succeed in buying Randerson out of the business.

'The kids would love a holiday messing about in a boat,' John said.

'I know, but Carolyn doesn't fancy it. She wants a hotel holiday. Four star of course.'

John was all too familiar with that kind of demand from Carolyn, and he understood very well the pressure Steve felt at being unable to satisfy her longing.

John smiled as he began a story from his early married life

'A friend once invited me and Lynda for a weekend on a gin palace he'd hired on the Broads. Lynda thought it was great.'

Carolyn, hearing this as she came back into the room, interrupted him. 'Oh, yes, I've seen the photos. Her in a bikini waving to all the weekend sailors.'

'Only for a laugh. All she wanted was a laugh,' John said, silently pleading with his daughter to listen, to be willing to have her judgements about her Mother questioned. But, like her Mother, Carolyn had never been very good at listening.

'I wish you'd stop it,' she cried, 'trying to pretend that you and my Mother were happy together.'

It had been a long time since John had lost his temper, he'd had to learn to keep it in check in the past few months, for the sake of his health if nothing else. But he was in danger of losing it now.

'We were happy,' he insisted, his voice getting louder. 'All three of us when you were little. There were good times, when we were very happy, Carolyn, and I wish you'd start remembering that!'

Carolyn wasn't going to have him re-writing history.

'All I remember are the rows, and her banging the door on her way out!'

John could hear that sound even now, and could picture Lynda's face tight with desperation, and sometimes also wet with tears as she walked out. He'd allowed it to happen so many times, but he had to defend her now.

'She got sick of us ganging up on her, Carolyn, you and me, and my Mother,' he said more calmly.

This was nothing but a travesty of the truth Carolyn, and she wouldn't let him get away with it, even though he was the father she had loved so much all her life.

'She was selfish, Dad. She didn't give a damn what we thought. She wanted all her own way, all the time.'

Steve gave a shout of laughter, but there was bitterness in his voice as he said, 'That's rich, coming from you!'

Carolyn glared at him. 'Don't you start defending

315

her as well!' she cried, and felt stranded as she looked from Steve to her Dad, seeing both men were against her.

John saw Carolyn's face turn pale and her eyes deadened and dejected. He'd seen that look before, and didn't want his daughter to be the one to walk out of the house this time.

He stood up and put his arm round Carolyn's shoulders.

'I'm sorry, love. I didn't mean to cause trouble, especially on your birthday. You're supposed to be going for a night out.'

'Are we still going?' Steve asked.

'Yes, of course we are,' Carolyn replied, but knew that the romantic evening she'd hoped for was already ruined.

Both Jean and Lynda had been upset when they'd found out that John was going to babysit alone on Carolyn's birthday. Lynda had sent her daughter a card, but Steve had had to warn her that a present would be viewed by Carolyn as nothing but an attempt at bribery. Carolyn wasn't happy about Lynda buying presents for the children, but she knew she couldn't refuse them.

Lynda was desperate to spend more time with her grandchildren. She loved them very much, and wanted to do what she could for them. She'd never forgotten how her Grandma had always found a few shillings for treats like going to see a pantomime at Christmas, and Lynda wanted to do the same for Michael and Gemma.

She knew she could, in fact, do much more than that, she could enable their Dad to become a successful businessman, with all the benefits that would mean for his family. It would be wonderful and she wasn't going to let Carolyn get in the way of her plan.

Also Lynda was still determined that her daughter would realise what a different person she'd become, and hoped that Carolyn might even, one day, be proud to have her as a Mother.

But all this depended on being certain that she'd have enough money to achieve these aims, and as Lynda walked into Philip Lawson's office that morning, that was what she was hoping he would tell her.

'First the good news, Lynda,' he said, leaning forward on his desk. 'I've consulted my friend, and he was fairly confident that you'd not go to prison if the bigamy charge was ever brought against you.

He believes that, in the circumstances, you could have reasonably assumed that you were free to marry. It would be difficult for a prosecutor to prove otherwise, if the matter did ever come before a court, which, if left to me, it never will.'

He paused, and the look he and Lynda exchanged tacitly signalled that he would let the facts she had confided in him slip quietly out of his memory.

'The bad news I have to impart, is that the question of your inherited money and property might be more complicated.

If Tom Meredith's will were to be contested, his son might be able to make a case for your not being entitled to the part of the inheritance you received as his wife.' He paused, and then added, 'Particularly if he were to learn that you and his father were, in fact, not legally married.'

Lynda's throat was dry, and she took a sip of coffee before asking, 'Would that apply only to the

317

money I was left in Tom's will?'

'I would hope so, as you were using the name Lynda Collins before your 'marriage' and all the transactions were made to that name. Does this reassure you?'

'Not as much as I'd like. You see there is a danger the will could be contested.'

'Oh. And that would affect your ability to help Steve set up his own business, if,' he added with a knowing look, 'the opportunity arose.'

'You know about that?'

He winked at her. 'Let's just say I'm very good at listening, and guessing. I want to help, and I think I can.'

'How?'

'By giving you information you might not have. Do you know, for example, who owns Victoria Mill?'

'Randerson.' Lynda hated even uttering the name.

Philip grinned and leaned forward even further to speak in a conspiratorial tone.

'Tony Randerson likes people to think he does, and that he owns the company. But when his father-in-law, Ralph Bentham, died he left it, and everything else, to his daughter. Just to his daughter. Everything. Ralph didn't trust Tony Randerson.'

Lynda's eyes widened as her mind raced.

'Do you think I could meet Mrs Randerson?'

Philip was delighted and waved his hands with a flourish, saying, 'I'll arrange it whenever you like. Her mother was a friend of my Mother, so I know Angela Randerson quite well.'

'You seem to know everyone, and everything in Milfield, Philip,' Lynda said, relaxing enough to tease him now.

'It's one of my many talents,' he boasted.

Steve was finding it difficult to concentrate on the routine of producing kitchen units, and so he was quick to notice Bob Horton strolling into the workshop, very much at ease, but his eyes assessing everything.

Randerson, having a leisurely cup of coffee, had looked out of the office window and seen him arrive. He'd cursed as he'd scrambled to grab his jacket and then thundered down the stairs. Horton had, however, as he'd planned, a few minutes alone with the men in the workshop.

'How are things?' he asked, and noted the way they looked at each other, wondering if they could tell him the truth.

'Not too bad,' Steve said, his eyes letting Horton know this was a not quite accurate statement.

The visitor ran his hand along a cutting machine that had earned its retirement, 'Your boss says you're getting some new equipment.'

Gary snorted his disbelief, 'First we've heard.'

Horton's eyebrows moved slightly upwards but, very sure of himself, he continued, 'It's a long time since I've been here, thought I'd come and have a look at the new design Randerson's been telling me about. One of yours?'

The question this time was directed exclusively at Steve, who was proud to claim ownership and invited Horton to follow him to the far end of the workshop to show him more of his work. Before they had taken more than a couple of steps, however, Randerson galloped towards them and, thrusting Steve aside, he shook Horton by the hand and eagerly showed him the new style unit.

Randerson tried to explain the new features, without giving Steve credit for the design, but when he hesitated over details, Steve was able to step forward and explain his ideas.

'You've got a good team here, Randerson,' Horton said, 'Hope you look after them.'

'I do my best,' claimed Randerson, with a smile which sickened Gary.

Horton, looking over their boss's shoulder, was quick to catch the expressions on the men's faces before Randerson ushered him towards the door.

'Come on up to the office, Bob. I've got some new figures to show you.'

Horton's response was not warm.

'Hope they're better than the last ones.'

Randerson laughed too heartily, and guided his customer out of the workshop, leaving behind irritation and resentment. Gary, knowing it was Matt's turn to make it, decided they should declare an unofficial coffee break. Matt didn't argue but collected up the dirty mugs and went to the back room of the workshop to make the drink. Gary grabbed Steve by the arm and spoke with urgency.

'We're going to have to move fast to stop Horton signing that contract with Randerson. You need to talk to Horton now.'

'I'll try to have a word with him before he goes.'

It wasn't easy, as Randerson solicitously escorted his client to his car, but Steve managed to catch Bob Horton's eye for a moment, and signalled that he would phone him.

Fortunately Carolyn was going to spend an hour with Ellen Heywood again that evening, so Steve was able to make the phone call his future depended on.

It didn't go as well as Steve had hoped, but when he told Lynda about it later, she reassured him. It was only to be expected that a smart man like Horton would want to see a business plan, and evidence that

Steve had the necessary funds to finance such a take-over. She was more hopeful now that she would be able to promise Steve that money very soon. She'd had a letter from a friend.

On the last Thursday in May Lynda went to the estate agents and was given the keys to 21 Bennett Street, her new home. On an impulse she called in at Lawson and Broadbent's and asked Jenny if she'd like to go with her to the house.

'Oh, Lynda, I'd love to. Ever since Katie told me about looking round it with you, I've been dying to see the place again. I'll just ask Philip if I can leave early.'

'What about the girls?'

'I've left their favourite meat and potato pie in the fridge for them to warm up.'

'You are organised.'

'I've had to be with two girls to bring up on my own.'

'I hope they appreciate you.'

Jenny laughed dryly, 'Sometimes.'

'We'll get fish and chips on the way, if you like, and I've got a bottle of wine in the car. I thought we'd celebrate,' Lynda said, as Philip came out of his office.

'I thought I heard your voice, Lynda. Celebrate what?'

'Me getting the keys to Bennett Street.'

'Can I join in this celebration?'

'Sorry, Girls Night,' Lynda told him. 'Now you won't object if I take Jenny off a bit early, will you?'

Philip, putting on his most woebegone expression, sighed heavily, 'I suppose not. Go off and have fun, girls. Don't worry about me staying here to finish the pile of work on my desk.'

Jenny laughed out loud. 'That'll be the day!'

CHAPTER THIRTY-SEVEN

Lynda and Jenny spent over an hour walking through the rooms which held so many happy memories for them both. Then they sat on the dilapidated sofa and Lynda opened the bottle of wine.

'Good to be here again,' she said.

'Yes.' Jenny held out her glass and smiled affectionately at Lynda.

She looked round her parents' old front room and up at the cracks in the plaster on the walls and ceiling. The previous owners had ignored anything which would require a serious effort to restore.

'You've taken on a challenge with this place. It needs quite a bit of money spending on it.'

'I know. But I've learned to rely on my instincts and just go for what I've wanted. And this feels right, doesn't it?'

Jenny nodded, 'My Mum and Dad would have been very happy to see you move into their old home.'

'Well, I had to have somewhere to live, and where better than here?'

'Yes. Steve said you were shocked at coming back and finding Beechwood Avenue wasn't yours any more. He feels a bit guilty about it.'

Lynda was surprised that Steve confided so much in Jenny, but could understand it. Jenny, like her Mother before her, was the kind of person you knew you could entrust with confidences, and talk to about your feelings.

'He's no need to feel guilty. When I walked back

322

into that house I could feel the bad memories coming out of the walls at me.'

'Like me at The Oakwoods house,' Jenny said.

'Yes. I remember you were desperate to get out of there. I'm so sorry that I deserted you like I did, leaving you to deal with it all on your own.'

'You'd already helped me a lot after Richard was killed. And you needed to get away.'

'Yeah. And then I needed to come home.'

Jenny saw the despair on Lynda's face, and perceived how lonely she was. She raised her glass.

'Well, you're here among friends now. It's great to have you back, Lynda.'

'Thank you. I wish everyone felt the same. But what about you, Jenny? Are you having a better life now?'

'Yes. Apart from having two teenage daughters to cope with,' Jenny laughed, 'not to mention a mother-in-law who thinks she's got the right to constantly criticise you, and tell you how to live your life.'

'Yes, Ellen Heywood's good at that. And Dan tells me she expects you to remain a widow for ever.'

'Expects? Demands, you mean.'

'That's appalling. You've a right to find love again, a lovely woman like you. Who is Ellen Heywood to tell people what to do? She's made mistakes, just like everybody else.'

'She didn't marry the wrong man like I did, though.'

'She would have done, if he'd not had a wife already.'

Jenny looked at her in amazement. 'What?'

'Ellen ran away from home with a married man.'

Lynda didn't know why she chose this moment to betray a secret she'd kept for almost forty years. It may have been because of her anger at the way Ellen had swallowed up this young woman's life, or because she felt guilty at not having stayed to defend Jenny when she needed her, or simply that fate decreed this was the right time.

'Ellen?' Jenny stuttered. 'I can't believe it!'

'She was young, and didn't know he was married,' Lynda explained, forcing herself to be fair to her enemy. 'It was like one of those bad Hollywood movies,' she laughed.

'Ellen wanted to be a singer. He promised he'd make her a star, but all he did was send her home pregnant.'

Jenny couldn't imagine the elderly, autocratic woman she knew being seduced and becoming pregnant. 'Ellen?' she repeated. 'Are you sure?'

Lynda nodded.

'Yes. Ellen's father, Alexander Buchanan, made sure it was kept secret. You can do that if you have the sort of money they had.'

'But you know.'

'Yeah, but only because my Mother told me, not long before she died. She used to work as a cleaner at Kirkwood House, and she happened to be in the next room when Ellen broke the news. The Buchanans realised she must have overheard the row.'

'But your Mother never told anyone except you?'

Lynda's expression hardened as she remembered how frightened her Mother had been, even at the memory.

'No. Mr Buchanan put the fear of God into her. He had a lot of influence, and knew how to make people keep a secret.'

'And you've never told anyone?'

'No, my Mum made me promise not to. I don't know why I've told you now, except that you're family, and someone should know.'

Jenny sat quite still, trying to comprehend all this. It was a moment or two before she could ask the question, but she had to confirm what had been racing through her mind.

'Did Ellen keep the baby?' she whispered.

'Yes. And she got married, in a hurry.'

'To Geoff Heywood.'

'Yes. Apparently he'd been in love with her for a long time, and suddenly he was acceptable as a husband. I'm not sure if he knew Ellen was pregnant, but I think he must have had some suspicion.'

Jenny was silent for a moment, hesitating to confront such a significant fact. 'So he wasn't Dan's real father.'

'No.'

'Lynda. Are you going to tell Dan?'

Lynda sighed. 'I've thought about it, many times when she's been cruel to him. But Dan adored Geoff Heywood, and Geoff loved him. I don't want to spoil Dan's memories of the man he thinks was his Dad.'

'I think you were right not to tell him,' Jenny said. 'I don't know what it would do to Dan if he found out. He finds it hard enough to cope with the way Ellen treats him.'

Lynda felt tears in her eyes as she thought of how Dan had suffered. 'It seems to me like she's been punishing him all his life for what wasn't his fault.'

Jenny shook her head in disbelief.

'And do you know the latest thing she's demanding of him? She wants him to sing for her at Alex's party. Alex says she'll die of embarrassment if that happens.'

'I can imagine,' Lynda sympathised with a grimace. 'Ellen made him sing once before, or rather Richard did, at her fiftieth birthday party, because he knew it was what his Mother wanted.'

'Really? I've heard Dan sing, in the pub when he's had a few drinks, and he's good, but he wouldn't want to perform in front of Ellen and her entourage.'

'No, he didn't. He told me he only sang at that party because Geoff couldn't cope with singing on his own. But he did dream of becoming a singer at one time. He even took lessons for a while when he was a teenager, but Ellen put a stop to it, because he would have been better than Richard.'

'Well, he's not going to sing at this party, he's said 'no' to her for once.'

'Should be an interesting evening, your Alex's party,' Lynda said. 'With me and Ellen Heywood in the same room. I'm surprised she's allowing me to come along and lower the tone.'

Jenny laughed. 'You're my guest, and Dan's, you'll be very welcome.' Then, trying not to show how important this was, she added, 'Steve hasn't said if he and Carolyn are coming yet. Do you know if they are?'

Lynda sat back and observed Jenny shrewdly as she thought of all the small intimacies she had witnessed between Jenny and her son-in-law. She was very fond of Jenny Heywood, but all her instincts drove her to protect her daughter, and the future happiness of her grandchildren.

This had to be dealt with, and it might as well be now. Because it was Jenny she tried to make her voice gentle, even though the statement was unequivocal.

'You can't have him, you know, Jenny.'

Jenny was stunned. 'How do you know I'm in love with Steve?'

'It's in your eyes every time you say his name,' Lynda explained quietly, 'and when you hugged at the football match, I could see how things were between you.'

'Lynda, I didn't want to fall in love with him, but I have, and I think he loves me.'

For a moment, she allowed herself to hope that Lynda would be sympathetic, and that it would all work out.

'I'm sorry, Jenny. And I am your friend, but I'm also Carolyn's Mother. And I'm telling you now, he's not for you.'

'Yes, he is,' Jenny said, her voice shaking a little.

'Steve's married,' Lynda continued firmly. 'He's married to my daughter, and they've got two lovely children. End of story.'

'Is it?' Jenny countered, defending her dream of happiness.

'Yes. It has to be. You can't break up a marriage.'

There and then Jenny Heywood made up her mind that, even if her conscience told her it was wrong, she would fight for Steve Sheldon. She loved him and she could make him happy.

It wasn't as if this was anything unusual, she told herself, it happened all the time, couples getting divorced, and everyone being happier in the end.

Jenny's voice was calm, and resolute now.

'No, I wouldn't want to break up a marriage,' she agreed. 'But I don't see why I shouldn't pick up the pieces.'

Lynda stared at her. 'What do you mean?'

Jenny bit her lip, she didn't want to upset her friend, but Lynda had to know the way things were.

'Ask your daughter, not me.'

Jenny refused to say another word and left straight away. Lynda was very angry, but she was also frightened at the thought of what might have given Jenny cause to talk like that, and with such hope in her eyes.

327

The next morning a letter arrived which gave Lynda even more to worry about.

'Whatever is the matter?' Jean asked.

'It's from Mark, warning me that his Mother is determined to contest the will, and has been to see a solicitor.'

'Oh, dear. You could lose a lot of money if she does that, couldn't you?' said Jean, still struggling with the concept of Lynda being a wealthy business woman. 'What are you going to do?'

'There's nothing I can do yet, but Philip will give me good advice if her solicitor writes to me. No good worrying till you know what you're worrying about, is there?' she said trying to sound confident.

'We don't have to go shopping today. I don't want you spending money you might need.'

'Stop worrying, Jean. I have more money than you've ever dreamed of, whatever happens over this will.'

'It's really generous of you, Lynda. Especially when I'm going to the cinema with your grandchildren, It should be you taking them.'

Lynda's face clouded over for a moment.

'Yeah, but it's not your fault, and I suppose Carolyn was trying to help, fixing it up as 'a date' for you and John.'

'But you're their Grandma.'

'It's all right, I'll see them some other time. And like I said, I'll be happy if you and John get back together.'

'I don't know if that will ever happen,' Jean said. 'He didn't seem too pleased about Carolyn organising this, but he couldn't refuse the children.'

'Wait till he sees you in the dress we're going to buy today. He'll realise then he'd be lucky to get you.'

'It's really kind of you, Lynda.'

'I'll come and get you at one o'clock, and we'll go and see if we can find something in Milfield. Otherwise it's a trip to Manchester.'

'I should be buying something from the shop.'

'No you shouldn't. We've had a look, and like I said, they're all frumpy frocks!'

'I just hope Frances Horton's not coming to the party.'

'Stop worrying, Jean, it gives you wrinkles. Now, you're sure 'Francesca' said you could have the afternoon off?'

'Oh, yes. She won't let me near these customers she's got coming in later today, they're the wives of two business men Bob Horton's trying to set up a big deal with.'

'Oh, does that mean he's got more housing developments in mind?'

'I assume so. Why do you want to know?'

'I'll tell you later. Now, are you sure you don't want a lift?'

Alice Smith didn't have any reason to be in Milfield town centre that Friday, other than to be 'out and about' rather than sitting in her kitchen wondering whether to clean out a cupboard.

A dull day suddenly became entertaining, however, when she saw Lynda and Jean emerging from The Moonstone Boutique, each carrying one of the smart, glossy bags which advertised that they were 'Moonstone' customers.

'Good afternoon, ladies,' Alice trilled. 'And what have you been buying?'

'Just a little treat,' Lynda said.

'May I see?' Alice squeaked, stepping forward to take hold of Jean's bag.

Jean pulled it away from her, 'No, you can see it next Saturday.'

'Oh, a dress to wear at the party, is it? You'd better not let Frances Horton see you carrying a Moonstone bag.'

'No, and you'd better not tell her, Alice,' Lynda warned her.

'I won't, I'm not one to make trouble. But I think you two could be a bit more sociable,' she said, looking hurt.

'Sorry, Alice,' Jean apologised. 'How are you?'

'Not too bad. How is your Carolyn?' she asked Lynda. 'I was sorry she wasn't well enough to go to the special Bank Holiday Concert, though her loss was my gain. I hadn't booked because they always put the prices up for the Bank Holiday ones, but Ellen gave me Carolyn's ticket, and said I didn't need to pay because she couldn't have got a refund.'

She finally stopped talking, and noticed the look which passed between Jean and Lynda. 'Have I said something wrong?'

'No. See you next Saturday, Alice,' Lynda replied, and took Jean's arm to hurry her away.

'Where are we going?' Jean asked, slightly out of breath.

'Well away from Little Miss Curiosity,' was Lynda's reply. 'Let's go and have a coffee, somewhere we can talk. Where's that new place you told me about?'

As they sat at a small table tucked away in an alcove of the Vienna Café, Lynda observed her friend looking across the room with a slightly sorrowful expression.

'What is it, Jean?'

'Nothing. I'm just remembering sitting in here and John asking for his key back.'

'That was just him being stupid. Forget it. He'll change his mind when he sees you in that gorgeous dress you've just bought.'

'That you've bought, you mean. It's really kind of you, but I can't keep letting you pay for things.'

'Why not? It gives me a lot of pleasure.'

The waitress brought their coffee and slices of chocolate fudge cake, and Lynda waited until she'd gone before continuing. 'And like I said, I'm not short of money. In fact, don't tell our Carolyn, but I've offered to lend some to Steve so he can set up his own business.'

Jean put down her cake fork.

'Is that wise? You're talking big money there.'

'I know. But it will be an investment more than a loan. And he's my son-in-law. I'll be investing in my family's future.'

Jean toyed with a piece of cake, avoiding looking at Lynda as she asked, 'Have you thought, that Steve might not always be your son-in-law?'

Lynda folded her hands in front of her, and regarded Jean calmly.

'You're thinking about what Alice told us.'

Jean didn't like to raise such doubts, especially about Carolyn whom she loved, but she had to say it.

'Yes. If Carolyn wasn't at that concert, then where was she?'

Lynda's heart felt heavy as she considered her suspicions. 'That's what I want to know. And there was that night you were baby-sitting, when she came home late.'

'Yes.' Jean had added that into the equation, too, but said, 'It might all be totally innocent, of course.'

Lynda put down her cup and saucer, her hand shaking a little.

'You know as well as I do that it's not. She's playing around, the stupid little fool.'

An image came into her head, Paul Ferris standing in the doorway with Carolyn, and the predatory look in his eyes.

'I bet it's him, that guy she works with. When I saw them together, I thought there was something going on.'

Jean, clutching her napkin in her hand, shrank back in her chair and asked tremulously, 'What can we do about it?'

'I'll have to go and see her.'

'Will you?'

'Yes. Tonight, while you and the children are at the cinema. Steve's going to be out as well, a snooker match or something. So I can go and see our Carolyn, and tell her we know what she's been up to.'

'Oh, don't mention me.'

'All right, I won't. There's no need for you to be involved in this row. It'll be just between me and my daughter. God help me.'

CHAPTER THIRTY-EIGHT

After the madness of that Saturday she'd spent with him, Carolyn had been glad that Paul Ferris had been going away on holiday for two weeks, it had given her time to try to rescue her marriage.

She had been embarrassed when Paul came back from his holiday, and began to be much less discreet about their relationship. She saw that Julie and Michelle were noticing that he took every chance to make physical contact, and to have moments alone with her. Julie made it clear that she'd guessed, and was disappointed, that Carolyn had become another of Paul's victims.

Julie was also worried about the re-organisation, and how it would affect her and the other female members of staff.

When the office was quiet that Friday afternoon, she took the opportunity to talk to Carolyn.

'It was very good of head office to postpone the interviews till Paul got back.'

Carolyn looked at her in that cool, superior way which always irritated Julie.

'The postponement was entirely due to the re-structuring, not Paul Ferris's holiday,' Carolyn said.

Julie's laugh expressed her scepticism, and then she quizzed Carolyn further.

'Are you sure you want him to drive you to the interview on Tuesday?'

'Yes, of course. It wouldn't make sense for us to travel separately when we're both going to head office.'

'Of course,' echoed Julie in a sardonic tone. 'And it will give Paul a chance to pick your brains about those latest financial management techniques that you've been studying.'

Carolyn looked at her, and Julie was pleased to see that she'd had that thought, too, even though she quickly denied it.

'You have such a suspicious mind, Julie. And you seem to have forgotten that there are several jobs on offer, and it's not as if Paul and I are in competition for any of them.'

'I'm glad to hear it, if that is the case,' Julie replied, sounding unconvinced.

Carolyn collected her papers together, signalling that the conversation was over.

She was glad she would have the evening to herself and be able to work on her presentation for the interview. She'd arranged to leave the office early so that she could cook a meal for her family and Jean before they went out that evening, so she didn't see Paul and their boss drive off together in Paul's car.

The restaurant Gerald Critchley had selected for this out-of-office meeting was in the style of a gentlemen's club and was very expensive. It was also, Critchley knew, within a short driving distance of both his house and Paul Ferris's apartment, so there would be little chance of Paul being caught if too much wine and brandy were enjoyed during their tête à tête.

Critchley was speaking very softly, and Paul had to lean forward across the table to catch all the nuances of what he was saying. Critchley had chosen a dimly lit corner of the luxurious restaurant, which was the only one in the area capable of serving an approximation of genuine French cuisine.

He liked to compensate himself for the self-generated misfortunes in his life by frequently dining as well as possible, and today he knew that Paul would insist on paying the bill, in return for a favour which would never be mentioned to anyone else.

Attempting to disguise his partisanship, Critchley imparted the information in meandering prose, but allowed Paul to ask the right questions.

'So the re-structuring isn't yet complete?'

'No,' Critchley confirmed, and then watched for Paul's reaction as he continued with the key point which had instigated this intimate little conference. 'And they've decided that, at the moment, there is only the one post available.'

Their eyes met in steady collusion, and he perceived that the required understanding had been tacitly reached. Critchley sipped his glass of Merlot before adopting a more casual, but still exact tone.

'It will be Stapleton and Hanson conducting the interview.'

'I don't think I've met them,' said Paul.

He was trying hard to sound relaxed, but was tense with the awareness that what was now being presented as 'casual office gossip' would be invaluable at head office on Tuesday.

Critchley allowed Paul to refill his glass before continuing.

'Hanson is a very keen golfer, so you should be all right there.'

'Good,' Paul said, and waited for the inside knowledge on the other interviewer.

'Stapleton's the decision maker really. He's a bit more tricky, but you'll impress him if you can talk taxation.'

'Right,' Paul gave what he hoped was a confident smile, but they both knew who was the expert on taxation, Carolyn Sheldon. Carolyn, who had now become his rival for the post at head office.

Paul was already adapting to this new circumstance and had begun to consign any feeling of guilt to rarely visited areas of his consciousness.

Critchley took a certain satisfaction in visualising Carolyn Sheldon as he gave this next piece of vital information to the eager young man sitting opposite him.

'Stapleton's also very straitlaced. He got rid of one very competent secretary because her skirts were too short.'

He paused, giving Paul time to make the connection, and then stared at him intently as he delivered his final message.

'There are just the two of you on the short-list.'

'I see,' was all Paul said, but his look did not waver from Critchley's satisfied face.

Steve drove John and the children to the cinema and then went to the snooker club. He spent half an hour playing snooker with Gary, before disappearing into the gents toilet and changing into the suit he'd secretly put in the boot of the car.

Gary, who had suggested the snooker match as an alibi, saw him come out and gave him a thumbs-up sign to register approval of his appearance, and also as a gesture of good luck.

The meeting with Bob Horton was neither as tough nor as long as Steve had expected. Horton was surprised, but also very pleased, when he explained his plan to set up in his own business.

'About time,' he said bluntly. 'You're the one with the talent, there's no doubt about that, but have you got the business sense?'

Steve flinched, he knew his own limitations too

well, but Lynda had helped him prepare a business plan and a detailed estimate of the costs and production schedule. Horton read them carefully and then nodded, and Steve relaxed a little, until the next question.

'And who's putting up the money?'

Steve didn't want to tell him that, but there was no dodging away from a straight answer when Bob Horton fixed you with those direct, steel grey eyes of his.

'Lynda Stanworth, or Lynda Collins to use her business name.'

'Lynda!' Horton exclaimed, astonished to hear that Lynda was able to finance such a venture. 'I'd heard she'd come back a lot better off than when she went away, but I'd no idea she'd got into that sort of league.'

He slapped Steve on the shoulder and laughed.

'No, mother-in-law jokes for you then.'

'Oh, I don't know about that!' Steve said with a cheeky grin, but his expression grew more serious, as he willingly confessed to Bob Horton, 'I think the world of her.'

At Hadden Lea later that evening Jenny stood in the doorway and watched her daughters as they got into the car to drive to a party at a friend's house together. She'd at least got one thing right as a parent, she said to herself, she'd brought her daughters up to be close friends as well as sisters.

Jenny had always tried to do her best for Alex and Katie, but few parents are ever convinced that they haven't failed their children in some way. Jenny knew how she'd failed hers, by choosing the wrong man to be their father.

She sighed as she closed the door, thinking she could say to herself that she'd chosen the wrong man again, because he was married. Jenny had been upset about Lynda's warning, but she'd also seen that Lynda already had some knowledge of Carolyn's infidelity.

Jenny did believe that Steve and Carolyn's marriage was over, but she also knew that she wanted to believe it. And since that conversation with Lynda, Jenny had made a decision; she and Steve would make love that evening.

As he walked into the room, she was surprised to see he was wearing a suit.

'Are you going somewhere else tonight?' she asked.

'No. I've just had a meeting with somebody, that's all.'

'Oh?'

He wanted so much to tell her about what he and Lynda were planning, but he couldn't. He saw that Jenny was disappointed he wasn't willing to confide in her, and tried to make amends.

'I've been looking forward to coming here, though.'

'Have you?' she said softly, looking up at him.

They both knew that this was the moment. Jenny slid her arms round his neck, snuggled her body against his and kissed him tenderly, leaving him in no doubt that she loved him.

And for both of them nothing had ever felt so perfect, so right. They couldn't let go of this passion, and when Jenny suggested that they go upstairs Steve kissed her, holding her close against him, accepting gladly that they would become lovers.

Then he saw the photograph on the wall by the door, a childhood portrait of Alex and Katie. He paused and stared at it, and thought of his own

338

children and of what might happen if he allowed himself to love Jenny.

He didn't have to explain. Jenny knew instinctively what went through his mind as he looked at the photograph, and she didn't try to stop him leaving.

There were things she could have said which might have persuaded him to stay, and later she wished she had said them. But some inner voice had told her that she could not be the one to tell Steve Sheldon that his wife was having an affair.

CHAPTER THIRTY-NINE

The house was so quiet without Steve and the children. At first Carolyn was thankful for the silence, and the chance to spread out her books and files on the dining table and begin her preparation for Tuesday's interview. But gradually the unnatural stillness became oppressive, and strangely depressing as her thoughts kept drifting away from the excitement which awaited her in Leeds. She began instead to think about Steve, and then about Paul Ferris and the contrast between the two men.

She had resolved to end the affair as soon as Paul came back, but the excitement she'd felt on seeing him again made her unsure whether she really wanted to.

He'd been so attentive that morning, and had even slipped a small box of her favourite Belgian chocolates into her desk drawer. He had waited for her in 'the oasis' and kissed her, and told her he was looking forward to having time with her on the drive to the interview and, he hoped, afterwards.

She'd brought the chocolates home with her, keeping them hidden in her briefcase and she reached for them now, delighting in the quality of the dark blue box with its gold satin ribbon. She loved receiving gifts like this, and couldn't help wondering why Steve couldn't appreciate and cherish her like Paul did.

Over the past few weeks she'd been trying so hard to please her husband, but it didn't seem to have improved things very much.

He was so closed off from her, and there was obviously something he was keeping secret.

She tried again to concentrate on figures and examples, but instead she found herself getting angry with Steve; the interview on Tuesday could change their lives, and she couldn't even talk to him about it.

She was again thinking about Paul, and the pleasures of his attentions and admiration when she heard the front door open. Thinking that Steve must have come home early, Carolyn hastily hid Paul's gift and, with thoughts of his caresses still in her mind, her feeling of guilt was very apparent to Lynda as she marched into the room.

Carolyn's immediate reaction was shock that her Mother had been able to invade her home without warning.

'What are you doing here? And how did you get in?'

'I've got a key. This used to be my home, remember?' Lynda said, her anxiety for her child converting itself into anger.

'The home you walked out of!' Carolyn stood up and shouted, 'How dare you barge in here like this? Get out!'

'How dare you mess around with another fella?' Lynda shouted back, forgetting all her good intentions of talking to her daughter in a calm and reasonable manner.

Carolyn was so stunned by this forthright accusation that she had to sit down again. Lynda stood looking down at her, trying to feel in control.

'I assume it's that guy I saw you with outside your office. I could see he could hardly keep his hands off you.'

'Don't be disgusting.'

Lynda realised she needed to calm down, she'd

come to help, not to have a row with her daughter.

'I don't know how you can even look at him, Carolyn, when you've got a husband like Steve. What can he give you that Steve can't?'

Remembering the comparison she'd been making between Steve and Paul only a few minutes earlier, Carolyn found herself still feeling angry with Steve, blaming him for causing this situation.

'A helluva lot, if you must know.'

'Such as?'

'Appreciation and admiration for a start! Steve can't think of anything but himself and what he hasn't achieved.'

Lynda was quick to speak up for her vulnerable son-in-law.

'He's trying his best, he always has done. It's tough for him to have to work for a lousy boss like Randerson.'

'I work hard, too. But all I get from Steve is resentment and envy.'

'That still doesn't give you the right to cheat on him.'

'I'm not,' Carolyn said, instinctively lying to defend herself. But she was afraid, and needed to know what had caused her Mother to make this accusation. 'Who's been telling you this rubbish?'

Lynda didn't want Carolyn to be able to make up lies to deny what she and Jean had found out. She wanted Carolyn to be worried enough to give up Paul Ferris, so her answer was infuriatingly enigmatic.

'You can't keep these things a secret, Carolyn. You can't go sleeping around and not expect to get found out.'

As had so often happened in the past, Lynda had chosen the wrong words.

'I am not 'sleeping around'. And how dare you

come here making that kind of accusation? You of all people! A woman with no standards, no morals.'

Lynda felt as if she'd travelled back in time, standing here in this room, with nothing but antagonism between her and her daughter.

'Do you know who you sound like?' she cried, 'Your flaming Nana!'

'And why shouldn't I? She was the one who brought me up, who looked after me, she was the one who loved me. Which is more than you ever did!'

'What?' Lynda gasped.

Carolyn stood up and moved away from her Mother. Determined not to cry, she dug her fingernails hard into the palms of her hands, but her throat was tight as she uttered the terrible words she'd spoken so often in her mind when imagining this moment.

'You never loved me. You're my Mother,' she was crying out now, 'you're my Mother, and you have never loved me.'

It was as if the walls of the room were holding their breath, not daring to break the silence as Lynda tried to absorb what her daughter had just said to her.

'Of course I loved you.'

'Liar! Oh, why did you come back? My Nan was right about you. She said the only person you really loved was yourself. All you cared about was 'having a good time'. I used to be so ashamed, seeing you going out dressed like a tart!'

Lynda sank down on to the sofa, afraid of what Carolyn might say next. She told herself she was being stupid, being frightened of her own child, but she remembered feeling like that when Carolyn was a teenager, and had stood there as she was now, staring at her with contempt.

She began to feel angry, to want to defend herself.

343

And then she remembered why she had come here this evening. She concentrated on keeping her voice quiet and calm.

'Like I said, Carolyn, you listened to your Nana too much. Sheila Stanworth not only took you away from me, she taught you to look down on me. Yes, I wore cheap clothes, I didn't have the money for anything else. And yes, I suppose I did have bad taste in those days, but I didn't go around having affairs.'

Carolyn almost laughed, and stepped towards her now.

'Don't you sit there telling me lies! I heard the rows you had, I heard you and Dad talking about splitting up.'

'When? What are you talking about?'

'When I was a teenager, when I came back from that skiing trip. I could see that you'd really upset my Dad, and something bad had happened.'

Lynda felt as if a cold hand had gripped her heart as she remembered what had happened that night.

'It wasn't what you thought, Carolyn. I wasn't having an affair.'

'I don't believe you. Why else would Dad have reacted like he did? Nana said it was obvious what you'd done.'

'What I'd done?' Lynda said, and saw the judgement in her daughter's eyes, reminding her how Sheila Stanworth used to look at her.

'Yes. You. The so-called Mother who walked out on me and your baby grandson when we needed you!'

Lynda bowed her head.

'I know that was wrong. But there were reasons.'

'Excuses, you mean,' Carolyn said in a voice full of disdain. 'I don't want to listen to them, or to your lies. Just get out, will you!'

Lynda stood up to face her.

'Not till you promise me you'll put an end to this affair, right now, before Steve finds out. Please, stop this, Carolyn, before it destroys your marriage.' She paused as the pain from the past made it hard to breathe. 'I don't want you losing everything, like I did.'

For a moment Carolyn felt a touch of pity for this woman who seemed, surprisingly, to be pleading with her; but she immediately rebuked herself for forgetting that this was the woman who had abandoned her family to pursue her own pleasures.

'Losing everything?' she mocked scornfully, 'From what I've heard, you've done pretty well for yourself, going off and finding yourself another man, one with money this time.'

She saw her Mother turn away, just as she used to when she was a child. Carolyn felt a powerful need to hurt her, to gain some revenge, and so she went too far.

'And that's why you thought you could come back, because you have fancy clothes and money now.' And then she could not resist what she knew was a cheap and cruel jibe, 'Which you got for 'services rendered', I assume.'

Lynda felt herself turning pale. Her body became still and cold as she heard Carolyn defiling the memory of the love between her and her beloved Tom Meredith. The pain of her loss, and the anger at Carolyn's ignorance and condemnation, overwhelmed her and she raised her hand, ready to hit her daughter hard across the face. Then she saw her child's frightened eyes, and instead put her hand to her mouth, and she backed away from Carolyn.

'Is that really what you think of me?' she asked, in a voice heavy with the burden of her grief, and filled with bitterness. 'I came here to help you, Carolyn. And as for the money my darling man left me, do you know what I'm doing with it?'

'No, and don't want to know!' Carolyn shouted, but Lynda ignored her.

'I'm helping Steve, your husband, so he can take the Horton contract away from Randerson, and set up his own company. He'll be able to build a wonderful future for you and my grandchildren.

I loved Tom Meredith and he loved me in a way I'd never known before. He made me a new person, gave me a new life.'

She had to stop and fight back her tears, but then stood tall and proud in front of her daughter.

'And we worked hard together to earn that money, so don't you dare look at me with judgement and contempt in your eyes.'

Lynda felt herself losing control again, and was unable to cope with the turbulence of thoughts and feelings that had overwhelmed her. She turned away from her unforgiving daughter, and walked out of the house which had once been her home, wondering, as she had so many times before, whether she would ever enter it again.

Carolyn watched her leave. Then she curled up in a corner of the sofa, like a little child, and wept as she gave way to the shuddering heartbreak she'd held back for so many years.

CHAPTER FORTY

Loveday Manor had regained its serenity, with only the satin bows still tied to the stable doors and gateposts, and drifts of confetti as reminders of the joyous celebration which had taken place there that weekend. As the last of the guests reluctantly took their leave on Monday morning, Patrick Nelson hurried out to help them load their suitcases in the boot of their cars. He went back into the hotel and walked angrily up to the reception desk where Suzanne was languidly turning the pages of reservations.

'Where's Jamie?' he demanded.

Suzanne eventually looked up at him and, pausing to lift her still luxurious glossy brown curls from her neck, she yawned and stretched a little.

'I sent him to mow my lawn.'

'He's supposed to be here, looking after the guests.'

'They were leaving,' she argued, with the slight petulance which had established itself in her vocal range during her indulged childhood, and which frequently emerged when she felt any need to defend her actions.

'I've told you before, Suzanne, our guests should feel they have our full attention right up to the moment they drive out of the gate. Having their luggage taken care of is a priority, and Jamie should have been here to do that.'

'Oh, Patrick, do stop making such a fuss. And please don't speak to me like that,' she added as she saw her son walk into the foyer.

'What's the matter?'

'I asked Jamie to do some work for me, but apparently that's not allowed.'

'It's a matter of priorities, and the guests come first,' Patrick insisted, looking at Mark for support.

Mark nodded. 'Absolutely. You need to check with Patrick or me before you send anyone off on other duties, Mother.'

Suzanne's look let her son know she was disappointed in him, and she was pleased to see that he was not comfortable with that. She made a show of being in charge of reception.

'The Tylers arrive today,' she announced. 'I've put them in Room 9.'

'No,' Mark contradicted her again, 'they always stay in Room 6, it's the one Lynda re-furbished for them.'

When, a few hours later, the Tylers were having coffee with Mark in a quiet corner of the large conservatory, Helen, a dainty but determined little lady, confirmed his decision.

'We want everything to be just as it was when your Daddy and Lynda were here,' she said with tears misting her eyes. 'We were so sorry we couldn't come over for Tom's funeral.'

'I had business commitments I couldn't get out of,' explained her husband, his usually commanding tone altered to one of gruff apology.

'We understood. But it was great that you were here for the wedding.'

'Yes,' Helen agreed, with a thoughtful look. 'And now Lynda has gone back to her folks in the North for a while.'

'Yes, but it looks like it may be for longer than I'd

348

hoped,' Mark told them regretfully. 'She's bought a house in Milfield. In fact I'm taking a van load of furniture up for her next week. After Epsom of course.'

'Oh?' Helen turned immediately to her husband, 'You and Peter could help with that, couldn't you?'

'I guess so, if it's next week, after my business meetings in London.' He turned to Mark, 'We're planning to take a look at that area, anyway. Helen has a list of some more of her hysterical houses we just have to see,' he teased.

'Stop it, Nathan. He means historical, and he pretends they bore him so much he has to find the nearest pub to help him recover.'

Mark laughed. 'I could help you there, Nathan.'

'Don't encourage him,' Helen protested. 'But, seriously, we do want to visit the North of England, and Nathan wants to look at property there.'

Nathan, who liked to keep his ideas to himself, adopted a slightly diffident attitude.

'Just so that this 'cultural tour' you've bullied me into won't be entirely a waste of my time,' drawled the man whose leather jacket and jeans belied an astute and ambitious business brain.

'Would you like me to ask Lynda to find you a hotel? Her house isn't furnished yet or I'm sure she'd want you to stay with her.'

'It's O.K, I can give her a call,' said Helen.

'Oh, have you got her new mobile number?' Mark asked, slightly surprised.

'She sure has, she and Lynda are always sending texts and letters, and making secret, and hellishly expensive long-distance calls,' Nathan complained.

'Nonsense, we like to keep in touch, that's all. I miss her, she's a good friend. I can see you miss her, too, Mark.'

'Yes. I wish she'd never gone back to Milfield, even though it was what Dad had told her she needed to do.'

'Yes, she told me,' Helen said, blinking back a tear.

'She was living with a friend in her tiny terraced house when I called in to see her. It looked to me as if things hadn't worked out the way she told me. I need to talk to her, and persuade her to come home. Loveday isn't Loveday any more without her, and without my Dad.'

Ellen Heywood often found Mondays very difficult, they always seemed so quiet after the weekend. The rain streaming down the window added to her feeling of isolation and boredom, making the afternoon stretching before her seem intolerable.

She reached deep down into the capacious black leather handbag she always kept with her, and took out a large set of keys, the possession of which she had kept secret for many years. She made her way, with considerable effort, up to the second floor of the house, an area she had not visited for a long time.

Her motivation for this expedition was to satisfy her curiosity about the boxes which Dan had told her, after relentless interrogation, contained some of Lynda Stanworth's private possessions. These had been stored in a room on this floor, and her son had locked the door and put the key in his pocket, not realising that his Mother had this spare set of keys for every room in the house.

She would have condemned such behaviour in others, but told herself that any means of gaining an advantage over the woman who was threatening her son's future would be justified. Ever since Dan had brought the boxes home she had known that, one

350

day, she would have to find out what they contained.

She was disappointed to find that they were too securely sealed, and there was only one which she could open without resorting to a knife or scissors. This box, however, held the prize she had been seeking, for it contained a white and gold framed photograph of Lynda and Tom Meredith, sitting hand in hand on the sofa in their apartment at Loveday Manor. It was their wedding photograph.

Ellen uttered a small cry of triumph as she gazed at the happy couple and fully comprehended what had taken place, an act of bigamy. She had little time to enjoy her discovery, however, as she was startled by the rat-tat of the heavy iron door knocker, followed by the ringing of the doorbell. She hastily pushed the photograph back into the box and made her way down the stairs, cursing under her breath at being disturbed before she had the chance to examine the rest of the contents.

Alice Smith had timed her visit to Wellington Road very precisely, She'd calculated that the topics of conversation she had listed in her head, plus preparing and partaking of a tray of afternoon tea for herself and Ellen, would stretch to five o'clock. Dan would then arrive as he was coming home early, she knew, because he would be bringing with him the two birthday cakes.

Alice had already covered these with the base layers of marzipan and Royal Icing, in preparation for the elaborate decoration she would carry out in the kitchen of Kirkwood House this week. The discussion of the decoration was her pretext for this visit. And, with any luck, she would still be there at six, and Dan, being kinder than his Mother, would invite her to stay for dinner.

Alice was very excited at the prospect of the

birthday party. Not only would it be an occasion which would garner praise for her cake decoration, but there would be a wonderfully combustible combination of guests.

Alice, established on Ellen's sofa with her first cup of tea, couldn't deny herself a flavour of the enjoyment to come, and so began to talk to Ellen about the fact that Lynda Stanworth was to be among the guests.

'I didn't think Lynda would be invited,' she commented boldly, and then tossed in an observation which she knew would be provocative. 'Though I suppose she has come up in the world.'

Ellen's derision was instantaneous. Arching her back, and folding her hands piously in her lap, she said, 'She thinks she has. I wasn't the one who invited her, I assure you.'

'No.' Alice paused to give full honours to the information she'd managed to acquire from her cousin. 'Lynda has been running her own business down South, you know, a hotel.'

'Really,' Ellen said, implying a lack of interest, but smiling to herself at the thought of the secret she had unwrapped that afternoon.

As Alice helped herself to another cream cake, Ellen was allowed time to sip her tea and mull over the memory of that discovery for a minute or two before Alice began to cover the list of topics she had prepared.

She worked hard at trying to encourage comment and confidences from her hostess, and was annoyed by Ellen's reticence and condescension, but nevertheless she persevered.

'My cousin Jean is looking forward to the party, she's even bought a new dress, from the Moonstone Boutique. I don't know what Frances Horton will say about that.'

'She may not find out, as she and her husband are not on my guest list.'

'Oh? They will be disappointed.'

'No doubt, but one has to limit the numbers, especially as Alexandra will, of course, need her friends to be there.'

'Of course,' Alice agreed, before quickly returning to her chosen topic. 'I think Jean's bought the dress with John Stanworth in mind. I hope she hasn't wasted her money.'

Ellen leaned forward with interest now. 'But John Stanworth has not yet divorced his wife, has he?'

'No. But I think Lynda will be divorcing him. She's made a different life for herself. It's sad, but I don't see what John Stanworth has to offer her now. And, in any case, he'd probably be happier with my cousin Jean.'

'Indeed.'

Ellen looked at her watch, as a clear signal that it was time for Alice to leave. Her guest, however, jumped up as she heard the sound of a van approaching the house.

'Oh, here's Dan, earlier than I thought. And we haven't even started to discuss the decoration of the cakes yet,' she exclaimed with some satisfaction. 'We'd better go and have a look at them.'

Ellen reluctantly followed Alice to the kitchen to examine the cakes which Dan placed on the table. There was an exchange of ideas as to the proposed decoration.

'Nothing too elaborate,' Ellen stipulated. 'It's not a wedding cake.'

'No. I'm hoping the next wedding cake I'll make will be for my cousin Jean and John Stanworth,' Alice simpered, watching out for Dan's reaction. Seeing that the idea pleased him, she continued, 'Your Mother and I were saying that it looks like they will get married.'

'You can't marry again until you are free to do so, and John Stanworth hasn't divorced his wife yet, Alice,' Ellen reminded her, watching her son as she said this.

Fortunately Dan didn't see her looking at him, and so didn't give any reaction.

'Oh, but he will,' Alice insisted, and then, wishing to exact some small revenge against Ellen for being less than forthcoming during the afternoon's gossip, she said, 'But Lynda won't want to be on her own for ever. She'll need a man, too.'

The two women both saw the light in Dan's eyes, and heard him breathe in deeply to take in the oxygen of hearing his secret hope expressed out loud. Watching Ellen out of the corner of her eye, Alice cocked her head on one side and enthusiastically stirred up the atmosphere in the room.

'I don't think you've ever really got over Lynda, have you, Dan?' she cooed.

Ellen glared at her. 'That's nonsense!' she exclaimed loudly.

There was a brief silence as Dan summoned his courage and calmly contradicted his Mother.

'No, it's not.'

Ellen, as determined as ever that she would never allow her son to fulfil his longing for the woman she regarded as her enemy, had no hesitation now in using, albeit obliquely, her recently acquired knowledge.

'Lynda Stanworth has secrets in her past, the kind one should not have, Daniel,' she said and then added the decree, 'She's not for you.'

Daniel looked steadily into the eyes of this

imperious duchess who was his Mother and, with a conviction nourished by years of loneliness and longing, gave his reply.

'I think I'm old enough to make my own decision about that.'

Alice wasn't going to wait for the aftermath of this rebellion, she knew she had to act quickly or her plan for the evening would fall apart. She decided to blithely ignore the stony silence.

'What else would you like on your cake, Ellen? Roses, like I did for your fiftieth?' she twittered. 'And we haven't discussed the other catering you want me to do yet, Dan, but I wouldn't want to interfere with your evening meal.'

Dan, taking care not to look at the thunderous expression on his Mother's face, suddenly saw a way of avoiding the horrors of a dinner consumed in an icy chill, an experience which usually ended in his grovelling for forgiveness.

'Oh,' he said, trying to seem unaware of any tension. 'We can talk about all that over dinner, Alice, if you don't mind staying?'

Alice didn't mind at all.

CHAPTER FORTY-ONE

Paul Ferris listened attentively to Carolyn sitting in the car beside him and talking about taxation. She really did know her stuff, he thought. He looked at her admiringly, she really was the perfect partner, in business and in love. Perhaps, he thought, the future could work out for both of them, as a couple.

But Paul wasn't the kind of man to let himself be distracted by fantasies of that kind, not when there was an immediate goal to be achieved. He wanted this post at head office, it was the next essential step in his career, and nothing was going to prevent him from taking that step, even though he felt a little guilty about Carolyn not knowing they were in competition with each other today.

They drove through the lively, money-making streets of Leeds, past tall, modern offices of glass and steel, contrasting with the majestic Victorian rose-pink brick and sandstone façades. As he drove into the car park at the AFS head office, Paul could see Carolyn was feeling very nervous.

He took hold of her hand for a moment to reassure her. It fascinated him that she could be so intelligent and ambitious, and yet also seem vulnerable and in need of protection. It made him feel so powerful, and it made him want to hold her, to caress her, but he wasn't going to let those feelings take control of him now.

'I hate interviews,' Carolyn confessed as they looked up through the windscreen at the shimmering glass and black marble of the AFS office.

'You'll be fine. You do want the job, don't you?' Paul asked, half hoping that she'd release him from his guilt by telling him she'd changed her mind about this promotion.

'Of course,' she confirmed, her eyes brightening with hope.

'Ready for somewhere new, and a lot more exciting than Milfield.'

'Oh, yes,' she nodded.

'I won't come in with you, if you don't mind. There are some papers I need to look through and it would be better if I read them here, rather than in the foyer.'

'Yes, of course. Wish me luck,' Carolyn said and leaned over to kiss him, but stopped as she saw him draw back and glance nervously up at the windows of the office. She understood and told herself that he was right, they didn't want anyone to see any intimacy between them, especially not here. She was, of course, unaware of any other reasons.

'I'll have a look round the shops while you have your interview,' she suggested, 'Meet you in the foyer at one?'

'Make it around two o'clock. I've got the midday slot, remember, so they may want me to have lunch with them,' he said, hoping, and feeling pretty sure that they would. He'd been very pleased when he'd learned the time of his interview, and he'd seen that Critchley, too, considered it a favourable sign.

Carolyn, until that moment had not been aware of that advantage, but thought it was just the luck of the draw.

'Oh. Well, good luck Paul,' she said as she opened the car door. She was surprised when he leaned across and swiftly re-arranged the collar of her shirt, laying it further out on the lapel of her jacket.

'That's better, it looked a little creased,' he said, 'You look wonderful. Good luck.'

Carolyn gave him a grateful smile as she stepped out of the car and Paul felt a little ashamed, but he quickly overcame such sentiment.

He had been pleased when he'd picked her up and seen that, as hc had suggested, she was wearing one of his favourite suits, with a skirt rather than trousers. He smiled now as he leaned back against the leather seat to watch her walk round to the main entrance. Stapleton would be sure to notice the length of her skirt, and the display of cleavage he had just so carefully arranged.

When he came out of the AFS head office after his interview and a very pleasant lunch in the executive dining room, he felt like jumping up and punching the air with his fist. He was in. He knew it from the way he'd been treated after his interview.

Now he wanted to celebrate by taking Carolyn back to his flat and making love to her. It would all work out. She'd be disappointed at not getting the job, of course, but after a while she'd come round, and he might even be able to fix it for her to get a promotion to head office after all.

He didn't want to lose Carolyn if he didn't have to. Looking at her sitting beside him as they drove back from Leeds, Paul thought again that Carolyn Sheldon had the ability to help him professionally, as well as being attractive and sexy enough to make him feel good in other ways.

She was on a high, as well, after her interview, and it made her look terrific. It would be wonderful to spend the rest of the afternoon with her.

But Carolyn said no. She didn't tell Paul but she knew she had got the job, she was convinced of it.

She'd performed really well in the interview, and although Stapleton had been rather cold and patronising towards her, Hanson had been much more sympathetic, and even complimentary. After the interview Hanson had been quite charming, and had asked his PA to offer her coffee and a tour of head office before the journey back to Milfield.

Carolyn had eagerly accepted the invitation, and had been exhilarated as she'd been shown glimpses of the world she might soon inhabit. But she wasn't going back to Paul's flat, all she wanted was to get home, to see Steve.

She'd phoned her Dad and arranged for Michael and Gemma to stay with him for tea, so she'd have the chance to talk to Steve without the children there. The job at head office was a reality now, and that had changed everything, Steve would see that. They could start making plans to move to Leeds and make a fresh start, both financially, and in their marriage.

Paul let her know that he was very disappointed, and hurt, when she turned him down, but that didn't really matter to her now. She was careful not to show it, though; after all they would probably be working together at head office, for Paul, though he tried to hide it, seemed confident he'd also got his job.

Carolyn could hardly wait for Steve to get home, and he was early for once. Carolyn had had time to change out of her suit, but she didn't want to, it was part of the aura of success that had wrapped itself around her since she came out of the interview, and she wanted to enjoy it a little longer.

It was a mistake.

When Steve, his clothes hanging limp and heavy with the dirt from Randersons, walked into the living room at Beechwood Avenue, he was a man without a job, without the means to provide for his family.

The previous evening, at a Chamber of Commerce dinner, Tony Randerson had tried unsuccessfully to clinch the deal with Bob Horton.

As everyone was leaving, he had taken an opportunity to chat with Horton's wife, to try and find out why he was hesitating. Frances Horton, who had drunk more wine with the meal than she was used to, was ready to be indiscreet. Having heard rumours, Frances had decided she didn't particularly like Tony Randerson, and giggled foolishly as he made his clumsy enquiries.

She had misunderstood what little her husband had confided in her, and so told Randerson that he wouldn't be getting the contract because Steve Sheldon was going to work for another company.

Still furious at being made to look a fool Randerson had marched into the workshop and sacked Steve. And when Gary had told him he couldn't do that, he'd sacked him as well.

Carolyn, standing there, still looking immaculate in her smart expensive suit, the light of triumph in her eyes, was everything Steve was not. He felt ready to collapse in a useless heap on the floor, but Carolyn didn't stop to see how he was feeling, she ran across the room and threw her arms round him.

'I think I've got it,' she cried, her smile full of love and excitement. Steve stared at her, as if he couldn't understand what she was saying. She told him again.

'I've got the job, Steve. I was really on top form, there was nothing they could throw at me that I didn't have an answer for.'

She was reliving those moments of high performance in her mind, and continued to pour out her joy and elation. 'I think it really surprised them, coming from a woman.'

Then she realised that his face was heavy with misery, and the flood of happiness swiftly disappeared.

'Steve, aren't you pleased for me?' she asked, still holding on to his shoulders. He closed his eyes for a moment and then moved away from her, wanting to find some quiet, dark place where he could hide.

'Congratulations,' he said, knowing he sounded half-hearted, but was glad that the bitterness he felt hadn't penetrated into that single, unfelt felicitation.

She faltered now, losing energy in her concern for him.

'Well, it's not certain yet, but I'm pretty sure I've got it.'

She watched him sink down into the armchair, his whole being depressed and weary. It was a minute or so before he gathered any thoughts, and the first priority was clear.

'Where are the kids?'

'Still at my Dad's. I phoned him to ask if they could stay there for tea, so we'd have a chance to talk.'

He looked up at her as he spoke, his eyes still weary but harder now. 'Talk? What about?'

'The future. Our wonderful future.'

It sounded so simple, put like that, but as they looked at each other they both drew breath for the fight they knew now had to come. Carolyn launched into it.

'Leeds is a brilliant city,' she enthused, 'lovely shops and everything else you could want. The kids would love it,' she told him, determination adding edge to the opinion.

It was as if he hadn't heard her.

'I got the sack today,' he said, his voice harsh with anger, 'That bastard Randerson gave me and Gary the sack.'

'Why?'

'Because he heard I was planning to leave.'

'Well, you can if I've got this job. Randerson doesn't deserve to have you. And there'll be plenty of better employers in Leeds who'll want you.'

'How many times do I have to tell you, I'm not going to bloody Leeds?'

'Oh, for heaven's sake, Steve, will you stop being so pig-headed? And anyway, you've no choice now you've lost your job,' Carolyn told him bluntly.

Steve's pride had been damaged enough by Randerson's brutal treatment of him today, and he was damned if he was going to be spoken to like that. He stood up and shouted at her.

'I have got a bloody choice!'

Carolyn felt her mouth tighten with frustration. 'Oh, really?' she said in that patronising tone which drove him crazy.

'Yes. Lynda and I are going to take over Randerson's.'

'Don't talk rubbish.'

'It's true, Carolyn. We're having to keep quiet about it for a while yet, but it is going to happen. Lynda's got the money.'

'And you're going to take it?'

'Of course, it's the chance of a lifetime. I'll have my own company, like I've always dreamed of.'

'I don't want my family living off that woman's money. You'll have to tell her you can't accept it.'

'Don't talk daft!'

'I mean it, Steve.'

'I'd have my own company, Carolyn.'

'And no experience. You're talented, Steve, but I

can't see you running a business.'

'Thanks for the vote of confidence.'

'We've got two children and a mortgage. We can't afford to take risks. This job in Leeds is our best chance for the future.'

She paused and looked round the room again. She saw the shabby carpet, the cheap vase she'd bought because she couldn't afford the crystal one she'd wanted, and she knew she had to tell him, now, how she felt.

'I've had enough of being short of money, Steve. All the time I've lived in this house there's never been enough money.'

Steve was silent. He knew she was right, but he also knew he deserved this opportunity Lynda was offering.

'That's why I want this chance. You're wrong, Carolyn, I can make a success of my own business, and earn the money we need. I promise, I can do it.'

Carolyn saw the doubt in his eyes as he spoke, and was ashamed that she'd caused that. But she also had reason to be proud.

'Oh, Steve,' she pleaded. 'Why take the risk, when I can earn really good money?'

Beginning to move round the room like an animal trying to avoid capture, he said, 'Oh, yeah, we all know about what you can earn. But that's not what's important here.'

Carolyn, trying to keep calm, argued back.

'Yes it is. You're being unreasonable, Steve.'

'No, I'm not,' he said quietly, 'I'm just wanting to be happy. And that, to me, means staying in this town, with all our family and friends. Can't you be happy, just staying here?'

Carolyn looked out through the window across at the row of identical semi-detached houses which stood opposite theirs; neat, adequate homes, sheltering lives that were, and always would be, forever the same. The frustration she felt overwhelmed her.

'No. No, I damned well can't be happy here!'

She turned towards him, to let him see how much she meant it.

'I'm bored out of my mind living in this rubbish town, and not going anywhere, not doing anything with my life.'

She turned her face away from him again, so that he shouldn't see the tears she was fighting to suppress. So Steve saw only a stubborn child demanding her own way.

'You're never satisfied, Carolyn, and you never will be. And I wish you'd stop being so bloody selfish,' he shouted.

She looked at him now, with bitter resentment.

'And I wish you'd be the man I thought I'd married.'

He recognised that resentment. He'd seen it often enough in a brief glance, heard it often enough in her voice when they were arguing with each other. He sometimes imagined he'd even seen it on their wedding day, as she'd walked down the aisle in a second-hand dress that didn't disguise the reason for their hasty marriage.

It was that resentment which told him, had been telling him quietly all through their married life, that she didn't really love him. He wanted to cry, but the sorrow transformed itself somehow into anger and a bitterness so strong he could taste it like a poison.

'You married the man who got you pregnant,' he snarled. 'And that's all there was to it. All there ever has been.'

She felt as if her whole being was fading into

nothingness as she looked at Steve now. He was the man she had loved, helped, cared for, and now he was telling her that all he felt was that their marriage had been a pretence.

She stared at him, trying to take in the horror of his accusation, work out what this could mean. And slowly, with all the echoes of their rows clamouring round her, she realised that it meant that he didn't love her.

'Is that what you think?' she whispered. 'After all these years together, is that what you really think?'

He gave no reply, and so she made her decision, clear and final.

'If I get this job in Leeds, I'm going.'

He'd made up his mind, too.

'Well, you'll have to go on your own, then,' he said callously. 'Or find somebody else to go with,' he added with a dry, coarse laugh.

'Is that your idea of a joke?' Carolyn demanded, 'Do you think our marriage is a joke?'

The blood rushed to her head and the words came out on a surge of madness. 'In that case, all right, perhaps I'll do that, find somebody else to go with. Perhaps I already have!'

Steve was very still, not even breathing as he stared at her.

'Who?'

Carolyn was terrified. She had never intended, never meant to say any of this. But it was too late now. All the fragments of suspicion and rumour came together in Steve's head and he nodded with certainty as he said, 'That guy at work. Paul Ferris.'

Carolyn wanted to scream out, to deny his cold, quiet and deadly accusation, but she knew he wouldn't believe her, and that she didn't deserve to be believed.

Steve looked at her, and she stood there as if waiting for him to hit her. He took a deep breath. He would not cry, he'd lost enough pride today, so he made himself speak slowly and deliberately in a voice filled with hatred and scorn.

'O.K. If that's what you want. Go ahead, do it. Walk out on me and the kids. Just like your Mother did!'

That evening was a nightmare of pretence for both of them, chatting to John and the children and making it look like everything was fine, and being careful not to let John or the children know about what had happened today.

For Steve the worst time was after the children had gone to bed and Carolyn had tried to talk to him. She had wept, and gone down on her knees, begging him to forgive her.

'Please believe me, Steve. I know it was really stupid, but it's just been a silly flirtation. I haven't made love to him,' she pleaded, again using the words that she told herself were the truth, for, in her mind now, what had happened between her and Paul had been only sex, there had been no love. Just as there was no love now in Steve's eyes, only scorn and contempt.

'Do you really expect me to believe that? A bloke like Ferris doesn't waste his time if he's not getting what he wants. Well, as far as I'm concerned, he can have you!'

Carolyn was stunned, not just by the cold harsh tone but by his indifference. It hurt so much that he could cast her aside so abruptly, without a second chance, refusing even to contemplate trying to save their marriage.

What she felt at that moment was absolute

humiliation, but it was accompanied by anger.

'You don't even care enough to fight for me,' she said accusingly.

Steve wondered if this woman, his wife for so many years, had ever known him at all. He wanted to knock her against the wall, and he felt his hands tighten in an action which brought terrible memories searing into his brain. He was struggling to stay in control of instincts he knew he possessed as strongly as any other man.

'What do you want me to do, use my fists like my Dad used to? Turn up at your office and beat him up?'

For a split second that was what Carolyn wanted, but instead she said 'Of course not.'

Steve turned away, and by chance fixed his gaze on the black leather briefcase, the symbol of his wife's achievements and ambitions.

'He's what you've always dreamed of, isn't he, Ferris? He's what you've always wished you'd married, a man in a suit, with a flash car and a gold credit card. Well, you've got what you wanted now and,' he paused, making sure she got his full meaning, 'obviously, so has lover boy.'

'No. Steve, you've got to believe me. Why won't you believe me?'

He stood up and looked down at her with sorrow and contempt.

'Because there's something you seem to have forgotten.'

'What?'

'This isn't the first time, Carolyn, is it?'

Steve walked out of the house. The children were asleep so he took care not to slam the door. To Carolyn the slow, deliberate sound of that closing made it seem very final.

CHAPTER FORTY-TWO

Walking through Milfield the following morning Carolyn thought to herself that she had never felt so lonely. It was as if all her life, all her connections with the world had been stripped away from her. She'd never truly realised how much she depended on Steve, and on his love for her. And now she had destroyed that love, and Steve didn't even want to look at her any more.

As she entered the office Carolyn told herself she had to accept that, from now on, her future was with Paul, it had to be. She even wished she hadn't refused to go back to his flat yesterday after the interview. He'd been annoyed and upset that she didn't want to take the opportunity to be together, but she would make it up to him, she'd have to now.

Suddenly she was filled with anger against Steve, she would never forgive him for the swift and callous way he'd given her up to another man.

Paul was surprised at the change in Carolyn's behaviour towards him in the office that morning, she seemed to have stopped worrying about concealing any hint of a relationship between them. She didn't care whether Julia and Michelle noticed when she went out to 'the oasis', giving Paul a clear signal she wanted him to follow her. Remembering his frustration yesterday, he pushed her a little roughly into the shadows, his body crushing her against the wall.

'This is more like the Carolyn I want,' he murmured as moved his hips against hers, 'I was beginning to wonder if you'd changed your mind about me yesterday.'

'That was yesterday,' she said firmly and made sure he had no doubt how much she wanted him.

'This is very enjoyable,' he whispered, 'but not, satisfying.'

Carolyn did not hesitate. This was to be her revenge against Steve.

'There's a party on Saturday,' she told Paul, 'and I've decided not to go to it.'

He looked at her, raising his eyebrows in a hopeful question.

'There'll be no-one at home except me,' she said, ignoring the flutter of fear inside her.

'Your place? Wow, that would be living dangerously. Exciting!' There was delight in his laughter. 'This is marvellous, Carolyn. Oh, you are so wonderful.'

She hung on to his words and clutched at him, desperate for reassurance. 'It is good, isn't it, you and me?'

The anxiety in her voice made him look at her a little warily, but with the ease of practice he gave her what she needed.

'Yes,' he breathed as his lips moved down her neck and his fingers dug into her breast, 'very special.'

'Special enough to last?'

'Of course.' He said the words without thinking, his mind fully focused on the anticipation of their night together; he felt the invitation was an exciting confirmation of his total conquest of her. He was not expecting what came next.

'Good,' she said, her voice catching in the dryness of her throat, 'Because, I've told Steve.'

She saw the panic in his eyes. Choking back tears, she broke free of him, and ran to the privacy of the ladies cloakroom, leaving Paul Ferris facing the kind of commitment he had never really envisaged.

When Steve had dropped his children off at school, he wondered where he could take the heartache and anger he was burdened with now. John Stanworth had always been his friend as well as his father-in-law, and Steve was desperate to talk to someone.

The morning was cloudy and John's living room seemed dark and gloomy, but neither of the two men felt like switching on the light as they sat facing each other.

'What are you going to do?' asked John.

Steve stared at him, unable to find an answer.

'I don't know. Go round and give the bastard a belting is what I feel like doing.'

'Don't do that. Carolyn would lose her job.'

'Talking of which,' Steve said, 'Randerson gave me and Gary the sack yesterday.'

'What for?'

'I'll tell you later. I hate Tony Randerson.'

'So do I.'

'I know,' Steve said, looking steadily at John. 'Lynda told me, about what happened.'

John sat back, open-mouthed. 'Did she? We've never talked about it, to anybody.' He shook his head, 'I should have killed him.'

'You couldn't do anything about it, neither of you, Lynda said.'

'No. But we can do something about this situation. You can get over things, you know. Me and Lynda had to find a way.'

He stopped talking then and looked away, knowing that, in truth, they'd never succeeded in dealing with that terrible event.

'Me and Carolyn can't. Our marriage is over,' Steve stated flatly.

'No. You have to stay together. You can't split up. Think what it would do to the kids!'

Steve bowed his head and brushed away tears as he tried to listen to John, to whom all this was a nightmare he was desperate to bring to an end.

'If you love somebody enough, you can forgive them anything,' John said as Steve sat in front of him, grim-faced and silent now. John sighed and tried again.

'It just takes time, that's all, Steve. You have to forgive.'

'I can't.'

'You've got the kids to think about.'

'I know!' Steve cried, becoming angry in the frustration of his dilemma. 'But how can I stay with Carolyn? She's done this before, remember. How many times am I supposed to forgive her, and take her back when she cheats on me?'

John put his head in his hands, and then looked up as another thought came pounding into his brain.

'You haven't told Lynda, have you? She mustn't find out or she'll want to go and sort it out, and it'll just make for more trouble between her and Carolyn.'

Not knowing that Lynda had already confronted her daughter about the affair, they both agreed that she should not be told. Steve felt guilty about his own, ignoble reason for not telling her, his fear that she would not be willing to lend money to him if she knew that he might, one day, not be her son-in-law.

On Thursday morning, in Philip Lawson's office, another marital affair was being dealt with. Angela Randerson was finalising the details of her divorce.

371

She casually flicked her expertly styled, bronze tinted hair away from her face as she finished reading the small print.

Philip shook his head in admiration. 'For a lady going through a divorce, you seem very composed, Angela.'

She leaned back and smoothed the folds of her eau-de-nil linen jacket.

'I've thought this through carefully, Philip, and it's something I've considered doing more times than I care to remember.'

'I can understand that. But, excuse my curiosity, would a certain Charles Sutherland have had any influence over your finally making this decision?'

Angela leaned forward and smacked her solicitor's wrist.

'When will you learn to be more discreet, young man?'

Philip pretended to be affronted.

'I am discreet, as a solicitor, but you are, I hope, more a family friend than a client. And as it was I who introduced you to Charles, you can understand why I'm interested.'

Angela smiled. 'I'll allow you that. And you're right, Charles has had an influence over my decision to divorce Tony. But there is another reason, some information I was given recently.'

Philip saw her eyes darken with a sadness he could only guess at, and, for all his sometimes cavalier approach to confidentiality, he was sensitive enough to know when not to probe any further. Instead he leaned forward to take the documents.

'If you're quite satisfied that everything is in there, I'll be happy to deliver them personally to your husband at his office. He's bound to react badly when he reads the divorce papers, so I'd like to prevent your having to experience that initial unpleasantness.'

To his surprise Angela drew back, holding the documents against her chest. 'Oh, no. Just give me one of your impressive envelopes to put these in, please. I intend to deliver them personally.'

'Do you think that's wise?'

'Perhaps not, but it will be deeply satisfying. Don't worry, I won't put myself in any danger, I shall choose my moment carefully, and he won't want to antagonise me further, as money is involved, my money. Speaking of which, do you also have the copies of my new will?'

'Certainly, I'll just ask Jenny to bring them in.'

Angela smiled and her eyes twinkled.

'To find them for you, you mean.'

'You know me too well,' Philip laughed as he gave Jenny the request over the intercom.

'Yes, I do, I'm glad to say. And I'm well aware that there's not much going on in this town that you don't know about. So tell me, if I were to look for some enterprise in which to invest some capital, what would be your suggestion?'

It didn't take Philip more than a couple of seconds come up with an idea, but he got up and walked over to the window to make it look as if he'd had to think.

'Would you be interested in the take-over of a local manufacturing business? I think you'd get on rather well with the people planning this, a talented young man, and a business woman of your own age. Both friends of mine.'

'That sounds intriguing. Who is this business woman? Do I know her?'

Jenny entered the room just as he was saying, 'Probably not, but Jenny does. Lynda Collins is an old friend of yours, isn't she, Jenny?'

'Yes,' Jenny replied, taken aback at this sudden

mention of Lynda. She was even more surprised, or rather dumbfounded, when Philip imparted the next piece of information.

'You do understand that this is completely confidential business intelligence I'm giving you, Angela? And you, too, Jenny?'

'Of course,' they both agreed in chorus.

'Lynda, who, as I said, is a successful business woman, wishes to invest in a local, and family business.'

Jenny's immediate query was, 'Family?'

'Yes. Steve Sheldon, the young man in question, is Lynda's son-in-law,' Philip explained to Angela. 'You may know his name, he's one of your husband's employees.'

Philip Lawson leaned back and grinned as he rubbed his hands together in delight at his scheme.

'Steve Sheldon,' Angela Randerson repeated, nodding her head thoughtfully. 'Yes, I do know him. He fitted my new kitchen a while ago, and he's also done excellent work for some of my friends. As you say, a very talented young man.'

Philip's tone was very definite. 'A man who is a hundred per cent reliable, and who deserves to have his own company, and benefit justly from his skills and talents.'

'A take-over, you say?'

'Yes, of a company you know very well.'

Angela gave a slow smile, but there was no humour, just cool wickedness in her eyes.

'Would that be the company badly managed by my husband, but which, in fact, belongs to me?'

'Yes, that would be the one,' Philip cried, smirking now.

'In that case, I would be very interested in meeting Steve Sheldon and, what name was it?

'Lynda. Lynda Collins.'

'They would, however, have to be willing to agree to my retaining an interest, as part-owner of what has always been, as you know, my family business.'

'I'm sure they would be honoured to have a lady like yourself involved. When would you like me to arrange a meeting?'

'As soon as possible.'

Philip ran a hand across his desk diary.

'Here, on Friday morning at eleven o'clock? Would that suit you?'

'It would suit me very well.'

'Right, could we put that in the diary, please, Jenny?'

She nodded, unable to speak, as her mind scrabbled to sort out the implications of all this.

That evening she still needed time to think. The showers of rain had gone and the sun made a late appearance, promising a lovely sunset, so Jenny decided she'd take Tigger for a walk.

There had been a tension over the evening meal, which Jenny assumed was caused by Alex's forebodings about the awful event that her birthday was threatening to turn into.

As they'd driven to school that morning there had been more arguments about conceding to Ellen's demands. Then Alex had criticised her Mother for failing, yet again apparently, to show her appreciation of Katie, who had made the dresses she and Alex were to wear to the party. Jenny was, therefore, very surprised when they both decided to join her for the walk.

They strolled along in silence for a while, just lifting their faces to the sun, and taking time to enjoy the gold of buttercups and sunshine.

'This is lovely,' Jenny sighed. 'It's so good to have you coming for a walk with me like this.'

'Instead of arguing and criticising like we did this morning,' Katie said, giving her sister a dig with her elbow.

Jenny smiled. 'We all have to let off steam sometimes. And you were right, I haven't been paying you enough attention recently,' she apologised. 'I've a lot on my mind with the party arrangements.'

With a sardonic smile Alex added, 'And Steve Sheldon coming, with his wife.'

They'd had this conversation before, and again Jenny pleaded with her daughter.

'Please, Alex. Steve isn't happy with Carolyn. Sometimes people marry the wrong person.'

'Like you did, you mean?' Alex retorted, and nodded to Katie. 'Let's sit down over here,' she said leading the way to some moss covered stones. 'We're going to do some talking, Mum, now.'

Jenny found that her daughters were strongly united in their determination to know the truth. And so, sitting in the middle of a meadow, gazing out over beautiful countryside, they at last had the conversation Jenny knew they were entitled to, but which she had dreaded.

"We know you don't want to tell us about Dad, but we've decided we've waited long enough.'

'Yes,' Katie joined in, with her usual bluntness. 'We're sick of all the careful answers, and the lies.'

Jenny was shocked at this, but she couldn't deny that at times she had told them lies.

'We've guessed some of it,' Alex continued, 'and there are things I remember.'

Jenny stared at her daughter, and experienced again the flashback of seeing her as a small sleepy child, peering round the edge of the kitchen door, her

376

eyes opening wide with fear. She had gathered little Alex up in her arms and carried her back up to bed, hoping that the child hadn't realised, and wouldn't remember, what had happened a few minutes earlier.

Jenny shuddered as she saw the knowledge in Alex's clear blue-grey eyes, and eventually she said softly, 'Yes. I see that you do remember, Alex, but I wish so much that you didn't have such memories.'

Jenny didn't want them to feel shame at whose daughter they were, or to fear what nature they might have inherited. She hesitated again, but saw that they needed to know.

'Like I said,' she repeated, 'some people marry the wrong person. I was the wrong person for your father.'

Alex, always astute, knew why her Mother was defending the memory of Richard Heywood, and wasn't going to let her take the blame.

She cut in, quick and sharp, 'And he punished you for it.'

'Yes.' Jenny admitted, knowing her daughters would accept nothing less than the truth now.

'Why have you kept things secret, and always pretended he was O.K.?' protested Katie.

Jenny had asked herself that question so often, and was still not sure her explanation was adequate, for them or for herself, but it was the only one she had to offer.

'I felt it was hard enough for you to be without a father, and hard enough for Ellen to have lost her son.'

'Yes, we understand that. But we're old enough now, and have a right to know,' Alex said firmly, 'the right to know everything.'

So Jenny began to tell them about Richard, how he

377

had wanted to be a success, how nothing was ever enough for him, and how frustrated he became. She paused, hesitating to reveal the worst of his behaviour, but they insisted she should tell them everything, no matter how bad.

Jenny looked at her brave, forthright daughters and nodded her agreement, but she knew that there were some things she would never tell them. They would never know the pain and degradation she had had to endure.

She had tried so hard to understand Richard Heywood, and had partly succeeded, and she'd also blamed herself. When he'd started to hit her she had, at first, forgiven him his loss of self-control. Then she had realised that he'd begun to enjoy it, the violence. He had needed it like other men need drugs or alcohol. Drinking had been part of the problem, too.

When she'd finished telling them all she was prepared to let them know, Jenny took a deep breath and said, 'And while we're talking frankly like this, I'd also like to talk to you about Steve.'

Alex got to her feet. 'I don't want to know about Steve Sheldon,' she informed her Mother.

'I do,' said Katie who hadn't realised that there was more than friendship between her Mother and Steve.

'I love him,' Jenny said, and then turned to her eldest daughter, willing her to accept what she was saying. 'And his marriage is over anyway, Alex.'

'You don't know that,' Alex insisted.

'I do. But we don't have to discuss that now. Let's just try to enjoy the walk back, and have a quiet evening together, just being a family.'

The two girls looked at each other, and realised that, after so many revelations, that was what they wanted, too.

378

As they walked back, quietly and calmly, Jenny felt a huge sense of relief. That evening was a turning point for her. It marked the end of her silence about her life with Ellen Heywood's son.

CHAPTER FORTY-THREE

Everyone who participated in that Friday morning meeting in Philip Lawson's office came out of it feeling positive about their future. Lynda and Angela had immediately recognised that they could not only be business partners but also friends, and went to have lunch together and begin developing that friendship.

Gary had persuaded Steve to meet him for a pie and a pint in The Red Lion, and was impressed when Steve told him about the deal he and Lynda had set up with Angela.

'When do you think we'll be able to tell Randerson?' Gary asked. 'I can't wait to see his face when he finds out that, in spite of his threats, we have taken the Horton contract off him.'

'Shush, keep your voice down,' Steve told him, looking round the pub to make sure no-one had heard. 'We've got to keep all of this under wraps till it's all signed and sealed.'

'Sorry,' Gary apologised, 'I am learning to keep my mouth shut, though, Steve. I haven't even told Jackie what's going on,' he boasted. 'Have you told Carolyn?'

All the hope and excitement disappeared from Steve's eyes.

'Yes, I have told her some of it, but she's not interested.'

Gary gawped at him. 'You what? She's got to be interested. It's the start of a great future for you and her, and your kids.'

'Our future's a bit more complicated than that,' Steve said, and the look on his face was a shock to Gary.

'Tell me about it,' he said quietly. 'I'm your mate, Steve. You can tell me. And if I can help you, I will.'

'Thanks.'

Gary stood up, and put a hand on Steve's shoulder. 'I'll get us another pint. You need to talk about this, don't you?'

Steve looked up at him. 'Yeah. Yes, I do.'

Gary listened, and when Steve had told him all he wanted to tell him, he was absolutely certain about how to react.

Gary Pearson, like Steve, was the child of an unhappy marriage, and in Gary's book you did anything to stop your children being the victims of a broken home. At this point there was only one issue that was crucial as far as Gary was concerned, and that was to save the marriage. He compelled Steve to listen to him, and was persuasive, and insistent.

'You don't know that she's slept with Ferris.'

Steve's expression became mutinous. 'Don't I?'

'She says she hasn't and it might be true. This is about your family, Steve, not just you and Carolyn. You've got to sort it out.'

'How?'

'If it were me, I'd just knock seven bells out of this Ferris guy, and then forget about him. He's not worth chucking away a marriage for.'

Steve said quietly. 'It's not just about him and Carolyn.'

'Perhaps not,' Gary said, guessing that Steve was thinking about Jenny Heywood. 'But you're a married man, like me, Steve, and we've all been tempted. In the end you just have to realise you can't have everything.'

381

'No.'

'You and Carolyn aren't that bad together.' He grinned and nudged Steve in the ribs. 'Bloody hell, if I can stick it out with Jackie I'm damned sure you can stay with Carolyn.'

Steve tried to smile, but Gary could see the problem was nowhere near being resolved. He leaned forward to advise his friend.

'Let's just deal with what's really hurting you, that bastard having it off with your wife. Or not?'

Steve took another drink of his beer, and as he put down his glass everything seemed a little clearer.

'Yeah, you're right. I need to know,' he said finally.

Gary gulped down the beer that remained in his glass and made ready to leave.

'Right, we'll try the direct approach, shall we? I remember Jackie saying Ferris puts himself on show at the sports centre in his dinner-break on Fridays. We'll go and flatten him against the wall and ask him, shall we?'

Steve pulled Gary back down into his seat.

'And get arrested for assault?'

Gary's look was a lads' back-street challenge.

'Don't you want to belt him one?'

Steve's male pride was offended, but he'd thought about this before. 'Of course I do,' he declared, 'but I'm not going to. My kids have already got a Dad with no job, I don't want them to have a Dad in jail as well.'

Gary knew he was talking sense, but he didn't want to see all this fizzle out to nothing, he wanted a result. He leaned his arms on the table, and adopted the reasonable, muted tone of a counsellor.

'O.K.' he conceded. 'You don't have to hit him. But you do have to find out the truth, don't you?'

Steve nodded. And so, half an hour later, the two

of them were waiting for Paul Ferris as he walked out of the sports centre and along a quiet pathway. It was Gary who called out to him.

'Ferris, could we have a word?' he asked, playing it very cool.

Paul turned to face them, looking first at Gary and then blanching as he recognised Steve Sheldon, standing very still and tense behind him. Gary, unable to resist bravado when he saw that flicker of fear, swaggered up to him.

'You look worried, Paul,' he said in his best 'Godfather' manner. 'I can understand that. Only natural when you've been knocking off somebody else's wife.'

Steve stepped forward, and pulled Gary gently aside. He looked at Paul Ferris's smooth, handsome face and hated him. He wanted to stay cool, to be in control, say something clever and devastating, but his hatred got in the way of the words. Gary spoke for him.

'Is it true? Have you been shagging Carolyn Sheldon?'

At first Paul couldn't believe that he was being asked such a crude question, but then he saw the look between the two men and knew how vital his answer would be.

'No,' he said flatly, and then held his breath as Steve continued to stare him in the face.

Gary, trying to be sensible now, was willing Steve to be satisfied with that answer, and began to hustle for an end to this.

'Right, Steve. That's what you needed to know. Come on, we can leave it now.'

He took his friend by the arm and Steve allowed himself to be guided away. Paul Ferris stood there, watching them, and was startled to see Steve suddenly turn and walk back to him.

Hesitantly Paul decided to try a smile, but it was obliterated under the impact of Steve Sheldon's clenched fist. Steve marched away, leaving his enemy lying on the ground. Gary, aware that there could be just the kind of trouble Steve had wanted to avoid, told him to go while he ran back to check that Ferris was all right.

Gary helped Paul to his feet and inspected the damage.

'You're O.K. just a bit of blood from your lip. No teeth broken, are there?'

Paul ignored him, and looked to see if by some chance there might be a policeman around. There wasn't, so he took out his mobile phone and began to punch in 999.

Gary grabbed his arm and, looking coldly into his eyes, gently took the phone out of his hand.

'Never a copper around when you need one, is there? I'd leave it if I were you. It'd only cause more trouble, for everybody.'

Paul knew he was right. Gary handed the phone back and Paul put it away.

'A small price to pay, really,' Gary commented wryly. He saw Paul's mouth twist a little, and it made him seek confirmation of what he now suspected more than ever.

'You know, Paul, I can't believe you're a man who'd not get what he wanted.'

Paul Ferris carefully brushed some dust from his charcoal grey suit, and picked up his sports bag. He stared coolly at Gary, and then gave a self-satisfied smile which left no room for misunderstanding.

'You're not as stupid as you look, are you?' he said, and strode away, leaving Gary with a secret.

On Friday evening Jenny Heywood arrived at Kirkwood House with her two daughters and met Dan as they entered through the kitchen door.

'Hello. I'm just on my way to the bakery to finish preparing the party food. Then I can leave it in the fridges overnight. She's waiting for you in the drawing room. Good luck with those,' he said, looking at the balloons and other party decorations they were carrying.

'Why?' asked Alex.

'She's not in the best of tempers, and she's already complained about the balloons I've blown up. I've had to leave them in the conservatory.'

'We'll cope,' Jenny assured him.

'See you later. Oh, Alex, Lynda's given me some money for you, like she promised. So you'll have plenty to treat your friends with when you go off into town. I wouldn't tell your Gran about that yet, though. Some things are best kept as a surprise.'

Alex gave him a kiss. 'Thank you. Don't worry, I'll wait till she has some of her 'important' friends round her, then she won't dare make a scene.'

They'd brought flowers as well as the decorations, and worked hard at creating a bright and celebratory atmosphere in the rooms the guests would enter during the party. It was not an easy task, especially as Ellen was feeling depressed as well as tired, but was determined to supervise their efforts.

Being extremely tactful, Jenny managed to obtain Ellen's permission to move some ornaments and pieces of furniture out of the way but disapproval was etched into every contour of Ellen's matriarchal countenance as she watched them preparing to put up the balloons.

'I love balloons, they remind me of the parties we had when we were little,' Alex said cheerily, attempting to deflect her Grandmother's disapproval.

Ellen's expression became tender. 'Yes, you were very fortunate. Your Father had a great talent for organising parties. He was so good to you.'

Jenny was grateful for the sympathetic look Alex gave her, and felt more able to withstand Ellen's cloying reminiscences now that her daughters knew the truth about the past.

They had talked long into the night, and had discussed everything, with the result that Alex had even come to accept her Mother's relationship with Steve Sheldon. So much so, that when Ellen confirmed that both Carolyn and Steve would be coming to the party, Alex grinned wickedly at her Mother.

'That should be interesting,' she muttered sotto voce. She immediately regretted this indiscretion, for Ellen, whose hearing was extremely acute, picked up on the comment.

'In what way interesting?' she enquired frostily. 'Is there something I should know?' she demanded, turning her glittering eyes on her daughter-in-law.

Jenny concentrated on moving ornaments and avoiding meeting those eyes. Ellen, however, had decided she would not be denied an answer.

Over the past few weeks she had perceived that her position as head of the family was being undermined, and she blamed Jenny for this. Now all the jealousy and resentment she harboured against this younger woman mounted within her, and she was ready to regain her power, whatever the cost to Jenny.

Holding herself very erect in her high backed chair, Ellen prepared herself for the pleasure of a little drama, and confronted Jenny with her suspicions.

'I did not wish to say this in front of your daughters, Jennifer, but I have noted your unhealthy interest in Carolyn's husband. And I find it despicable.'

Hearing a gasp from her two granddaughters, she turned to them and said, 'Your Mother is a very self-centred person, who thinks all that matters is what she wants.'

'That is just not true!' Alex cried, wanting to defend her Mother against Ellen's venomous attack, but only provoking Ellen to continue her accusations.

Turning back to Jenny, Ellen said, 'You've made up your mind to take Carolyn's husband from her, haven't you? Just as you made up your rapacious little mind to take my son from me.'

Ellen expected Jenny to flinch away and bow her head in humility as she had so often, but this time Jenny was not intimidated.

'I haven't taken anything from your precious Carolyn,' Jenny declared, surprising both Ellen and herself with her belligerence. 'She's the one who's wrecked the marriage, she's the one who's having an affair.'

'Nonsense! How dare you tell me such a lie?' was Ellen's response, even though she was already recollecting the night she saw Carolyn getting into a car driven by a good-looking man.

Jenny spoke more gently now. 'I don't tell you lies, Ellen. I've always told you the truth, but you never have believed me. Right from the start, when I tried to tell you the truth about Richard.'

Ellen felt her heart contract, for she knew what Jenny was going to say. And she would not hear it, for, once uttered, it would be out in the open, exposed and given credence.

'Truth?' she cried, 'Filthy lies about my son! My son and your devoted Father.' She turned to appeal to her granddaughters, but found them stony-faced.

'Devoted?' Alex said coldly, 'I don't think so.'

Ellen was shocked at her granddaughter's tone, but knew who was the cause of this insurrection. She turned on Jenny.

'What have you been saying?'

'Ellen, all these years I've kept quiet,' Jenny began, but then shrank away from the pain and the fury on Ellen's face, and could not continue.

Alex, however, remembering how often she'd seen her Mother cowed by this domineering woman, wasn't going to let it happen again. She'd inherited the incisive manner of the Buchanans, and her voice was controlled but very forceful as she confronted her Grandmother.

'All our life she's had to listen to your lies. You, telling us how wonderful he was, your precious son. Mum would never say anything against him, but I knew the truth.'

Ellen stood up and raised her hand.

'Be silent, child!' she commanded. 'You were only five years old when he, when we lost him. You cannot remember him, and how. . . .'

'I remember Mummy screaming.'

Ellen stared open-mouthed at her granddaughter, and then gasped for breath as her heart began to beat hard against her chest. Jenny ran to her and Ellen signalled to be given the inhaler she kept beside her chair.

They phoned Dan, and by the time he'd returned home, Ellen had recovered and was still insisting that the doctor should not be called.

'And I wish you three to leave my house immediately,' she told Jenny and her daughters. 'My son will take care of me.'

CHAPTER FORTY-FOUR

Carolyn had thought she would phone Ellen to tell her that she wouldn't be able to go to the birthday party, but on Saturday morning she decided it would be cowardly to make excuses over the phone. She also felt that she needed to talk to someone, someone who would be on her side.

Ellen greeted her with even more affection than usual and asked Ruth Dawson, the girl who helped with the housework, and who was on extra duty today, to bring them coffee immediately.

'Come and sit down, my dear, I've been expecting you.'

'Have you?' asked Carolyn as she sat in her usual place by the fire.

'Yes. You have come to tell me you will be unable to come to my birthday party.'

Carolyn stared at this woman who had been her mentor for so many years, and marveled yet again at her insight.

'Yes. I'm so sorry to disappoint you, Ellen. I seem to have been doing that a lot lately.'

'Carolyn, I quite understand,' Ellen said. 'I assume there are changes taking place in your life, in your marriage, and that you have to be elsewhere.'

'Yes.' Carolyn was beginning to wonder how much Ellen knew.

'Let us not waste time,' Ellen said, enjoying this intrigue. 'You have met someone else. Someone more suitable, I hope?'

'How do you know?'

'Never mind about that. Tell me about this young man.'

Carolyn, embarrassed at first, described Paul Ferris and the way he had pursued her.

They halted their conversation when the coffee was brought in, and Carolyn was glad to have a moment to reflect on what she had told Ellen. She waited until Ruth had closed the door, and then leaned forward to apologise again.

'I know there can be no excuse. I can only say, that he was very persuasive.'

'Carolyn, please don't worry about this. I just want you to be happy, and Paul Ferris sounds the kind of man who appreciates a beautiful and intelligent woman like you.'

'Yes, he does. But I don't know what to do, I keep changing my mind, about everything. I never meant this to break up my marriage. I don't want to lose Steve.'

Ever since she'd seen Carolyn getting into Paul Ferris's car, Ellen Heywood had been making plans for Carolyn's future and knew precisely what advice she needed now.

'Carolyn. You know my opinion of Steve Sheldon. He was never good enough for you, and never will be. This is your chance to start a new life, the kind of life you should have had. And don't worry about the children, you will get custody of them, the mother always does.'

Carolyn shook her head.

'Not always, not now. And anyway, I don't want a divorce,' she said, blinking back tears. 'Steve and I can get over this, we had a good marriage before I began this madness.'

Ellen decided that if she was to win the fight for Carolyn's future, she must play her trump card. She walked over to the piano, fingering Richard's photograph and striking a pose she considered appropriate to this high drama she was creating, and which held the extra dimension of a secret sense of revenge.

She spoke with the confidence of being certain she was right.

'Carolyn, you must listen to me. You're assuming that Steven will want to save your marriage. You are also assuming that you're the only guilty party.'

Carolyn was dumbstruck as Ellen continued, 'I happen to know that your husband has succumbed to temptation.'

'What do you mean?'

Ellen Heywood pronounced her accusation in a slow, deliberate tone. 'He is involved with another woman.'

'Who?' gasped Carolyn.

'I am ashamed to say this. My daughter-in-law.'

'Jenny?' Carolyn whispered.

Ellen spoke again, placing her final ace on the table.

'A temptation set before him by your Mother, I believe. Apparently it was at her instigation that they began spending time together.'

Carolyn felt as if she were sitting motionless while the world fell to pieces in front of her. Ellen continued talking, and it was almost as if she'd forgotten Carolyn was there, so absorbed was she in her own pain and grief.

'Jennifer has always wanted to marry again. It seems the memory of my son means nothing to her.'

Carolyn was shaking her head like a bewildered child. 'I can't believe this. Steve has never even looked at another woman.'

Ellen was losing patience with her protégée and

interrupted her sharply. 'I think, Carolyn, you have to accept that your marriage to Steven is over. You must move on. Marry Paul Ferris.'

'I don't know if he wants to marry me.'

Ellen had already decided how to deal with that particular difficulty. She offered her generous solution.

'You won't have to be dependent on that. You have your career, and I shall help you financially.'

She held up her hand to halt Carolyn's attempt to refuse any such offer.

'I had already made some provision for you in my will, but I've now decided that my bequest to you should be considerably increased.'

Carolyn began to protest again. 'But what about your own family?' she asked.

'My family will still be well provided for. And I wish to help you.' She paused before going against her nature and confessing her own sorrow. 'I never did have what I wanted from life, Carolyn, but I'm determined that you shall.'

Carolyn looked at this proud, unhappy woman and felt great pity for her. Ellen held out her arms in a rare gesture and held Carolyn close for a moment.

'Say goodbye now, my dear, I need to rest before this evening.'

Carolyn kissed Ellen's cheek which was pale and cold, and Ellen cupped her face in her hands, and gazed intently at her favourite child as she said goodbye. Then, as Carolyn reached the door, Ellen smiled and said quietly,

'I don't think you will have to wait too long for your inheritance.'

Carolyn turned and looked at her in dismay, suddenly aware of how frail she looked. She wanted to comfort her, but Ellen dismissed any such intention with a wave of her hand and her well-practised wry smile.

That smile was very precious to Ellen Heywood; all her life it had enabled her to hold on to her dignity, and it was now her shield against the unforgiving onslaught of old age.

Carolyn had changed her mind again when she'd arrived home from Ellen Heywood's. She would go to the party, she was Steve's wife, and no-one was going to break up their family.

The silky dress the colour of cornflowers was over ten years old. Carolyn had been surprised that, although it did cling a little tighter than it had before, it still fitted her. It was a very special dress. Steve had bought it for her to wear on their first wedding anniversary, the year after Michael was born.

They had never been closer than they were then, in those terrible months after her Mother had left them. That was why she'd taken the dress out of the wardrobe and hurriedly put it on, knowing that Steve would be coming upstairs to get his wallet which he'd left on the dressing table.

'What do you think?' she asked. 'Shall I wear it for the party?'

'Please yourself,' he said, barely glancing at her.

Carolyn saw that he'd not remembered the dress was special, at least she hoped he hadn't because that would have made his indifference even more painful.

'I'm taking the kids to their friends' now. Have they got everything they need for their sleep-over?'

'Yes, it's all in their bags. I won't come down, I've said goodbye to them,' she said, knowing she was close to tears.

She had cried as she'd taken the dress off.

When they'd discussed the birthday party Steve had insisted he would be going whether she did or not. After what Ellen had told her, she knew why.

And she definitely couldn't go now. She couldn't let other people witness the cold indifference of a husband who had already chosen another woman to replace his unfaithful wife. Ellen was right, it had to be Paul from now on.

When Steve came back half an hour later he was surprised to find Carolyn sitting in the living room, wearing her dressing gown.

'Why aren't you ready? Ellen Heywood won't want us to arrive late.'

'I've told her I'm not going.'

'Why not?'

'Lots of reasons.'

'O.K,' he said with a shrug. 'If that's what you want, stay here on your own.'

Carolyn was horrified to feel herself blushing. Steve noticed the colour on her cheeks and the guilt in her eyes.

'Oh, I see. Got other plans, haven't you? You and him,' he said in disgust.

Carolyn watched Steve putting on his jacket and preparing to walk out of the house, and out of her life. For a moment she wanted to get down on her knees and beg him not to go, but instead her pride and anger took over.

'Enjoy the party,' she said, 'I'm sure my Mother will be glad to see you there, and Jenny Heywood, of course.'

He froze, and the look on his face told her that what Ellen had said about him and Jenny was true, and condemned her to a future she did not want.

Without saying another word he walked out. For a while Carolyn sat there, neither moving nor thinking, just looking at her hands clenched in her lap. She began to tug at her wedding ring, forced it off her finger and put it in the pocket of her dressing-gown.

Then she went up to the bedroom, hung the cornflower blue dress at the back of the wardrobe, and put on a low cut black dress she'd bought in a sale a year ago but had never dared to wear.

She went slowly back downstairs and opened a bottle of Côte du Rhône she'd hidden in the sideboard cupboard. She carried it into the front room, poured herself a glass and arranged herself on the sofa to wait for Paul.

The curtains of Kirkwood House were usually closed as soon as darkness descended over the streets of Milfield, but not this evening. Ellen wanted all the lights in the house to be visible to any passers-by, so that they could pause and admire the prestigious event, and wish they could have been among those chosen to attend.

There was an air of restored glory about the room. There were vases of white carnations and gypsophila displayed against a background of laurel leaves, and on the sideboard crystal glasses sparkled on a white damask cloth. Dan, wearing an apron over his best silk shirt and tie, was polishing the last of the wine glasses when his Mother made her entrance into the room.

She paused in the doorway waiting to be admired. She wore a full length dark blue dress, and the impressive three strand pearl necklace and earrings inherited from her mother.

'You look splendid,' her son said dutifully, but Ellen was too much on edge to respond graciously. It had been a long time since she had played hostess on such an occasion, and she was feeling tired in spite of

Dan's insistence on her taking an afternoon nap.

Dan nervously placed the glass next to the others. He had made a promise, to himself, as well as to Katie and Alex when he'd seen them that afternoon. They'd told him about the talk they'd had with their Mother, and all that had been revealed about their father.

They knew he had tried to help Jenny during those terrible years, but he felt ashamed that he'd been able to do so little. He had confronted Richard, tried to make him stop his cruelty, but he'd been no match for a brother who had always been able to beat him easily in a fight.

His nieces had not wanted him to blame himself, but Dan wished he could have been more of a hero for them, and had resolved that there would be no more secrets in the family, no more pretence about the past. Jenny didn't deserve to be disparaged and humiliated by his Mother, and Dan had vowed that he would put an end to it, today, before Alex's birthday celebration.

It was not proving easy for him to find the courage, but then Ellen paved the way for the confrontation. With an air of sadness she walked slowly round the room.

'If only Richard could have lived to see his daughter's eighteenth birthday,' she sighed. 'But I am here, and I shall make sure he is remembered as he should be.'

Dan, trying to keep his voice steady, asked, 'Why didn't you tell me the real reason for your argument with Jenny yesterday?'

Ellen was looking out of the window, and he couldn't see her face, but he noticed that she stood very taut and still for a moment before turning to face him. She breathed in deeply before she spoke.

'And give credence to her lies?'

Dan wanted to run away and hide from those wrathful eyes, but he stood his ground.

'I'm sorry,' he said, cursing himself for stammering, 'I don't want to hurt you, Mother, but we've all been doing too much pretending, and Jenny was quite right to say what she did.'

He stopped, realising he was beginning to gabble.

'Do you mean you believe her?' Ellen was already condemning him for treason, but her son knew it was now or never, and he had to complete the mission he had set himself.

'Yes. Because I know it's true. I've tried before to tell you, and this time you have to listen.'

'Do I, indeed?' she mocked.

'Yes. You have to know the truth about him. All his life Richard made people suffer. Jenny had a terrible time.'

Ellen's voice was full of scorn as she declared, 'Whatever he did to her, it was no more than she deserved.'

'You can't say that!' Dan protested. 'You've got to realise what she went through with him. You've got to realise what he was really like.'

He felt himself instinctively stepping backwards as Ellen moved like one of the Furies towards him.

'Daniel, you will say no more. You will not defile the memory of my beloved son!'

His Mother stood in front of him, her fist raised as if she would strike him to the ground. Dan shrank away from this spectre from his childhood.

Seeing the fear in her son's eyes made Ellen catch her breath. She lowered her hand and, feeling very weak and a little faint now, she moved towards her chair by the fire. Dan reached out to help her but she cast him away. She sat there for a few moments to

397

recover, and then lifted her head to look at him, first with contempt, and then with sorrow.

'Do you really think I didn't know he was selfish and cruel?'

She looked at the fire and blinked back tears as she thought of her youngest child.

'But he was my son, my beautiful boy,' she continued proudly, 'and I loved him.'

She paused then, and suddenly wanted to take some kind of revenge on the son who was still alive, and who seemed willing to tarnish the memory of her favourite child, his brother.

'I loved him,' she repeated. 'I loved him, as I've never loved you.'

'I know that.'

Dan's face crumpled and he thought he was about to cry like a two year old. Almost all his life he had known that his Mother had felt this way about him and his brother, but to hear her say it caused him more pain than he could bear. He had to fight to free himself from that pain, had to hit back.

'But why?' he shouted 'Why did you love him more than me? He was a bastard!'

Ellen was both shocked and enraged at her son's rebellion, and for once lost control.

'No.' she cried. 'You were the bastard!'

Dan stared at her in a stunned silence. He could see from the look on her face that there was something which had never been told, but which he needed to know. The doorbell rang, but the silence was more powerful than the instinct to answer its summons.

'What do you mean?' he asked.

Ellen had intended that Dan should never know this secret, but she felt too old now to carry the burden of it any longer. And he had a right to know.

398

'Geoffrey Heywood was not your Father.'

Too late she realised how cold her words sounded, but there, it was done.

'Of course he was,' Dan heard himself laugh at the preposterous notion, though he didn't feel any laughter inside him. The doorbell rang again, and Ellen pushed herself up out of her chair as if she would go to answer its clamour.

'Mother?'

Ellen could not look at him. She knew she'd been cruel to tell him like that, and she was ashamed. And it had been wrong to tell him, for his sake and her own. She did not have the courage to dismantle the past and destroy the treasured memories which, sometimes, were the only sweetness in her life.

With a slight tremor in her voice she said, 'Our guests are arriving.'

She went to stand by the piano, next to the photograph of her dead son, and detached herself from the emotions of the past few moments. Dan shook his head in disbelief.

'You can't say something like that and then . . . .'

He stopped. It was no longer his Mother standing there; she had withdrawn out of his reach and become the society hostess waiting to receive her guests.

'They're waiting,' Ellen said in a voice sharpened with demand.

The self-control inherited from her father did not waver as she saw Dan's desperation. Her unflinching eyes demanded obedience as she pointed to the door, and, numb with shock, Dan obeyed.

CHAPTER FORTY-FIVE

Ellen Heywood greeted and graciously welcomed her guests, and there was no doubt who was to be the centre of attention that evening. Alex had already retreated into the company of her friends who huddled themselves protectively around her, trying to alleviate her embarrassment at the bemused or patronising attitude of some of Ellen's older guests.

Jenny and Dan had been quickly relegated by Ellen to the roles of butler and parlour maid rather than co-hosts, and they spent most of their time alongside Alice Smith, circulating with trays of food and glasses of wine.

Dan kept watching his Mother, but whenever she saw him looking in her direction she turned away. Jenny noticed his agitation, and the cold way Ellen kept avoiding him, but Dan wouldn't tell her why he seemed to be so shaken and preoccupied.

She herself was constantly looking at the doorway, waiting for Steve to arrive. Ellen had informed her that Carolyn would not be coming, and had expressed the hope that Jenny would be suitably ashamed of her role in creating this circumstance. At half past eight Steve had still not arrived, and Jenny was beginning to worry that he'd decided to stay at home with his wife.

Alex noticed her anxiety and whispered to her, 'Don't worry, he'll be here soon.' She grabbed her by the arm, 'Come on, Mother of an eighteen year old. Head up, hide the double chins,' she teased as she swept Jenny across the room to introduce her proudly to some more of her friends.

Lynda had made sure that Jean looked gorgeous and, thanks to a couple of large Martinis, felt wonderful before they set off. She also decided that they would arrive at the party a little late, and make an entrance.

Two of Ellen's friends from church were wishing her 'Many Happy Returns' and congratulating her on having arranged such a delightful soirée, and she was smilingly accepting their compliments. The smile withered on her lips when she saw Lynda and Jean enter the room. Almost everyone turned to admire Lynda, magnificent in a stunning, full length, shimmering white dress, and antique gold necklace and earrings.

Jean was wearing the beautifully tailored green velvet dress Lynda had bought for her. She felt, for once, that was dressed for the occasion, but nevertheless she was a little uneasy. Lynda, however, was perfectly composed as she looked round the room, seeking out her hostess. Ellen pretended that she hadn't noticed their arrival, and continued her conversation, leaving Dan to step forward and greet his guests.

As he poured them both a glass of wine Jean glanced over his shoulder and saw John standing by the fireplace. He was so entranced by the sight of Lynda that he seemed not to have noticed that she was standing next to her.

Jean gave him a little wave and, gratified to see his astonishment at her appearance, she bobbed a cheeky little curtsey. John was taken aback, but then gave her a big appreciative smile.

She and Lynda made a tour of the room, and both enjoyed the surprise, and sometimes dismayed, expressions of several people who hadn't been aware of Lynda's return, or her change of fortune.

It was quite a while before Ellen deigned to approach them.

'So glad you could come, Jean,' she said, pointedly ignoring Lynda.

'We were very pleased when Jenny invited us both,' Jean said. 'This is lovely wine. Lynda likes Chablis, don't you, Lynda?'

'My favourite,' Lynda said. 'I've acquired some good taste while I've been away, don't you think, Ellen?' she asked provocatively, stepping back to invite her hostess to admire her.

Ellen found her self-possessed manner extremely vexing and immediately sought to gain the upper hand.

'You seem to have acquired many things,' she said, in a way which alerted both Lynda and Jean to the significance of the remark.

'Such as?' Lynda asked coolly, even though her heart had begun to beat less steadily.

Ellen gave an enigmatic smile as she countered with her own enquiry. 'Will the young man from the South be bringing the rest of your possessions?'

'Eventually,' Lynda replied, wondering what Dan had told Ellen about Mark. 'I hope storing a few of my belongings is not proving inconvenient.'

Ellen smiled with satisfaction as she realised there was a game to be played here.

'Not at all,' she said smoothly. 'One needs to take good care of such personal items. I'm sure they hold many precious memories, and perhaps even a secret or two?'

Lynda couldn't stop herself from revealing a moment of panic, and Ellen eagerly collected this reaction like a small trophy. 'Now if you'll excuse me, I think it's time for the birthday cakes and the toasts,' she purred and walked away, leaving her opponent trying to assess how much Ellen Heywood might know about her past.

Steve had driven around for at least half an hour before finally stopping the car in a quiet, dark street. Sitting with his arms resting on the steering wheel, he bowed his head and grieved for his marriage. Like Carolyn, he'd realised that when he'd walked out of the house they had broken the last fine thread of hope that held their marriage together.

With tears finding their way down his cheeks he'd thought his way through the joys as well as the hardships of the past, and struggled to understand the reasons for the dilemmas he was facing now. He had tried to think clearly, rationally, but his whole being seemed taken over by the fact that his wife was, in their home, waiting to continue her affair with another man.

It began to rain as he drove along Wellington Road, but the lights in the windows of Kirkwood House seemed to welcome him as he approached it. As he slowly got out of the car he heard the distant sound of music and conversation. Jenny was in there, celebrating her daughter's birthday, and waiting for him.

He walked in just as Dan, forcing himself to behave normally, was beginning to usher the guests from the dining room into the drawing-room for the traditional lighting of the candles on the birthday cakes.

Jenny, still watching out for Steve, was standing at the back of the throng of guests. When she saw Steve her beautiful smile told him he could, at last, have the love he deserved. She moved quickly to stand by his side and he put his arm round her, eager to feel the warmth of her love.

'Are you all right?' she asked noticing the shadows in his eyes.

'I am now,' he said pulling her closer. 'What about you? Are you coping with your little girl becoming an independent adult?'

'And leaving home before too long,' Jenny added with a touch of sadness.

'You'll still have Katie. And me, if you want me.'

Jenny stared up at him, but before she could speak to him again everyone was called to order by Alice Smith, obeying Ellen's signal and chiming a teaspoon loudly and insistently against a glass.

Ellen, her arm round Alex's shoulders, waited regally for the hushed attention of everyone in the room.

Dan could see Alex looking round the room, searching for her Mother and he, too, tried to find Jenny, wanting to bring her forward to her rightful place by her daughter's side. Ellen, however, was already beginning her speech.

'Firstly, I would like to express my gratitude to you all for coming to my home to celebrate my birthday, and for all your gifts and good wishes.

This is, of course, also a celebration of the eighteenth birthday of my granddaughter, Alexandra. As some of you may know, she was named after my dear father, Richard Alexander Buchanan, a much admired man who had great intelligence and strength of character, and those are qualities which I believe Alexandra has inherited.'

Ellen paused to acknowledge the murmurs of agreement, and as her gaze moved around the room she saw her daughter-in-law, with Steve Sheldon. Her resentful eyes met Jenny's as she continued her speech.

'But there is another man who must also be part of this celebration, Alexandra's father, my beloved son Richard. His memory should be honoured here today.'

The emotion in her voice increased and she stared intently at Jenny as she declared, 'He will never be forgotten. He would have been so proud of his daughter, and so, on his behalf, I give you a toast, to Alexandra.'

The guests, glad to be released from the intensity of Ellen's speech, raised their glasses of champagne and drank the toast. Alex forced herself to smile and thank them, but she was struggling to suppress her anger.

Lynda saw that Jenny's face had grown pale and that Dan, too, was extremely upset. There was a smile of satisfaction on Ellen's lips, and when Lynda observed this she decided to put an end to her reign over the proceedings.

She walked across to Jenny, put her arm round her and led her to stand by her daughter's side. As they passed Dan Lynda saw that he was hesitantly holding a cigarette lighter.

'Light the candles, Uncle Dan,' she said loudly.

Jenny took her place next to Alex, who had wrenched herself from her Grandmother's bony fingers. Lynda waited till Dan had lit the candles on both cakes, and then, linking arms with him, to give him the support she saw he needed, she and Dan led the guests in singing 'Happy Birthday'.

Ellen was furious at Lynda's intervention but had to, belatedly, join in the singing of 'Happy Birthday' to Alex. There was a silence afterwards, because Dan couldn't bring himself to start the singing again in honour of his Mother.

Alice Smith, however, piped up, 'What about Ellen? Come on everybody, 'Happy Birthday to You' again.'

And so the guests hesitantly began to sing the celebration for their hostess, who tried to listen to the slightly half-hearted chorus graciously, but found it difficult to hide her annoyance at Lynda's behaviour.

An hour later it required all of Ellen's self control to prevent her losing her temper, when she discovered that Lynda had also played a part in sabotaging her evening of glory even further, and that Alex and all her friends were leaving the party to continue their celebration in town.

Ellen then saw her 'soirée' draw to a close earlier than she had intended, as almost all of her carefully chosen guests took the opportunity of leaving in the wake of this lively exodus.

When Ellen had closed the door behind the last of her friends, she saw Dan was waiting to speak to her, but walked straight past him.

'I am going to bed,' Ellen announced and went swiftly towards the staircase. Dan stepped in front of her.

'Mother, you have to talk to me, about what you said.'

Ellen dismissed his plea with one sharp word. 'No.'

She began to climb the stairs but he took hold of her arm, asking in a voice full of anguish, 'If Dad wasn't my father, then who was?'

Again Ellen attempted to move away, but he held on to her.

'I need to know,' he pleaded.

Ellen looked at her son as if he were a stranger accosting her in the street.

'There is nothing you need to know.'

'How can you say that?' he cried, 'You've got to explain.'

'There is nothing I wish to tell you,' she said and attempted to pull her arm away from him. 'Now will you please let me pass. I'm extremely tired.'

For once Dan wasn't going to give way to her, so she began to breathe as if gasping for air.

'Let me go. I must go to bed. Can you not see that I'm not well?'

He released her and, frustrated and perplexed, watched her slowly climb the stairs.

Jenny had been outside, laughing with Alex and her friends as they left in cars and taxis. She was shocked when she came back in to find Dan sitting at the foot of the stairs, close to tears.

She sat beside him, putting her arm round his shoulders, and begged him to tell her what was wrong.

He struggled to his feet and looked up the stairs. His voice shook as he cried, 'She, she says Geoff Heywood wasn't my Dad.'

There was a small sound from the top of the stairs where Ellen had paused to listen, but Dan didn't hear it. He was looking at Jenny and wondering why she wasn't shocked, or even surprised.

'Did you know, Jenny?'

'No. Not until the other day.'

'Who told you?'

'Lynda.'

Ellen Heywood gripped the rail at the top of the stairs, and leaned forward, standing very still as she waited to hear what Lynda had divulged.

She had always suspected that Lynda had learned the secret from her Mother, it was another reason she disliked and distrusted her. She wanted no-one to know how she had ruined her life, just as she hadn't

407

wanted Dan to know the truth about his father.

Ellen had cursed herself for inflicting that on him in a moment of temper. She knew how much he had loved Geoff Heywood, the man whom she had not appreciated until it was too late. Now all she could do was stand there, hiding in the shadows, and wait for Dan to learn the rest of her shameful story.

Dan felt as if the ground was shifting beneath his feet. There was no hesitation now, he needed to know everything.

'Who was my Father?' was his first, and most heart-stopping, question, and one which Jenny couldn't answer.

'I don't know. You'll have to ask Lynda, Dan. She knows the story.'

Jenny heard Ellen's footsteps, and looked up, but Ellen had fled. She'd already taken refuge in her room, where sleep would again be denied her by the voices from the past.

CHAPTER FORTY-SIX

Lynda, Jean and John were the only guests left in the drawing room, and were making conversation to fill the silence in their unfamiliar surroundings.

'Where's Steve gone?' John asked Lynda.

'I don't know.'

'He was talking to Jenny Heywood the last time I saw him,' Jean volunteered.

'Was he?' Lynda said with a frown.

'He might have gone home, to see how Carolyn is,' suggested John. 'It's a shame she wasn't well enough to come to the party. Good news about Steve's job, though, isn't it?'

'What's that?' asked Jean.

'He's had a phone call,' Lynda told her, 'to tell him he's got his job back.'

'That doesn't sound like Tony Randerson,' John commented.

Lynda smiled knowingly.

'No, I think somebody else might have had a say in that.'

John looked at her. 'Do you? Who?'

'I'll explain later.'

She walked over to the stereo system and the pile of CDs which Dan had set out.

'Let's put some music on. This is supposed to be a party and I haven't had a dance yet.'

Jean, fearful of taking a liberty, said, 'Do you think we should? Dan's not here, and neither is Ellen.'

Lynda grinned.

'All the more reason.' She selected a CD, 'Here

you are, Jean, just what you need, a bit of Elvis.'

The three of them were dancing when Dan entered, followed by Alice Smith bringing a tray. She began to collect the last of the plates and glasses scattered round the room, but paused to speak to Dan. Alice had noticed the tensions among the family and was desperately trying to find out what was going on.

'You didn't sing tonight, Dan. I told everybody I hoped you'd be giving us a song, like you did at your Mother's fiftieth birthday party, you and your Dad together, it was lovely. Did she not ask you to sing tonight?'

Dan shook his head.

Lynda had seen the stricken look on Dan's face and quickly stepped between him and his inquisitor.

'You're a great singer.' She turned to John and Jean who'd stopped dancing. 'We were saying earlier, weren't we, that Dan ought to offer to sing at the Carlton Dance. Harry Benson's looking for someone to act as vocalist for his band.'

'It won't be me,' Dan said quickly.

'He wants everyone who used to go to the Saturday dances to be there.' Jean said excitedly. 'Are you going, Alice?'

'Oh, yes, I shall be there,' Alice said, 'I wouldn't miss the last dance at the Carlton for anything. Such a shame it has to close.'

'Yes, we had some good times in that ballroom,' John said, looking at Lynda. 'We had our first dance together there.'

'So did you and Jean,' she reminded him.

'Yes, I remember that night,' Alice piped up again, putting down the tray of crockery, and eager to join in an interesting conversation.

'Shall I help you wash up, Alice?' Lynda asked,

410

picking up the tray.

'No, thank you. I'll do it,' Alice insisted, taking it from her. 'The taxi Dan's ordered for me will be here soon, and I've got things to see to,' she said, thinking about the basket of left-over treats she hadn't quite finished packing. 'See you in the morning, Dan, to help you clear up like I promised.'

'Yes. Thank you, Alice.'

Dan closed the door behind her and walked over to the sideboard to pour himself a brandy.

'Does anybody else want one?', he asked holding out the bottle.

'Why not?' Lynda said brightly, and went over to join him. 'Are you going to the Carlton dance, Danny Boy?'

'Yes, if you'll go with me.'

The need in his eyes at that moment was so great that she couldn't refuse. 'It's a date,' she said, and raised her glass to him. Then she turned to John. 'Dan's taking me to the Carlton Dance. Are you taking Jean?'

Jean, who'd taken advantage of the rare treat of free champagne that evening, came over to accept Dan's offer of a brandy.

'Doesn't look like it,' she said, the alcohol adding a certain shrill defiance to her voice. 'I think it's you he wants to take, Lynda. It's always been Lynda, hasn't it, John? And always will be.'

Lynda put her arm round her friend. 'Don't get upset, Jean.'

'I can't help it,' Jean said, brushing away a tear. 'He still wants you, Lynda, not me.'

'No. He doesn't, not really.' She looked at John. 'You know we're not right for each other, don't you, love? And that we have to get divorced.'

John, who'd needed a few beers to get him

411

through Ellen Heywood's uncomfortably formal 'soirée', was almost shouting. 'So you say. But what's the flaming hurry?'

The pain he was inflicting on Jean made her cry out. 'Shall I tell him why you want a quick divorce, Lynda?'

'No, love,' Lynda said firmly, 'I will. John, I married Tom Meredith.'

John stared at his wife. 'You can't have.'

Dan contradicted him. 'She has. So the sooner you can put things right by signing those divorce papers, the better.'

John was annoyed now.

'Does everybody know about this, except me?'

'Of course not,' Lynda said, trying to speak calmly. 'And I have to keep it quiet John, I could go to jail for bigamy. But I had to marry Tom, and I wanted to. I loved him.'

She sat on the sofa, sipping the brandy and trying not to give way to the grief that was threatening to engulf her again.

John stared at her, and then strode over to Dan. 'Give me that bloody bottle.'

His hand was shaking as he poured the brandy.

Lynda, watching him, said gently, 'I'm sorry you're upset, John. But we've got to move on. And there is an up-side to this. I'm going to use some of the money Tom left me to help Steve take over Randerson's.'

John almost dropped his glass. 'What?'

'And Steve wants you to be chief electrician for him.' Lynda told him. 'You'll be back where you should be. And it will be a family business, for you and our grandchildren.'

John enjoyed a moment of hope, but then pride pushed the hope aside.

'I'm not taking that Meredith guy's money.'

'Don't be like that, John. And anyway, it's not just his, it's my money. I earned it and I want to invest it for the benefit of my family. But I could lose a substantial amount of what I own if Tom's family find out he and I weren't married, so we all have to keep quiet. And you and I have to get divorced as soon as possible.'

'Bloody hell!' was John's verdict as he knocked back his brandy.

'Please, John,' sighed Lynda. 'Start thinking straight and accept what has to happen. You could have a lot to look forward to now. You and Jean.'

Jean had been listening and watching but, observing that the mention of her name had no impact on the man who had been her lover, she headed for the door.

'There is no 'him and Jean'. He's finished with me,' she cried. 'And I've finished with him now. So goodbye, John Stanworth. Will you call me a taxi, please, Dan? I'm going.'

'No, I'll take you home, Jean,' Dan said. 'I haven't had much to drink. Though, God knows I felt like getting drunk tonight. I'll get your coat.'

He turned to Lynda.

'I need to talk to you, Lynda. There are some questions I really need answering, and Jenny says you're the one who can help me. Can I take you out to lunch tomorrow?'

Lynda was going to joke about him asking for a second date, but the way he spoke told her this was very serious, and she wondered what had put that bewildered, desperate look in his eyes.

'O.K. Dan. I'll look forward to it.'

'Thank you. I'll call for you at about eleven.'

As he followed Jean into the hall, Lynda looked at John.

'You'd better go home as well now, with Jean. Unless you want to lose her for good. Do you?'

He stood there, looking at the woman he had dreamed of for years, and finally realised that, for him, that was what Lynda Collins had always been, a dream.

'No. I don't. I'll go with her.'

'You'll have a lot of talking to do, and a lot of apologising.'

'Yes. Wish me luck.'

Lynda kissed him on the cheek.

'She just wants you to love her, John. And I think you do already. Am I right?'

He looked at her, 'You always knew more than I did.'

'Yeah,' she laughed, and gave him a little push towards the door. 'Now, go on. And choose your words carefully for once!' Then she added tenderly, 'Goodnight, love. And God Bless.'

When he'd gone Lynda found herself alone for the first time in this cold, unwelcoming room. She looked round at the antique furniture, the fine glass and silver, and then at the piano Carolyn had played as a child, during the weekly lesson with Ellen Heywood which Sheila Stanworth had arranged, against Lynda's wishes.

Drinking her brandy slowly and thoughtfully, she took a long look at the straight backed leather armchair, the throne from which Ellen, and her father before her, had ruled for so many years.

She turned away from it and noticed the silver-framed photograph of her daughter. Steve had refused to explain why Carolyn hadn't come to the

414

party, and she wondered if he, too, had now gone home. She put down the brandy glass, and went into the hallway. She heard Steve's voice coming from the conservatory and walked towards that familiar, homely sound.

The door was ajar and when she pushed it open wide, there in front of her was her son-in-law, with his arms round Jenny Heywood, holding her as if he'd never let her go.

'What the hell's this?' Lynda shouted, and then said accusingly to Jenny. 'I thought I told you to leave him alone.'

Jenny turned to Steve in surprise. 'Doesn't she know?'

'What?' Lynda demanded.

'Carolyn's been having an affair, with that guy at work, Paul Ferris,' Steve told her, glad that he didn't have to feel so guilty now about his love for Jenny. But Lynda's response shocked him.

'Yes, I knew that, but it doesn't mean you have to do the same. You and Carolyn have to sort this out.'

'No. It's over. She knows about me and Jenny, and I know about her and Ferris. So we'll be getting divorced,' he announced, still holding on to Jenny.

'You can't do that!' Lynda cried. 'What about the children?'

Steve flinched, and had no answer.

Lynda was fighting now. She knew what was at stake here for her grandchildren, and she was going to defend their future at all costs.

'You don't give up on a marriage just like that,' she said, snapping her fingers.

Steve shook his head slowly. 'No, you don't. But what do you expect me to do, Lynda? Keep on trying, like you did? Waste half my life being miserable and still end up having to leave?'

415

Lynda didn't want to listen, but she could see that Steve wasn't going to back down, not standing there with his arms round Jenny Heywood.

'Go home, Steve,' she pleaded. 'Go and talk to Carolyn before it's too late.'

'You don't understand, Lynda,' he said stepping towards her, grim-faced. 'Carolyn didn't come to the party tonight, because she'd arranged to spend the night at home, with lover boy! And there's something else you don't know; this isn't the first time. She had an affair while you were away, and I'm still not sure whether Gemma is that fella's child or mine!'

'What a terrible thing to say!' Lynda protested loudly, but she felt as if the floor was rocking beneath her feet. 'I'm not going to stay here listening to your lies and excuses, Steve. I'm going to see Carolyn, now, and tomorrow I'm going to talk to the two of you, and find a way to save your marriage.'

She marched out of Kirkwood House, slamming the front door behind her, and drove at breakneck speed to Beechwood Avenue.

Carolyn had spent a lot of time that evening staring down the empty street. She'd heard a car approaching once, and had gone to the window to see if it was Paul arriving. The car had stopped at a neighbour's house and Carolyn had quickly moved away from the window, and decided to close the curtains. She'd poured herself another glass of wine and, looking at the empty glass next to it, had begun to wonder if Paul was coming.

After more than another hour of waiting, she'd gone into the living room and, being careful not to look at her children's photographs, she'd picked up the phone and dialled Paul's number. But when she'd heard it ring she'd put down the receiver again.

He would be on his way, she told herself, because if he wasn't able to keep their date, he would have phoned to let her know.

He wanted her, she knew that. He'd told her again and again how much he wanted her. She phoned again an hour later, and this time instinctively knew that Paul was at home, sitting on the sofa, staring at the phone and letting it ring.

What she didn't know was that Gerald Critchley had observed his protégés success in seducing Carolyn Sheldon, and had wondered about the cause of the injury Paul had received that lunch time.

At the end of the afternoon Critchley had called him into his office, and had made it clear that now was the time for Paul to relinquish the pleasures of his conquest, for the sake of his career.

Carolyn went up to the bedroom, and not liking what she saw in the mirror, she took off the sexy black dress, got ready for bed and went downstairs in her dressing-gown. She sat on the sofa in the living room, to wait for her husband to come home.

CHAPTER FORTY-SEVEN

Carolyn didn't hear Lynda park the car quickly outside the house, she was sitting on the sofa, remembering the look in Paul's eyes when she'd told him Steve knew about their relationship.

She stood up as she heard the front door open.

'Sorry I didn't ring the bell, love,' Lynda apologised as she walked into the room, 'but I didn't think you'd let me in, and I had to see you.'

Carolyn didn't move, she felt numb, and there was no anger or strength in her voice. 'I thought it was Steve.'

'No, love.'

'Is he with Jenny?'

'Yeah. I'm sorry.'

'Not your fault.'

Carolyn stood there, helpless as a child, and burst into tears. Lynda took her in her arms and sat down with her on the sofa. She held her little girl until she stopped crying.

'Oh, Mum, I've been such a fool,' Carolyn whispered. 'Why did I do it? I love Steve. How could I do this to him?'

'Hush, it'll be all right.'

'No. He won't forgive me, not this time. I've done this before. Did you know?'

'Yeah, Steve told me.'

'I didn't sleep with Nick, but Steve never really believed me. And this time, I have. I've slept with Paul Ferris.'

Lynda was thinking fast, desperate to find a way to help her daughter. 'Does Steve know that for sure?'

'I don't know. I don't think so.'

'We'll keep it that way, then. I'll tell him you haven't, and he'll have to believe me.'

'But it's a lie.'

'Yeah, and I'll feel ashamed to be deceiving him. Just as I'll be ashamed to blackmail Steve into staying with you, but if that's what it takes to keep your family together, I'll do it.'

'Blackmail?'

'Steve wants to own his own company. He always has wanted that, more than anything. And I'll make it happen, on condition that he stays with you and the kids. I'll sort this out, love, don't you worry.'

Carolyn looked up, with hope in her eyes. 'Will you?'

'Of course I will. I'll do anything I can to help you.'

'Thank you.'

'Oh, don't thank me. I've a lot to make up for, like walking out on you when you needed me, remember?'

'I shouldn't have said that.'

'Yes, you should, you were right. But I didn't intend to abandon you like that, you know.' She shook her head sadly at the memory.

'I'd like to explain. I need you to understand. Oh, I'm sorry. This isn't the right time.'

'It's all right. I'm just glad you're here. And I'm ready to listen now.'

Lynda gave her daughter a grateful smile.

'Thank you, love.'

She took a deep breath and began her story.

'I thought I was just going away for a few days, to do some thinking. But once I got away, I was so relieved. I went to pieces really. And when I got better, I found I was somewhere where I was happy, and so I stayed a bit longer, and then a bit longer, until I was scared to come back.

I told myself you and Michael didn't need me, that I'd only make you miserable. I knew Sheila and your Dad, and Steve would look after you. But I'd still no right to leave you.'

Carolyn took hold of her hand.

'And I'd no right to tell you not to bother coming back. But I did. I remember that phone call, Mum. I told you we never wanted to see you again.'

Lynda looked away, so that Carolyn wouldn't see how much that memory still hurt her.

'Yeah. But we all say what we don't mean, sometimes. And like I said, I'd found a place where I could be happy. And then I found Tom Meredith, and he was the love of my life, he was my life.'

She couldn't stop the tears then. And mother and daughter held each other to try to ease their pain.

After a while Lynda said gently, 'I did love you, Carolyn, but I never felt I was any good as a mother. I knew that right from the start, when you were a baby, and you cried, and you always stopped when your Nana picked you up. I knew nothing about babies, I was hopeless. When you did let me cuddle you later, it was wonderful, but all I can remember being good at as a mother was reading you stories.'

Carolyn looked at her lovingly. 'Yes, I remember that.'

Lynda tried to laugh, 'I did wish I knew how to be classy, though, the kind of mother you could be proud of.'

'I'm so sorry, Mum,' Carolyn whispered. 'I said such terrible things that night you came here. And you were right, I did listen too much to what Nana said about you.'

Lynda looked at Carolyn, and decided she needed to hear it all.

'Sheila had a point, you both did; I suppose I did dress like a tart.' She shuddered. 'And it got me into trouble. Not like Sheila assumed, though. I didn't have affairs. But I did go out to have a good time, and one night I let Tony Randerson get me drunk, too drunk to stop him. And, well you can guess the rest.'

Carolyn put her hand to her mouth in horror as she realised what her Mother was telling her.

Lynda swallowed hard, and then said, 'And that was what you heard me and your Dad rowing about, what your Dad couldn't forgive me for.'

'Tony Randerson did that to you?'

'Yeah. I hate him for what he did, and I hope I'm about to get my revenge. But never mind that for now, it's you and Steve we need to think about. And what you've got to remember is that he loves you.'

'No, he doesn't, not now.'

'He did before, and he will again, once you're both over this craziness. Loads of couples go through rough patches in their marriage and get over them. And you and Steve have to, for the sake of your kids. Steve will realise that.'

'I hope so.'

Lynda laughed as she saw Carolyn yawn.

'Come on, you, time for bed. You need to get some sleep. I'll stay here in case Steve comes back. And I'll talk to him if you want me to.'

'Yes, please. He'll listen to you. You've always been such good friends, he thinks the world of you.'

'And I think the world of him. Or used to.'

'This isn't his fault, Mum. Oh, what if he doesn't come home?' Carolyn wondered fearfully.

'Then I'll go to Jenny's first thing in the morning. Don't worry, love. Tomorrow this will get sorted out,

421

and we'll all make a fresh start. There's too much to lose here.'

She took her daughter upstairs, and tucked her into bed like she used to when she was a child. Carolyn looked up at her and said softly, 'I'm so glad you've come back, Mum.'

'So am I love, so am I,' Lynda said and tenderly kissed her goodnight.

Lynda didn't sleep much, she found herself looking round that room and remembering all the bad times. At seven o'clock she took Carolyn a cup of coffee, and told her she was going back to Jean's to change, and would then drive to Hadden Lea.

Her confrontation with Steve and Jenny didn't go well. Steve had made up his mind that his marriage was over, and Lynda's spelling out what the consequences of that might be only made him defiant. But Lynda saw the doubt in Jenny's eyes, and resolved to talk to her again later, when there'd be just the two of them.

On her way home she phoned John and arranged to meet him in Alexandra Park. When they got there he grumbled at being summoned out so early after the party the night before.

'I needed a bit of fresh air,' Lynda said.

'Why? Is something wrong?'

'Yeah. Did you notice Steve spending a lot of time with Jenny last night?'

'Not really. Why?'

'Because he went home with her. He's leaving our Carolyn.'

'Oh, hell, no! Because of Carolyn carrying on with that bloke at work?'

'Yeah. You knew about that, did you? You didn't say anything to me.'

422

'Well, I didn't want you having another row with our Carolyn. But I didn't know Steve was seeing Jenny Heywood.'

'Neither did I till last night. Though I knew Jenny was in love with him.'

'What are we going to do about it?'

'I don't know. I've just been to see them, and warned Steve that if he leaves Carolyn the Randerson deal is off.'

John looked shocked. 'Hell. That's tough talking.'

'I know. And I didn't want to do it, but I'd no choice.'

'Our Carolyn is such a bloody fool. Why couldn't she be satisfied with what she'd got?'

'She and Steve weren't wanting the same things. Like you and me. So I can understand how Carolyn was tempted.'

'Well, I can't!'

Lynda laughed. 'This is different, isn't it, you playing hell about Carolyn, and me defending her? It used to be the other way round.'

'Yeah. I spoiled her, I know that.'

'Yes, you did, but that's all in the past now. And you haven't realised, have you, John, that me and Carolyn are talking again?'

He stopped and stared at her. 'No. When did that happen?'

'I went round to see her after the party, to tell her Steve wasn't coming home. And she, she let me hold her, like she used to when she was little.' Lynda wiped away the tears as she smiled at John. 'I'm her Mother again, John. I can't tell you what that means to me.'

'Some good's come out of a bad situation then,' John said, struggling to comprehend all this.

'I suppose you could say that. But we've got to help them get over this. I want you to take Steve to

423

the pub this lunchtime and talk to him. He might listen to you.'

'All right, I'll talk to him, but it will have to be later. I'm going out this lunchtime. With Jean,' he added hesitantly.

Lynda beamed at him. 'Oh, I am glad. It should always have been you and Jean.' Then she grinned cheekily, 'I've got a date as well, remember? I'm going out for lunch, with Dan.'

John looked at her and nodded.

'Perhaps that 'should always have been' as well, you and Dan.'

CHAPTER FORTY-EIGHT

Kirkwood House seemed very still and sombre to Dan as he walked round taking down the balloons. He was glad of Alice Smith's company as well as her help. He'd stored away the left-over food last night but hadn't been able to face the clearing up, and had gone to bed, even though he'd known he wouldn't sleep.

Now, finding it an effort even to push the Hoover round, he was moving slowly compared to Alice, who was flitting about collecting the remaining glasses, and restoring ornaments to their rightful places.

Alice had woken up this morning with her head full of speculation; the party had been most informative and entertaining. Hardly anyone had taken any notice of her, of course, but she'd had a wonderful time sitting in the small tub chair in the corner and watching everyone.

There had been plenty going on: Ellen insisting on being top dog, and sparring with Lynda Stanworth, her cousin Jean dressed to the nines, Jenny making eyes at Steve Sheldon who had come without his wife, and Dan looking as if the world had caved in on him.

He still looked like that this morning, and Alice was dying to ask what was wrong, but she was very experienced in eliciting information, and was waiting for a suitable opportunity.

She didn't have to wait too long. Dan took her up on her offer to go and see how his Mother was. Dan

425

had taken Ellen's breakfast up to her as usual, but she'd refused to speak to him and he'd been glad to get out of the room. To tell the truth, he'd been afraid his feelings would drive him to attempt to shake the truth out of her.

All night he'd been thinking back over his life, looking for clues as to who his real father might be. He had to know, he couldn't cope with the strange, empty feeling he'd had since his Mother had told him that she and Geoff Heywood had been lying to him all his life. He felt he had lost his identity, and somehow he didn't feel whole any longer.

Alice was surprised to see how pale and quiet Ellen was. She had expected her to be tired after the party, that was only natural at her age, but there was more than that. Ellen seemed troubled and, if it had been anyone else, Alice would have said, almost tearful.

'Dan, your Mother doesn't seem like herself at all,' she announced when she came back downstairs.

'Oh. Do you think I should call the doctor?'

'No. She seems more upset than ill. Have you and your Mother had a row?' Alice enquired, emboldened by Dan's asking for her advice.

She was amazed at the range of emotions which passed over his face before he replied, 'Nothing as simple as that.'

'If you fall out with your Mother, she'll come back and haunt you, like mine did,' Alice warned him. 'You don't want that.'

'No,' Dan agreed, knowing that Alice took all that sort of thing quite seriously.

He paused as he moved Richard's photograph, which had been pushed out of its usual position.

'There are enough ghosts in this house,' he

426

muttered bitterly.

'Yes,' said Alice. 'She loved him too much,' she commented, looking at the photograph.

Then, confiding thoughts which she usually kept private, she sighed, 'I'm glad sometimes that I never had children. It seems so hard to get it right, being a mother. You either love them too much or not enough.'

The early showers had discouraged many people from making an excursion into the countryside this Sunday and so, in spite of the sunshine now, there weren't yet any customers at the tables outside The Grey Horse. Dan was relieved; this needed to be a very private conversation.

He and Lynda sat on one of the benches which looked out on to the hillside. She held his hand as she told him about his real father.

'His name was Lawrence Cameron. He was Scottish, like your Grandad Buchanan, and quite a well-known singer in the 1940s, and very charming and handsome.

She waited for Dan to respond but he was staring at her blankly.

'Anyway,' she continued, 'he was appearing at the Milfield Empire and the Buchanans invited him for Sunday lunch.'

Trying to ease the tension, Lynda paused and tried to laugh, as she said, 'I bet they wished they hadn't.'

Dan didn't manage to smile back at her, he was too anxious to have all his questions answered.

'And my Mother fell for him?'

'Yes. She was a young woman, remember, and from a very strict and suffocating household according to my Mother. Ellen was desperate for excitement, and almost twenty-one, so she was due to inherit a fair bit of money. And it's the usual story; my Mum reckoned he promised to make her a big star, she had a lovely singing voice in those days. He kept coming back to visit, and in the end she ran off with him.'

'And came back pregnant.'

'Yeah. She told your grandparents that he'd forced her, but my Mum said she thought they'd only pretended to believe her. Mr Buchanan hardly spoke to Ellen for years after that. He left her Mother to deal with it all.'

'My Nan.' Dan blinked back a tear as he remembered Constance Buchanan, with her soft and gentle voice, and those arms which had cuddled him as a child.

'How did Geoff Heywood come to marry my Mother?'

'Apparently, he'd always been crazy about her. He'd already proposed a couple of times, and suddenly he was good enough. A marriage was arranged, as they say, and in this case pretty damned quick.'

Dan heard the cynicism, and shared it. 'They dropped lucky, didn't they, finding her a husband like that. Did he know she was pregnant?'

Lynda was aware that this question was even more important to Dan than the rest.

'My Mum reckoned he must have done. And he was in love with her.'

'And he loved me,' Dan spoke strongly but his face crinkled as he repeated, 'And he loved me, even though I wasn't his son.'

He couldn't go on, but sat there with his head in his hands and began to sob quietly.

'But my Mother didn't. She didn't ever love me.'

Lynda grabbed hold of Dan, holding him fiercely in her arms.

'She should have, though,' Lynda said vehemently. 'She should have adored you, not hurt you like she has all these years. Somebody ought to tell her she has no right to treat you so badly.'

She became aware that Dan was trembling, and kissed him before gently urging him to stand up. 'Come on, love. You need a drink. And so do I.'

They managed to find a table in an alcove in the Grey Horse, and enjoyed the meal as much as was possible, given the circumstances. They ordered coffee and Dan, quiet and subdued, drank it slowly.

'I don't want to go home, Lynda. There's nothing there for me now. There wasn't before, but I tried to pretend there was.'

'What are you going to do?'

'I don't know. Marry you, eh? That'd upset her,' Dan said, forcing himself to laugh like the mischievous little boy he had once been. But they both knew he was serious.

Lynda laughed as well, keen to maintain the illusion that Dan was joking, but in vain. He reached across the table and took hold of her hand, and Lynda didn't pull it away.

'I know it's too soon for you to even think about that, and I don't expect an answer. I just need to have something to hope for at the moment. You understand that, don't you?'

She nodded. They sat there in silence for a few minutes. When Dan spoke, that note of anguish was in his voice again.

'I can't live with her any longer. I feel as if I have no Mother. And it turns out I've never known my father.'

Lynda couldn't let him think this way.

'Geoff Heywood was your father.'

'I wish he had been,' Dan said mournfully.

Lynda had no doubt about what she was saying now, and that strong conviction was in her voice.

'Listen, Dan. Geoff Heywood brought you up as his own son. He loved you, and taught you what he knew, made you what you are. That's what a father does. Geoff Heywood was your Dad.'

Dan looked into his memory and saw the face of the man who had given him so much love, he remembered Geoff Heywood's strong arms holding him, guiding him, and he knew he was hearing the truth.

'Yeah. Yes, you're right.' He lifted up her hand and kissed it tenderly. 'Thank you. Oh, I'm so glad you came home, Lynda.'

She gave a little smile. Then the emotions she'd been going through ever since she'd returned to Milfield, grieving for her lost love, suddenly swept over her. She closed her eyes tightly for a moment, trying to hold on as she felt herself losing all the resilience and self-control which had enabled her to cope.

When she opened her eyes again Dan was startled to see they were glistening with tears, and full of uncertainties. His lovely Lynda was as lost as he was.

'Home?' she said. 'Where you belong. Where is that for me?'

CHAPTER FORTY-NINE

When Carolyn arrived for work on Monday morning Paul was already in Critchley's office. She sat at her desk and tried to concentrate but was aware of Julia and Michelle watching her, concerned about how exhausted and stressed she looked. They were also curious to know what had so obviously upset her, but Julia thought she could make a shrewd guess.

Julia was also able to guess the reason for the ill-disguised look of elation on Paul's face as he came back out of Critchley's office. She saw him trying hard to hide his delight from Carolyn as she went to talk to him, on the pretext of discussing a document.

'What happened on Saturday?' she whispered. 'Why didn't you come?'

She sat very still as he told her what she already knew but did not want to believe. The office was the last place Paul would have chosen to tell her, but his excitement made him reckless and eager to clear away the past, so that he could be free to enjoy the future which had just been granted to him.

'It's over, Carolyn,' he said just loud enough for her to hear. 'It has to be.'

He hardly dared look at her, afraid that she might cry out. But the next voice he heard wasn't Carolyn's, it was Gerald Critchley's, inviting Carolyn into his office to hear the bad news.

Julia noticed that there was a gleam of satisfaction in Critchley's eyes. His mouth curled into a little smile, bestowed in Paul's direction as Carolyn walked into his office almost as if in a trance.

Paul was relieved that he'd avoided a scene with Carolyn, but then Julia spoke to him, and as he turned towards her his guilt spread across his features like a stain.

'You got it, didn't you?' she said.

'Yes.'

'And what did Carolyn get?'

Paul was embarrassed. He took refuge at his desk, but he wasn't safe there. When, a few minutes later Carolyn emerged from Critchley's office, Julia and Michelle hurried to stand protectively beside her as she sank down on to her chair.

At first she'd not been able to take in what Critchley was saying, and now, answering Julia's questions, it felt as if she were struggling through a chaos of words and concepts. Eventually it came down to one simple sentence.

'There was only one job, and they've given it to him.'

She stared across at Paul who registered in her brain as only a hazy figure, but Julia and Michelle could see him clearly enough, and they made sure he could hear them.

'Why?' Michelle demanded loudly, 'You're loads better than he is!'

Julia shouted sarcastically across the office.

'Congratulations, Paul, you creep!'

Paul Ferris looked anxiously at the door of Critchley's office, and decided he had to deal with this. He walked over to Carolyn and, ignoring the glares of her vengeful colleagues, said quietly, 'Come with me, please, Carolyn, we need to talk.'

Still clinging to some fantasy of hope, she allowed him to put his arm round her and take her into the relative privacy conferred by the once romantic cluster of ferns and palm trees.

432

She tried not to be overwhelmed by the desperate panic that was taking hold of her.

'Congratulations,' she said bitterly. 'When do you go to Leeds?'

'They want me as soon as possible. Maybe next week.'

'And you don't want me with you.'

She'd tried to state this calmly but heard the tremor in her voice. Paul heard it, too, and for a moment she thought her prayer was being answered as he took her in his arms.

'I do care about you, Carolyn.'

He saw the hope as she looked up at him, but all his decisions had been made, and so he continued, 'But it's not going to work, is it, for either of us?'

He saw that she was close to tears and found himself stroking her cheek. 'I'm so sorry,' he murmured.

They'd accidentally left the door ajar, and Julia had gone to stand quietly behind it and listen. She had to stop herself from flinging the door open and hitting Ferris when she heard what he said next.

'There'll be another job.'

Carolyn stared at him, and the whole vision of what she had lost was suddenly painted vividly in front of her.

'Yes,' she said. Her eyes held his and tried to burn her anger and pain into him. 'But there won't be another marriage.'

She ran down the stairs and out of the building. Julia opened the door and set off after her, but paused at the top of the stairs to speak to Paul Ferris.

'I want you to understand what you've done here, Paul,' she told him.

'I was lucky, all you took from me was a bit of self-esteem. For Carolyn, it's her career, marriage, and family. Well done, Paul,' she said with bitter sarcasm. 'What a man you are!'

Lynda had been anxious when Philip had phoned that morning and asked her to call in at his office, but she relaxed a little as he gave her some reassurance.

'The friend I've consulted about your inheritance is pretty sure that, as most of the money and shares you have in Loveday Manor were given to Lynda Collins, they are yours. It's only when you become Lynda Meredith that problems arise.'

'So I've got the money to take over Randerson's?'

'To take over a majority share in Randerson's, yes. But it will take a large proportion of your assets, and you need to think about that. You need security for the future, Lynda.'

'So does my family.'

'I'm just having to warn you, that there is still the threat that Suzanne, or Mark, could contest Tom's will and your right to that inheritance.'

'Suzanne might, but Mark wouldn't want to go against me.'

'I'm glad to hear that, but my experience has taught me that there is rarely a full guarantee when it come to people. And the fact that you weren't legally married may present difficulties at some point in the future. I'm sorry, but you just never know.'

'I understand. What you're saying is that I'd better be careful what I say on Wednesday.'

'What's happening on Wednesday?'

'Mark, and some friends of ours, are bringing my furniture to Bennett Street.'

'Oh. So you're moving out of Loveday Manor. Are you sure that's what you want to do?'

'I don't think I have a choice. It can't really be my home any longer. Not in the circumstances.'

'What a shame.'

'Yeah,' Lynda said, her voice almost a whisper.

She stood up to leave, not wanting Philip's sympathy to make her cry again as she thought of Loveday Manor and her life there with Tom.

Philip saw her need, and announced brightly, 'Something a bit more positive before you go. Angela phoned me and said it looks like everything should be dealt with by the end of the week. She wanted to ask you how you'd feel about delivering the news to Randerson on Friday. Friday 13th.'

Lynda laughed.

'Tell her that sounds like a very appropriate date!'

She was still smiling as she left his office, but her expression changed as she saw Jenny sitting at her desk.

'I've just been talking to Philip about taking over Randerson's. It looks like it could happen on Friday.'

Jenny looked at her warily. 'Oh.'

'Have you thought about what I said to the two of you yesterday?'

'Yes.'

Lynda saw the misery in Jenny's eyes, and remembered how she'd comforted her when she'd suffered before. She couldn't offer any comfort to her friend's daughter now. Her own daughter had to come first, but Lynda had to steel herself to deliver her challenge.

'If you really love him, Jenny, you'll let Steve have what he needs, his dream, and his family.'

As she walked out on to the street Lynda felt exhausted, but she straightened her shoulders and took a deep breath. She had another battle to fight yet. She couldn't let that woman hurt Dan any more.

CHAPTER FIFTY

Ellen Heywood was sitting in her chair by the fire, pretending to read a book but also watching Alice Smith casting covetous glances at the piece of gâteau which remained on the tray of food Dan had set out for their lunch. Ellen had not been feeling well since the party, and had reluctantly given her son permission to invite Alice to come and keep her company, so that he wouldn't have to worry about her while he was at work.

Still feeling frail, Ellen had even allowed Alice to insist on placing a rug over her lap. However, her main problem now was the wearying hours of boredom. She had had enough of Alice's chatter and was pleased to hear the doorbell ring. Silently praying it might be someone interesting, Ellen sent Alice trotting off to see who the unexpected caller might be.

Alice, enjoying being 'in charge' of the invalid and her home, was not particularly pleased to have a rival visitor. Also, having put up with Ellen's high-handed manner all morning, she was not amused by Lynda's jaunty greeting.

'Hello, Alice. Playing nursemaid, are you, or is it parlour maid? Where's your little white apron and frilly cap?'

'I am here as a friend, not a servant,' Alice replied tartly and decided she had the authority to turn away this unwelcome intruder.

'Ellen's not well enough to receive visitors,' she said, beginning to close the door.

Lynda, knowing how to handle Alice, said, 'I've just come to collect some things being stored here for me.'

As Lynda had predicted, this pretext switched on Alice's curiosity.

'Oh, what are those?'

'Let me in and you might find out,' Lynda said sharply, stepping past Alice while she was trying to decide whether to take offence and prevent her entering.

On hearing Lynda's voice Ellen Heywood hastily removed the rug from her knees and concealed it under her chair. She sat up very straight and fixed her eyes, already alight with the prospect of battle, on the doorway.

Lynda entered, assuming an air of confidence bordering on arrogance, and Alice followed, nervously trying to excuse herself for having allowed this intrusion.

'I'm sorry, Ellen, but Lynda says she has some things to collect.'

She was mightily relieved when Ellen seemed amenable to receiving her visitor.

'Ah, yes, the boxes which Daniel brought here. They're upstairs.' Ellen spoke in an equable manner which disguised her anticipation of sparring with her old adversary.

Alice quickly observed the tension between the two women, and saw that some entertainment was imminent. With too much eagerness she said, 'I'll go and get them, shall I?'

But Ellen was only just beginning the game. 'Not just yet.'

'They're in boxes and too heavy for you, Alice,' Lynda said, not wanting Alice Smith's prying eyes to have sight of her possessions.

Ellen, watching Lynda carefully, made her first thrust.

'Yes,' she purred, 'they're very full. I'm afraid one of them burst open.'

She had the satisfaction of seeing Lynda failing to hide her anxiety, before her eyes hardened with suspicion.

'Did it really?'

'Yes,' Ellen replied silkily, 'it was a box containing special photographs.'

'Oh,' Lynda tried to sound unconcerned, but Ellen was going to change that.

'There was one of you and a handsome companion,' she continued, and directed a look of shrewd assessment at Lynda. There was no misunderstanding of what was being revealed here, as Ellen gave an apologetic little laugh.

'I couldn't help but see as I put it back.' She paused. 'You made a lovely couple.'

Lynda's face darkened briefly with anger at what felt like a violation, Ellen Heywood had no right to look upon the face of the man she had loved. Then she and Ellen both became aware that Alice Smith, sensing some scandal here, was clasping and unclasping her hands, so enthralled she couldn't keep still.

'You can go now, if you like, Alice. I'll sit with Mrs Heywood.'

Alice wasn't going to allow Lynda to dismiss her, and deprive her of participation in this drama. Without hesitation she jumped up and asserted squatter's rights.

'No, I don't mind staying,' she said, picking up the tray. 'I'll make us all some tea, shall I?'

Ellen smiled at this display of the thickness of Alice's skin but she wasn't going to let her witness this private combat. With an extravagantly gracious smile, and a wave of her hand, she said firmly, 'No, Alice. You have been very kind, but I mustn't keep you any longer.'

Alice stood her ground, but when Ellen, in her most superior 'lady of the house' tone, said, 'Thank you, Alice,' she had to accept that she was dismissed.

Observing that Alice had carefully left the door ajar, both Ellen and Lynda waited in silence until they heard her reluctantly retreating footsteps, and the front door closing.

Lynda walked across to the window, and made sure that Alice was not coming back before she turned to face her opponent.

She was so angry when she thought of the pain Ellen had caused Dan, that she forgot what Tom Meredith had taught her, and showed no mercy.

'Dan doesn't know I'm here, and he probably wouldn't want me to be. He thinks you're not well. I think you're just a good actress.'

Ellen looked at her with contempt.

'Indeed?'

Lynda didn't shrink back at Ellen Heywood's disdain, not this time. She went to stand in front of Ellen. 'You may be a good actress, but you're a lousy Mother.'

Ellen began to speak, but Lynda wasn't going to let her, not until she'd told her about her conversations with Dan yesterday, and castigated her for being a cruel and unnatural mother.

Once or twice Ellen looked as if she were going to struggle to her feet and order Lynda to get out, but she didn't. Instead she listened until Lynda ended her tirade. Then Ellen sat very still, and when she did speak at last, her voice was low and harsh.

'He should never have been born.'

439

'How can you say that about your own son,' Lynda gasped, 'and about someone as loveable and kind as Dan?'

'I am not denying that Daniel is a good man.'

Ellen looked away; an image of Dan standing there, trying to please her, made her clutch at the folds of her dress, but other more painful, more selfish images crowded into her mind and it was of herself she spoke now.

'His birth marked the end of all my dreams,' she whispered. 'I was young and did not want to have a child. It was my Mother's decision, not mine,' she declared vehemently. 'Just as Carolyn's hasty marriage was your decision, not hers.'

'That's not true.'

Ellen glared at her.

'She should not have had that baby, just as I should not have had Daniel. Carolyn would have had the life she was worthy of, if you hadn't made her marry Steven Sheldon.'

Lynda was being distracted from her purpose, and driven along paths she didn't want to go down. Her voice grew louder now.

'I haven't come here to talk about Carolyn.'

'No, quite right!' Ellen's manner was haughty and confident now. 'You are hardly qualified to talk about her. She ceased to be your daughter many years ago.'

Lynda's words flowed like pure acid. 'And became yours? She's not yours, Ellen Heywood, not your flesh and blood, but Dan is.'

Ellen gripped the arms of her chair and pushed herself to her feet.

'I don't think you and I have any more to say to each other,' she said icily.

'I've plenty to say.'

'You always did have, 'Lynda Collins', Ellen

440

sneered, 'but nothing worth listening to.'

Lynda was determined to speak out for Dan, but knew she needed to keep calm.

'You have no right not to love your child. No-one has. Dan has always loved you, Ellen, he's worshipped you ever since he was little, you and the man he thought was his Dad.'

Ellen Heywood knew that what Lynda was saying was true. And the mention of Geoff Heywood, the man she had failed to love as he deserved, was too disturbing for her. She walked over to the window and leaned on it for support.

'Will you please go? I am exhausted.'

But Lynda wasn't going anywhere until this tyrannical woman had heard what she'd come to say.

'Geoff Heywood loved Dan, even though he hadn't fathered him. But you,' she continued, giving full rein to her scorn and disgust now, 'Dan's spent his life looking after you, trying to please you, just as Geoff Heywood did. But you'd no love to give to either of them, had you?'

Ellen wanted to say that Lynda was wrong, but could not. She shut her eyes against the shame, and folded her arms tightly around her body to comfort herself against the pain.

Lynda knew she was winning, and couldn't resist claiming a moment of superiority against this woman who had helped turn her daughter against her.

'Do you know something? I pity you.'

If there was one thing Ellen Heywood could not, would not countenance, it was pity, especially from this vulgar woman she despised so much, and whose secrets she had discovered.

Her tone was imperious as she delivered her retort.

'And who are you to pity me, or to judge me?'

441

She breathed in deeply as she gathered herself for the attack. 'You! A woman with no morals, a woman who married when she had no right in law, or in the sight of God. A woman who was not good enough to nurture her own child!'

Lynda, hearing too much truth in that, tried to speak but couldn't, and turned away.

Ellen's tone became triumphant. 'Carolyn didn't want you. She came to me. You ruined your daughter's life. And now you are ready to ruin the lives of two good men.'

Lynda, walking towards the door, stopped and faced Ellen again.

'What are you talking about? What men?' Lynda snapped out the question on a shout of mocking laughter.

Ellen delivered her explanation with confidence, and the belief that she was saving her son.

'You will ruin Daniel's life if you marry him. And John Stanworth's if you prevent him from marrying Jean Haworth.'

Lynda smiled slowly.

'You've been misinformed, Ellen. I'm divorcing John, and actually encouraging him to marry Jean Haworth.'

'And my son? Will you promise me you will never marry Daniel?'

Lynda stared at her, and was disturbed to find that she could not make that promise.

She walked quickly out of the room, through the front door and away from that overpowering house, and the woman who had once destroyed her dream.

CHAPTER FIFTY-ONE

On Sunday Steve and Carolyn had hardly spoken at first, but when they saw the children were noticing the atmosphere they'd tried to make everything seem more normal. On Monday, however, as they sat having their evening meal together they learned that they hadn't succeeded. They'd finished eating and in the silence which followed Michael blurted out, 'Are you getting a divorce?'

Both her parents were shocked at the question, but before they could answer, Gemma added her plea.

'Oh, please don't. Melanie Holden's parents are getting divorced, and she's says it's horrible. Her Dan doesn't live with them any more, and her Mum cries all the time. You don't want a divorce, do you, Mum?'

'No,' Carolyn replied, looking at Steve, who was wondering what to say to his children.

'What about you, Dad?' Michael asked. 'What do you want?'

'You two to stop worrying, for a start. Your Mum and I have got some talking to do, that's all. Now go and do your homework. Your Mum and I will wash up.'

Pleased to be excused from their usual task, the children went upstairs, leaving Steve and Carolyn to go into the kitchen and talk quietly about the future.

'It seems crazy, doing the washing up while we have a conversation about something so scary,' Carolyn said, trying to smile and to persuade Steve to look at her. He concentrated on carefully drying knives and forks.

443

'I meant what I said, Steve,' Carolyn repeated, 'I don't want a divorce. And the kids would be heart-broken if we split up.'

'You should have thought of that before you started sleeping with Paul Ferris.'

Carolyn lied again to save her marriage. 'I didn't sleep with him, I swear I didn't. It's you I love, Steve, you I want to spend my life with, here in Milfield.'

'Milfield? What about Leeds?'

'I didn't get the job,' she admitted quietly. 'But I'll be happy to stay in Milfield for ever, if that's what you want. And I'll help you make a success of Randerson's, if Mum can set that up for you.'

'Oh, Mum, is she now? Not 'that woman'.

'Yes. She is, my Mother, who's come back to us, for a second chance. I know how wrong I was about her. And she's forgiven me, for everything. Can't you forgive me as well, Steve?'

When he didn't reply, she stumbled on, 'I don't mean now. I know it will take time. But we can make our marriage work. And for the sake of the children, shouldn't we at least give it a try?'

Steve stared out of the window, remembering the panic in his children's eyes. 'I don't know,' he muttered. 'I've promised to go round to Jenny's tonight.'

'Oh.'

'I've got to go. But I'll wait till the kids are in bed.'

Hesitantly she asked, 'And will you come home?'

'Yes.'

Jenny did her best to make it easy for him. She'd been for a walk with Tigger, who had seemed to sense her anxiety; the usually wayward dog hadn't raced away from her, but had stayed close, looking up at her as if to enquire what was wrong.

The colours of the sunset were fading from the sky when Steve arrived. Jenny opened the door and Alex and Katie came downstairs to greet him.

'I gather you're moving in,' said Katie, 'we don't mind, do we, Alex?'

'No. Mum's explained it all to us, and we're fine with it,' her sister agreed.

'Thank you.'

Jenny noticed his embarrassment, and also that he wasn't carrying any bags. 'Is your suitcase in the car?'

'No,' he said, and the way he looked at her told her daughters there was a problem. They tactfully made excuses and both disappeared back upstairs.

Jenny kissed him gently on the cheek and went to make coffee. Steve sat on the sofa, wishing he could stay in this house for ever. Jenny sat in her rocking chair, watching Steve and locking away in her heart the image of him sitting there, knowing that she might never see him in her home again.

'It's hard to find the words, Steve, but we both know it has to end, our little fantasy.'

He looked at her with desperation in his eyes.

'We love each other, Jenny.'

'Yes. And I'm so glad to have had your love, but I have to let it go. Your life is with your children. I can't take their Dad away from them. And you can't leave them, can you?'

'No.'

'I want you to be happy, Steve. And I want you to have the dream that Lynda is going to make possible for you.'

Steve's voice was heavy with bitterness, and defeat. 'If I stay married to her daughter. I feel as if I'm selling myself.'

'You mustn't think like that. You must believe this is right, for you and for the future of your children.

445

You've waited so long for this chance, Steve. I couldn't be happy, even living with you, my love, if I knew I'd deprived you of that chance.'

He stood up, looking round as if for some salvation.

'There has to be a way for us to be together.'

'Perhaps, one day. But for now, we have to say goodbye, and just be grateful for the memories. You've too much to lose, Steve.'

She got to her feet, a little shakily. 'Let's do this now, and quickly. I don't want you to remember me with tears in my eyes.'

She stepped towards him, and they clung to each other, holding on so tightly that Jenny, when she could take no more of this longing, struggled to move Steve's body gently away from hers.

'Go now, Steve, please,' she said, the words catching in her throat.

He moved slowly backwards, away from her. As he reached the door, he said, 'I love you, Jenny, and I always will.'

'And I love you, and always will.'

Jenny couldn't bear the pain of going to the window and watching him leave. She curled herself up on the sofa, and wept until the sky darkened into night.

When the removal van drew up outside the house on Bennett Street Lynda surprised Nathan Tyler by running down the steps of her new home and giving him a hug.

'Lovely to see you, Nathan. And thanks for helping Mark bring my furniture.'

'You're very welcome. And we've brought the Cavalry, too,' he told her, indicating the elegant but muscular young man stepping out of the silver Range

Rover he'd parked behind the van.

'Hi, Lynda, good to see you again,' Peter Tyler called out as he helped his Mother down from the passenger seat.'

The petite, curly haired little lady hurried to greet her friend.

'How are you, Lynda, dearest?' Helen enquired as she gave Lynda a hug and an appraising look.

'I'm fine, and so happy to see you all again. But please excuse me while I hug my adopted son.'

She ran to Mark who was grinning at her as he unfastened the back of the van. 'Thank you for coming, love, and for bringing everything.'

Hugging her, he said, 'Not everything. I've made sure there's plenty for you to come back to. We're going to take her back to Loveday, where she belongs, aren't we Helen?'

'As soon as she's ready,' Helen responded quietly, and then asked cheerily, 'Now, is it O.K. if Lynda and I just go and have a cup of tea and a chat, and leave you guys to do all the heavy work?'

'I guess so,' Nathan agreed, 'But first of all, I hope you've got a beer or two in your fridge for us, Lynda?'

'Of course,' Lynda smiled. 'And one of my meat and potato pies in the oven for later.'

'You spoil him, Lynda. Your Daddy is crazy for Lynda's pies,' she told her son as they all followed Lynda into the house.

They sat down at the kitchen table and looked around as Lynda made the tea and handed out the beers.

'As you can see,' she apologised, 'there's a lot of work to be done here. Steve's going to put in a new kitchen for a start. He's coming round this evening to discuss it, and to meet you, of course.'

'Is he the guy we're about to trust with our money?' Nathan asked.

'Yes, if that's all right,' Lynda answered, looking up at him a little nervously.

Nathan looked doubtful. 'Well, I tell you plainly, Lynda, it wasn't my idea. I came to the North of England with a view to investing in property, not risky small businesses.'

'Stop your complaining, Nathan Tyler. And remember you owe this lady an apology.'

'An apology? What for?' asked Lynda.

'Tell her, Nathan,' Helen instructed her husband, and then turned to Mark. 'You don't mind, do you, honey?'

Mark shook his head, but nevertheless looked a bit uncomfortable. Nathan Tyler, however, shifted from one foot to the other as he made his shame-faced confession.

'Lynda, I have to tell you I had a little bit of a cash-flow problem at the end of last year, temporary, of course. And somebody offered me a good price for my shares in Loveday Manor, too good a price for me to refuse in the circumstances.'

Lynda had not expected this.

'Who did you sell them to?'

'My Mother,' sighed Mark.

'So that means, that Mark and Suzanne could out-vote you, if they wanted to,' Helen revealed, giving her husband a baleful look.

Mark spoke up quickly.

'Yes, but we wouldn't, I'd never vote against your wishes, you know that, Lynda.'

'Thank you, love. But how are things between you and your Mother now?'

'Fine. She's trying hard,' he said, embarrassed, 'and she's enjoying helping out at Loveday.'

448

'I'm glad,' Lynda said, ignoring Helen's raised eyebrows.

It didn't take the three men long to empty the van and, following Lynda's instructions, carry into various rooms the boxes and pieces of furniture. These included Lynda's long dreamed of chaise-longue which Tom had laughingly bought as a surprise, and the 'golden sofa' they had shared on most of their evenings at Loveday.

The largest item was the double bed, on which Helen and Lynda placed familiar fine bed-linen and big soft pillows. Helen put her arm round Lynda, and handed her a packet of tissues.

'Let them flow, those tears you've been holding back, Lynda. You're entitled to have a good cry at moments like this.'

She kept her arm round her as they sat on the edge of the bed.

'I can't bear it, that he won't be here, next to me,' Lynda whispered. 'I keep looking for him, even so far away from Loveday. You understand, don't you, why I can't go back, and not find him there?'

'Yes. But are you sure this can be your home?'

'This run-down old terraced house, you mean?' Lynda said, trying to smile. 'I feel safe here, Helen, and it's more of a home than anywhere else at the moment.'

'Because of your friends who owned it.'

'Yes, there are so many happy memories here, more than sad ones.'

Helen patted Lynda's hand. 'Happy memories are good, but you also have to live in the present, and to have hope for a future. That's what's so good about this business venture, for your son-in-law and your family.'

'Yes.'

'And have Steve and your daughter sorted out their problems?'

'They're working at it. Steve has finished with Jenny.'

'That can't have been easy for him.'

'No, but necessary.'

Helen heard the unfamiliar hard tone in Lynda's voice, but decided to keep her thoughts to herself.

When they went back downstairs they found that Katie had arrived and had already made a pot of coffee for Lynda's friends, who hadn't been shy of introducing themselves.

'Hiya, Katie,' Lynda greeted her. 'Thanks for coming to help, love. I see you've got acquainted already.'

'Yes, once Katie had gotten over the shock of our American accents,' laughed Peter.

Katie, slightly self-conscious, admitted, 'I've never met any Americans before.'

'Katie is the granddaughter of my best friend who used to own this house,' Lynda explained.

'She makes good coffee,' Mark commented, giving Katie a smile which made her blush, and begin to dream.

Helen noticed and nodded appreciatively at the young girl.

'Thank you for looking after our boys. Are you pleased to have Lynda back?'

'Oh, yes. She's my honorary aunty, you know,' Katie said proudly, with a grin at Lynda, 'whether she likes it or not! And I'm hoping once she's got her divorce, she'll marry my Uncle Dan and make it official.'

Instead of the tolerant laughter she'd expected

would be the response, everyone caught their breath.

Mark broke the silence. 'A divorce?'

Katie went bright red. 'Oh, I'm sorry. I shouldn't have said that, but Mum said Lynda and John were getting divorced,' she stammered, knowing she was betraying confidences.

Mark turned to look at Lynda. 'I thought you were divorced.'

Lynda found it hard to speak. 'No. Not yet.'

'But you married my Dad.'

'Yes.'

'Do you mean you lied?'

'Yes, but not to Tom. He knew, but he wanted us to get married anyway.'

'So you weren't my Dad's wife.'

'Yes I was. But not legally. Mark, I can explain.'

'No, you can't,' he said, standing up and glaring at her. 'I thought I could trust you, Lynda, but you've told me lies. You lied about your family welcoming you back home, when you weren't even living with them, and now I find you've lied about being my Dad's wife.'

Lynda ran to stand in front of him as he reached the door.

'No, I was Tom's wife. Listen, Mark, please.'

But he was deafened by his anger, and the turmoil he'd had to endure. 'I've been going through hell trying to persuade my Mother to let you have everything. Telling her she'd no right to take things which belonged to you and Dad.'

'I'm sorry, I didn't mean to deceive you,' she pleaded.

'Of course you did! It's beginning to look to me like it's all been a pretence.' He gulped in air to stop himself sobbing as he forced out the next sentence.

451

'I thought you were so special, Lynda. I thought you loved my Dad, and me. But you've been telling lies. Was that a lie, as well, when you told my Dad you loved him?'

'No!' Lynda cried out.

Mark stared at her for a moment and then ran out of the house as Lynda reeled from the shock of what he'd said.

'Look after, Lynda,' Helen Tyler said urgently to her husband, as she ran after Mark. 'I'll deal with this.'

Mark had already opened the door of the van but Helen caught hold of his arm. 'Mark, where are you going?'

'Back to Loveday, to tell my Mother she was right. Lynda Collins is a liar, and we do have to contest my Father's will. I don't want her to have anything to do with Loveday Manor, she has no right!'

'She has every right, and you know that! And you know that she loved your Daddy with all her heart and soul.'

Helen made him look at her as she said, in a calm and gentle voice, 'Your Mother is full of jealousy and regrets, but that's no reason for you to allow her to hurt Lynda. Tom Meredith wanted Lynda to own Loveday Manor with you. He knew that Lynda loves you, and you know it, too.'

Mark pulled away from her, got into the van and drove away. But he had heard what Helen Tyler had said.

There was still silence in the kitchen when Helen walked back in.

'Has he gone?' Lynda asked, almost in a whisper.

'Yes. But don't worry, you haven't lost him, Lynda. He's just a young man who's had a lot to deal with in his life.'

452

'I'm so, so sorry,' Katie said.

Lynda shook her head. 'It wasn't your fault, love, you didn't know. But, for now, please don't tell anyone about this, about any of it.'

'I won't, I promise. I'd better go now, and leave you to talk.'

She picked up her bag.

Peter Tyler saw how upset she was. 'I'll drive you home, if you like,' he offered.

She looked at him with gratitude. 'No. But thank you. I said I'd meet Mum after work, and go home with her.'

When she'd left, Helen said quietly, 'Poor girl. But it's a good thing she left before Steve arrived, that might have been too much for her to cope with.'

'And me!' Nathan Tyler declared. 'What the hell is going on here?'

Helen stroked his head soothingly. 'It's way too complicated for you, honey,' she teased. 'All you have to do is stay a while longer, meet Steve Sheldon, and share Lynda's pie with him. We'll talk a little business, and then you'll shake Steve's hand, give Lynda a kiss and Peter will take us back to the hotel.'

'Oh, is that all?' her husband said with heavy sarcasm which Helen ignored.

'Yes, it's quite simple.'

'Don't worry, Dad,' Peter consoled him, 'Tonight you and I will go and find one of those English pubs you're so fond of, and reward ourselves for putting up with women.'

CHAPTER FIFTY-TWO

When Steve Sheldon arrived he made a good impression on the Tylers, but he was relieved when they shook hands with him and left.

'They liked you,' Lynda reassured him.

'It's great that they're willing to invest in the company.'

'Yes, I'd find it much harder without them. It's Helen we have to thank for that, she's persuaded Nathan to invest, as well as putting some of her own money in. She must have known that there was still a threat to my Loveday inheritance.'

'I'm really grateful, Lynda.'

'I know you are.'

Lynda saw how anxious he was, how much it all meant to him, and she didn't feel comfortable with what she was about to do, but the happiness of her daughter and grandchildren came before everything. Lynda pushed aside her love for Steve as she made sure he understood what was at stake.

'So you've seen Jenny, and ended it?'

'Yeah. But I didn't want to. And I'm not sure whether me and Carolyn can make a go of it.'

Lynda had always admired Steve's honesty, and she hated to see the misery in his eyes. She steeled herself to resist showing compassion.

'You have to. Like I've said before, Steve, this is a family business I'm investing in.'

He concentrated on packing his papers back into his shabby briefcase, so that he could avoid looking at her, but she knew him well enough to see by the way his head was bowed that he understood, and was brought down by what she'd said.

The compassion broke through, and she wanted to put her arms round him, and tell him she didn't mean to threaten him, but she had to hold back. Instead she tried to make some kind of compensation for her harshness.

'I'm glad you're going to find the time to do my kitchen for me. We've had some good times in this room.'

'Yes. I helped Bernie with the last kitchen he put in here. We didn't have much money to spend on it, but it was better than this cheap rubbish the new owners put in.'

'Bernie would be proud of the stuff you do now, and delighted you're kicking Randerson out.'

'Yeah. Is everything sorted out for Friday?'

All the papers are signed, ready for you to show him when he doesn't believe you. Angela and I will be arriving at eleven, so you need to have all the men out in the yard by then.'

'Angela's coming?'

'Oh, yes, we both want to be there to take our revenge. So it's going to be quite a day on Friday, for everybody.'

'Yeah.' He took a breath to steady himself, and said quietly, 'I won't let you down, Lynda.'

'I know.' The look she gave him was full of love, and pity, and then she smiled as she said, 'You and me together, kid, just like the old days.'

Their eyes met and they remembered how they had always been allies, and friends.

On Thursday night Tony Randerson came home from another of his 'business and pleasure' trips, and found that he had moved out.

455

Angela had been very busy while he'd been away, she'd packed up every item which belonged to him and moved it all into a flat she had rented; it was near Milfield but as far away as possible from Langton Hall, the family home which her father had bought and which she had, foolishly, shared for too many years with Tony Randerson.

She'd had the locks changed, so he'd had to stand in the driveway and phone her to find out what was going on. She'd stood upstairs in her bedroom and looked down at him, taking some satisfaction from his shock and outrage, and helplessness.

He'd had to hold out his hands and catch the large envelope containing his new address and set of keys, the divorce papers, and the letter which told him she knew everything, including the most terrible lie he had told her all those years ago.

A chance encounter with Roger Fawcett, the now retired GP who had been their family doctor, had caused her to make the decision she'd hesitated over for far too long.

At the fund-raising party they'd both attended, Dr Fawcett had enjoyed enough glasses of whisky to overcome discretion. He liked Angela, and had casually commented that it was a shame her husband had not been able to give her any children. He had no idea, of course, that Tony had lied to her, had told her the results of tests had shown he was fine, and that she was the one at fault.

What she was doing now could never compensate her for all the unhappiness of her marriage to an adulterous husband, and all the heartache she'd suffered all those years, watching other women of her age enjoying the delights of motherhood.

She set off for Milfield early the next morning to meet Lynda Collins, who had been another of Tony's victims, and with whom she had quickly formed a friendship as well as a business partnership. They both wanted to be there to see the man they hated realise that he had lost not just his home, but everything.

Josie Williams smiled to herself as she calmly observed her soon-to-be former employer kicking the drawers of the filing cabinet and slamming the phone down on the unfortunate salesmen who'd called him that morning. Sipping a cup of coffee she looked out of the window and watched the men walk out of the workshop and into the yard, tilting their faces to feel the sunshine. Tony Randerson looked up as he heard the murmur of their voices growing louder, and a shout of laughter caused him to get up and look out of the window.

'What the hell is going on down there?'

He flung open the door and went quickly down the stairs. Josie followed him, and stood at the top of the steps which led on to the yard, waiting for what her friend Gary had told her was about to happen.

'Get back to work, you lot!' Randerson shouted and was perplexed to see them all look at each other and grin as they moved aside to let Steve Sheldon step forward with some papers in his hand.

'What are you up to, Sheldon?' snarled Randerson. 'Wanting the sack again?'

Steve didn't reply, but looked toward the entrance to the yard. The men fell silent, wondering what he was waiting for. Then came the sound of two pairs of high-heeled shoes striking against the old stone flags of the cotton mill, just as the iron-tipped clogs of countless working women had, many years ago.

Randerson stared in astonishment, then apprehension as he saw that the two women walking across the yard were his wife and Lynda Collins.

'Good morning Angela, Lynda,' Steve greeted them solemnly, and then turned to Randerson.

'We have some bad news for you, Randerson. We've taken over the company, and we'd like you to leave the premises immediately.'

'Don't talk rubbish, Sheldon,' was Randerson's response. 'You haven't the money or the know-how to take over anything.' He turned to the men. 'You'll all be out of a job if you stick with him. Nobody will give him work once I've put the word around.'

'I think you'll find you're wrong there,' Steve stated happily, 'We've already got the Horton contract.'

'You bastard!' Randerson yelled at him.

Angela's voice cut across the yard.

'Language, Tony, there are ladies present. And as Steve said, we'd like you to leave, now. No need to go back up to the office, there'll be nothing there that you have a right to. I am prepared to be generous and let you keep the car, if you go now.'

'Angela, please,' her husband pleaded. 'We can talk about this.'

'No point. There is nothing you can say to me, or to my friend Lynda. This is more than a business deal, it's a personal matter, isn't it, Lynda?'

She turned to Lynda who nodded, and then gave Tony Randerson a look which he would remember till the day he died.

'Hey, Randerson! Do you know what day it is?' Gary Pearson called out as his former boss, head down and fists clenched, marched over to his car. 'Friday the thirteenth, your unlucky day!'

Mark Meredith had always found that going for a walk helped him to think through problems, or calm emotions he found it hard to deal with, so on the

Thursday morning he set off early in the morning to go for a walk by the river.

Amy was already at work, setting out a new display of wedding merchandise in the shop at the far end of the courtyard. She saw him passing and called out.

'Hi, Mark! How was your trip to Milfield?'

'All right,' he replied in a tone so devoid of enthusiasm that she immediately knew something was wrong, and hurried across to him.

'How's Lynda?'

'Married!' he declared angrily, and was annoyed with himself because he hadn't intended to tell anyone that, at least until he'd had chance to think about it some more. He turned to walk away but Amy grabbed hold of his arm.

'What do you mean, married?'

Mark looked round, and even though none of the guests were around, he knew he and Amy couldn't have this conversation here. He allowed her to lead him into the café at the far end of the shop.

'We'll have a coffee and you can tell me what's upset you. You can tell Patrick as well, he's working in the barn, setting out some stuff for the wedding on Saturday. I'll go and get him while you make the coffee.'

Patrick and his wife listened carefully while Mark told them what had happened in Milfield. The way he talked reminded Patrick of when Mark had been a young boy trying to cope when his Mother and Grandmother had let him down. The rage and embarrassment were there again.

'She lied,' Mark said angrily 'So my Mother is right to be contesting my Dad's will. I'll have to support her in that now.'

'Whoa, just a minute,' Patrick exclaimed. 'You're forgetting something here. Lynda loved your Dad, and she worked her socks off for him. You wouldn't have Loveday if she hadn't come here and helped Tom rescue the place, and stopped your Mother and Nicki from selling it.'

Mark looked away, not wanting to remember those bad times, but Patrick hadn't finished.

'Your Dad wanted Lynda to have Loveday – you know that. He told you he wanted you and Lynda to run it together. Don't you dare go against his wishes.'

Amy placed her hand on her husband's arm as a signal to him to ease off a little, but Patrick was determined to set matters straight.

'Tom wanted Lynda to marry him years ago, and in the end she couldn't refuse him, she loved him too much. They were man and wife, and I'll beat the hell out of you if you try to tell me different. He was a good man and my best friend, your Dad, and Lynda's a very special lady, and she loves you.'

'He's right, Mark,' Amy joined in. 'You have to make your Mother see sense and stop paying solicitors to look for trouble. Please don't tell her what you've found out, she'd use it to try and destroy everything for the sake of revenge against Lynda. Now go for that walk, and think about all this.'

Mark took their advice, and walked for an hour through the woods and along the river as he had so often with his Dad.

He walked slowly back to the hotel through the rose garden which Lynda had planted in memory of the friend who had left her an inheritance. Lynda had, he knew, invested that money in Loveday Manor and the wedding business she and Amy had set up together.

He sat down for a few minutes to breathe in the scent of the roses. He remembered how many times his Mother had left him, and how, one day, he'd sat on this bench and surprised and delighted Lynda by telling her he loved her.

CHAPTER FIFTY-THREE

Dan was glad to be at work, enjoying the colours of the market stalls in July, and breathing in the scents of the flowers and fragrant summer fruits. For the past month there had been a cold, tense atmosphere in the house he no longer felt was his home.

He was delighted when Lynda walked into the kitchen at the café.

'Looks like you've been busy this lunchtime,' she remarked, noting the amount of dirty crockery piled up on the work-surfaces. 'Shall I give you a hand with the washing up?'

'No, I'll do it later. Let's go and sit outside in the sunshine and have a coffee.'

'All right, but I'll just clear a bit of this while you're making some fresh coffee, I'll enjoy it, just like old times.'

'I thought you'd be busy helping at 'Sheldon Interior Design', I hear Steve's doing well.'

'Yes, other contracts are coming in on the back of the Horton one, and he's going to have to take on more men. It's all a bit hectic, but he'll cope, and he's loving it.'

'And how are things with him and Carolyn? It's been over a month now, hasn't it?'

Lynda sighed. She wouldn't pretend to Dan.

'I'd like to say 'wonderful' but I'd be lying. But they'll make it work, they have to. How's Jenny?'

'Avoiding Steve, like you asked her to. But Katie says she and Alex still hear her crying at night when she thinks they're asleep.'

'I am sorry, Dan, really I am. But there was no choice.'

'I know.'

'And while we're talking about problems, how are things between you and your Mother?'

'She still won't talk to me about the past, and about my real father, so it's an even more strained relationship than before. And sometimes she seems almost as upset as I am.'

He put the coffees on a tray and led her outside.

'Come on, let's go and enjoy a quiet cuppa while we can. There'll be no chance once the schools break-up for the summer holiday.'

'Is the café still popular with the kids?' Lynda asked as she followed him.

'Yes, they love coming here for their ice-creams and a bit of 'café culture'. You started that, remember, putting tables outside and serving ice cream sundaes.'

She smiled happily as they sat together in the sunshine. 'I always loved running this café.'

'And you were good at it. There's a job for you here any time you like,' he chuckled.

Their enjoyment of each other's company was interrupted by the arrival of Harry Benson, the owner of the Carlton Ballroom. Harry was in his seventies now, and since the death of his wife the previous year had found it hard to waltz through life like he used to.

He still had the straight-backed elegance of a professional dancer, but these days there was an air of melancholy which kept pushing its way past the persona of the flamboyant local impresario he had always liked to present to his public.

Dan had known Harry for many years, and appreciated his 'joie de vivre' attitude to life, but Dan had also learned to be a little wary of him and his schemes.

463

Harry paused to greet several people as he glided between the tables and chairs of the café much as he progressed through life, weaving and side-stepping with a jaunty but elegant style. He bowed and kissed Lynda's hand, and sat down to chat to her while Dan went to get the coffee and the 'Danish tart' Harry had requested.

'You are coming to the dance a week on Saturday, aren't you, darling? It's the last one there'll ever be at The Carlton.'

'Wouldn't miss it for the world, Harry. It's very sad that you're having to close.'

'Yes, the end of an era. But it's been a marvellous life, and it will be a wonderful night, as long as Dan will do me this favour I've come to ask him.'

'What favour is that?'

'The guy I had lined up as my vocalist has let me down. I've phoned everyone I can think of but they're either booked up or on holiday, so I'm hoping Dan will come to the rescue. I've heard him sing at parties, and in The Red Lion a few times, and he'd be ideal. But whether I can get him up on that stage is a different matter.'

When Dan came back and heard what Harry wanted him to do, he refused to even think about it, but Harry turned to Lynda for support.

'He can't say 'no' and let us all down, can he, Lynda?'

'I can,' Dan contradicted him swiftly, 'Get somebody else, Harry.'

'There is nobody else, you're my last hope.'

'I'm very flattered,' Dan said sardonically.

Harry's next ploy was to ooze admiration.

'Dan, they'd love you. You always had the potential to be a singer, you know you did. Take this opportunity to show what you can do. You'll never

464

get another chance like this, not at your age.'

'Thanks very much! I'm not that old!'

Harry didn't even blink.

'You can't say no,' he insisted. 'This will be the last big Saturday night dance at the Carlton. I'm just wanting to give everyone a night of wonderful memories. We're doing every kind of music from the history of the Carlton. I need you. Me and my band and the people of Milfield need you, Dan.'

Lynda saw Dan was hesitating in a confusion of panic and longing. 'I'm not up to it. You've only heard me sing in The Red Lion, with my mates, Harry. I'd be no good on a stage.'

Lynda remembered him talking about how he would have loved to have been a singer. He needed to do this.

'Tell you what, Danny boy, if you will, I will,' she offered.

Harry clapped his hands in delight.

'Of course! You used to sing in your Mum and Dad's pub, didn't you, Lynda? Come on, Dan, you can't refuse to sing with such a beautiful partner.'

Dan had already begun to imagine what it would be like to be up on that stage, it was an old dream, but a powerful one. And he would have Lynda by his side. He smiled at her, wishing he could kiss her.

'All right,' he said, with a sudden calm resolve, 'I must be crazy, but I'll do it.'

His Mother seemed pleased that evening when he told her about singing at the Carlton, and they had a discussion about which songs he should sing.

'Always' is a very good waltz,' she said. You and Geoffrey sang it for me at my fiftieth birthday party, do you remember? And it was your Nana's favourite song.'

'Yes. Would you like me to sing it at the Carlton?'

'I would like that, yes.'

Dan and his Mother looked at each other, again both aware of their need for reconciliation. His heart quickened with hope and hesitantly he asked, 'Would you like to come to the dance to hear me sing?'

'No. I'm afraid that won't be possible,' she replied, offering no explanation.

He turned away, disappointed by what he saw as yet another rejection, and as a small revenge he told her something he knew would displease her.

'That's a shame. You'll miss me and Lynda singing together.'

'Lynda Collins? Oh, is that why you've agreed to do this, because it's an excuse to spend time with that woman?'

'Yes.'

Ellen was determined to make Dan see sense about Lynda and declared, 'There are things you should know about her.'

Dan looked his Mother coldly. 'Are there?'

'The woman is a criminal,' Ellen told him with smug satisfaction. 'She has committed bigamy.'

'I know,' Dan answered, enjoying showing her that he was unperturbed by her revelation.

'Oh, do you? And what are you going to do about it?'

He saw that, in spite of her challenging tone, his Mother was ruffled, and that sign of weakness gave him the courage to repeat his intention, so that she would have no doubt.

'Marry her.'

Ellen's face darkened with anger. 'Don't be a fool.'

Dan, for once, could match her anger.

'Why not? Geoff Heywood was!'

Ellen, stirred by guilt, and the memory of her

466

husband and his kindness, defended him. 'He was not. He was a good man.'

Dan was sure of his ground.

'And Lynda's a good woman. She's made mistakes, like we all have, but she's generous and loving, like my Dad, like Geoff was. And I'll marry her if she'll have me. You can't stop me this time,' he finished defiantly.

Ellen Heywood was not used to being disobeyed, and hearing him speak to her like that raised all the fear and ill-temper which her age and her illness had been nurturing within her.

'No, I cannot stop you. But,' she threatened, 'I can change my will.'

With that she turned and swept out of the room, holding on to the dignity that seemed, she felt, to be all that was left to her at this decline of her life. And decline it certainly was.

She had not been willing to reveal the true state of her health, and so Dan never knew that his Mother wanted very much to go to the Carlton to hear her son singing.

The following day she was still upset when Jenny came to see her. She always dreaded visiting Ellen but she'd promised Dan she'd call in and make sure she was all right.

When she went to Kirkwood House in her lunch hour, she found Ellen in a prickly mood.

'You need not have come,' she insisted. 'I am perfectly well and able to cope on my own. Indeed, it is a situation I shall, it seems, soon have to get used to.'

In response to Jenny's puzzled look she explained, 'Daniel intends to marry Lynda Stanworth. And I have told him that if he does, he will have to move

467

out. I will not have that woman in my house.'

Jenny could see that Ellen was regretting having had yet another row with her son.

'Don't upset yourself, Ellen. I know that Dan loves Lynda, but I also know she may not ever want to marry again.'

'Unlike you,' was Ellen's retort.

'I won't be marrying again either.'

'Because Steven Sheldon is remaining with Carolyn?'

'Yes.'

'And you no longer see him?'

'No. I haven't seen him since he made his decision to stay with his family.'

'Oh. I can see that is hard for you,' Ellen said, surprising Jenny with her sympathy, 'but it is the honourable thing to do. And you may find someone else one day, someone who is free to be with you.'

Jenny was taken aback that Ellen seemed to have changed her mind about her re-marrying, and was completely unprepared for her next statement.

'You deserve to be happy, Jennifer. And I know that my son did not make you happy. You made a mistake, marrying Richard, didn't you?'

Jenny saw that Ellen was ready for her to be honest.

'Yes,' she said softly.

It took Ellen a moment to regain control of her emotions, but she knew that this might be the last chance to talk to Jenny, to make her peace with her, and so she continued.

'I made a mistake too, when I was young. I didn't want to accept the consequences but, my Mother begged me to.' She faltered at the recollection of that painful time.

'To have the baby,' Jenny said gently. 'Daniel.'

Ellen was still a little perturbed that Jenny had been told her secret, but found that now she was glad. She had longed to be able to confide in someone, to explain what had made her the way she was.

'That mistake I made is, I think, the reason I've always felt compelled to prevent others from making mistakes that might ruin their lives.'

She turned to gaze at Richard's silver framed photograph. Clasping her hands in her lap she composed herself.

'I know that Richard was not the best of husbands, and to be truthful, he was not the best of sons. He found it hard to love people.'

Jenny, seeing how painful it was for Ellen to admit any of this, took pity on this lonely, bereaved old lady, and sought to reassure her.

'He loved you,' she said simply.

'Did he?' Ellen Heywood looked at the daughter-in-law to whom she had never shown kindness or appreciation, and renewed her resolve to carry out the task she had set herself.

'Jenny, I think the time has come for us to set the record straight. I did know that he, that he ill-treated you.'

'You knew?' Jenny gasped.

Ellen caught her breath as she pleaded, 'I must ask your forgiveness.'

'It wasn't your fault,' Jenny said, feeling sorry for this proud woman.

'I feel it was. Somehow I failed Richard, but I gave him everything I could.'

She stared at the photographs again, and her eyes lighted on one of the few of her Mother with Daniel as a chubby, dimpled child, struggling to push a large wheelbarrow.

She remembered how it had been her Mother, not

her, who had picked him up and comforted him when the task had proved beyond his strength. It had always been his Nana who had held him and cuddled him. Ellen bowed her head.

'And I gave Daniel so little,' she whispered.

Jenny knew what was needed here.

'Talk to him, Ellen.'

Ellen remembered her confrontations with her son, and felt both ashamed and afraid.

'That doesn't seem possible,' she said wearily.

Jenny knew how vital a reconciliation was to both mother and son, and so she persevered.

'A few kind words, Ellen, that's all he needs, all it takes, a few kind words.'

Ellen was finding it too difficult to cope with all the emotions that were assailing her, and decided that she needed to be alone, to calm those memories, and to consider how best she could reach out to her son. She looked at the clock.

'Philip Lawson will be expecting you back at the office.'

'Yes,' Jenny agreed, seeing that Ellen needed to rest. She put on her coat. 'But will you be all right?'

'Of course,' Ellen replied. Her tone was sharper than she intended, but Jenny heard the frailty beneath the words. She looked at Ellen Heywood, and found she no longer feared this woman who had so dominated her life. With pity in her heart she leaned over and kissed her.

The gesture surprised and touched Ellen, and she momentarily placed her hand on Jenny's cheek. Then she felt tears again threatening to betray her, but would not give in to them. She straightened her back and looked away.

Jenny, perceiving that she could not reach her any further now, walked to the door.

470

As she opened it, she heard Ellen's voice, a little tremulous, calling out to her.

'As I said, Jennifer. You deserve to be happy.'

Jenny turned and wanted to go back to offer comfort, but Ellen lifted her hand in a brief, and final, farewell.

CHAPTER FIFTY-FOUR

The Teddy Boy suit Lynda had hired as a surprise for John was a spectacular, deep purple success. When she went to the flat on the Friday night before the dance to deliver it, John put it on straight away.

'What do you think?' he asked, a 'Jack-the-Lad' grin on his face as he stood with his hands in the pockets of the drainpipe trousers, and pushing back the long, velvet collared Edwardian style jacket.

She beamed at him, 'Very smart.'

'I'll put a record on, got to have a dance in this.'

As the music started he began to move to the rhythm of 'Jailhouse rock'. Seeing him dressed up and full of energy and confidence like that moved Lynda almost to tears. It created a flashback in her mind of John, taller and more handsome than all the other young men, moving in the spotlight that used to ride over the crowded dance floor at the Carlton on the Saturday nights of their youth.

She, too, felt some of the energy of those days revive within her as she took hold of John's outstretched hand and danced with him. She suddenly felt confident that everything would be all right, it would all work out for her in Milfield.

'Oh, I'm really looking forward to this dance tomorrow night,' she sighed happily.

'Yes. I feel really good in this outfit. 'When I was a young teenager I used to envy the older lads wearing this sort of gear.'

'I remember you saying that, so I thought now's your chance.'

'Yeah, and you've got to take your chances, haven't you?'

'I've always thought so,' Lynda said confidently.

John stopped dancing.

'I always remember you telling me off, saying that if I carried on the way I was doing life would have passed me by before I realised I was supposed to join in.'

'Did I say that? I'm sorry.'

'No, you were right. That was partly what went wrong between you and me, wasn't it, me not wanting to do things, and not being willing to take risks?'

'And me taking too many!' Lynda laughed.

His expression was serious as he said, 'But you want me to play safe now, and marry Jean.'

'I think it'd be a good idea. If it's what you want?'

'Yes, it is. So you won't mind if I ask her?'

'I'd be really happy for you both. And Jean's waited long enough.'

'Yes. Our Carolyn will be pleased as well.'

Lynda stopped smiling.

'Do you think they're all right, her and Steve?'

John sighed, 'He's kept his word, you know, he hasn't seen Jenny.'

Lynda was worried. 'He'll see her tomorrow if he goes to the dance.'

'Perhaps Steve shouldn't go,' John suggested.

Lynda shook her head. 'They can't avoid each other for ever. And he's got to go to the dance, the kids are really excited about it. Gemma's been wearing her outfit already.'

'And they're looking forward to seeing their Grandma up on that stage singing.'

'Yeah. I'm not sure Carolyn is, though. I think she's frightened I might make a fool of myself. And so am I!'

473

'Dan will be too scared to do it without you.'

'I know.'

'You'll be fine, just imagine you're in the piano room in The Black Bull again.'

'Yeah.'

John hesitated but decided she had to know.

'Sit down a minute, Lynda.'

'What's bothering you now?' she asked.

'Steve's told me he's not sure he can make it work, him and Carolyn.'

'He has to.'

'Yes, I suppose so,' John said, sounding doubtful. 'He's a good lad. I don't like to see him so miserable.'

Lynda took John's hand to reassure him. 'Our Carolyn loves Steve, and she needs him. She won't let him down again.'

John looked at Lynda, and when he spoke she heard the despair he felt about his child.

'Steve's found out she's lied to him again. She did sleep with that Ferris guy.'

'Oh, no! I told her not to tell him.'

'She didn't. It was his workmate, Gary Pearson. He kept it quiet because of the children, but the other day he decided he had to tell him. He couldn't stand seeing how unhappy Steve is without Jenny.'

'How does Gary know? Is he just guessing?'

'No. Apparently Ferris told him after Steve had hit him that day. So there's no denying it now.'

Lynda felt all the hope and energy disappear.

'Oh, hell.'

Everyone would remember the last Saturday night dance at the Carlton Ballroom, but not just because of the music and the memories of younger and more carefree days.

Harry Benson was delighted that he'd managed to

sell all the tickets, and that he wasn't having to dip any further into his savings to make it all happen.

Dan had been persuaded to do the catering, and he in turn had recruited Jenny and his nieces to support the event in every way they could. Lynda had agreed to help them decorate the ballroom, and on Saturday morning she took Gemma and Michael along with her, as both their parents were working.

Steve was finding out what it was like to be in charge of a company, and have responsibility for his employees' ability to repay their mortgages, but he was happy to give that commitment.

Carolyn was upset at having, again, to go into the office on a Saturday. Critchley was making it hard for her, and Carolyn guessed it was a kind of petty revenge for causing a scandal in the office. However, she was also aware that Critchley needed her.

A great deal of work had been left unfinished by Paul Ferris, who had taken up his post in Leeds as soon as possible. Carolyn was the only person qualified to complete his work, and she couldn't refuse; it was essential that she should keep her job, at least until Steve had the business properly under control.

When Lynda arrived at the ballroom with her grandchildren, she found Katie and Jenny had already set out small tables round the sides of the room, and larger ones in the raised area where the bar was. They were taking a break from the heavy work and sitting in the centre of the dance floor untangling a great pile of ancient garlands and streamers.

She was a little taken aback when Michael and Gemma ran straight across to say hello to Jenny and Katie and begin to help them. Jenny looked up and smiled at Lynda a little warily.

475

'Some of these garlands belong in a museum,' she said jokingly. 'I remember Mum and Dad having ones like these when I was a kid.'

She held up a garland of red and white paper concertinas.

'Yes, I remember those too,' Lynda said, smiling at the memory.

Jenny got to her feet and, pointing to the pile of decorations, asked the children, 'Could you two take over untangling these, so Katie and I can get on with sorting out the tables for the supper?'

'O.K.' Gemma and Michael agreed happily.

'I'll give you a hand, Jenny,' Lynda offered, 'and show you where the table covers are, if Harry still keeps them in the same place. And shall we have some music on?' she suggested, wanting to dispel the feeling of tension still there between them.

'Great idea,' Katie said, 'you show me where the CDs are and I'll sort it out.'

'You might have a bit of old technology to deal with,' Lynda said with a grin, 'I suspect a lot of Harry's music will be on ancient tapes.'

They found a CD player and stereo tape deck hidden round a corner of the stage, and Lynda got some CDs and tapes out of the cupboard which, she remembered, would open for anyone who knew exactly where to give it a kick. Soon they had sixties music blasting out from the speakers.

Katie set herself the task of blowing up balloons, while Lynda and Jenny covered the large tables with paper tablecloths on top of the old velvet covers, ready for the food which Dan was bringing later. Then they found cloths for the small tables, and as they worked together Lynda paused to look round with a pleasurable, but also wistful nostalgia, at the ballroom which held so many memories.

476

It had hardly changed from when she'd danced there as a teenager. The small stage was still draped with the midnight blue velvet curtains on which Harry's wife had sewn silver stars; the curtains were faded now and the red plush seats along the walls were a little frayed and shabby, but it was still all you needed a ballroom to be.

Jenny held a rickety step-ladder steady while Katie balanced on it to attach garlands, twisted ribbons of silver foil and bunches of balloons to the beams and curtain rails. When they'd finished Lynda found the switch and turned on the old mirror ball which still hung from the centre of the ceiling, and they all danced together. Lynda delighted her granddaughter by teaching her to jive, and promising she would be her partner to show off their steps at the dance.

Lynda watched Jenny with the children and noticed how relaxed and happy they were with her. Then she mentally gave herself a shake, reminding herself that Jenny was a threat to her daughter's happiness.

Jenny watched Gemma and Michael go off with Katie to bring in the candle wax encrusted wine bottles she and Alex had made as sixties-style table centres, and turned to smile at Lynda.

'They're great kids,' she said.

'Yes. And they'll be here tonight with their Mum and their Dad. How are you going to cope with that?'

'I have to come, Lynda, to support Dan.'

'I know.'

Jenny hesitated, but her happiness was at stake.

'And I want to see Steve. I've kept my promise and not seen him Lynda. But I do still love him, and I want to be with him.'

'You can't.' Lynda hated to use this argument, but she had to.

'What would your Mum say, Jenny about you trying to steal another woman's husband?'

There was a quiet defiance in Jenny's eyes.

'She'd say that sometimes you can't stop your heart choosing. She used to say her heart chose my Dad, and the Lord knew that she didn't want it to. But it did. And that was that. And they loved each other, for ever. And that's me and Steve. We'll love each other for ever. We have to be together, Lynda.'

'No. Think of the cost to those children.'

'I have thought, and I know it will be horrible for them at first, it already is. But we can make it all right for them, and I love them already, just as you love Tom's son.'

Lynda looked away then, she didn't want to think about Mark and the last time they'd seen each other.

Jenny was pleading now.

'I'm not a bad person, Lynda.'

So sorry that she had to take away the chance of happiness that this kind and loving woman deserved, Lynda put a gentle hand on Jenny's shoulder.

'No. I know you're not. But you can't have him, Jenny.'

Jenny knew the arguments Lynda was going to present, she'd worked her way through them herself so many times in the past weeks, but she had an answer which, in her heart and mind, overcame any argument, any reason. And she knew that Lynda would understand.

'It's special, what me and Steve have, Lynda. Like you and Tom Meredith. You told me there was a kind of magic between you. Well, that's how it is between me and Steve, a special magic, a love neither of us have known before.'

Lynda's heart softened but, for her daughter's sake, she would deny Jenny.

'You can make do without magic,' she insisted strongly.

Jenny looked at her sorrowfully. 'Yes, you can live without it. But can you be happy?'

Tears ran down Lynda's cheeks as she drove back to Jean's. She was crying for Jenny, and the love she had to lose, and also for herself, and the lover she had lost.

When she arrived back at Bridge Street she found Jean in her bedroom, standing in front of the mirror and holding the frothy dress of pale pink taffeta in front of her.

Jean turned and gave her a beaming smile.

'Thank you so much for this, Lynda.'

'My pleasure, love. You always said you'd give anything to wear a dress like the girls on 'Come Dancing' and here's your chance!'

'You always were good at giving me presents that were just what I wanted,' Jean said, remembering how Lynda had always taken care to remember small details of people's dreams and desires. She put aside the dress and threw her arms round Lynda's neck, overwhelmed by the memories of other moments of kindness.

'I'm so sorry, Lynda,' she whispered, 'for all the times I haven't been a good friend.'

Lynda held Jean tightly, and there were tears in her eyes, too.

'We're friends again now, that's what matters,' she said and picked up the dress. 'You'll look fabulous in this. We'll have something to eat and then get ready. We'll have a bubble bath, and do our hair and put our make-up on, it will be just like old times.'

'Oh, yes!' Jean cried. 'I'm so looking forward to this dance, and to meeting your American friends.'

'Yes, it's great that Helen and Peter are coming. I wish that Mark was, too,' she sighed, 'but you can't have everything.'

'It'll all work out, Lynda, don't worry,' Jean said gently. 'And it'll be fantastic to see you and Carolyn together in your Abba outfits.'

'Yes, me and my daughter, and my grandchildren dancing together, that's what I'm looking forward to.'

Jean gave a wicked smile. 'And the look on Sylvia's face when she sees what a smart lady her sister-in-law has turned out to be.'

'Yeah.' Lynda gave a little laugh. 'But to be fair, I think she was only against me because her Mother was. And being married to Graham has changed Sylvia. Made her into a better person, like Tom did with me.'

Jean saw that look of loneliness and sadness in Lynda's eyes again, and gave her a hug.

'We'll have a great time going to this dance together, and you'll be with all your family, and lots of friends. It'll be like a celebration of you coming home.'

She was surprised to see Lynda looking doubtful.

'What's the matter?'

'Nothing. Just that word, 'home'. It can make you feel lost sometimes.'

Jean was struggling now. 'I don't understand.'

'It's just that, I've had to do a lot of thinking lately, about me and my life, and where I belong.'

She stared out of the window. 'Perhaps I just need to go for a walk to sort myself out, look at a view over the countryside and get that space inside me. You feel you've had some freedom then, a chance to find yourself again.'

Jean could only look at her friend, and feel bemused.

'I've always done that, you know,' Lynda continued, 'even when we lived in the Black Bull I'd take myself off, and go for a long walk in the fields at the end of Park Lane.'

'Park Lane? That was a helluva walk from the Black Bull!' Jean exclaimed.

'Yeah.' Lynda stood very still as she threaded her memory through all the layers of her past. 'I remember it always seemed a long way back, but lovely when you get home and have a cup of tea by the fire.'

She paused and gave Jean a rueful, sideways smile.

'But it's no good unless you have someone to come home to.'

CHAPTER FIFTY-FIVE

Ever since Jenny's visit, the phrase 'a few kind words' had been echoing in Ellen Heywood's head. She had tried on several occasions to talk to her son, but time was against them. The combined extra demands of catering for the dance and rehearsing with the band had put a lot of pressure on Dan. He'd had much less time to spend at home with his Mother, and Ellen, knowing how important the dance was to him, had worked hard at pretending that she was quite well now.

She would not let him know that her heart had been repeating its warnings to her much more frequently in the past few days. She didn't want Dan to be concerned about her, he'd spent enough of his life worrying about her and her needs. She had tried to tell him that, but he had been preoccupied and, in any case, was very wary of what she might say to him. And so he had not properly heard his Mother's tentative efforts to reach him.

Even though it was a summer's evening she had asked him to light the fire, she found its cheerful warmth a comfort. Sitting watching the flames wrap themselves round the logs that Saturday evening, Ellen could hear Dan singing as he dressed himself in his velvet jacket and bow tie. Ellen began to sing softly as the lyrics drifted down into her drawing room, 'I will understand, Always, Always'.

Then too much emotion caught at her throat, and caused a tight dryness which made the notes trickle away into silence. Geoff Heywood had always made an effort to understand, had always loved her. She knew she had taken his love and understanding, and never told him that she cared for him.

The man who had married her knowing that his was the only love in their marriage, had gradually nurtured a kind of love in Ellen's heart. It was, like the love she felt for Daniel, sustained by gratitude, but it was a kind of love, nevertheless.

She had left it too late to let Geoff Heywood know how she felt about him, but she had promised herself and her God that she would not now make the same mistake with her son. She'd resolved to tell him before he went to the Carlton Ballroom this evening.

That was her intention but, as so often in such human endeavours, the words would come out spoiled by the wrong shade of meaning, the inappropriate nuance.

Dan entered the drawing room looking like a bright-eyed, shining faced choir-boy dressed up in a dinner jacket. Ellen wanted to smile and share his excitement, but the effort of trying to subdue the pain burning in her chest deprived her of the strength to lift her spirits.

Dan paused a little self-consciously as he entered the room, hoping for an admiring smile from his Mother when she saw him looking so smart. But all he saw was her frown.

As he placed a tray of delicacies on the table next to her, to try once more to tempt her to eat, he thought again how her skin seemed to be acquiring a kind of translucence as it stretched even more tightly over that autocratic face.

'I'm going now,' he said anxiously as he retrieved the tartan travel rug that she was allowing to slip off her lap. 'I'll give you a ring if I can, to make sure you're all right.'

483

'No,' Ellen commanded, and dragged the rug out of his hands. 'For heaven's sake, stop fussing about me.'

The intention was to prevent his spending his special evening worrying about her, but Dan heard only the irritation in her voice.

He began to protest, 'I'm only trying to. . .' but then stopped himself, he didn't want to argue with her, not tonight, nothing must spoil tonight. 'Call me if you need me. I'll leave my phone switched on.'

She interrupted swiftly, 'Not when you're singing, surely?'

Ellen saw him recoil, and she felt exasperated that she had made this, too, sound like a rebuke. She tried to make amends.

'Just have a wonderful evening,' she said and even managed to summon up the energy to attempt a little humour. 'No bum notes, is that the expression?'

It touched her heart, and also shamed her, to see how just a hint of benevolence could make her son's face light up with pleasure.

'Yes,' he laughed, and then said wistfully, 'I do wish . . . .'

Ellen's habits were her enemy now. The sharp, automatic retort came against her will. 'We all wish,' she said.

She dug her fists into her lap, she would not let him go like this. She raised the pitch of her voice, determined that she would get through to him.

'You, you look very smart.'

Dan, surprised and delighted, stood shifting from one foot to the other, like a small boy eagerly hoping for more sweets. Ellen struggled to say the words she knew he needed to hear, but her feelings for him became intertwined with those for her dead husband, and so she only managed to say, 'Geoffrey would

484

have been so proud of you.'

'Yes.' Dan was pleased but at the same time disappointed, and too afraid to try to induce her to say more. 'I'll say goodnight, then, Mother,' he said, standing stiffly aware of his formal dress and feeling self-conscious.

Then something told him to find the courage to step forward and kiss her on the cheek. Ellen was too taken by surprise to respond to the clumsy embrace, and Dan didn't hear her calling him back as he stumbled quickly from the room.

The Carlton Ballroom had the air of a blowsy courtesan, well-rouged, over-dressed, and with a suspicion of alcohol in her breath as she awaited her entrance into high society.

Dusty red velvet curtains were drawn across the windows, silver spangles corkscrewed their way down from the ceiling and sent out rainbow reflections even though the dance floor was not yet fully lit. Harry had set a tape playing through the stereo system and gentle rhythms from the dance bands of the thirties and forties echoed across the empty dance floor.

Michael, like his Dad, had reluctantly agreed to wear fancy dress for the dance, as long as it only consisted of a pair of jeans and a not too brightly coloured shirt. He held back in embarrassment as he watched Gemma and his Mother and Grandma make quite an entrance in their satin flared Abba outfits.

His Grandad was also feeling self-conscious, but encouraged his grandson. 'Stop looking so worried, Michael, we're all just going to have a bit of fun. Do you like my outfit?'

Michael was having trouble adjusting to his Grandad's new image, but he responded with a grin

485

to the twinkle in John's eyes.

'Yeah, it's not bad. Just don't tell anybody we're related!'

When Dan arrived Lynda saw straightaway that he was upset, and went to talk to him.

'Are things no better between you and your Mother, then?'

'No,' he sighed, 'and I can't see that they ever will be.'

'Never mind, love, you've still got me. Come on, let's show these people how to dance.'

She led him towards the dance floor to the sound of Brenda Lee singing 'Let's Jump the Broomstick', as Harry had decided rock and roll music was required to shake his clients out of their shyness. Quite a few people had already arrived, but they were following the tradition of having a drink, and waiting for everyone else to take the first steps.

Dan held Lynda back. 'Nobody else is dancing.'

'That's just the way I like it, more room for me to show off!'

She laughed, 'Look at Harry, the daft beggar, up there conducting a tape recorder with his baton. Come on, Danny boy, let's go for it!'

Dan looked at this beautiful woman holding out her hand to him, smiled, and swung her into a jive.

'I'd forgotten how good a dancer you were,' Lynda told him as he twirled her under his arm.

'So had I,' he laughed.

Helen Tyler arrived with her son and stood by the door for a minute or two, watching Dan and Lynda dancing together. When the music ended she gave a little wave and Lynda hurried towards her.

Then she stood still as she saw someone following

Helen and Peter.

'Mark!'

He stepped forward and took hold of her hands. 'My Dad wouldn't want you to come to this dance without a partner.'

With tears in her eyes, Lynda flung her arms round him and held him as if she'd never let him go. Then she introduced him and Helen and Peter to her family, and to Jean and Dan.

There was an awkward moment when Mark met the man who was still legally Lynda's husband, but he could see that John was finding it even more difficult than he was. He shook John's hand firmly and talked about safe topics like John's colourful outfit.

'Peter and I decided we weren't brave enough to go for the fancy dress option,' he apologised.

'You would have been, if Lynda had been there to persuade you,' John laughed, 'let me buy you both a drink,' he said, leading them towards the bar.

Helen stayed to talk to Dan. She had taken an instant liking to this gentle, good humoured man, whose eyes followed Lynda's every movement.

'So you're the famous Dan Heywood Lynda talks about so fondly.'

'Oh, she does talk about me, then?' he asked eagerly.

'A lot. You're a very special friend, I think.'

'But just a friend?'

Helen heard the need in his voice, and looked at him thoughtfully. 'Yes. Lynda still belongs to Tom Meredith, and part of her always will.'

'Oh.'

Helen smiled at him, 'Don't give up hope, Dan.'

'I won't, not as far as Lynda's concerned. I never have done.'

He saw Helen was worried about him, and didn't want it to spoil her evening, so he gave a little bow, and said,' But in the meantime, would you like to dance? I've never danced with an American lady.'

Helen laughed, 'Except in your dreams, or so I've heard.'

Dan was surprised at how much Lynda had told Helen about him. 'Oh, you know about me and Rita Hayworth, do you?' he grinned.

'Oh, yes. And Mae West!' she joked as he led her on to the dance floor. Helen's smile faded a little when she saw her son had already asked Lynda's daughter to dance.

Carolyn was looking fantastic in gold flared trousers with a pale gold and white satin tunic. She'd been hanging on to Steve's arm, leaning her head on his shoulder or smiling up at him, but was becoming upset at his lack of response. Peter, as astute as his Mother, had noticed this and had gone to her rescue, and Carolyn was grateful.

Lynda, chatting with Gemma and Michael, watched her daughter dancing. She, too, had noticed Steve's detachment from his wife, though he was doing his best to smile and join in the banter with everyone.

He was pleased to see John's brother-in-law, Graham Laycock arrive, and went across to join him and John and his sister Sylvia.

'Hello, Graham, nice to see you again.'

'Good evening, Steve, good to see you, too. And congratulations on becoming your own boss. I'm sure you'll make a great success of the business.'

'Thank you. Hello, Sylvia, how are you?'

Sylvia, wearing an elegant 1950s style cocktail dress her Mother would have admired, turned to Steve with a look of condescension which she had inherited from Sheila Stanworth. It was a mannerism which her husband had still not yet managed to help his wife erase from her repertoire of reactions.

'I'm very well, thank you, Steven. I hope you do very well with your company. Sheldon Interior Design sounds quite classy.'

'The name was Lynda's suggestion.'

'Was it?' Sylvia looked across to where Lynda, wearing silver and dark blue satin flared trousers, and a pale blue satin tunic with flashes of silver, was dancing with her grandchildren.

'Yes. She and I are running the business together.'

'With a lot of help from Carolyn, I assume.'

John, wanting to correct his sister's attitude a little, joined in the conversation. 'She helps when she's got the time. But it's Lynda's money and know-how that's made it all possible.'

'Really?' Sylvia said, and both Graham and Steve observed the re-assessment that Sylvia was obviously having to make.

Jean, discreetly holding on to John's arm, had noticed this, too, and spoke up for her friend proudly.

'Yes, she's come a long way from the girl who used to pull pints in The Black Bull, hasn't she, Sylvia? Lynda always had it in her to be a big success if given the chance. She owns a four-star hotel near Guildford as well, you know.'

Sylvia stared at Jean, who was also a revelation to her, in her glamorous dress, sophisticated make-up and bouffant hair-style which Lynda had insisted was all part of 'the look' for that very special night out.

'A four-star hotel?' Sylvia exclaimed, her voice a little faint.

'I'll get you a drink, dear,' said Graham, suppressing a smile and walking with Steve in the direction of the bar.

John was glad that Carolyn came to keep her Aunty Sylvia company then because Harry Benson, who'd just ushered his quartet of musicians on to the stage, announced that Elvis would be allowed one last number before giving way to the superior entertainment of a live orchestra.

'This is a special request,' he confided loudly over the microphone, for Mr John Stanworth and his chosen partner, Jean Haworth, who, I believe is an ardent Elvis fan. The song John has chosen for her, is a romantic slow waltz, 'Love Me Tender.'

Helen stood next to Lynda and they watched John lead Jean on to the dance floor. John hesitantly began the waltz, and Jean beamed as they joined the other dancers and managed to do the steps in time to the music.

'I didn't know you could waltz, John,' she said, gazing up at him lovingly.

'Lynda taught me a few days ago. Am I doing all right?'

'You're doing great,' she said and sighed with happiness as he held her closer, singing the words softly to her. As Elvis sang the last few notes John stopped dancing but didn't let go of Jean.

'Will you marry me?' he asked.

Jean Haworth had heard him say those words so many times in her dreams that her answer came instantly.

'Oh, yes, John. Yes, please.'

They were unaware that the other dancers had moved away, and they were standing alone in the centre of the ballroom.

Harry Benson had seen this scenario often over the years, and didn't hesitate to embarrass the couple by speaking in a husky tone into the microphone.

'Hello, young lovers. Has someone asked somebody to marry them?'

John stared at him in shock, but Jean's beautiful smile gave Harry the answer he wanted.

'Did she say 'yes' John?' he asked boldly.

John found his voice at last. 'Yes, she did.'

He looked round the room as everyone applauded and cheered. Sylvia joined in, clapping but looking round a little apprehensively as her brother led his fiancée back to the family group.

'John,' she whispered, 'You can't get married, you're still married to Lynda, aren't you?'

'Not for long,' Lynda reassured her.

'And are you all right with this?' was Sylvia's next question.

Lynda smiled at the happy couple, 'Oh, yes. It should have happened a long time ago.'

CHAPTER FIFTY-SIX

Everyone was still congratulating Jean and John when Lynda saw the door open and Jenny Heywood walk in. She had her daughters by her side in close support, and Alex's boyfriend, Jamil, and his parents were also with them, but Steve Sheldon saw no-one but Jenny.

He thought how lovely she looked in her white cotton 'gypsy' top and fifties-style flared skirt which swished against the net underskirt beneath it. He remembered how excitedly she'd laughed as she'd told him her outfit was to be a surprise, but that she thought he'd like it. He loved it, and he loved her.

Carolyn saw the look on Steve's face, and so did Lynda, and Helen Tyler. The music began again, and the dancing continued as Jenny led her party to the table she'd reserved for them. She sat and made polite conversation with Jamil and his parents, but Katie and Alex saw their Mother catching a glimpse of Steve whenever she could. He was watching her all the time, and when their eyes met, the love and longing was clear for everyone to see.

Later, Jamil's mother, still not quite sure she wanted to be at this particular social gathering, gave her husband permission to dance sedately with Jenny, while she sat and made an effort to approve of her son dancing with Alex. Katie politely stayed with the Indian matriarch, but couldn't hide the fact that she was watching Mark Meredith.

'Do you know that young man?' Jamil's mother enquired.

'Yes. Well, I've only met him once,' Katie said,

aware that she was blushing.

'He is several years older than you. But that is quite a good thing for a woman sometimes.'

'My Mother wouldn't agree, I don't think.'

Jamil's mother gave a little laugh. 'It seems to me that these days, unfortunately, children think they have a right to disagree with their Mother,' she said, watching her son dancing with Alex.

Harry Benson's quartet were playing better than they had when they were much younger men, and Harry, his eyes shining with success, assumed full command of his audience as he stepped forward to introduce his star singers.

'And now, ladies and gentlemen, it is my pleasure to announce a real treat. For one night only Miss Lynda Collins and Mr Daniel Heywood will sing for you.'

Dan gripped Lynda's hand tightly as they stepped up to the microphone. She gave him a smile, and amazed him with her confidence as she announced their first two songs.

'Good evening everybody. We'd like to sing Helen Shapiro's 'Walking Back to Happiness' and then one of my friend, Jean Haworth's favourite Elvis numbers, 'The Wonder of You', in celebration of her engagement to John Stanworth.

It was as if she and Dan had been singing together for years, and his confidence soon matched Lynda's as they were lifted by the smiles and waves from the couples of all ages who danced to their music. There was such a sense of the joy of being in this ballroom which held so much history for the dancers and their families.

Lynda had also chosen a Tina Turner number, 'It Takes Two' which had everyone singing as well as dancing, and then Dan was going to sing 'Always'.

He knew it was going to be difficult, but he felt he had to sing it tonight, in memory of the times he'd sung with Geoff Heywood, the man who had loved him, and whom he would never stop loving and remembering as his Dad. He was also singing it for his Mother.

He took a deep breath as Lynda made the announcement.

'And now Dan is going to sing the beautiful waltz which Irving Berlin wrote in 1925 for his wife, it's called 'I'll be Loving You, Always'.

Dan began the melody, but then emotion made his voice falter. Lynda put her arm round him, and began to sing with him, looking at Dan with so much love in her eyes that his voice rose with a strength and quality it had never reached before.

In the drawing room at Kirkwood House Ellen Heywood lifted the telephone receiver, and slowly and deliberately placed it on the table next to her chair. She would not have her son phoning her, not tonight. She had prayed that he wouldn't be too nervous, that he would sing well and receive the applause he so deserved. She hoped that God would forgive her for praying for something so worldly, but it was for her son.

And there was nothing else she could do for him, not now, not with this heart of hers telling her that, whatever part she had thought she was playing in the world, it was now over. And she had not done what she wished to do more than anything.

She struggled to her feet and, holding on to the furniture, managed to get across the room to the piano. She took hold of Richard's photograph and looked at it with sorrowful but loving eyes.

Then, smiling tenderly, she reached across for the photograph of Geoff Heywood with his arm round Dan's shoulders. But, before she could take hold of this, she fell to the floor and died, holding only the photograph of her eldest son.

Jenny had promised to help Alice with the buffet, making sure that the platters were kept filled with the traditional 'Carlton supper' of sausage rolls, cubes of cheese and pineapple on sticks, and dainty sandwiches just like the ones Harry's late wife, Betty, had boasted of preparing with her 'own fair hands'. Tonight they had, like the gâteaux and apple pies, been supplied by the Heywood Bakery.

Helen Tyler was standing with Lynda in the queue for the buffet and Steve was a little way in front of them. They saw him stop, and he and Jenny looked at each other, unable to move. Lynda said his name, and he looked at her and walked away, looking down at the floor.

When she and Lynda were again sitting at their table, Helen spoke to her quietly.

'Lynda, you're tearing apart two people who obviously are in love with each other. That's not the Lynda I know. You can't do this.'

Lynda, grim-faced said, 'I have to.'

Later she tried again to help her daughter, saying to her son-in-law, 'Steve, aren't you going to ask your wife to dance?'

Steve looked at her mutinously for a moment, and then slowly got to his feet and obeyed. Carolyn smiled beseechingly at him, holding him close as they began to dance.

Steve stumbled through the steps, but then saw Jenny, alone by the door, putting on her coat. Steve stopped dancing. He gently let go of his wife, and shook his head.

'I can't do this, Carolyn. I'm sorry.'

Carolyn stood there and watched him walk across the room and put his arm round Jenny Heywood. As they left, Carolyn knew that Steve was walking out of her life. She could feel the beat of the music pounding in her head, and thought she was going to fall into the whirlpool of lights and stars.

'Carolyn!' Lynda called out as she swiftly crossed the dance floor, and took her daughter in her arms. She led Carolyn back to their table where the children had been sitting with John and Jean, and watching what had happened.

'Are you all right, love?' John asked, as Carolyn sank down on to the chair next to him. Carolyn couldn't speak at first but just held on tight to her Mother's hand.

'John, I'm going to take Carolyn and the kids home,' Lynda said. 'I'll just go and tell Dan he'll have to sing the last numbers on his own. I'll be back in a minute,' she reassured her daughter who was still sitting there numb and shocked.

John, picking up the need to remain calm and get his family away from the curiosity of the people in the ballroom, stood up and held out his hand to his grandchildren. 'Come on, kids, let's get your coats.'

'Where's Daddy?' Gemma wanted to know.

'He's had to take somebody home,' Jean explained, 'He'll be back soon,' she added, wishing she could believe that.

It wasn't until the morning that Carolyn managed to dry her tears and quietly explain to her children

496

that their Daddy might be staying away for a while.

'Staying where?' Gemma demanded to know.

Carolyn looked at her Mother, who nodded. They had talked until the early hours, and in the end Carolyn had tearfully accepted that Steve had left her. What had scared her the most was having to tell the children, but she decided it would be best to do that now.

'He's gone to Jenny Heywood's,' she said calmly.

Gemma, as usual, came back with a straight question, 'Why?'

Carolyn took a deep breath, 'Because he wants to be with her rather than with me.'

Michael's voice was little more than a whisper.

'Do you mean he's left us to go and live with Jenny?'

Carolyn nodded.

'That doesn't mean you won't see him,' Lynda said quickly. 'And it certainly doesn't mean he doesn't love you. He'll still be your Daddy, only he won't live here.'

'That's right, I'll still be your Daddy, and I'll still love you,' said Steve as he quietly entered the room. He'd left Hadden Lea very early, wanting to come and reassure his children. Now he stood there, not knowing what would happen next, but expecting an onslaught of emotions from Carolyn. She stood up, drawing her children close to her, but there was no outburst of anger, only sadness as she tried to keep her voice steady.

'You've come for your things.'

'Yes, if you don't mind, I'll just go and pack.'

Carolyn did mind, very much, but she and her Mother had done a lot of thinking, as well as crying last night. What was important was for everyone to accept that there would be a divorce, and to make it

497

as easy as possible for the children to live with all the changes that would mean, and to feel secure in the love of both their parents.

When Steve had gone upstairs, leaving an unhappy stillness behind him, Lynda forced herself to smile brightly, and said, 'While your Dad's doing that, shall we all go to the park and then find a nice pub for lunch?'

'Yeah!' Michael said with relief as well as enthusiasm.

'Shall we, Mum?' asked Gemma, looking anxiously at her Mother, who gave a smile that looked like a reflection of Lynda's, and nodded.

'Shall we invite your Grandad and Jean as well?' Lynda suggested. 'We need to celebrate their engagement, don't we?'

Carolyn hesitated. Celebrating was not what she felt like doing today, but then she realised her Mother was right, it was just what they needed to do.

'Yes,' she said. 'I'll give your Grandad a ring now.'

'Can Dad come to the pub as well?' asked Michael.

Carolyn looked at her son, who didn't know what he was asking of her, and replied gently, 'No, not this time, Michael. Not today.'

Lynda saw that Michael was unhappy with this and created a diversion.

'It's exciting, isn't it, to have a wedding to look forward to? And if you ask nicely, Gemma, you might be allowed to be a bridesmaid.'

Gemma squealed with excitement at the idea, but Michael's face remained sullen as he asked, 'I won't have to be a page-boy or anything daft like that, will I?'

'No!' Lynda and Carolyn reassured him, and Carolyn was amazed, and pleased, to find herself laughing.

They were laughing again as they returned to Beechwood Avenue that afternoon, until Lynda's phone rang. It was Dan.

CHAPTER FIFTY-SEVEN

Carolyn had immediately burst into tears when she was told of the death of Ellen Heywood. She had wept, heart-broken, for at that particular moment she was mourning not only the death of her dear friend, but also the end of her marriage.

Lynda hadn't shed any tears, but had left straight away to be with Dan. It was strange to walk into Kirkwood House and know that Ellen Heywood would never again be sitting there, holding court from her chair by the fire. Lynda was alarmed when she saw Dan trembling as he told her how he'd come home from the dance and found his Mother lying dead on the floor.

They were sitting in the conservatory as Dan couldn't bear to go back into the drawing room. He was stumbling over his words, talking too fast, trying to cope with it all.

'I wasn't here, I should have been here, though the doctor said there was nothing I could have done. He'd been expecting it, she'd been expecting it, but she wouldn't let him tell me. And I wasn't with her. I should have been here.'

'I'm sorry love. I know that's hard, after all the times you've stayed to look after her, and this time you couldn't.' She held him tight, and then asked, 'How are Jenny and the girls?'

'They're like me, they can't take it in. I waited till this morning to tell them. No point in waking them up, better to let them have some sleep first.'

'Yes, quite right,' Lynda agreed, trying not to think about Steve sleeping in Jenny Heywood's bed last night.

'They came straight here, and we sat round the kitchen table, trying to sort out what we should do. There'll be the funeral to arrange, she left strict instructions for that.'

Lynda suppressed a wry smile, trust Ellen to want to be in control right to the end.

Dan was still stammering out his thoughts, 'There'll be such a lot to sort out.' He paused. 'I keep expecting her to walk in,' he said, looking round fearfully.

Lynda couldn't bear to see him like this, huddled in this large, echoing house which, to her, had always seemed designed to crush one's spirit.

'Let's go out, Dan, love. Let's go for a walk in the countryside, get some fresh air and sunshine.'

'Oh, that's a great idea. That's what I need, to get out of this place.'

Lynda drove and could sense Dan relaxing as they parked the car and set off walking through the fields, still golden with buttercups. He held out his hand to help Lynda over a stile and kept hold of it as they continued their walk. They wandered along familiar paths by the side of hedgerows of hawthorn and holly, and across streams forming miniature waterfalls over ancient stones.

'It's a long time since we did this,' he said. 'Do you remember when we came here courting?'

'Of course I do.' She looked at him, and wanted to stop and smooth away the frown on his forehead. Instead she just smiled gently, and said, 'We were so young then, and I knew so little.'

His look was full of admiration. 'You've made up

501

for it now. You've achieved a lot, Lynda.' He sighed, 'I wish I could say the same.'

'Don't think that way, Dan. You've made a good life for yourself here, you've got loyal friends and a job you enjoy, and Jenny and the girls think the world of you.'

'Yes, sorry. I have got a lot to be thankful for. But it's not been the life I wanted. I had such dreams, Lynda, but I ended up staying in Milfield and looking after my Mother. And now she's gone, and I don't know what comes next.' He gave a hollow laugh. 'Apart from the funeral, of course.'

'Yeah. That won't be easy for you, in spite of having instructions!'

'Yes, though it won't be a big affair. Like we said before the party, there aren't that many of her friends left.'

'Yes, that's sad for her.'

'I'd like you to come, Lynda, if you don't mind.'

'Your Mother won't like it.'

'No, but I'll need you to be there.'

'Then I will be.'

'I don't know why she hated you so much.'

'Because she was a bully, and I stood up to her. Sorry, shouldn't speak ill of the dead, should you?'

'It's only the truth. She bullied me all her life, and I never really had the courage to stop her. But I couldn't stand her being nasty about you, there was no need for that, especially after she managed to split us up.'

'I think deep down she must have felt guilty about that, because she knew neither of us were happy.'

'Our lives would have been so different if I'd defied her and married you.'

'No point in having regrets, Dan. Concentrate on the future, it always brings something good, at least, that's what I've found.'

He gave her a hug.

'Oh, I'm so glad you're here, Lynda.'

'So am I.'

It rained on the day of Ellen Heywood's funeral, making Kirkwood House look even more dark and bleak than usual. In accordance with her wishes, there was a buffet lunch set out in the dining room and it was, as Dan had predicted, a small gathering. Eventually Alex insisted everyone should follow her into the drawing room, in which the air seemed very still and cold.

Alex stood resolutely, and alone, in front of the fireplace and was glad when Edwin Lawson went to stand beside her. Looking towards the straight-backed chair, he raised his glass in respectful salute.

'Somehow, one could never imagine this house without your Grandmother.'

'No,' Alex replied somewhat tersely.

Edwin observed her hastily brushing away a tear, and said gently, 'It is always hard to lose a member of one's family. I hope you didn't find the meeting yesterday too upsetting.'

Obeying his client's command he had invited the family, and also Carolyn Sheldon, to his office the previous day and made known to them the contents of Ellen Heywood's will. He now spoke, less formally than he had on that occasion, to Ellen's eldest granddaughter.

'It must feel very strange to be standing here as the joint-owner of Kirkwood House.'

'Yes. But it's not right, it should belong to Uncle Dan, not me and Katie.'

'I think your Grandmother knew that Daniel would not wish to own the house. She felt that you

503

were her father's rightful heirs to the family home. And, under the terms of the will, Daniel and your Mother will be able to live here as long as they wish.'

'My Mother's already said she won't come to live here, and I don't know what Uncle Dan will do. He's found it very hard to stay here since she died, even with me and Katie moving in to keep him company.'

'No-one should make hasty decisions. That has always been my experience in these circumstances. And you are very welcome to ask my son's advice,' he added, nodding towards Philip, who was deep in conversation with Jenny.

'Philip, not you?'

'Yes, he will take care of you from now on. I can truly retire now that I have carried out my duties for your Grandmother.' He paused, seeking a less funereal subject of conversation, 'She was so proud, you know, that you are going to Cambridge.'

'That will depend on my results, and I'm still not sure. But everyone seems to think it's the right thing for me. In the meantime there'll be a lot to sort out here.'

'Quite so, but you will, I am sure, do everything as your Grandmother would wish. Now, may I once more offer my condolences, and say my farewells to you and your family?'

Alex watched him walk away with slow, measured steps and turned to find Alice Smith standing next to her. Holding a tray of sandwiches as a pretext, she had been standing as close as she could without being noticed. Alice was disappointed that, even with her sharp hearing, she had missed some of Alex's conversation with Edwin Lawson. She had, however, already quizzed Dan on his inheritance, so she knew some of the details of Ellen's will.

504

'Would you like a sandwich, Alex?' she enquired sweetly.

'No thank you, Alice.'

'Oh, you sound so like your Grandmother, so like the lady of the house, which, of course, you are now.'

'No, I'm not.'

'Well, you and your sister then. And it's nice that Dan is being allowed to stay on. And your Mother, though she'll want to stay at Hadden Lea, I would imagine, with Steve Sheldon.'

Alex had not had much contact with Alice Smith before today, and was taken aback by her assumption of the right to talk of such private matters.

'I see Carolyn hasn't come back with us,' continued Alice. 'It's a shame. She should be here, she was very fond of your Grandmother.'

Alex tried to move away but Alice shuffled closer to her, lowering her voice to a confidential tone. 'But I can understand her not wanting to be in the same room as Jenny. It's terrible to see a marriage break-up, isn't it. Those poor children.'

'The marriage did not break up because of my Mother,' Alex informed her sharply, 'but because of Carolyn Sheldon's adultery. Not that that is any of your business!'

She stormed away from Alice, who watched her for a moment and then, unperturbed, sat down on the sofa, placed the tray on the coffee table and began to munch her way through the sandwiches, lifting the corners to identify all the ones filled with her favourite, fresh salmon.

Noticing Lynda standing looking at the photographs on the piano, she signalled to her, and Lynda, feeling tired, accepted Alice's invitation to sit beside her.

'Lovely photos, aren't they? Expensive, those

silver frames. Nice one of your Carolyn.'

'Yes.'

'She seemed really upset in church. Well, she would be, with Jenny Heywood there. I wasn't sure she'd come.'

'Neither was I,' Lynda admitted, and immediately cautioned herself to be more careful what she said to Alice Smith.

'I expect she'd have liked to come here this afternoon, for one last time. Your Carolyn has spent many a happy hour in this room. Ellen was very fond of her, I wouldn't be surprised if she left her some money, or at least some jewellery.'

She paused, but saw that Lynda wasn't going to tell her anything and so continued, 'I was hoping she'd have left me something, but apparently she hasn't. I thought she would have done, some small token, after all, we'd been friends since schooldays.'

Lynda was surprised to see Alice's lower lip tremble, and realised that the little woman would miss coming to enjoy the warmth of this house on winter afternoons, the treat of afternoon tea, and the pretence of being a part of a grand household.

'If you ask Dan, I'm sure he'll find something for you as a keepsake.'

'Do you think so?'

'Yes. Dan will take care of it.'

'As he took care of his Mother.'

She smiled across at Dan who was standing with Jenny and her daughters, saying goodbye to the remainder of the mourners.

'He's been a wonderful son.'

'Yes, he has.'

'He'd have made somebody a wonderful husband, too, if she'd let him,' mused Alice, her look letting Lynda know that she was aware of the history there.

506

An image came, vivid and painful, into Lynda's mind, an image of herself in this room as a teenage girl in cheap clothes, and with wet, bedraggled hair, perched on the edge of a sofa, clutching Dan's hand. She had never forgotten Ellen Heywood's snobbish disparagement and disdain that night, it had haunted her, and made her doubt herself for years.

As if she'd read her mind, Alice said, 'You never stood a chance of marrying Dan, not while his Mother was alive. Nothing to stop you now, though,' she speculated.

Lynda stood up, pretending she hadn't heard that last remark.

'I'd better be going now, I'll see you later, Alice.'

'Yes, it was great at the Carlton dance, wasn't it,' Alice called after her, 'you and Dan singing together.'

Dan heard her and smiled.

'It seems a long time ago, that,' he said to Lynda. 'Are you off to Beechwood Avenue now?'

'Yes, I told Carolyn I wouldn't be long. I'm going to be spending a lot of time with her and the kids.'

'Yes, I know you have to make them the priority.'

'I'll see you whenever I can. Will you be all right, love?'

'Yes, I've got these girls to look after me,' he said, smiling at his nieces standing close by. He and Lynda both saw the look between Katie and her sister.

'It'll be just me, I'm afraid, Uncle Dan,' Alex told him. 'Katie's got a job this summer, but don't worry, I'll help you out at the café.'

'Where's this job?' asked Jenny who had joined them in time to hear the last part of the conversation.

Katie watched for Lynda's reaction as she said, 'Loveday Manor.'

'Loveday!' gasped Lynda.

'I'm sorry it's a shock. Mark was going to tell you,

but then he heard about Steve and Carolyn, and thought he'd better wait a bit.'

'What is this job?' her Mother wanted to know.

'I told Mark at the dance I was looking for some hotel experience, and he offered me a job at Loveday Manor in the summer holiday. I was going to tell you, Mum, but with Gran dying it didn't seem the right time. I can go, though, can't I? Please.'

Jenny turned to Lynda. 'So you didn't know about this either?'

'No.' Lynda said, still picturing Loveday Manor with the garden and trees in their full summer glory.

'Is it all right with you?' Dan asked anxiously.

'Yes,' Lynda said, 'Yes, I suppose so. It's Mark who's in charge of staff now anyway. He'd have assumed it was all right as I know you. So, yes, if you're happy for her to go, Jenny?'

It was the first time she'd spoken to Jenny that day, apart from murmuring the formal condolences required at the church door. Jenny was in a daze at having to make a decision like that at this moment, but couldn't deny the pleading in her daughter's eyes.

'Yes. I'm sure it will be a good experience for you. Will you be going to Loveday Manor this summer as well, Lynda?'

'I don't know,' Lynda replied quietly. 'I hadn't intended to, not yet. And I'm taking Carolyn and the children to America in August for a couple of weeks. Helen invited them before she left, and they're keen to go.' Her eyes fixed on Jenny, as she added, 'They need to get away for a while.'

Jenny's face reddened.

'I'm sorry. I'm so sorry, Lynda,' she whispered.

Lynda looked at the woman whom she had known since she was a child, and whose life had been made so hard by Ellen Heywood and her son, whose grave

508

she now shared.

She remembered the days and weeks after Richard's death, and how Jenny had had to fight to prevent Ellen completely taking over her daughter-in-law and her children.

Life had not been easy for Jenny, and Lynda resolved there and then, that she wasn't going to make it any harder.

'I know you are, love,' she said, putting her arms round Jenny and holding her close like she used to.

CHAPTER FIFTY-EIGHT

As soon as he got home from work Jenny, with tears in her eyes, told Steve about Lynda giving her a hug. He was relieved, and it made him less anxious when he went to Bennett Street the following week to talk to Lynda about the work she wanted him to do while she was away.

'I'm sorry to make you come out this evening after a busy day at work,' she apologized as he took measurements in the front bedroom for the fitted wardrobes she wanted.

'Not a problem. I might be working hard but I'm enjoying it so much I hardly notice being tired. It feels so different, being my own boss.'

He paused and the tape measure snapped back into its case as he lost concentration.

Lynda saw his anxiety. 'Don't worry, Steve. I won't back out of the agreement. I know I have to accept that you and Carolyn can't be together.'

'Thank you, Lynda,' he said solemnly. 'I really am grateful.'

'I know. I don't want to invest more than I have done, though. I've got to think of the future.'

'And doing nice things like taking your grandchildren to America. They're so excited about that.'

'So am I!'

'And I should be able to manage financially with what you've already put into the business,' Steve said, wanting to reassure her.

'Good. But if you do need more, Angela is ready

to make a further investment.'

'Yes, she told me, and she's got some good ideas. She seems keen to get more involved.'

'Yes, and she's keen on her new boyfriend as well,' Lynda laughed. 'Have you met Charles?'

'Only briefly, but he seems a nice bloke. It's good that she's found someone else.' He hesitated, but then gave Lynda one of those steady looks of his. 'I hope Carolyn will find somebody one day.'

'So do I.'

Lynda knew she shouldn't say this, but she and Steve had always shared a wicked sense of humour when on their own, and she dropped back into that old habit now.

'Helen's hoping it won't be her son, Peter.'

'Why not?'

'Because he's already had one wife who went off with other men.'

'Oh.'

'Sorry. Don't tell Carolyn I said that! I obviously haven't quite managed to cure my wickedness.'

'You were always good enough for me, Lynda.'

She became more serious. 'I'm hoping Carolyn will have learned her lesson. John gave her a good talking to, you know, about how it was her fault you split up.'

Steve was surprised. 'Did he?'

'Yes. I've never heard John telling her off like that before.'

'It wasn't all her fault,' Steve said generously. 'We wanted different things out of life.'

'I know, like me and John. And she's selfish sometimes, like I am.'

'You're not selfish, Lynda.'

'Oh, no? What about when I went off and decided I'd found a better life for myself?'

'They drove you away. I could see that.'

'I know, and I've always been grateful for you being on my side. But I was selfish. We're all selfish, that's the trouble. It's always a case of trying to balance your needs against the needs of others. And it's about what choices you make.'

'That sounds like a wise woman talking.'

Lynda's smile held pride as well as sadness.

'No, just a woman who met a wise and generous man and remembers what he said. Now, let's go downstairs and have a drink.'

'And look at those designs I've brought?' he reminded her.

'Yeah. And start putting the world back together again. Helen Tyler was right, we have to accept what's happened and create an extended family, and a happy one.'

The Heywood family, especially Dan, had been surprised at how much money Ellen Heywood had left in her will. Although she'd given her beloved Richard a large portion of her wealth, she had, since his death, secretly saved money.

Ellen had always enjoyed having money, and the sense of power it gave her. She had decided, as she'd grown older, that saving money was an interesting thing to do, and had decided to economize, for example, by not spending more than absolutely necessary on Kirkwood House. And, in addition, she had preserved the funds and stocks and shares which her father, Richard Alexander Buchanan, had insisted his daughter should set aside to safeguard the family's reputation and status.

Dan had, at first, been furious that his Mother had kept this wealth secret, even when the bakery had been short of funds, and that she could have saved him so much worry.

512

But he'd been very glad to learn that she had, towards the end of her life, changed her will.

It seemed that she had wanted to make amends to the son who had kept her and cared for her. She had made sure there would be enough money for Dan to be financially very well provided for after her death.

The family were all also surprised that, although she had left instructions about Kirkwood House, she had not stipulated that it could never be sold. Dan and Jenny, and the girls had had many long conversations about the house, but in the end admitted that none of them wanted to live there permanently in the future.

Alex and Katie therefore decided that Kirkwood House would eventually be sold. They felt guilty about that decision, which they knew would not have been Ellen Heywood's wish.

They had also felt a little guilty about deciding to spend a small amount of their inheritance, and make a holiday out of taking Katie to Loveday Manor.

They spent a weekend in London, seeing the sights and going to the theatre before leaving on the Monday to drive through the Surrey countryside to the hotel.

'It feels strange to be down here again,' Dan commented as they took a detour to have a look at the lovely town of Richmond.

As drove along enjoying the view of the river Thames and the elegant Georgian mansions, Jenny turned to see whether Dan was upset.

'This was where Sandra lived, wasn't it?'

'Yes,' he said grimly.

'Who's Sandra?' chorused Alex and Katie.

'My ex-wife. I thought I'd told you about her.'

'Not much,' said Katie.

'Well, I don't like to talk about it. It was a big mistake,' he sighed.

'Like me and Jamil,' Alex chipped in sympathetically.

'Not really,' her sister contradicted her. 'You just decided after the dance, that you were in danger of being approved of by his parents, and that took the fun out of it.'

Alex glared at her. 'I decided I didn't want a serious commitment to him, that's all. There's nothing wrong with that.'

'Jamil doesn't think so, poor bloke,' said Katie.

Jenny turned round. 'Stop it, you two. And it was very sensible of Alex to end the relationship before she goes off to university.'

'Anyone seen a sign for Guildford?' enquired Dan, just to change the subject.

When they saw Loveday Manor, gracious and serene in the late afternoon sunshine, they were all as enchanted as Lynda had been on that first day, when Tom Meredith had brought her to his home.

Patrick Nelson came hurrying out to welcome them and introduce himself. Alex shook his hand but then, looking round, couldn't stop herself exclaiming, 'Wow! And this belongs to Lynda.'

Patrick corrected her.

'Not all of it,' he said. 'This young man owns a chimney or two,' he grinned as Mark also came hurrying out.

'I'm so glad you could come,' he said with a beaming smile which embraced all of them.

'I'm sorry we couldn't bring Lynda with us,' Jenny apologized. 'I know what you really want is to have her here again.'

'She'll come back when she's ready,' Patrick said

with confidence. 'She loves this place.'

'I can understand that,' said Jenny.

'So can I,' Dan agreed, 'Milfield can't compete with this,' he decided unhappily.

Mark stepped forward and took Katie's suitcase.

'Let me show you to your rooms.'

'Not me, I'm not a guest,' Katie said, a little embarrassed.

Mark smiled at her in a way which made her heart flutter.

'You are for the next couple of days. Lynda wants you to just enjoy the place before you start work, and so do I.'

Jenny saw the way Mark Meredith smiled at her daughter and it worried her, but for the next two days she pushed that anxiety aside and, like the rest of them relaxed into the pleasures Loveday Manor had to offer.

The rooms Mark had chosen for them were all ones which Lynda had re-furbished, and Jenny was particularly appreciative of the fabrics and colour schemes she'd chosen.

'I never realised Lynda had all these talents,' she said to Amy, who proudly showed Jenny and her daughters round the wedding venue she and Lynda had created in the old stables, and the shop from where they sold all the accessories.

'She didn't know she had until Tom brought her to Loveday. She told me this was a magical place for her, it inspired her and gave her a new life.'

'And a man who loved her,' said Jenny, thinking how much she was missing Steve.

'Yes, it was pretty special what they had together.'

'Don't tell my Uncle Dan that,' Katie pleaded. 'He's still in love with Lynda, isn't he Mum?'

Amy picked up on this. 'Dan and Lynda?'

515

'It's a long story, going back to when they were teenagers,' Jenny said, 'but we all hope it will have a happy ending one day.'

Alex, not as romantic as her Mother or sister,' shrugged her shoulders. 'I think Uncle Dan knows he can't compete with this, or with the memory of Tom Meredith.'

'He's a lovely man, I think Tom would have liked him,' said Amy. 'And Tom told Lynda that after he died, she should go back to Milfield and her family, at least for a little while.'

Jenny was surprised. 'Did he?'

Amy blinked back a tear. 'Yeah. He was the kindest and most unselfish man in the world, Tom Meredith. He told me and Patrick that all the love Lynda has to give, should be shared, and that he didn't want her to be alone. He wanted her to find someone else one day.'

'Did he tell Lynda that?' asked Jenny.

'Yes. And perhaps Dan should know, too.'

'I'll tell him one day soon,' Jenny promised, 'but I think Lynda needs more time yet.'

'I'm sure you're right,' said Amy. Then she turned to Alex and Katie, and grinned mischievously. 'And I think we need some time to go shopping now, girls. How about I take you to Guildford this afternoon? I want to show you my little gift shop, which is where Lynda and I first met and started having crazy ideas.'

The trip to Virginia had been a great success, not just as a holiday, but also as a time of healing. The love and trust Lynda was slowly creating between her and Carolyn was growing day by day. It had begun to ease away the painful memories and the feeling of rejection they had both suffered for too long. And

516

Lynda was building a strong bond between her and her grandchildren.

After seeing them happily settled back in Milfield at the end of August, Lynda was eager to go and talk to Dan about his visit to Loveday Manor, but the death of Princess Diana brought the world to a shuddering, heartbreaking halt. On the 6th September the streets of Milfield were silent as everyone stayed at home to watch the funeral and weep.

Lynda, hunched on the sofa with her arms clasped around her body, felt as if she had lost someone very dear to her. She remembered how she'd sat with Jenny Heywood and watched Diana's wedding, but she couldn't mention that now because today it was Carolyn sitting next to her.

Lynda was avoiding contact with Jenny as much as possible because of the divorce which was progressing step by painful step. She wanted so much to talk about Loveday and her life there, and knew that Jenny would have been thrilled to have a chat about it.

When she eventually saw Dan, she tried asking him about their stay at the hotel, but he just said he'd been very impressed, and seemed unwilling to add to that. He was more willing to talk about her trip to Virginia.

'I'd like to go there one day,' he said. 'I'm going to be making a few trips to America myself.'

'Are you?'

'Yes, you know I've always wanted to go, and there's nothing to stop me now.'

She understood what he meant. 'Yes, you go, Dan. And call in on Helen, I'm sure she'd give you a great welcome.'

Dan smiled as he remembered the perceptive little

American lady who had sympathy with his aim in life.

'I liked her a lot. She's got the world sussed, has Helen Tyler, she's a woman to be listened to.'

'Yes she is,' Lynda agreed, nodding thoughtfully.

She had listened to Helen during their visit, and they had talked about Dan. 'I know you're not ready to hear this yet, but you still have a life, Lynda, still have a future. And Dan Heywood might be the one to share it with, Helen had told her.'

Lynda hadn't been ready to think about that possibility then, and she still wasn't, and so she quickly changed the subject.

'I saw Alice the other day, she invited me and Jean to her house for a cup of tea.'

Dan was surprised. 'She doesn't often invite people round.'

'She wanted to show off the silver teapot you'd given her, as a memento. It was very kind of you, that.'

'Well, she'll miss all those afternoon teas with my Mother.'

'Yes. How is life at Kirkwood House now?'

'Pretty quiet. And it'll be quieter still when Alex goes off to university.'

'Are the girls still sure they want to sell the house?'

'Oh, yes. We all want to move on, especially me. Anyway, what about you? Are you happy at Bennett Street?'

Lynda found it hard to answer that. 'Happy' was not a word she could use to describe herself.

'It's good to have my grandchildren visiting me, gives the place a bit of life. And Peter Tyler is coming to stay when he comes over on business in October.'

'Oh? Is he still interested in property investment in the North of England?'

'His Dad is. Helen's promised me Peter will stop Nathan demolishing the town. That husband of hers can be pretty ruthless when it comes to business.'

'Milfield could do with somebody investing money in it, though.'

'Tell you what,' Lynda joked, 'I'll send him round to have a look at Kirkwood House, and see if Nathan Tyler can turn it into a night club or something.'

'No thanks! My Mother's ghost is giving me a hard enough time as it is! I daren't even ask you round,' Dan laughed, but there was some truth in what he'd said.

'You come round to me, then, and I'll cook for you. It'll make a nice change from you catering for everybody else.'

She was surprised, and touched, to see how that modest invitation drove away the shadows on Dan's face.

'Oh, Lynda, I'd love to,' he said, his eyes shining with delight and affection.

That first evening at Bennett Street soon became one of many, full of laughter and wide-ranging conversation as well as confidences. But it took all of Dan's will power to limit himself to affectionate friendship. His passionate love for Lynda was even stronger than it had been when they'd had to meet in secret all those years ago.

Just to see her walk towards him in the street still made his heart beat quicken with love and longing. But whenever Lynda saw that look in his eyes she turned away; there was no place for that kind of love in her grief-locked heart.

CHAPTER FIFTY-NINE

Carolyn's way of dealing with the heartbreak of divorcing Steve was to work hard, and there was plenty of that kind of distraction at AFS these days. One of the outcomes of the re-structuring of the company was making Gerald Critchley redundant.

It was presented, of course, as early retirement, but Critchley refused to go through the charade of insincere speeches. Instead, he collected together all the days he was entitled to and, without notice, went on a very long vacation.

This caused a slight panic at head office, and it was necessary to swiftly promote Carolyn Sheldon to act as manager of the Milfield Office. This was a temporary appointment, until the senior managers realised that she was much more competent than Critchley had ever been.

By October they had made her position permanent, with only a monthly supervisory visit from a head office executive as an extra reassurance for those such as Stapleton. He was the only one who grumbled when Carolyn, having worked long hours to rescue the Milfield Office from the mess Critchley had abandoned, informed them that she would be taking a week's leave to cover her children's October half-term holiday.

Carolyn had decided early on in the divorce proceedings that there would be no difficulties about sharing time with the children. And, although she knew she could never have Steve's love again, she aimed to have his friendship. And so there was no tense atmosphere to be feared by their children when their parents were together.

They were sitting in the living room having a cup of coffee while waiting for Gemma and Michael to finish packing for a weekend at Hadden Lea, when Carolyn told Steve about the holiday arrangement she'd made.

'Thank you, I'm really grateful,' he said. 'I wasn't going to ask, but it will be a great help.'

'I thought it would be. It's a crucial period in the company's development and, for all our sakes, I want you to make a success of SID.'

They both smiled at the acronym Lynda had suggested they use to refer to the family business.

'My Mum will be helping me entertain them, and Dad and Jean offered as well, but they'll be busy with the last minute details for the wedding.'

Steve laughed. 'Yes. I think it's hilarious how guilty Jean feels about her and John living together at her place, she makes such a point of telling people that they are getting married, as soon as possible.'

Carolyn laughed, too. 'It's just the way she is. But it's wonderful to see how happy they are. And they've had their offer accepted on that bungalow now that Dad's sold his flat.'

'Oh, that's great news. It'll be good for your Dad to have a garden again.' He paused and looked at her a little anxiously.

'You know they've invited me to the wedding? Not Jenny, just me. Is it O.K. with you if I come?'

'Yes. Dad asked me before he invited you. Gemma would be upset if you weren't there to see her be a bridesmaid.'

'Yeah, she would. Thanks, Caro.'

Hearing him use the name only he had ever used

made her feel like crying. She looked at this good man who had once been her beloved husband, and had to struggle not to despair as one of those waves of regret overwhelmed her again.

Making an effort not to show her feelings, she asked, 'Can I leave the kids with you from Friday afternoon till Sunday night at the end of half-term week, though? Peter Tyler has offered to drive me and Mum to Loveday Manor for the weekend.'

'Yes, sure. How long is Peter staying?'

'A couple of weeks yet, but he's travelling about quite a bit on business. He said he wanted to call in and see you, too.'

'Yes, Lynda said he'd do that. She's enjoying having him staying with her.'

'He's good company.'

'Yeah, so I've heard. The kids keep going on about how 'cool' he is.'

Carolyn looked pleased.

'Yes, they got on well when we went over to Virginia.'

Steve thought again how his wife and family seemed to have moved into a world which was very different from his. He didn't feel entirely comfortable with that and so, instead, focused on his concern for his mother-in-law.

'So Lynda's ready to go back to Loveday Manor at last, is she?'

'Not to stay. Just to visit. She wants me to see what she calls 'her other life'.

'It won't be easy for her, going back,' said Steve, a little worried.

'No, I think that's partly why Peter offered to drive. But at least Suzanne won't be there. She's decided the Côte d'Azur is where she'll spend the winter.'

'Like you do,' Steve said sardonically.

'Like a lot of people would like to. Including me!'

They looked at each other, and remembered how they had so often had different dreams. With no resentment in his voice, Steve said, 'Perhaps you'll get to do that one day.'

'Everything is possible, that's what I feel now,' Carolyn stated, more confidently than she felt.

Steve's smile was gentle. 'I'm glad.'

Lynda, Carolyn and Peter arrived at Loveday Manor just as the sun was setting. Lynda was delighted to see that Carolyn was impressed when she saw the hotel, with its graceful Georgian windows glittering in the golden light.

The sun's rays highlighted the autumn colours in the trees, and the fading blue streaks of sky were being pushed aside by huge, luxuriant clouds layered one against the other, and lit from beneath by the setting sun so that they glowed with many shades of pink and gold.

As they got out of the car, Lynda stood and stared at the sky.

'What is it?' asked Carolyn.

'This sunset, it reminds me of a special one I saw when I was a teenager. I've never forgotten it. I was such a romantic then, I remember hoping my future would be like that, rosy and golden, and with excitement on the horizon, like a Hollywood dream.'

She expected Carolyn to laugh at her fantasy, but she didn't. Instead she said softly, 'But that wasn't what happened, was it?'

'No. Not till I came here.'

Since his Mother had left for France, Mark had moved into The Gatehouse. Peter was to stay there with him during their visit, but noticing the way Peter looked at Carolyn, Mark wondered if he should have let her stay there, too. Instead he showed her and Lynda into the room he'd chosen for them.

'There's the apartment, of course, we've kept that ready for you, Lynda, but I wasn't sure whether you'd want to stay there.'

'No,' she murmured. 'Too soon for that.'

'This isn't our best suite,' he apologized to Carolyn, 'but most of the rooms were already booked for the wedding tomorrow.'

'We shouldn't have come when you've a wedding to cater for,' Lynda said, 'but it will be lovely to be here for it. I loved doing weddings,' she told Carolyn.

Mark grinned cheekily. 'I'm glad you said that. We could use some help, if you don't mind.'

'Try and stop me!' Lynda said, her eyes alight with excitement.

Carolyn was admiring the pale green, silver and white decor.

'It's a beautiful room, so elegant and restful, and I love all the details, the vases of flowers and the little quilted baskets.'

'All your Mother's work, like the rest of the rooms in the hotel.'

'Really?' Carolyn turned to Lynda in surprise.

'A labour of love,' Lynda said simply, and needed to turn away from them and stare out of the window for a moment.

They had supper in the kitchen after the guests had been served in the two dining rooms, and Peter and Carolyn enjoyed not just the excellent food, but also the banter and camaraderie between Lynda, Mark and Patrick. Carolyn had never seen her Mother so animated, and so at ease as she was with these friends.

Lynda had forgotten how much she could laugh with Patrick and Amy, and how much she loved the way of being together, as well as working together, which they'd brought with them to Loveday from Cornwall, and the days at The Springfield Hotel.

Carolyn also noted how confidently Lynda joined in the allocation of tasks involved in the organization of the wedding. It was to be an Austrian themed event, as the bride and groom had met in Vienna.

Patrick and Amy and the rest of the staff had had to work hard on the decorating of the venue, including placing Austrian style painted wooden gables and flower-filled window boxes on the stable doors, in imitation of mountain chalets.

'There'll be plenty of Strauss waltzes, and quite a few cow bells, Patrick laughingly informed them. 'I was going to get a bell for the bridegroom's mother,' he added wickedly, 'but fortunately she's calmed down a bit.'

Leaving Carolyn sleeping peacefully, Lynda was up early the following morning. She wanted to give herself the time to quietly wander round special places in the hotel grounds and by the river, just to be with Tom Meredith again.

She was going to work on the wedding that morning, but she'd arranged for Carolyn to enjoy a relaxed breakfast with Peter, followed by a stroll through the garden.

As they returned to the hotel, Carolyn caught sight of Lynda arranging flowers in the Springfield Room, and Peter tactfully left her to spend some time alone with her Mother.

The room was an extension which Lynda and Tom had had built in 1995, when the law had been changed to allow different venues to be licensed for wedding ceremonies. Softly gathered white voile was draped along the cornice, and also round the large white windows which looked out on to the garden.

'What a beautiful place to get married in, said Carolyn. 'I know it's not a church, but somehow you get the feeling you're in a private chapel as well as a lovely room.'

'Tom and I wanted it to remind us of the chapel in St Benedict. That had lovely views, and stars like those,' she explained, pointing up at the deep blue ceiling decorated with gold and silver stars.

Later that morning Mark found the time to show Carolyn round the hotel, and the stable courtyard with the barn they had converted into a wedding venue. For this occasion there were crystal chandeliers as well as gold and silver balloons, and magnificent flower arrangements, the whole decoration designed to give the atmosphere of a Viennese ballroom.

'Not all our weddings are as elaborate as this, but the couple wanted no expense spared, so we took them at their word, and tried to create their dream.

'Oh, I think you've succeeded,' sighed Carolyn.

'It's so satisfying if you manage to achieve the perfect wedding day. And we usually do, but there's a tremendous amount of work behind the scenes. Like the baking and washing up that Lynda's probably doing now.'

Carolyn looked at him in amazement.

'Is that where she is, in the kitchen?'

'I think so, but that's Lynda, not afraid of hard work.'

'No. She's always worked hard, all her life. We didn't really appreciate her efforts at home,' Carolyn confessed ruefully.

'Hope you don't mind my saying, but that was what my Grandma Meredith told me. It was partly the reason Lynda left Milfield and came to Cornwall, where I met her. I was too young to understand what was going on, but my Gran said Lynda had needed to find a new life.'

'And she found it in Cornwall, and then here,' Carolyn accepted quietly.

'My Gran used to say that if you're lucky you find the place you need to be, the place where you can be happy. St. Benedict was that for her, and Loveday Manor is that place for Lynda. I know you need her, but I still hope she'll come back to us eventually.'

No-one noticed when, once the dining tables had been cleared away and the dancing had begun, Lynda slipped away. She went back to the hotel, and taking her new key out of her bag, quietly let herself into the upstairs apartment she had shared with Tom Meredith.

The large, soft woollen shawl which had belonged to Tom's mother, was still in its place on the back of the little sofa. Lynda wrapped it round her as she had so many times before, and sat by the open window listening to the music and laughter from the wedding.

She also listened to the silence of the apartment, and let the tears stream down her cheeks, hugging the soft warmth of the shawl against her heart and wishing she were holding Tom instead.

She fell asleep, and it was almost midnight when she heard the welcome sound of Mark coming up the stairs and entering the room.

'I thought I'd find you here,' he said softly and stepped across to close the window against the cool night air.

'I will come back,' she whispered. 'When Carolyn

doesn't need me so much, I'll come back and spend time here. At the moment, though, I can't seem to think about the future. I'm just getting through every day as best I can.'

She shuddered and pulled the shawl more tightly round her.

'I can't bear it that he's not here. I can't bear it.'

Mark sat beside her, took her in his arms, and they cried together for a while.

Lynda gradually became calmer, and even started to try and imagine how she might go about including both Milfield and Loveday in her life. Mark took a deep breath and quietly spoke the words he knew his Dad would have wanted to say.

'I don't know what your future will be, Lynda, love, but I do know it will be better if you're not on your own. And I don't mean just being with me or your family, but being with someone who loves you and will take care of you. That's what my Dad wanted for you.'

She looked at him, at that face so like Tom Meredith's, and brushed her fingers down his cheek. Mark took hold of her hand and held it tightly as he looked into her eyes.

'Nobody is asking you to forget my Dad. None of us will ever forget him, but he would want you to, one day, be happy again.'

CHAPTER SIXTY

John and Jean wanted a quiet wedding, and Jean had risked offending her entire family by not inviting any of them, but they'd never kept in touch with her since she'd been widowed, and so she felt justified in not including them on the guest list. Her cousin Alice was, however, so disappointed that they had relented and invited her.

The wedding was to be at ten o'clock, but Alice arrived at the registry office almost half an hour before that, wearing her best winter coat, and with new crimson silk flowers attached to her ancient navy straw hat.

When she walked in she found Lynda was already there, arranging the posies and vases of red roses and white carnations she'd ordered to decorate the sombre, oak panelled room which hadn't changed much since her own wedding there in the 1960s.

'What a lot of flowers. Did you buy them?' Alice enquired.

'Yes.'

'That's very generous of you, especially as Jean is marrying your husband.'

'With my blessing,' Lynda reminded her.

'Yes. It should have been Jean who married him in the first place, shouldn't it? Like it should have been you marrying Dan Heywood. I'll never forget the look on poor Dan's face when he had to stand there as best man, and watch his father give you away to his best friend instead of him.'

'That was all a long time ago, Alice,' Lynda said firmly, determined not to allow Alice to turn this wedding into a raking over of the past. However, John's sister, Sylvia, too, was in 'remembering mode' when she and Graham also arrived early, to be sure of a parking space.

'The last time we were in here was for your wedding, Lynda. My Mother was so upset,' Sylvia remarked tactlessly. 'She wouldn't have been there at all if Graham hadn't gone to fetch her, and insisted that she had to come. Graham can be very firm sometimes,' she sighed proudly.

'The flowers are lovely, Lynda,' said Graham Laycock, as he removed his smartly tailored black overcoat to reveal a grey pin-striped suit, and beneath it a ruby red silk waistcoat, to match the rose in his buttonhole.

'I like the waistcoat, Graham, will you be wearing it to the Bank on Monday?' Lynda teased.

He smiled, 'You never know. If they think I may be turning a little unconventional, perhaps they'll offer me the early retirement I'm hoping for.'

Sylvia brushed a speck of dust from her husband's shoulder. 'I don't think the Bank will ever want to be without you, but it would be nice for us to have more time together.'

She pulled back her coat to reveal her dress.

'I'm wearing red, too. Well, wine-coloured really. We were told Jean wanted the wedding to look a bit Christmassy, to counteract the miserable November weather.'

'That's right, red and green and white,' Lynda said. 'Gemma's thrilled to bits that she's got a little white fur cape and muff to wear over her red dress.'

'I heard you bought that,' commented Sylvia.

'Yes, the only thing I have been allowed to buy, apart from the flowers and this outfit I'm wearing.'

Sylvia had been admiring Lynda's beautifully cut pale gold trouser suit. 'Very smart, and a trouser suit is sensible, this weather.'

'Yes. And I thought perhaps I ought to look a bit masculine, as it's still traditionally a man who gives the bride away.'

Graham put out a hand to steady his wife as she took a slightly staggering step backwards. 'You're giving Jean away?' Sylvia said, almost squealing with shock. 'I thought it would be one of her brothers.'

'Peter is living in Australia now, and she lost touch with Dennis once he started to turn into a younger version of her Dad.'

'Oh. But, still. Being given away by your husband's ex-wife!'

Graham decided the sentence needed finishing appropriately. 'Shows Lynda's generosity, and true friendship.'

Lynda smiled at him gratefully.

'I was very touched, when she asked me. She wanted me involved, and I'm too old to be a bridesmaid, unfortunately,' Lynda laughed.

Sylvia decided she needed to establish that there would be at least some etiquette observed at this ceremony.

'Dan is best man again, isn't he?'

'Yes,' Lynda replied, deciding not to mention that John had originally intended to have Steve as his best man.

'Who will he walk out with, as there's no chief bridesmaid? Little Gemma?'

'No, with me. Gemma decided she wanted to walk out on her own, have her moment of glory.'

'Oh. Well, I suppose that's all right,' Sylvia

531

conceded, and then thought of another problem. 'Who is Carolyn going to stand with?'

'Steve, and Michael.'

Sylvia, still influenced by her late Mother's view of Carolyn's husband, was astounded.

'Steve?'

'That's good,' commented Graham. 'I was hoping they'd manage an amicable divorce, and that we weren't going to lose Steve from the family. Weren't you, Sylvia?'

She stared at him for a moment, then swallowed hard before agreeing.

'Yes. Yes, of course.'

It was a simple, relatively short ceremony, and Carolyn was glad when it was over. That morning she'd received the letter she'd been dreading, but had decided she wasn't going to talk about it, not on her Dad's wedding day.

Standing with Steve so close, and listening to those vows they had once made to each other was very hard for her. Steve was more relaxed, looking down proudly at his son who had recently become a teenager, and who was now wearing his first formal suit.

Lynda had to hold back tears, and thoughts of Tom Meredith, as she watched Jean gazing up at John Stanworth with such love in her eyes. Dan, finding it a little surreal to be acting as John's best man again, was trying not to think about that previous wedding, which had taken Lynda Collins away from him for the rest of his life, until now.

There were only a few shivery photographs outside the registry office before everyone gratefully got into their cars and headed for Ashton House and the wedding reception.

Lynda's heart sank as they walked into the dark and cold foyer. She'd heard that the hotel had been losing its reputation for a while, as its current owners had neither the experience nor the enthusiasm to make a success of it, and this was reflected in the atmosphere today.

Fortunately John and Jean were still outside, having a few photographs taken in front of the fountain in the garden. Lynda asked Steve to quickly fetch the flower arrangements they'd brought from the registry office.

She looked Dan, and he nodded his understanding. Without having to speak to each other, they each set off and spoke to the staff, issuing a few instructions, making sure lights were switched on and that the log fires were quickly lit in all the rooms.

The staff had been glad of the booking and, with Dan and Lynda's encouragement, soon abandoned the stiff and slightly snobbish formality demanded of them by their absent employers. They began to work hard, and help the occasion to develop into a lively, warm-hearted family celebration.

As there were only nine guests, John and Jean had decided that they didn't want the embarrassment of formal speeches. They all dined at one large oval table in the conservatory which was converted into a private dining room for such small events. Jean had gratefully accepted a wedding cake as a present from Dan and Alice, who had excelled in the decoration, and as the cake was placed in front of the bride and groom, Dan stood up.

'Ladies and gentlemen,' he began, 'Mr and Mrs Stanworth,' he said, smiling round at everyone, 'didn't want a lot of formal speeches, but they have given me permission to say a few words.

As all of you know, this has been a long-lasting romance. There have been lots of complications along the way, but today we have these two good people starting a new life together.

John and Jean have found out for certain what it is they need to make them happy, and that's each other. So, as the bride and groom cut the cake, could I ask you, please, to drink a toast?'

He waited until everyone was standing and then raised his glass.

'To John and Jean, the new Mr and Mrs Stanworth. May they have a long and happy life together.'

Later, as everyone moved around to have a chat, Dan went to talk to Lynda who was standing alone, looking round the slightly shabby room.

'Not like Loveday Manor, is it?'

Lynda shook her head ruefully, 'No, it isn't. But it has potential. You could do a lot with this house, and the garden of course.'

Dan saw Lynda's imagination had fired her interest, and he asked eagerly, 'Are you tempted to buy the place? As a wedding venue, I mean. Is that what you're thinking of doing? If it is, I'd be interested in that, we could work on it together?'

She backed away.

'I don't know what I want to do with my life yet.'

'Oh,' he said, taking this as a rejection.

He looked so crestfallen that she forced herself to smile and take hold of his arm.

'I know what I want to do with this wedding, though, organise a bit of dancing. Did you find out where they've hidden the disco equipment?'

'Yes, I've got them to set it up over there. And I've brought those CDs you asked me to.'

'What are we waiting for, then?'

She took hold of his hand and led him across the room. They cleared chairs and tables aside to make some space available for dancing, set the music playing, and got everyone to join them on the dance-floor.

Jean and John were delighted to see their guests enjoying themselves before they left for their honeymoon, which was Lynda's wedding present to them, a week at Loveday Manor.

Shortly after they'd gone, Steve, having danced for almost an hour with his daughter, decided he needed to be home with Jenny. Before he left, however, he went to speak quietly to Lynda.

'Are you going back to Beechwood Avenue with Carolyn and the kids?' he asked.

'No, she said she'd be all right on her own. Dan's asked me to go out to dinner with him tonight.'

'Oh.'

'What's the problem?' Lynda asked, seeing his concern.

'Could you stay in with Carolyn instead?'

'Yes, of course, but why?'

'She'll have received a letter this morning, like I did. Divorce papers, the decree nisi.'

It wasn't until after the children were fast asleep under their duvets that Lynda, opening one of the leftover bottles of wine she'd brought back from the wedding reception, mentioned the subject to her daughter.

'Steve told me you'll have received a letter this morning.'

'Yes,' Carolyn said quietly. 'I've been thinking about it all day. It was such a shock, seeing it there in black and white, the end of our marriage. I'm no longer Steve's wife, and now he's free to marry Jenny Heywood and be happy without me.'

She looked up at Lynda, and there were tears on her cheeks as she asked, 'And what am I going to do, Mum? I don't know what I'm going to do with my life.'

Lynda sat down beside her and placed the glass of wine in her hand. 'You're going to drink to the future, like me. We don't know what it's going to be, but we both know we have the strength to make the best of it.'

'I'm not sure I have,' Carolyn whispered. 'When I was standing next to Steve today, listening to all those promises I'd broken, I felt so alone.'

Lynda put her arm round her shoulders.

'You're not alone, you have the children, and me, and your Dad and Jean. We're still a family.'

'But not together. I keep thinking about things like Christmas, what do we do at Christmas?'

'We all come round here, and you and I cook Christmas dinner together for the kids, and your Dad and Jean.'

'But not Steve. Steve won't be here. The kids will be so upset when their Dad's not here.'

'He'll be here, if you ask him. Steve will come to see his kids on Christmas Day, I know he will. It might only be for an hour two, but he'll come.'

Carolyn was thoughtful for a while, but then said, 'I suppose we can make it work.'

'You'll have to,' Lynda insisted. 'You've made a good start, there's been no arguing over the house, or anything like that.'

'No, Steve's been very fair.'

Carolyn drank her wine sorrowfully.

'What I'm finding really hard is getting used to the

idea that he belongs to Jenny now. But I've no-one to blame but myself for that. And I have to admit, she's a lovely, kind-hearted woman.'

'Yeah, she is. She takes after Kath, her Mother,' said Lynda wistfully.

'I used to be so jealous of Jenny, you know, when you went to take care of her after Richard was killed.'

'I know. I shouldn't have spent so much time with her when you needed me to be with you really.'

'You were just being kind, and keeping a promise. I understand that now.' She placed her hand on Lynda's, 'I don't blame you for going away, you know, Mum.'

She tried to laugh as she got up to refill their glasses.

'In fact, looking round the place today, and comparing this wedding with the one at Loveday Manor, what I don't understand is why you came back!'

Lynda stood up and put her arm round her daughter. 'For you, and my grandchildren, and for forgiveness.

Lynda hesitated to ask the question, but she did need the reassurance. 'Have you forgiven me, Carolyn?'

'Of course I have.' She kissed her Mother. 'I'm just so sorry it took me so long. But I'll make up for it, we'll have some great times together. Speaking of which, have you told Helen we'll take her up on her invitation to spend New Year with them and her sister's family in New York?'

The last thing Lynda wanted to do now was disappoint Carolyn, so she just said, 'No, I haven't let her know yet.'

Carolyn gave her a hug. 'But really you want to have a party at Bennett Street instead, don't you?'

'Who told you that?'

'Dan. I mentioned how excited I was about the idea of going to New York for New Year. I asked him if he thought you'd like to do that, so he told me you'd mentioned having a party at your house. For old times' sake, he said.'

'I don't have to.'

Carolyn laughed. 'You don't have to come to New York, either, just to please me. But would you mind if I took the children on my own? Peter said he'd pick us up from the airport.'

Lynda had noticed that Carolyn seemed to be in regular contact with Helen Tyler's son, but thought it best not to comment on it. She was delighted at how confident Carolyn sounded about going to New York.

'No, it would be a great adventure for you and the kids. Tom and I always used to love going over there, and it's even better when you're visiting friends, isn't it?'

'Yes, they're lovely people. It's opened up a whole new world for me, going to America.'

'It did for me, too.'

'You mustn't give up all that, Mum. There's not enough in Milfield for you.'

'Are you talking about me or you?' Lynda teased.

'Both of us. I am your daughter, after all.'

'Yes,' Lynda laughed, giving her a hug. 'And I'm so glad. Now, talking about parties, it's my birthday on Thursday, and I was wondering if I could celebrate it here.'

'Wouldn't you rather we took you somewhere special?'

'Like Ashton House?' mocked Lynda.

'Yes, it was a bit disappointing, but Dad and Jean were happy enough. You ought to buy it and turn it into a stylish wedding venue.'

'Is that you talking to Dan again?'

'No,' Carolyn said, 'Well, yes, but only about your birthday cake which he's insisting on making for you.'

'Oh, lovely. As long as he doesn't put any numbers on it! So can I have a little birthday tea here? Just you and the kids, and John and Jean of course? That's what I'd really like to do.'

'O.K. if that's what you want. We'll have to ask Dan as well, though, as he's making the cake. That's all right with you, isn't it? After all he's practically family.'

Lynda shook her head in mock reproach.

'Not you as well!'

'What?'

'There seems to be a campaign to get me and Dan together.'

'Not from me. I know better than to try to push you into doing anything you don't want. On the other hand, it doesn't seem a bad idea,' Carolyn said, joking, but watching her Mother's face closely to see her reaction.

Lynda looked away, and then spoke softly.

'We both had an emotional time today, Carolyn, at that wedding ceremony, remembering when we last made those vows.'

She paused, and closed her eyes to seal in that memory once more.

'I love Dan Heywood.' She stopped, surprised to hear herself saying those words, but then continued, 'I love Danny, he's a wonderful man, but he's just a very special friend.'

CHAPTER SIXTY-ONE

Christmas happened just as Lynda had predicted, slightly awkward at first, but then a joyous realisation that they could enjoy being together as a complete family again. When Steve left to spend the rest of the day with Jenny and Dan and the girls, Lynda said goodbye to him at the door.

'So you're all spending Christmas at Hadden Lea?'

'Yes, it's a bit of a squash, but none of us wanted to be at Kirkwood House, especially Dan.'

Lynda pictured the large house standing dark and empty. 'Ellen won't be happy about that, God rest her.'

Steve shrugged. 'She wouldn't be happy about Peter Tyler and his Dad buying it and turning it into flats either, however, up-market they are.'

'No,' Lynda agreed, 'but at least her granddaughters will be living in one of them.'

'Yes, for a while, anyway. Everyone wants to move on, and that's the way it should be.'

'Yeah. I'm glad you could come here today. It's going to work out, Steve, for all of us,' she reassured him. 'Helen Tyler was right, it will just mean a bigger family.'

He smiled, 'Yes, I hope so.'

'I'll see you and Michael on New Year's Eve at my place, then. Is Michael all right about Carolyn going to New York with Gemma?'

'Yes, he didn't want to go. He says he'd much rather be at your house.'

Lynda laughed.

'Well, yes, much fancier than New York!' Then she said quietly, 'Carolyn was a bit upset when he told her he wanted to stay here with you.'

'I know, and I'll miss Gemma. But I suppose it's the kind of thing we'll have to cope with. But, as long as they love us both.'

'Yeah, that's the main thing.' Lynda paused for a moment, and then said quietly, 'Tell Jenny I'm looking forward to seeing her at the party as well.'

'Are you sure?'

'Yes. I've asked Carolyn about it, and she understands. She doesn't want me to lose my friendship with Jenny.'

'And me, Lynda? What about your friendship with me?' he said, looking at her searchingly.

Lynda reached up and kissed him.

'You and I will always be the best of friends, Steve. You're still family as far as I'm concerned.'

She kissed him again on New Year's Eve, under the big bunch mistletoe which hung in the entrance to 21 Bennett Street. She kissed Jenny, too, as she followed Steve into the hallway.

'I'm keeping all your Mum and Dad's traditions,' Lynda declared.

Jenny looked up at the mistletoe and smiled.

'They'll be blessing you for it. It's wonderful to be here again, tonight of all nights.'

'I hope you and the girls will come here often from now on. Good to see you, Alex and Katie,' she said, welcoming them with a hug. 'Your Grandma and Grandad Kelly would be delighted to see you here, especially with baskets of food in your hands.'

'We've been told we had to keep up that tradition, too, and it's all home-made,' Katie said happily.

'Mark sends his love,' Lynda told her, winking mischievously at Alex, who grinned back as Katie blushed.

'And is this William?' she asked as a tall, curly haired young man with a grin almost as wide as his shoulders followed Alex into the house.

'Yes. William, this is Lynda Collins.'

He held out a broad, strong hand.

'Pleased to meet you, Lynda, and thank you for inviting me. I hear you are the proud owner of a piano.'

'I am indeed, the house felt unfurnished till I bought one.'

'William plays twelve bar blues and jazz - much more popular than my classical stuff,' Alex boasted proudly.

'And some old music-hall songs,' William volunteered.

'Then you're even more welcome, Bernie would be delighted to hear that, particularly if they're saucy ones!'

She turned to grin at Jenny.

'There can't be a Kelly-Style New Year's Eve party in this house without someone thumping hell out of the piano, and the rest of us singing at the tops of our voices, can there, Jenny?'

'I'll be only too happy to oblige,' William assured her.

Lynda nodded approvingly.

'Sounds like you've found a good one, here, Alex.'

Jenny expected her eldest daughter to wince with embarrassment at such forthright comment but, to her surprise, Alex smiled and gazed up at William.

Lynda gave Jenny a knowing look, and then led them all into the kitchen to set out the food. She was still there a few minutes later when Dan arrived.

He'd been hoping Lynda would be there to greet him under the mistletoe, and Jenny, coming back into the hall, noticed his disappointment.

'You'll get your chance later,' she promised, looking up at the white berries and reading his mind.

'Do you think so?' he asked doubtfully. 'She seems to have been avoiding being alone with me ever since John and Jean's wedding.'

'Perhaps she had some thinking to do,' Jenny suggested. 'You'll have to give her time, Dan, it's been less than a year since she lost Tom Meredith.'

'I know.'

Jenny placed a reassuring hand on his arm.

'You will be together one day, you and Lynda, I'm sure of it, but you might have to wait, like I did for Steve.'

'I've already waited half my life,' sighed Dan. 'She does love me, you know. I see it in her eyes every time she looks at me. She loves me.'

'But not the way you want her to love you.'

'No.'

The curtains were left wide open in the front room at Bennett Street, so that the neighbours who had been invited but had been too shy to accept, could see the fun going on inside and change their minds.

Philip Lawson pushed open the door and he and Tricia nudged each other and grinned as they saw their companions, Angela Bentham and Charles Sutherland, hesitate as a roaring wave of loud music and shouts of laughter came at them.

'It's all right, go straight in, Angela,' Philip urged her, 'and be ready to wear a silly hat.'

'And drink snowballs!' Lynda called out, waving a large glass of Advocaat and lemonade, with a paper parasol and a plastic sword full of bright red cocktail cherries balanced precariously on top.

Angela quickly took off her coat and handed it to Charles before pushing her way through to Lynda and giving her a kiss.

'I'm so happy to be here, Lynda,' she said. 'And I've got something to show you.'

She waved her left hand in front of her friend so that the diamond ring flashed in the light.

'Charles and I got engaged at Christmas! And his children are thrilled, I'm glad to say.'

'Wonderful! I'm so happy for you.'

Philip, gathering all their coats, said, 'It's all thanks to me, you know, I was the one who introduced them. Shall I take these coats upstairs?'

'Yes, back bedroom,' Lynda told him, 'and be quick, we're just about to start the games.'

'Games?' said Charles, a little apprehensive now.

Lynda, assessing this tall, immaculate gentleman, decided he wouldn't mind a bit of teasing. 'Yes, we're starting with strip poker.'

Dan came forward to rescue him.

'Don't believe a word she says. Come with me, you'll need a drink before you can hold your own at this party.'

They followed him into the kitchen where they found Michael enjoying acting as barman, supervised by his Grandad. Jean took the boxes of cakes Angela had brought.

'Oh, you shouldn't have, but it's very kind of you. I'm Lynda's best friend Jean, Jean Stanworth now.'

Dan smiled at Jean's delight in using her married name.

'We're the staff for tonight,' he explained, 'unpaid of course!'

John laughed. 'And it won't be this organised for very long, it'll turn into a free for all after the games.

You'll just have to help yourselves then.'

'We'll cope,' Angela said cheerily, 'and we'll be happy to help with the washing-up, won't we Charles?'

'Yes, good practice for married life, so I'm told,' quipped Charles, eagerly accepting a pint of bitter John had drawn from the keg on a shelf to one side of the sink.

'That fits in well,' Charles commented.

'Bernie, our friend who used to own this house, put the shelf up years ago for this very purpose,' John explained. 'He would be very glad to see it still being put to good use.'

'So you've been to parties here before?'

'Yes, many times, like quite a few of the people here, including some old neighbours of the Kellys, and some of Lynda's friends from when she ran the Copper Kettle.'

'The café which Dan Heywood owns,' said Charles, wanting to clarify the relationships in this new group of friends he was being introduced to.

John leaned forward to whisper noisily in Charles' ear.

'I reckon Dan kept that café open in the hope Lynda would come back one day,' said John, who was in a confiding mood after several pints from the keg.

Charles nodded. 'And lo and behold, she has come back.'

John, marvelled at his new friend's perception.

'Yes, she has. And everything's going to be all right now!'

Charles smiled, 'Glad to hear it. Now I believe we're required to go into the front room to play silly games.'

Jenny, who had perched on the wide sill of the bay

window with Lynda, just as her Mother used to do, watched as everyone took childish delight in playing pass the parcel and musical chairs.

'Always gets the party going,' Jenny said.

'Yes,' Lynda smilingly agreed. 'We used to do this at The Springfield Hotel, too, and at Loveday. Everyone loves the excuse to go back to their childhood.'

'Even my sophisticated elder daughter. I'd never have believed Alex could be so full of fun.'

'I reckon that new boyfriend from university is a good influence on her. He's good company, and he's promised to play the piano again for a sing-song later on.'

Jenny took hold of Lynda's hand. 'I'll be in tears, singing 'Auld Lang Syne' in this house again after all these years.'

'So will I, love. But there'll be such good memories among the tears, and we'll make a lot more happy memories in the future.'

'You're staying here for good, then, Lynda?'

'Yes. This is where I belong.'

'What about Loveday?'

Lynda's smile was gentle and certain.

'I belong there as well. And I'll spend quite a bit of time there, I can't abandon what Tom and I created together.'

'I understand that. But please always come back to us.'

Lynda squeezed her hand.

'I will.' She laughed softly, 'Do you know, I spent years thinking I'd never really belong anywhere, and now there are two places I can call home.'

'That's good.'

'Yes, it is. What more could you ask of life?'

Jenny smiled across at Steve, who was rolling around on the floor laughing with his son.

She looked at Lynda.

'The right person to share it with.'

'Yeah.'

Jenny did cry all the way through 'Auld Lang Syne' as everyone linked arms in a double circle round the front room. When the circles broke up she sought out first Steve, and then her daughters, kissing them and wishing them Happy New Year.

She looked for Dan and found him standing pensively by the door, watching Lynda going round making sure she gave everyone her good wishes.

'What am I going to do, Jenny?' he whispered, 'I need her so much.'

Jenny put her arm round him.

'My Mum always used to go outside just after midnight, and make a wish. She believed that those wishes were special, and always came true. Go outside, Dan, stand in the back garden like she used to, and make your special wish.'

'Yes, I think I will.'

She watched him make his way towards the kitchen which opened on to the back garden, then she moved purposefully across the room to Lynda.

It was a very still night, with hardly any breeze to coax the delicate wisps of cloud across the starry sky. Dan was gazing up at the moon when Lynda came to stand beside him.

'Jenny told me you wanted to see me, and that I'd find you here.'

Still looking at the stars, he said, 'Her Mother used to believe that if you made a wish after midnight, under the moon and stars, it usually came true.'

'Yes, I remember,' Lynda said softly. 'Kath and I always used to come out here and make a wish together on New Year's Eve.'

'I've come out to make a special wish.' Dan took a deep breath and turned to look at the woman he loved so much. 'I expect you can guess what it is.'

When she didn't say anything, he began to be afraid, but eventually she gave a little sigh, and then lifted her face to his. He kissed her very gently, but with all his love.

She took a step back and, as if something had taken her by surprise, she opened her eyes wide.

'What is it?'

'I'm happy,' she whispered.

Lynda smiled at him, the way he'd always wanted.

'I never thought I would ever feel happy again. But that's how I do feel now, Dan, here with you. I'm home, and safe, and happy.'

She hesitated, then reached up and kissed him tenderly.

He didn't dare move, didn't want to break the spell of this moment. She looked into his eyes with such tenderness, and kissed him again. It was a special kiss, which made a very special wish come true.

The Lynda Collins Trilogy
by
Liz Wainwright

Book One
~~~~

The Girl who wasn't Good Enough

Book Two
~~~~

Second Chances

Book Three
~~~~

A Long Way Back

www.lizscript.co.uk

Made in the USA
Charleston, SC
30 October 2015